D0610840

Loans are up to 28 days. Fines are charged if items are
not returned by the due date. Items can be renewed
at the Library, via the internet or by telephone up to
3 times. Items in demand will not be renewed.
Please use a bookmark

Date for return		
12 DEC 2015		
09 SEP 2017		

£1.99
(32)

GLS

16.8.17

Check out our online catalogue to see what's in stock,
or to renew or reserve books.
www.birmingham.gov.uk/libcat
www.birmingham.bov.uk/libraries

Birmingham City Council

Q45612r1

The author of the terrifying serial killer thriller, *The Girl he Adored*, also featuring FBI agent E. L. Pender, Jonathan Nasaw lives in Pacific Grove, California.

JONATHAN
NASAW

FEAR
ITSELF

POCKET
BOOKS

First published in Great Britain by
Simon & Schuster UK Ltd, 2003
This edition first published by Pocket Books, 2004
An imprint of Simon & Schuster UK Ltd
A Viacom company

1 3 5 7 9 10 8 6 4 2

Simon & Schuster UK Ltd
Africa House
64–78 Kingsway
London WC2B 6AH

www.simonsays.co.uk

Simon & Schuster Australia
Sydney

A CIP catalogue record for this book is available from
the British Library

ISBN 0 7434 5064 7

Printed and bound in Great Britain by
Cox & Wyman Ltd, Reading, Berkshire

This one's for Mom.

I

Six Suites for Cello Solo

1

Wayne Summers opened his eyes to find himself in
the dark, surrounded by the chirring and rustling of
unseen birds. He tried to tell himself it was only a
dream, but the feel of the rough mattress-ticking
beneath him and the fetid, faintly ammoniacal smell
of feathers and old newspapers and bird dung argued
otherwise.

Wayne struggled blindly to his feet, heard a shrill
hiss only inches from his head, then felt the buffeting
of heavy, silent wings, followed by a sharp blow to his
ear. He threw himself back onto the mattress and
curled into a ball with his arms thrown up to protect
his head—he didn't know he'd been screaming until
he stopped and heard the silence.

Then, filling the silence, the unbearable chirring
and rustling again, the nervous tip-tap shuffle of hard
claws on cage floors, the shuddering noise of birds
ruffling their feathers for grooming. And, intermit-

tently, the muffled beating of those heavy wings only a few feet away in the dark.

Unless, of course, it wasn't dark. Wayne brought his hand toward his face until his palm touched his nose—there was no change in the quality of the blackness. For the first time it occurred to him that he might have gone blind—but how would you know, how could you tell? He tried to think back, to remember how he'd come to be here, but the memories were so wispy that trying to catch hold of them was like grasping at smoke rings: the harder you clutched, the quicker they dissolved.

Whimpering softly, Wayne fingered his torn earlobe. Sliced clean through—a razor-sharp beak or talon. Raptor, most likely: Wayne, an ornithophobe, knew from the studies he'd undertaken as part of Dr. Taylor's desensitization therapy that it had to be either a raptor or a carrion eater, and of the two, only the raptors had need of silent wings. Noise was not a problem for the carrion eaters—their prey wasn't going anyplace.

The mattress beneath his ear was damp with blood by this time, and the panic was coming in waves, one big roller after another. Wayne knew he could forestall a panic-induced blackout (or, as Dr. Taylor called it, a vasovagal syncope) by breathing slowly from the diaphragm while tensing and relaxing his muscles. He also knew he could stop the bleeding by pressing the edges of the wound together with his fingertips. But he wasn't sure he wanted to do either. After all, he told himself as his consciousness slipped away, there are worse things in life than bleeding to death while you're asleep—if he hadn't known that before, he knew it now.

But bleeding to death was not going to be an option for Wayne—at least not yet. After only a few minutes of sweet unconsciousness, he was awakened by a sharp pinching sensation in his left earlobe. And since pinching that same ear was how Wayne's mother always brought him around after what she referred to as one of his "faint'nin' spells," he allowed himself the momentary luxury of pretending he was back home in the apartment they shared on Fillmore Street, and that he'd had a blackout and she was pinching him awake.

Then he opened his eyes and found himself lying in the dark with his hands now cuffed behind him. Someone or something was indeed pinching the torn edges of his earlobe together, and when he tried to pull his head away, the grip only tightened.

"Who are you?" Wayne asked into the darkness.

"Sssh, hold still."

Man's voice—sounded like an older white guy. Familiar, but Wayne couldn't quite place it. "Why are you doing this to me?"

The pressure on his earlobe eased. "Looks like the bleeding's just about stopped."

Looks like? Oh, God, no. "Am I blind? Have I gone blind? Please, I have to know."

No answer—just a pager beeping in the darkness, followed by the sound of receding footsteps.

"Please, can't you even tell me that?"

Footsteps, climbing stairs.

"Please, I—"

But by then Wayne had his answer: a door opened at the top of a flight of open-treaded steps, admitting just enough light to assure him that his eyes still functioned, before closing again, leaving him with only the afterimage of the ghostly white, heart-shaped face of an enormous barn owl tethered to a perch above his head.

2

From the highway, the unremarkable three-story building on the lightly wooded rise looked like just about every other new office building in the Virginia suburbs west of Washington.

Which was exactly the point, noted FBI Investigative Specialist Linda Abruzzi, formerly Special Agent Abruzzi, as she pulled up to the guard kiosk in her '93 Geo Prizm. If all government architecture can be divided into two periods, before Oklahoma City and after Oklahoma City, the Department of Justice's recently opened auxiliary office building, though small, was definitively post-O.C. in design and construction, and its first, cheapest, and most effective line of defense was anonymity. No signs, no visitors, no press, no exceptions.

It was only when you got closer that you began noticing a few subtle distinctions. The kiosk, for instance, anchored two reinforced steel gates and was situated at the bottom of the approach road, a hundred yards distant from the building, while the parking lot was another fifty yards to the west: no one would ever get a car bomb near *this* federal building.

Add to those precautions reinforced roof and outer walls, acrylic windows thick enough to withstand a direct hit from one of the smaller handheld mortars, additional load-bearing interior walls to keep the whole building from collapsing in case a larger rocket did make it through, and a self-contained environment that could be sealed off floor by floor in the event of a chemical weapons attack, and you had a facility that was as close to impervious as was practicable for an aboveground structure.

When she flashed her credentials, which included an access pass entitling her to park in the garage under the building rather than the distant outdoor lot, Linda expected to be summarily waved through. Instead the guard painstakingly compared her face to the photo on her ID, which he then compared to the picture on a computer terminal inside the kiosk. Next he had her press her forefinger to a touch-screen pad, both so the computer could match it digitally to her file prints, and also to have it on file in case she turned out not to be Investigative Specialist Abruzzi.

"Thank you," said the guard, handing her badge case back to her. "Can you open the trunk for me, please?"

"Not from in here," said Linda, taking the key out of the ignition and handing it over to him. "This wasn't exactly the bells-and-whistles model." Linda had been a rookie SA working out of the San Francisco field office when she bought the Prizm six years earlier. Given the climate, there hadn't seemed to be any pressing need for air-conditioning, so she'd passed on the deluxe package, which included a remote trunk opener, and saved herself a few grand.

Three months later, naturally, the Bureau transferred her to the resident agency in San Antonio, where AC was all but a necessity; she'd kept the car only out of sheer stubbornness.

After checking the trunk for explosives, the guard used a long-handled mirror to inspect the undercarriage, then stepped back into the kiosk and pushed the button to raise the right-hand gate. "Drive directly up to the building without stopping. There's a keypad at the garage door. Code today is three-two-zero-four—don't write it down. Take the ramp to the sub-basement—space nine is reserved for you."

"Three-two-zero-four, subbasement, space nine. Got it, thanks."

"No problem." Then, under his breath, as the blue Prizm rolled through the gate and started up the hill: "Who'd you have to blow to park up there?"

Inside, the security precautions were no less stringent. A guard met Linda in the subbasement garage and escorted her to an elevator that communicated only with the lobby, where he turned her over to Cynthia Pool, an efficient, perfectly preserved clerk-secretary in her late fifties wearing a dress-for-success outfit from the early eighties—tailored navy pantsuit, white blouse with a ruffled bow, black Naturalizers with stacked heels.

"Very impressive security," remarked Linda, as Miss Pool led her to a second elevator, which, to Linda's surprise, had buttons for six floors—three of them turned out to be underground.

"None of it's for us, hon. We're only here because they needed our office space at headquarters."

The elevator doors slid silently open; Linda followed her guide down a series of white corridors remarkable for their featurelessness. No nameplates on the doors, all of which were blue, all of which were closed. No art on the walls, and the only signs were for fire exits.

"Now, pay attention to the route," warned Miss Pool, turning right, then left, then right again. "If you lose your way and wind up somewhere you're not supposed to be, you could find yourself up in Counterintelligence being interrogated with a rubber hose." She stopped abruptly and slipped the picture ID hanging on a chain from her neck into a slot mounted outside yet another anonymous-looking blue door.

"You're kidding, right?"

"Only about the rubber hose—they're a little sensitive in Counterintelligence, these days. After you."

Exhausted from her long walk, Linda felt her legs start to weaken as she crossed the threshold, and sent up a quick prayer: *Please God, not here, not on my first day.* He'd screwed her over enough lately; she figured he owed her a favor.

And her prayer was answered, after a fashion: just inside the door stood a file cabinet tall enough for Linda to lean against casually while her legs recovered. It struck her as an odd place to put a file cabinet—then she saw that the little anteroom was so crammed with free-standing metal cabinets, white cardboard record boxes, precarious stacks of perforated computer printouts, and collapsing slag heaps of overflowing red, brown, or buff accordion file folders that there was scarcely room left over for the secretary's desk and chair.

Miss Pool edged past Linda without comment and rapped with sharp knuckles on the interior door of the suite. "Linda Abruzzi is here."

"Already? Jesus H. Christ, the body isn't even cold yet." The voice was a little too hearty for nine o'clock in the morning, which fit the stories Linda had heard about her predecessor's drinking, part of his legend by now, along with his size, his eccentric wardrobe, his mastery of the Affective Interview, his heroism in the Maxwell case, and his open contempt for the Bureau-cracy. "Come on in."

Linda let go of the file cabinet, found to her relief that her legs had regained their strength, picked her way across the crowded anteroom, and opened the door to see an enormous bald man in a plaid sport coat on his knees in front of yet another file cabinet.

"One question," said Special Agent E. L. Pender, FBI, soon to be Ret., marking his place in the roll-out bottom file drawer with his left hand, reaching up to shake Linda's hand with his right. "How bad did you have to fuck up to get sent here?"

"I take it you haven't read my personnel file," she replied. Even kneeling, he was so tall that Linda didn't have to stoop to shake his hand, which was roughly the size of a waffle iron.

Pender glanced pointedly around the windowless office—if anything, it was even more cluttered with printouts, file folders, record boxes, and file cabinets than the anteroom—and shrugged. "It's around here someplace. But I don't pay much attention to person-nel records—and if you'd ever seen mine, you'd understand why."

"I heard you had your own coffee cup hanging on

the rack over at OPR," joked Linda. The Office of Professional Responsibility was the Justice Department's equivalent of an internal affairs division.

"Only a rumor. But they do know I take it black. Have a seat, take a load off."

Linda hesitated—the only chair in the room was behind the desk, which was buried under yet another slag heap of computer printouts and file folders.

"Yes, ma'am," said Pender, reading her mind. "That's your chair, that's your desk, this is your office now." He took the file folder he'd been looking at and turned it sideways in the drawer before standing up.

"What about you?" Linda tested the stability of the desk chair, then lowered herself into it carefully, using both hands on the arms for balance the way the physical therapist in San Antone had taught her.

"I'm gone, I'm history. The eagle flies until the end of the month, but I had some vacation saved up, and it was use it or lose it. I only came in today to finish going through these old files, refresh what's left of my memory—some idiot publisher's paying me a shitload for my memoirs. They're also paying somebody else a shitload to write them, thank God."

"But aren't you supposed to be training me or something?"

"For what? They're shutting down Liaison Support at the end of the year, when Steve McDougal retires. It's outlived its function—everybody's on-line with everybody nowadays. That's why I asked how bad you fucked up—no offense intended."

"None taken. I was afraid it was something like that."

"Now that I've seen you motorvatin', though, I'm guessing it has more to do with that." Pender cleared off a space and perched one enormous cheek on the edge of the desk—his thigh was nearly as wide around as Linda's waist. "What's the story?"

Linda took a long, deep breath, let it out slowly. Might as well get this over. "MS," she said. "MS is the story—I was diagnosed with primary progressive multiple sclerosis a few months ago."

Pender didn't miss a beat. "Dang," he said. "I hate it when that happens."

Not quite the reaction she'd been expecting—Linda let out a startled laugh. "Yeah, me too," she said after a moment, then quickly changed the subject. "So what's my job exactly? What is it I'm supposed to do around here?"

"Do?" Pender snorted derisively. "Frankly, my dear, nobody gives a toasted fart."

3

"You okay in there, sweetheart?" Simon Childs tapped gently on the bathroom door. Sometimes Missy only wanted to be sure the pager would actually summon him; other times she did it out of pure mischief.

"Mo hah, mo hah."

More hot. Simon had never had any trouble understanding what his kid sister was saying. He

opened the door to see Missy stretched out in the
deep clawfoot tub, waving her pink plastic pager
over her head, and grinning from ear to ear—oh,
how that girl loved her bath. You had to keep an eye
on her, though. She'd stay in the tub until she was
one big wrinkle if you let her, but when the water got
cold, she'd start fiddling with the taps, no matter
how many times she'd been warned not to, and more
often than not, she'd end up either flooding the
bathroom or scalding herself.

And for a strange, out-of-time moment, as he
approached the tub, Simon saw his baby sister not as
she was now, but as he still held her in his mind's eye:
a darling, round-faced, whitey-blond five-year-old
Kewpie doll with a loving heart and an unquenchable
sense of wonder. Then she broke the spell by bleating
"Mo hah!" again in her deep-toned, uninflected
voice. Simon blinked and found himself looking
down at a naked, waterlogged, sparsely haired, morbidly obese, forty-nine-year-old idiot with a protruding tongue and slit eyes lost in folds of fat, whose pale
skin was tinged blue as a result of the cardiac condition her doctors had predicted would prove fatal
before another year had passed.

Best not to think about that, though. Simon and
Missy had been abandoned by their mother after their
father's death and were raised by a paternal grandfather as tyrannical as he was wealthy. After his death, it
was just the two of them, their trust funds, and the
hired help. Simon was fifty-one now; for forty-nine
years Missy had been the only constant in his life, and
no matter how often Simon told himself it was better
this way, more merciful for her to predecease him

than for him to leave her behind, he knew in his heart that he was going to be lost without her.

And so despite the doctors' warnings, Simon spoiled Missy outrageously—why make her stick to a diet if she was going to die anyway? It was like the way the trustees had wanted to send her to retard school after their grandfather's death. They said she'd never reach her full potential otherwise. What did *they* know about Missy's potential—or her happiness? If what made Missy happy was baths and food and Audrey Hepburn videos and staying home with Simon, then that's what she'd get. He'd had a huge water heater installed so she could bathe all day if she wanted to, and she had free rein in the kitchen, which he kept well stocked—not an easy task: oh, how the old girl could pack it away, and oh, how she could pack on the pounds.

But then, Missy had always been chubby. In fact, when he and Missy were kids, Simon used to think of her corpulence as just another symptom of her Down syndrome, along with her moon face, her sloping forehead, her slanty eyes with their yellow-spotted irises, her flat-ridged nose, her protruding tongue, and her low-set, folded ears.

He knew better now, of course. "Okay, okay, I'll run some more hot. Get your piggies out of the way."

Missy drew her legs up. Simon reached down and pulled the old-fashioned, rusty-chained, cork-shaped rubber plug.

"Hey, hey, you braa'," she barked tonelessly.

"Take it easy, I'm just letting some of the cold water out, make room for the hot." He replaced the plug, opened the left tap, swirled the water with his hand to mix the hot in gradually, the way their old nanny, Granny Wilson—Ganny, they called her—would have. Then, splashing his sister playfully: "And watch who you're calling a brat, you brat."

Missy giggled and splashed him back, paddling the water with her chubby hands, which had only a single crease across the palm.

"Is that better?" Simon asked her, turning off the water and wiping his hands on the bath mat. As he stood up and crossed to the sink to get Missy a washcloth, he caught a glimpse of himself in the mirror and smoothed back his wavy silver hair, which was receding decorously into a handsome widow's peak.

"Peedee keem." *Peachy keen.*

"Okay, then." He tossed the washcloth into the tub. "I have to go back down to the basement. Page me when you're ready to get out. And don't forget to wash your whoop-te-do." That had been Ganny's collective term for private parts, male or female.

"Wah *yah* whoodedo, you braa'!" Missy shouted angrily—after all, she wasn't a *baby*—and the washcloth hit the back of the door with a wet thud as Simon closed it behind him.

4

Last day on the job. For a secret sentimentalist like
E. L. Pender, the whole morning had been fraught
with significance. Alarm clock: won't need you no
more, you little bastard. Shaving: why not start a
beard now, after all these years? Hide those extra
chins, at any rate. Clothes: one last chance to nail
down his reputation as the worst-dressed agent in
the history of the FBI. Universally loathed plaid sport
coat, Sansabelt slacks that had spent the night on the
floor, and his most comfortable wash-and-wear
short-sleeved white shirt—comfortable because it
had been washed and worn to a point just short of
decomposition. No tie, of course: odd to think that
this was the last time that *not* wearing a tie would
carry any meaning.

Perhaps the strangest part of Pender's morning
came when he realized that he was strapping on his
calfskin shoulder holster for the last time. He'd
already decided he wouldn't be applying for a concealed weapons permit. Not much use for the Glock
.40 on the golf course. Anyway, he'd never really
bonded with it after the Bureau had taken away his
SIG Sauer P226 for display at the FBI museum. It was
the shoulder holster that really should have been
behind glass, though: Pender was one of the last federal agents to wear one; everybody else had switched
to the officially approved over-the-kidney holsters
years earlier.

Like most secret sentimentalists, Pender suspected

other people of being sentimental, too. Though he knew that save for Pool, the rest of the old Liaison Support gang were either retired or scattered by the Bureau to the four winds, he'd practiced acting surprised on the drive to work, just in case they had decided to throw a party for him.

The only surprise, however, had been the discovery that his replacement was a handicapped female who was no longer even a special agent—and even that felt more like the last piece of the puzzle finally falling into place. Obviously the Liaison Support Unit, *the* assignment for ambitious young agents back in the late seventies, had in its final days become a dumping ground for employees the Bureau didn't know what else to do with.

So when Pender told Linda that nobody would give a toasted fart how she spent her time, it was only the unvarnished truth. But when he saw the hurt in her eyes, he quickly added: "That's the bad news *and* the good news."

"Good how?"

"You have two and a half months to make whatever you want out of this assignment without Steve Too crawling up your ass."

"Steve who?"

"Steve Maheu, Steve McDougal's number two. Picture in the dictionary next to *holier-than-thou*. But with McDougal retiring, Maheu's too busy scouting a soft place to land to pay any attention to you, so you should be pretty much on your own."

"But for what? To do what?"

"To look for serial killers nobody else is looking for."

"Are there any?"

"It's a growth market, kiddo." Pender chuckled. "Now more than ever, it's a growth market."

Then he caught himself, and the laugh faded. "I'm sorry, that was bullshit of me."

"Why do you say that?"

"When we started Liaison Support over twenty years ago, I promised myself I'd never forget about the victims. Even if I was only going fishing in the MMRs, I told myself I'd never forget what the job was really about. And I just did."

Linda looked away, moved by Pender's passion and commitment; maybe this might not turn out to be such a dead-end assignment after all.

"So what do we got?" she asked brusquely, when she was sure of her voice again. All Bronx, all business.

"I want you to take a look at a letter that came in last Friday. It gave me a chill." He began shuffling through the papers stacked on the desk. "And if there's one thing I've learned on this job . . ." Now he was back down on the floor again, rummaging through a stack of buff file folders with one hand, trying to keep it from toppling over with the other. ". . . it's to trust the chill." Then, distractedly, still rummaging: "What scares you, Linda—what are you afraid of?"

"You mean, other than progressive paralysis, ending in death?" Linda tried to soften the bitter words with a laugh. When she'd first decided to fight for the right to keep her job, she had promised herself that if she won, the office would be a no-whining zone.

And it had been one hell of a battle: FBI regs

stated clearly that special agents were required to be in "excellent physical condition with no defects that would interfere in firearm use, raids, or defensive tactics." In the end, however, the brass agreed to a compromise: reassignment with the bogus job title of *investigative specialist,* rather than *special agent.* Badge, no gun, same pay level, desk job, monthly physicals, and, most worrying of all, monthly psych evaluations: first sign of cognitive impairment, a common enough MS symptom, and they would wash her out entirely.

"I mean before the MS. When you were a kid, say, what was the thing you feared most?"

"Like a phobia?"

"Exactly."

"That's easy, then—snakes."

"How severe?"

"What do you mean?"

"Did snakes just give you the creeps, for instance, or were you afraid to walk in the woods, or—"

"We didn't have much in the way of woods where I grew up. But I definitely stayed the hell away from the reptile house in the Bronx Zoo. I passed out in front of it on a field trip when I was in college."

"Well, if you . . . Here we go." Pender had found the envelope he was looking for, and winged it up onto the desk. "If you multiply your fear of snakes by about a thousand, you'll have some idea what life might be like for Dorie Bell."

"Gee, thanks," said Linda.

"Don't mention it. Give me a holler when you're done—I'll be down here someplace."

5

Johann Sebastian Bach's *Six Suites for Cello Solo* has long been considered a benchmark for cellists. Pablo Casals, who at age thirteen stumbled upon the suites in a secondhand sheet-music store near the harbor in Barcelona, practiced them every day for twelve years before he worked up the courage to play one in public, and it would be another thirty-five years before he felt ready to record the entire series.

Since then, every world-class cellist has had his or her go at the suites, but only the most gifted, the Jacquelines and the Yo-Yos, have even wrestled them to a draw, so it was probably an act of hubris for a twelfth-chair cellist like Wayne Summers to attempt them.

But Wayne, born poor and black in San Francisco's Fillmore District, had come late to his instrument, and as his teacher Mr. Brotsky always said, without at least a little *chutzpah,* a man never knows how good he can be or how far he can go.

Which was why every day for the past six years, whether he was working a day job, rehearsing with the symphony, or playing chamber music—or all three, as sometimes happened—Wayne made time to practice at least one of the dances from one of the suites. His favorite was the sarabande from the first suite—there was something so damn sweet and hopeful about it.

That, then, was the piece Wayne, lying in the darkness with his hands cuffed behind his back, chose to practice first, in order to keep himself from going mad. To begin with, he ran through the sarabande in his mind, his left hand twitching the fingering behind him, the muscles of his bowing arm tensing and relaxing rhythmically. Midway through, he began diddle-dumming along, which started the caged birds chirring and singing again. Not the owl though—the owl remained silent.

When he finished, Wayne heard polite applause— the sound of one man clapping, somewhere across the room. But the Bach had worked its magic on Wayne: his mind felt clearer than it had since he'd first awakened, however many hours ago.

"Who are you?" he asked into the darkness. "Why are you doing this?"

No answer—even the birds were silent. But the man was drawing nearer; Wayne could smell him now. He smelled like bubble bath. Cheap, strawberry-scented bubble bath.

"Are you going to kill me?" Wayne asked. It felt strange to be so calm at such a time.

"No." The voice was only inches away.

Thank you, Jesus. "What, then?"

"I'm going to let our feathered friends here do it for me—eventually."

On the surface, Wayne remained calm, perhaps because beneath the surface something had already died—hope, most likely—leaving him nothing to do but ask the question again: "Why are you doing this?"

Instead of an answer, a rank smell, then the unpleasant sensation of something cold and clammy being rubbed against his eyelids. It was all so bizarre and incongruous that it took Wayne a few seconds to recognize the odor, and a few more seconds for him to put it all together. Liver—the crazy fuck had just rubbed raw liver into his eyes.

And even then the significance of what had happened failed to dawn on Wayne until he heard a sound that drove every other thought, every other sensation but pure blind panic from his mind and consciousness: the rattle of the chain that tethered the barn owl to its perch.

A moment later came the buffeting of silent wings, and the strike. The first blow drove Wayne's head back violently against the mattress. The pain was indescribable—Wayne rolled over onto his stomach and began thrashing his head from side to side to protect his eyes. The owl, starved and frustrated, half hopped, half flew from one side to the other, stabbing with its beak, trying to get at the liver smell, the blood smell.

Then it found the ear it had struck accidentally earlier, and contented itself with tearing at that until the man who had brought it to this place hauled it away from its prey and dropped a burlap sack over its head.

"Who *are* you?" screamed Wayne again, through the pain.

"I'll give you a hint," came the answer. "You know how people are always saying you have nothing to fear but fear itself? Well, that's me, buddy—I'm fear itself."

6

Dorie is sitting on a couch somewhere, knees primly together. Across the room a television is playing, but she can't quite make out what's on the screen. Behind the television, a window. What floor is this? she asks herself. It makes a difference—if she's a few stories up, there's no danger, but if she's only on the first or second story, she mustn't look up, mustn't glance at the window.

In front of her, on a familiar-looking coffee table, there's a big, glossy coffee-table book. She leans forward and opens it at random, but she can't make out the words, can't quite bring them into focus.

There are pictures, though. The first one she turns to looks like a bird initially; the picture is the only colored object in Dorie's black-and-white world, and so vivid it's almost 3D. Then she leans closer and discovers to her horror that it's not a picture of a real bird, but of a bird mask—one of those elongated, feathered masks that a medicine man or a witch doctor might wear.

She quickly closes the book, then hears a tapping at the window. Don't look up, she tells herself—whatever you do, don't look up.

But she does look up. She always does. And sees what she always sees: the face at the window. Or rather, the mask at the window—the eyeholes are empty, there's no face behind it.

As always, Dorie Bell awoke from her recurring nightmare with the echo of her own scream ringing in her ears. And as always, there was no way to know whether she'd screamed out loud, or only in the dream. Fortunately, it didn't matter: she lived alone.

Of the approximately thirty million Americans who suffer from phobia disorders serious enough to require professional consultation at some point in their lives, forty-two percent are afraid of illness and/or injury, eighteen percent are afraid of thunderstorms, fourteen percent fear animals, eight percent are primary agoraphobics (people who are afraid of public spaces, largely because they fear they will experience a panic attack, sometimes involving a syncope, in public; there is, of course, an element of agoraphobia associated with almost all specific phobias—the fear of having a panic attack is always more debilitating than the fear of whatever inspired the phobia in the first place), a surprisingly small seven percent are terrified of death, five percent fear crowds, and another five percent are afraid of heights; comprising the remaining one percent are the more exotic phobias, such as amathophobia, the fear of dust, siderodromophobia, the fear of railroad trains, and prosoponophobia, the fear of masks.

Dorie Bell, age fifty-two, of Carmel-by-the-Sea, California, had been a prosoponophobe since age three. She had tried everything—prayer, analysis, desensitization therapy, behavior modification, more prayer—but had never been able to uncover either the source for her fear or a cure. The actual sight of a mask still triggered severe panic attacks, fear of accidentally encountering a mask still ruled her daily comings and goings, and mask dreams still haunted her nights.

And sometimes her afternoon naps as well—she had fallen asleep on the couch in her studio while waiting for Wayne Summers, who was supposed to be driving down from San Francisco that afternoon. They had met the previous spring, in Las Vegas, of all places, where nearly a hundred phobics (or, as they preferred to be called, Persons with Specific Phobia Disorder) had gathered for the PWSPD convention, and the two had become fast friends despite some rather striking differences between them, including age, race, religion, and sexual orientation.

Still struggling to shake off the psychic tatters of the dream, Dorie left the studio and went into the kitchen to make herself a cup of tea and check the time—there was no clock in the studio, intentionally. She was surprised to discover that it was nearly four in the afternoon, which left her in a minor dilemma, as she was anxiously awaiting a response to her letter to Agent Pender and hadn't yet dropped by the post office today. (There was no home mail delivery in Carmel, largely because there were no street numbers on the houses; Carmel-by-the-Sea was a town that worked at being quaint.)

On the other hand, Wayne might be arriving any minute—he was already several hours overdue—and he would absolutely pitch a syncope if he had to wait outside with the jays, crows, thrushes, juncos, and warblers that inhabited the live oak in Dorie's front yard.

Black guy passed out on the front lawn: wouldn't that give the neighbors something to talk about, thought Dorie, hurriedly scrawling a note that read, *"Wayne, come on in, back soon, Dorie,"* and tacking it to the front door, which she left unlocked for him—you could still do that sort of thing in Carmel. Then she set off at a brisk walk for the post office, an eight-block round trip from there for most people, but twelve for Dorie, who had to take the long way around in order to avoid passing the African masks in the window of the Ethnic and Folk Arts Gallery.

There were, as of October of 1999, ninety-six art galleries and forty-one gift shops in Carmel; of necessity, Dorie had memorized the location of all the ones that displayed, or might display, masks visible from the street, so that she could detour around them. A relatively minor inconvenience, she knew, especially compared to the lengths an ornithophobe like Wayne had to go to avoid his bêtes—as specific phobia disorders go, prosoponophobia wasn't the worst one to have. Except around Halloween, which, as Dorie was about to learn, had come two weeks early to Carmel that year.

No one watching Dorie Bell stride confidently down the hill toward the post office would have suspected her of being a phobic. She was a tall woman, broad-shouldered and full-figured, and she walked the walk in her Birkenstocks, paint-spattered overalls, and brown serape—head up, long strides, arms swinging, colorful straw Guatemalan bag swinging, waist-length brown braid swinging, too.

But as she turned west onto Fifth Avenue, having detoured down San Carlos to avoid the Ethnic and Folk Arts Gallery, she was ambushed. Overnight a faceless white mannequin wearing the medieval costume known as a domino (hooded robe and eye-mask, all the more dreadful to Dorie for its simplicity:

black and white, the mask stripped to its essence) had appeared in the window of Verbena, the upscale women's clothing shop on the corner of Fifth and Dolores.

Frozen in front of the window, unable to avert her eyes, just as in the dream, Dorie could feel her scalp tingling; bright pinpricks of color dotted her vision as the blood began to drain from her head. She knew what was happening—her sinoaortic baroreflex arc, the mechanism responsible for the vasovagal syncope, was overcompensating for the sudden increase in blood pressure by dropping the pressure just as suddenly. But she also knew, after all these years, how to take charge, how to reverse the process.

Breathe, she ordered herself, closing her eyes to the m—to the object that had triggered the attack. Deeeep and sloooow, deeeep and sloooow. Then up on your toes, back down, up and down, breathe deep; long, slow shoulder-rolls, get the blood circulating, never mind about making a public spectacle, you'd make more of a spectacle passing out on the sidewalk, and breaking your nose again for good measure.

Attagirl, can't be fearless until you've been afraid. Now turn away from the object, nice and slow, don't hyperventilate; now you can open your eyes . . . now you can take a step . . . now you can take another. . . .

And the danger was behind her, both physically and temporally. Nor did she abandon her errand, instead detouring another three blocks out of her way, only to return home empty-handed—no letters in her box, from Pender or anybody else—to an empty driveway and empty house: no Wayne, either.

By six o'clock, Dorie was concerned; by eight, she was worried; by ten she had already left three messages on Wayne's machine and another two on his mother's.

A few minutes after eleven the phone rang; Dorie snatched the receiver off the cradle, barked "Where the hell are you?" and was told, in no uncertain terms, to watch her language. Vera Summers, who double-shifted as a private nurse, was Dorie's age, a praise-shoutin', hymn-singin', tee-totalin', no-cussin' Baptist, and not to be trifled with. Dorie apologized. "Sorry, Vera, I thought it was Wayne."

"Apologize to Jesus, not me. But listen, sugar, I ain't seen Wayne since church yesterday morning. Didn't come home last night, didn't call, nothing. You do see him first, you warn him he better duck next time he see his mama. He show up there, you have him call me. Meantime I'm 'onna see if I can get hold of my brother Al, on the police, grease some wheels."

"Okay, stay in touch."

"I will. I wouldn't worry too much, though—it wouldn't be the first time that boy stayed out all night, tomcattin' around."

But Dorie did worry, because she knew something Vera did not know. God *damn* it, she thought, picking up the phone again—how many more of us have to die before somebody listens?

"Hello?" The man on the other end of the line sounded peeved.

"Hi, it's Dorie. Did I wake you?"

The voice softened. "Oh, hi. No, no problem—I'm a night owl. What's up?"

"Remember Wayne Summers?"

"Refresh me."

"He was the only black guy at the convention."

"Right, right, the ornithophobe. What about him?"

"He's missing," said Dorie. "He was supposed to be coming down today, but he never showed up."

"Maybe it slipped his mind. From what I recall of the boy, he did strike me as being just a tad flaky."

"No, I talked to his mother. She doesn't know where he is either—she said he didn't come home last night."

"Has she filed a missing persons?"

"Not yet—but her brother, Wayne's uncle, he's a cop, he's gonna look into it."

Attenuated silence, then the snick of a lighter and a hissing inhalation (the unmistakable sound of somebody toking up), followed by a spluttering cough (the unmistakable sound of somebody blowing a toke).

"You okay?" Dorie asked.

"Yes, yes," he snapped. "Just calming my nerves." It didn't sound to Dorie as if he'd had much success. "Listen, Dorito, I'm sorry to hear about Wayne—I'm sure he'll turn up—but I have to ask: why on earth are you calling *me?*"

Up until now—up until Wayne—Dorie had restrained herself from taking her suspicions to any of her new friends from the PWSPD convention. The phobic community was the last place you wanted to start a panic. And her theory—that somebody was going around the country murdering phobics and trying to make it look like suicide—did sound a little paranoid, if not downright fantastic, not just to the authorities she'd contacted, but to her own ears as well. The letter she'd sent Pender was an umpteenth draft, and the only way she'd managed to get that one off was to seal the envelope and drop it into the corner mailbox without reading it first.

But what had seemed like caution this morning felt more like denial this evening. Dorie took a here-goes-nothing breath and let 'er rip. She told him about the deaths of Carl, Mara, and Kim, about her correspondence with the Las Vegas, Fresno, and Chicago police, about the letter to Pender—she laid it all out, and when she had finished, the silence on the other end of the line was so complete she thought at first the connection had been broken.

"Hello? Hello, are you still there?"

"Yes, yes—just trying to find my Valium."

"Hey, take it easy on the meds," Dorie cautioned him. "I can't afford to lose any more friends."

"I'm more worried about you. If your suspicions are accurate—and I'm not at all sure they are, despite my now shattered nerves and pounding heart—you're in more danger than I am, a woman alone and all that."

"I think we're *all* at risk here," replied Dorie. "In fact, I'm thinking about posting this on the chat room."

"No!" The response was unhesitating. "There are a lot of unstable personalities who visit that chat room. Something like this might drive some of them over the edge. Panic attacks, agoraphobia, maybe even suicide."

"Then what—"

"First of all, calm down. I'm not without resources myself. I'll make a few calls, contact a few people. I'll let you know what I find out, you let me know what you find out. And in the meantime, let's keep this between us—we don't want to throw the whole community into a panic."

"You think so?" said Dorie doubtfully.

"I know so. Look, I have to go now—sounds like Missy just woke up."

"Say hi to her for me—and for God's sake, be careful."

"You too. Good night, Dorito."

"Good night, Simon."

7

Monday had been a lonely day for Missy. Simon had given Tasha, her attendant, the week off, then spent all morning in the locked basement. And after lunch, instead of taking her to the park as he'd promised, he'd installed her in her bedroom with her favorite Audrey Hepburn videos *(Charade, Breakfast at Tiffany's, Wait Until Dark)*, a snack tray, and strict instructions not to leave the room unless she had to use the toilet.

Then he was kind of distant all through dinner and hardly paid any attention to her. It was a good dinner, though: hamburgs, Tater Tots, applesauce, and Little Debbie snack cakes for dessert—she gobbled down three before he even noticed, and he *didn't* make her eat any green veggies. Plus Simon cooked it for her himself, which made it extra good.

After dinner Simon sent Missy back upstairs, then

went down into the basement, and didn't come back up until halfway through *The Original Ten O'Clock News.* Missy never missed *The Original Ten O'Clock News*—she had a major crush on Dennis Richmond, the handsome black anchorman. Once Simon took her to the telethon and she met him in person and gave him a dollar for those poor children in their wheelchairs.

But even after Simon came up from the basement, he didn't pay any attention to Missy—just went into his room and closed the door. Missy kept expecting him to come kiss her good night, but he didn't. She fell asleep with the light and the TV on but woke up in the dark with the TV off—she'd been awakened by the ringing of the telephone. From across the hall she heard Simon talking. She got out of bed and knocked on the door of the master suite. No answer—she opened it anyway, crossed the bedroom, and stuck her head into Simon's little office. He was at the computer.

"Who called?" A stranger would have heard *Hoohaw,* but as always, Simon had no trouble understanding Missy.

"Dorie. She said to say hi to you."

Missy decided to tease him a little. "Talking to your *girl*friend. *Si*mon's got a *girl*friend."

"Missy, I'm in no mood for your nonsense. Now, go back to bed before I get serious."

Uh-oh. When Simon said "serious," he meant "mad." When Simon was mad, sometimes he did things he was sorry for later. But the sorry didn't help much if you were the one he did the things to. "I love you?" she whispered cautiously.

"I love you, too," said Simon, turning his back to the door. It wasn't as though *he'd* had that great a day, either. That's what comes from trying to do too much too fast, he told himself. The total darkness, then that stunt with the liver—greedy, Simon, greedy. And now, what with Dorie Bell stirring things up, it would have to end sooner than he had planned. For Wayne and Dorie both.

Still, spilt milk and all that. And perhaps when Wayne knew the end was coming . . .

Simon could feel his pulse quickening at the thought. Yes, that's it, he told himself, that's what we're in this for. Then he realized Missy was still standing forlornly in the doorway. He spun his chair around again. "Hey, sis, what do you say, how 'bout pancakes for breakfast?"

"Peachy keen," replied Missy, picturing the Mrs. Butterworth's bottle, which always made her giggle. "I love pancakes."

"I know you do. Now, go to bed—I have to go back down to the basement."

"I don't like the basement. It's scary."

"I know," he said. "That's why you mustn't go down there, not ever."

"You do," she said intelligibly. She could manage her *oo* sounds pretty well. And as Simon knew, her speech difficulties stemmed from the way the congenital Down's flattening of the palate forced Missy's tongue to protrude, and were not indicative of her level of comprehension.

"I have to," he said.

"Ha hunh," she replied, waving a chubby hand.

Have fun. Simon found himself wondering, as he

slipped on his new D-303, single-tube, dual-eye, night-vision goggles with built-in two-stage infrared illuminator, whether somehow Missy didn't understand a lot more than even he gave her credit for.

8

Something was wrong.

Since regaining consciousness, pain, thirst, and hunger permitting, Wayne had spent the last few hours working his way through the Bach suites numerically, and doing rather well, too, until he got stuck on number five, the one Casals called the tempestuous suite. The problem wasn't that he didn't have the music with him—he knew the score by heart. But he just couldn't seem to get number five going.

Then, in his mind's ear, he heard old Brotsky: *the tuning, Mr. Summers, the tuning.* He'd forgotten to drop the A string down to G—a little trick Bach had employed to enhance the cello's sonority. After that, the piece went relatively smoothly, although it was interesting to note that even on an imaginary instrument he still sometimes stumbled over the same difficult intervals that had always given him trouble.

He played with his remaining eye firmly closed. Funny how total darkness made you want to shut your eyes, he thought. Otherwise it was too vast, like the blackness of space—you felt as though if you let go, you'd tumble through it forever.

But even with his eye closed, he was so sensitive to light that he knew when the door at the top of the stairs had been opened, however brief and faint the glow. He did his best to ignore it, concentrating all the harder on the Bach.

As for the birds, a curious thing had happened. It might have been the result of such an extreme application of Dr. Taylor's desensitization therapy. *Flooding,* the technical term for overwhelming a phobic with the object of his fear, was considered by some psychiatrists to be the most effective form of phobia therapy, but few patients or psychiatrists had the stomach for it, and the malpractice carriers weren't crazy about it either—when it failed, it failed big time. Or perhaps it had something to do with the fact that he and the birds were all fellow captives, but whatever the reason, Wayne's ornithophobia had vanished: he found that birds no longer frightened him. Except for the owl, but as that was no longer an unreasonable fear, it no longer qualified as a phobia.

Somebody probably should have locked me in a room with a bunch of birds years ago, thought Wayne during one of his more lucid moments. He even started to chuckle.

Think of the money I'd have saved on therapy.

Laughing out loud, now. LOL, as they said in the PWSPD chat room.

Miracle cure for ornithophobia. Not cheap, though—cost you an eye and an ear.

LOL a little too hard.

Also guaranteed to improve your cello playing. Play even the most difficult pieces with your hands tied behind your back.

Shrieking with laughter. Lucid no longer. Couldn't stop if his life depended on it. Birds skittering around in their cages.

My new friends.

Shrieking and sobbing.

My fine new feathered friends.

Just sobbing, until he'd sobbed himself out. Then it was back to Bach. Number six—the bucolic.

And this time, Mr. Summers, remember to retune your instrument before you begin.

Much better, thought Simon, when Wayne began to lose his composure. Fear comes in flavors, but the purer it was, the better—nothing chased away the blind rat, or made Simon feel more alive than the terror of a severe phobic. And these new Generation 2 technology goggles were really something—$1,899 over the Internet, but worth every penny. The detail was astounding, especially when you switched on the optional infrared spot/flood lens intended for use in total darkness. You could see every twitch, every quiver, every tear and every drop of fear sweat, and even the darkest blood. All in shades of green, of course, but you got used to that quickly enough, and the padded headgear distributed the one-and-a-half pound weight of the goggles evenly, and thus made it easy to bear—Simon thought of himself as having a long, aristocratic neck and a delicate build.

But when Wayne left off sobbing and went back to that intolerable, infernal finger twitching, Simon intervened for the first time since the owl attack.

"I think I'm going to let the smaller birds have you now," he said quietly.

"Fuck you, Simon," replied Wayne. He still didn't remember much after the recital Sunday evening, but the voice of the man who had called himself fear itself, particularly when he said the word *buddy,* had triggered one of those wispy, smoke-ring memories: standing out on Van Ness with his cello case, eyes averted from the sight of the Civic Center pigeons while he waited for a cab. Shiny silver Mercedes convertible pulls up to the curb, Simon Childs behind the wheel.

Hey, buddy, I thought that was you, what a coincidence, can I give you a lift someplace?

Wayne had always been a sucker for silver-haired white guys, not to mention silver convertibles; he'd almost made a move on Simon at the PWSPD convention last spring, but hadn't been able to decipher the decidedly mixed signals the older man was putting out.

The sexual signals weren't the only contradictions Wayne had noticed. Simon Childs was third-generation wealthy, obviously upper-crust, but though he was well-spoken, his speech was sprinkled with just enough street snarl to suggest that he'd spent some time mucking around down at the bottom of the pie as well. And yet he never swore—Wayne had never heard so much as a *hell* or *damn* escape from those elegant lips.

Wayne had never seen Simon in a tie, either, even at the PWSPD closing banquet in Vegas—his dress was always casual and comfortable, but expensive, and the drape of those casual, comfortable clothes could only have been achieved by a tailor. Part dandy, part roughneck, intelligent and well-read, but with little formal education, Simon Childs was also the most poised phobic Wayne had ever seen. Not a stiff white man's poise, either, but a loose, slouchy, long-limbed, easy kind of poise, so perfect it had to be studied.

But Simon's signals must have been clear enough last night, thought Wayne: he had a vague recollection of a wild ride in the convertible, top down, of wild laughter and champagne on a balcony, of undressing in a bedroom. But everything after that was a blank. Obviously Childs had slipped a roofie—a Rohypnol capsule—into the champagne.

Fuck you, Simon? Disappointed as Simon was to have been recognized so early in the game, he refused to stoop to Wayne's level. Simon took pride in not swearing, regardless of the provocation; it was his own private mental discipline, enforced at an early age by a few good beatings from Grandfather Childs, who didn't swear either, and reinforced when Missy began parroting his occasional epithet.

But Simon did feel rather foolish when he realized that Wayne had called his bluff. As part of his preparation for this latest round of the fear game (the preparation was as important, and nearly as engrossing, as the game itself), Simon had read a book on the making of Hitchcock's *The Birds* and learned that it was nearly impossible to get the smaller species, even the more aggressive ones, to attack on command. In the film it was all done with trick shots and chroma-key. And Simon would be the one who'd have to clean up the crap and get them back in their cages afterward.

"Wayne, listen to me—this is important."

"Fuck you," repeated Wayne, closing his eye and returning to the Bach. In many ways the sixth suite was the least satisfying to play, perhaps because it had originally been written for some unknown five-stringed instru—

Whap! A hard blow to the temple. Wayne toppled sideways onto the mattress, but made no effort to get up again. Fuck it, he thought as he tuned the imaginary top string back up to A. When you're practicing an imaginary cello with your hands cuffed behind you, it doesn't make all that much difference whether you're sitting up or lying down.

At-teck the gigue, Mr. Summers, don't snyeak up on it. If Wayne concentrated hard enough, he could almost *hear* old Brotsky's Russian-Jewish accent. *It's a dence, Mr. Summers, make it dence!*

And so Wayne attacked it, and he made it dance—in his mind his bowing action had never been freer, or more joyous, or, paradoxically enough, more under control. But there was a limit to his ability to maintain his concentration: he lost his place when Simon started kicking him.

"Wayne! Listen up, Wayne—you have to do something for me."

That got his attention. The *chutzpah,* as Brotsky would have said. The sheer *chutzpah.* "What?"

"I need you to write something."

"Then you'll leave me alone?" For some reason, finishing the entire cycle of suites had taken on urgency for Wayne.

"Yes."

"You're lying."

"Well, yes. But I'll make you a deal—if you do as I ask, I promise I'll make it quick and painless."

In the end, it was neither quick nor painless, though when Simon originally made his promise, he sincerely believed he was telling the truth. In the fear game, the payoff was fear, not pain—there was no advantage to prolonging Wayne's suffering.

But while Wayne was writing the note Simon required of him, Simon had a little too much time to think about what a disappointment Wayne had been and to convince himself that he would be entirely justified in making one last attempt to recoup his not inconsiderable investment of time, trouble, and cold, hard cash.

It was all to no avail, however—the smaller birds might as well have been origami sculptures for all the effect they had on the so-called ornithophobe. Simon went so far as to try stuffing one of the canaries into Wayne's mouth—no response other than that frenzied twitching of the fingers behind the back. Nor would the owl attack a third time, even after the blood started flowing again.

How long the beating lasted, Simon couldn't have said—when he lost his temper, he lost all sense of time. But for several minutes after Simon collapsed on the bloody mattress, sobbing for breath, Wayne's fingers continued to twitch. It was like a nightmare, something out of an Edgar Allan Poe story—Simon, who thought of himself as fearless, even managed to generate a little pretend terror by playing around with the notion that those blessèd fingers would continue to twitch long after he cut the hands off.

But to Simon's mixed relief, the twitching stopped of its own accord after a few more minutes. Then it was over, except for the cleanup, which would have to wait until morning. For one thing, Simon was physically exhausted and emotionally drained; for another, despite all the soundproofing he'd installed in the basement, the noise and vibration from the jackhammer still might leak up through the vents and awaken Missy.

II

The Blind Rat

1

Tuesday dawned clear and bright in Georgetown, where Linda Abruzzi was staying with her old college roommate Gloria Gee and Gloria's husband, Jim, until she found her own place. It was the sort of fall morning that made you forget winter was just around the corner. And the commute wasn't as bad as it had been on Monday—Linda was at her desk by eight, after another thorough vetting at the gate. The first thing she did was go over Dorie Bell's letter again.

Dorie Bell
Box 139
Carmel-by-the-Sea, CA 93921
(831) 555–1914

Oct. 1, 1999

Dear Agent Pender,

I don't know if this letter will even reach you, or if you will pay any attention to it even if it does, but in the article in the *Herald* last week about the Maxwell case, you talked about how your department helps track down serial killers who move around and kill people in different locations, which is exactly the situation I'm writing about. In any case, I don't know who else to turn to.

To begin with, I am not a nut. I know every nut who ever writes you starts out that way, but I can't help that. And just so you don't think I'm trying to hide anything I'll tell you right off the bat that I suffer from a psychiatric condition known as SPD, specific phobia disorder, which means an unreasonable fear of a particular situation or object, severe enough to detrimentally affect your everyday life.

I know it's probably hard for someone like you to understand how somebody can *know* a fear is unreasonable and still be negatively impacted to such a degree anyway, but as any psychiatrist will tell you, that's what it means to have a phobia.

In my case, I suffer from prosoponophobia, which means I am afraid of (I have to force myself to even write the word) masks. This probably sounds pretty lame to you, and as phobias go, it's surely not the worst, but believe me it's no walk in the park, especially around Halloween.

But that's not why I'm writing you. The reason I am writing is that this past spring I attended the PWSPD (Persons with Specific Phobia Disorder) convention in Las Vegas.

On the whole, it was one of the most positive experiences in my life. Not only did I pick up many new coping techniques, it was also very empowering to learn how many phobics there are. One speaker said 11 percent of the population.

And now I'll get to the point. Over the last six months, at least three people who attended the PWSPD convention have allegedly committed suicide. I say at least, because there may be others I don't know about, and I say allegedly because I don't think they committed suicide at all. I think they were murdered—but I'll just tell you the facts I know and let you decide for yourself. Which I'm sure you would do anyway.

One: Carl Polander. Las Vegas. Acrophobia. Fear of heights. Jumped or fell or was thrown to his death from a twelfth-story window on April 12th, the last night of the convention. The police say jumped, but those of us who knew him think differently. What would Carl have been doing on the roof of any building, when he couldn't even bring himself to enter an elevator or climb higher than the second floor?

Two: Kimberly Rosen. Chicago. Pnigophobia. Fear of suffocation. On June 15th, her mother found her in the bathtub of her apartment with a plastic bag over her head. There was a suicide note, supposedly in her handwriting, but I just don't buy it.

Three: Mara Agajanian. Fresno. Hemophobia. Fear of blood. Found in the bathtub on August 17th, with her wrists slit. But a hemophobe would no more have cut her own wrists than a pnigophobe would have tied a plastic bag over her head or an acrophobe would have thrown himself off a roof.

Agent Pender, something very strange and alarming is going on, but I can't get anybody to pay any attention. Maybe it's because I'm a PWSPD that the police in those three cities just won't take my fears seriously, but let me assure you that just because somebody has SPD does not make them paranoid. SPD and paranoid schizophrenia are two separate and distinct disorders that have no more in common than, for instance, measles and appendicitis.

I don't know what else to say, other than please, Agent Pender, won't you at least look into these cases? Because if you won't investigate three deaths in three different jurisdictions, I don't know who will, and if you don't, I'm afraid more of my friends are going to "commit suicide."

Sincerely yours,
Dorie Bell

And there it was. Didn't look like much in the cold, hard light of the morning, without Pender around to encourage her. But it wasn't as if Linda had anything else going on, so she spent the rest of the morning contacting the Vegas, Fresno, and Chicago PDs in order to verify the facts, then logging on to phobia.com, the PWSPD Association web site, in order to bone up on specific phobia disorders, and just before noon—nine A.M., California time—Linda, as she noted in her log, "initiated telephone contact with correspondent."

"Hello?"

"Dorie Bell?"

"This is Dorie."

"I hope I didn't wake you, Ms. Bell."

"Not at all. Is this about Wayne?"

"No, this is Linda Abruzzi with the Federal Bureau of Investigation. I'm calling in response to your letter to Special Agent Pender."

"Oh, thank God."

Not exactly the kind of response Linda was accustomed to getting when she called somebody at nine in the morning, their time, and identified herself as FBI. Still she stuck to Bureau-cratese: "Special Agent Pender has passed your letter on to me for disposition, and I need to ask you a few—"

The other woman cut her off in midsentence. "It's happened again."

"What's happened again, Ms. Bell?"

"My friend Wayne hasn't been seen since Sunday night. He was supposed to be *here* last night, only he never—"

"Wait a minute, slow down there, Ms. Bell—let's take it from the top."

So they did, they took it from the top, and by the time they reached the bottom, Linda was a believer. After promising to call Dorie back as soon as she had any information and deflecting her effusive and prayerful thanks, Linda clicked off the receiver, then called her old friend Bobby Emmett, who was still with the San Francisco field office.

Linda and Bobby had worked the Polly Klaas kidnapping together back in '93—what a cluster-fuck that had been. Old FBI truism: the more agents assigned to a kidnapping investigation, the worse the chances for a successful resolution—if by successful you mean finding the victim alive. The FBI's failures were loud and public, its triumphs often quiet and private—which was the way it had to be, of course.

And being a low-seniority agent in a high-visibility manpower rollout was no picnic. But if you had to spend eighteen-hour days canvassing neighborhoods, knocking on doors, fielding hot-line calls from wackos and publicity hounds, or, toward the end, cruising up and down Highway 101 looking for unmarked graves, there wasn't a nicer guy to do it with than Bobby Emmett.

True to form, Bobby agreed to get in touch with one of his contacts in the SFPD, then get back to Linda. But when he did, not long afterward, the news wasn't good—not for Wayne Summers, and certainly not for Linda's first Liaison Support investigation.

"Turns out Mr. Summers has an uncle pretty high up in the SFPD," Bobby explained. "They've been all over this one, and according to them, it looks like your boy drowned himself. They found his cello case out on Ocean Beach this morning, along with his clothes and a suicide note. Haven't found the body yet, but you know the riptide out there."

"The note—does it look legitimate?"

"His mother verified the handwriting."

"Can you get hold of it for me?"

"No can do. You're lucky you even caught me here—I'm off to Seattle in a few hours. Been loaned to Antiterrorism—they're beefing up for this Y2K deal."

"How about this afternoon, then? The fact that it looks like a suicide makes it a better fit for the profile."

"Linda, I have to go. If I were you, I wouldn't put a lot more effort into this one. Coincidences happen, you know? And suicides come in clusters."

"You're probably right," said Linda distractedly— she was trying to remember Ocean Beach from her San Francisco days. Dog shit, broken glass, murderous riptide, seals by the dozens on the rocks below Cliff House, and seagulls by the hundreds, wheeling and screaming and fighting for garbage and picnic scraps. Western gulls, California gulls, herring gulls, Heermann's gulls: you could throw a french fry in the air and nine times out of ten it would never hit the ground. "Thanks for the help."

But as she prepared herself mentally for the unpleasant task of calling Dorie Bell back and giving her the bad news about her friend Wayne, Linda was still far from convinced. Sure, suicides did sometimes come in clusters, and sure, coincidences did happen. But so did murder. And Ocean Beach was no place for an ornithophobe, thought Linda—especially a suicidal one.

2

"Watch out!" called Missy. She knew the man with the hook was hiding behind the door, and that as soon as Audrey Hepburn opened it, he would . . .

Ring ring ring ring, Simon, it's me, call me.

Missy rarely answered the telephone, partly because Simon didn't like her to, and partly because it was generally a frustrating experience. But all morning it had been *ring ring ring ring Simon it's Dorie, ring ring ring ring, call me I have news,* and finally she couldn't stand it anymore. She paused *Charade* and picked up the extension.

"Hello?"

"Hi, Missy. It's Dorie. Remember me?"

Of course she did—Dorie gave absolutely the *best* hugs. "Oh, hi."

"Hi. Is Simon there?"

"In the basement."

"What? I'm sorry, honey, he's what?"

"Basement. He is in the basement." But she could have repeated herself all day and not been understood. Stupid tongue. Stupid mouth. "Wait."

Even though the basement door was securely locked and bolted, you couldn't have dragged Missy near it with a team of horses. She beeped Simon with their two-way, then went back to her movie, leaving the receiver off the hook. A few minutes later, a frowning Simon showed up in the doorway wearing his kneepads and his rubber boots, smelling of wet cement. Missy waved the pager in the direction of the phone.

"Hello? . . . Oh, hi, Dorie, what's— . . . Oh, no. Oh, no . . . Listen, Dor', I want to take this in the other room. . . . Yeah, no sense getting the kid all upset." He handed the phone to Missy. "I'm gonna take it in my room—would you hang this up for me?"

And she did. Simon raised his hand as if he were going to strike her; then his mustache twitched; then he laughed. "I meant after I picked up the other phone."

"Then why didn't you say so?" Missy said coolly, without taking her eyes off the television screen, where Cary Grant (who with his silver hair and dimpled chin looked a lot like Simon, at least to Missy's eyes) was sliding, *clackety-clackety-clackety-clack,* down Audrey Hepburn's slippery, steeply sloped tile roof.

Simon, who'd been up since well before dawn—he'd driven to San Francisco and back to drop off the note and cello case at Ocean Beach, then worked like a galley slave all morning—still hadn't decided what to do with the birds when Missy summoned him up from the basement to take Dorie's call.

And while this afternoon's news update from the troublesome Ms. Bell wasn't entirely bad—according to the FBI agent she'd been in touch with, apparently SFPD had bought the suicide note, hook, line, and sinker—it was alarming to learn that she'd gotten the FBI involved in the first place. Simon would have to accelerate his timetable—a road trip was definitely in order.

But he couldn't leave Missy alone, and he'd given her attendant the week off in order to have more privacy with Wayne. Now he'd have to get Tasha back, but before he could do that, he'd have to do something about the birds in the basement. All on three hours of sleep. Busy, busy, busy, but at least he wasn't bored. That was the important thing—Simon had never encountered anyone who suffered from boredom to the extent he did, with the possible exception of Grandfather Childs, who'd known it well enough to have given it its name: the blind rat.

Only, the way Simon pictured it as a boy, it was more like a grub, a fat, blind, hairless grub gnawing away at him from the inside, robbing him of his peace, of his rest, and if he went too long without sufficient stimulation, of his sanity.

But with another session of the fear game to look forward to in the near future, the blind rat was not likely to be an immediate problem. And this game would be an easy one to prepare for: all he needed, really, was some Rohypnol, with which he was already well supplied, and a few masks, which shouldn't be all that difficult to procure, Simon reminded himself, not with Halloween less than two weeks away.

3

They got him. They got him good.

First they tortured him a little. No congratulatory messages at work Monday, no retirement luncheon, no gold watch.

But Pender had been determined not to let it get to

him. On his way home he stopped at the strip mall in Potomac and picked up videos of *Guadalcanal Diary, The Sands of Iwo Jima,* and *The Best of Mimi Miyagi,* enough Chinese takeout to feed the Red Army, and to wash it down, a fifth of Jim Beam. He'd left the pint behind in Abruzzi's desk drawer. She'd insisted she didn't drink, but Pender suspected it would only be a matter of time.

Since his divorce ten years earlier, Pender had been living in a ramshackle house on a hillside above Tinsman's Lock, Lock 22 of the Chesapeake and Ohio Canal, on federal land originally ground-deeded to former slaves after the Civil War and held now by Pender on a grandfathered National Park Service lease.

Among the advantages of living at Tinsman's Lock: a heavily wooded lot, no neighbors, and gorgeous views of the C&O, the Potomac, and the Virginia countryside beyond; it was also cheap. But chief among the disadvantages was the reason it was cheap: according to the terms of the lease, all visible improvements beyond the existing underground power and phone lines had to be period—any time between 1850 and 1890 would do—and not many people, it seemed, were willing to pay Montgomery County prices for a Tobacco Road home.

As for the interior, in the ten years Pender had lived there, more than one woman had tried her hand at decorating, but none of them had lasted long enough to make much of a dent, domesticity-wise. As his old friend Sid Dolitz once observed, the house was a lot like Pender himself: big, homely, and getting more dilapidated with every passing year.

So after convincing himself that he hadn't wanted

a damn party anyway, Pender had spent the first evening of his retirement watching videos, pigging down Chinese, and practicing his putting out on the spacious, if rickety, back porch, in preparation for his retirement present from Sid: a trip to California, two days of golf at Pebble Beach, two nights at the Lodge.

By Tuesday morning, a surprise party was the last thing on Pender's mind. He slept until ten, drowned his hangover with the hair of the dog (and why not?—he wasn't working), had leftover Chinese for brunch, and drove off in his jet black pride and joy, a '64 Barracuda he'd rescued from an abusive living situation and restored to health while drying out after his divorce, to meet Sid Dolitz at Sid's country club for their veddy civilized one o'clock tee time.

In many ways, Dolitz was the anti-Pender. Short, slight, a connoisseur of good food and fine wines, a faithful and uxorious husband to his beloved and extremely wealthy Esther until death did them part, and something of a dandy, at least by Bureau standards (even back in the FBI's mandatory conservative-suit-white-shirt-and-tie days, his suits were natural shoulder, his shirts were Egyptian sharkskin, and his Countess Mara neckties were always accessorized with a complementary pocket handkerchief), Sid had been playing a somewhat bemused Felix to Pender's Oscar for over twenty years.

Today he was wearing a pale green poplin windbreaker and perfectly creased khakis with a one-inch cuff; his iron gray toupee was unruffled by the fresh autumn breeze.

"Five bucks a hole," he called as Pender stepped up to the first tee.

"Ten," replied Pender, who then duck-hooked his first drive into the dogwoods to the left of the fairway.

Although Sid was ten years older than Pender, he preferred walking the course—possibly because he understood that the more tired Pender's legs became, the worse he hooked his drives. Once again, Pender barely shot his temperature. He paid up at the nineteenth hole; Sid left the money on the bar, and several rounds later, he insisted on leaving his own car at the club and driving Pender home in the 'Cuda.

Not a particularly subtle ruse: afterward, it occurred to Pender that if he hadn't suspected anything by the time he dragged his golf bag through the front door—at which point the thirty or forty people crowded into the vestibule or overflowing into the living room jumped out at him (those still young enough to jump) and shouted "Surprise!" at the top of their lungs—he probably *had* been too drunk to drive.

He had to fight back the tears as they crowded around him. "You got me," he kept saying. "You got me good."

4

September and October were what they called locals' weather on the Monterey Peninsula. Not only did the tourists clear out after Labor Day, but so did the fog—if the winter rains held off, you could generally count on two months of sunshine.

Dorie had been too shaken by the news of Wayne's death to get any work done Tuesday. Eventually, she knew, she'd end up painting it out, putting the fear and the grief, the whole mourning process, into one of her plein air scenes—just not during locals' weather.

But when she walked down to Carmel Beach around six o'clock that evening, Dorie found herself wishing she'd brought her gear. You don't need rain for mourning, she thought: a Carmel Bay sunset will do very nicely. There's sadness in so much beauty, especially when it's over so quickly. Then she remembered that Wayne Summers was only twenty-seven when he died.

Twenty-seven! And he was healthy, he had a job he loved and his career was flourishing; he was as close to taking charge of his ornithophobia as he'd ever been; and as if all that weren't reason enough to live, he got laid a lot more often than Dorie did, usually by breathtakingly gorgeous men—what possible reason would he have had to kill himself? Drown himself, at that. Wayne couldn't swim a lick. Dorie remembered how he used to joke that it was one of only three black stereotypes that could be applied to him. The other two, he added, were a good sense of rhythm and none-of-your-business.

Dorie found herself laughing through her tears at the memory. But after the tears came anger, and a resolution: She would not give up. She would keep trying, she would redouble her efforts, she would make a pest of herself at every level of law enforcement, until she had convinced somebody to open an investigation, and keep it open. Somebody like this female FBI agent. Because even if Abruzzi didn't believe what Dorie was saying yet, at least she sounded as if she *wanted* to believe. That was something, anyway.

5

Froot Loops, thought Linda—the Maryland countryside was in full autumn riot, yellow and crimson and orange, and it was almost too much, like driving through a box of Froot Loops, or an old Technicolor Disney cartoon.

Miss Pool proved to be as efficient at giving directions as she was at managing the Bureau (everybody knew it was the FBI clerks who really ran the place): from Virginia, follow 495, the Beltway, northeast into Maryland; then take 190, the River Road, north past Potomac and turn west on Tinsman's Lock Road. Pender's driveway was the first (and last) one on the left, on the far side of the sign marking the entrance to the C&O Canal National Historical Park and telling you what you could and couldn't do there.

It was dark by the time Linda turned down the long dirt drive. The other partygoers had parked in the overflow lot down by the canal and hiked back up the hill, so as not to screw up the surprise; the driveway was clear save for an old black muscle car—Linda parked behind it.

Some things never change, she realized, as she

heard the laughter and music spilling out from the big wooden house. Thirty-five years old, seven years with the FBI, and the prospect of walking into a party where she hardly knew anybody still reduced Linda Abruzzi to the emotional age of five.

It's okay, she reminded herself, you're not here to socialize. Find Pender, ask him what you came to ask him, wish him luck on his retirement, maybe grab a crab puff. Then *arrivederci,* Abrootz—you're out of there.

The front door was ajar; Pender, glass of Jim Beam in one hand and a shiny new beribboned Callaway driver in the other, was holding court on the far side of the rustic living room, over by the sliding glass doors that opened out onto the back porch. He saw her coming and proudly brandished the driver over his head. "Linda, what do you think of my gold watch?" Then: "Everybody, this hotshot here is Linda Abruzzi—she's gonna be filling my thirteen double Ds back at Liaison Support."

"If I can find them in that mess of an office, that is," said Linda, to polite laughter. The first retort that had come into her mind was something about not leaving quite that big a footprint, but she didn't want people looking down at her feet—she was still a little self-conscious about the shoehorn-style ankle braces built into the heels of her ugly orthopedic shoes, even though her slacks were tailored long to cover them.

And before she could ask Pender if they could talk privately, somebody tapped her on the shoulder; she turned to find herself face-to-face with another Bureau legend, Deputy Director Stephen P. McDougal. McDougal, according to scuttlebutt, had come within inches of being appointed director several years earlier, instead of Louis Freeh. Good-looking older man with tremendous presence and a head of thick white hair you wanted to walk barefoot through.

"How are you settling in, Abruzzi?"

"Excellent, sir. First rate."

"Office all right? Need any special accommodations?"

"No, sir, I'm fine."

"Good attitude," said McDougal. "Behind you all the way."

"Thank you, sir."

Linda was relieved when he turned away—she'd found herself feeling the way she'd felt back in high school, encountering the principal in the grocery store. When do *I* get to be the grown-up? she wondered. And now Pender had disappeared. She glanced around, saw him out on the back porch, engaged in earnest conversation with a dapper old guy wearing what looked like one of Sinatra's old toupees. She caught Pender's eye; he waved to her to join them.

"Linda Abruzzi, this is Sid Dolitz. Best forensic shrink who ever wore a badge. Never treated a patient a day in his life, though."

"Didn't care much for crazy people," Dolitz explained. "Bit of a handicap for a psychiatrist, but a plus as far as the Bureau was concerned."

"Nice to meet you."

"Nice to meet you, too." Dolitz had a neat little hand, not much bigger than Linda's, and much better manicured. "I understand you have MS."

"Yes?" As in *what of it?* In the few short months since her diagnosis, Linda had already met too many people who saw her disability before they saw her.

"So did my late wife. Would you mind terribly if I offered a suggestion?"

"I guess," said Linda dubiously.

"Get yourself a cane before you throw your back out."

"I'll take it under consideration."

"I'm sorry, I've offended you."

"It's okay."

"Friends?"

"Friends."

"In that case, can I offer you a glass of wine? I was just on my way into the kitchen to pop the top on a lovely looking Bordeaux—if you want good vino at Pender's, you have to bring it yourself."

"I'm on the wagon. But thanks anyway."

Dolitz left. Linda leaned out over the wooden railing; below her, the dark hillside and the shiny black ribbon of the canal. "Listen, Ed, I'm sorry to crash your party, but I needed to ask you a few questions, and Miss Pool said you were leaving town early tomorrow and that it would be okay to drop by."

"Well, if Pool said it, it must be so. What can I do you for?"

"It's about Dorie Bell's letter." Linda told him about Wayne Summers's disappearance and ostensible suicide.

"Oh, man," was Pender's only response—but it was an eloquent *oh, man*.

"The thing is," Linda continued, "I'm just not buying the suicide. Everybody else is—everybody but Dorie Bell. SFPD says drop it, Bobby says drop it, and the ASAC in San Francisco won't even talk to me—

he hung up when he found out I was with Liaison Support."

"That ASAC—his name wouldn't be Pastor by any chance?"

"Thomas Pastor—why, do you know him?"

"Ran into him a couple times during the Maxwell case. Empty suit—couldn't track down an elephant with diarrhea, but he'll look terrific at the press conference afterwards."

"So where do I go from here?" There weren't any courses at the Academy on liaising an investigation nobody seemed to want to conduct in the first place—but if there had been, Pender would have been the instructor.

"You have any more contacts in the field office?"

"Bobby was the last of my old gang."

"How about SFPD?"

"Nope."

"Then you're screwed," said Pender. "Unless . . ." And he leaned back casually against the precarious-looking railing, arms behind him, weight on his elbows—for some reason he seemed to be enjoying himself immensely.

"What? Unless what?"

"Unless you just happen to know two old farts named Pender and Dolitz, who just happen to be flying out to Pebble Beach tomorrow. We'll be five minutes from Carmel—no reason I couldn't drop by, have a little chat with Ms. Bell, at least find out whether she's with the MDF."

Linda gave him a never-heard-of-it shrug.

"When I first got to Washington, there was a huge

flap about a plot to blow up the Washington Monument," Pender explained. "Metro had a tip on a new group called the MDF. Antiterrorism shuts down the monument, plants snipers all around the mall, the whole nine yards. Then somebody actually goes out to interview the informant—turns out *MDF* stands for *Martian Defense Force*—the guy was intercepting messages from Mars through his fillings."

Linda forced a laugh. "I don't think Dorie Bell's with the MDF. In any case, I couldn't ask you to—"

"You didn't—I volunteered."

"But you're retired now."

"Not exactly," said Pender. "I still have two weeks before I'm officially a civilian."

"I don't want to get you in any trouble."

Pender shrugged. "What's the worst they can do, fire me?"

6

As a boy, Simon Childs had often been beaten by his grandfather for laziness—among other things. But he wasn't lazy, just subject to spells of paralyzing, unbearable, skin-crawling lethargy.

When not in the grip of one of his spells, however, Simon possessed a capacity for almost inhuman exertion; there were reserves of strength in that slender frame and surprising leverage in those long arms and legs. He worked all day and into the evening, and by the time he'd finished, the basement was so clean you could have held a prayer meeting down there.

Except for the God . . . blessèd . . . birds. Try as he might, he just couldn't bring himself to harm any of them. He tried to, starting with a mercy killing of the canary with the injured wing—the one he'd tried to stuff into Wayne's mouth—but holding it in his cupped hands, feeling the warmth, the softness, smoothing down the trembling yellow feathers with his long thumbs, he felt the same fullness in his chest and throat, the same bittersweet, painful yet pleasurable feeling that sometimes overcame him when he ran hot water into Missy's bath, or tucked her into bed at night.

Therefore, despite the fact that it was far more dangerous than simply doing away with the birds—or perhaps *because* it was more dangerous, and therefore less boring—he decided to set them free.

The first step was to consolidate the birds, by species—the parakeets, the pigeons, and all the canaries but one—into three cages, which he then loaded, along with the alarmingly apathetic owl in its burlap sack, into the Mercedes parked in the garage abutting the sound-proofed basement of the Julia Morgan–designed Childs mansion. There was barely room in the trunk for the canary and parakeet cages; he stowed the pigeons on the backseat of the convertible, covered the cage with a blanket, tossed the sack with the owl into the front seat, and put the top up.

Simon went back upstairs a little before nine-thirty. Missy was still in the bath. He helped her out, rubbed her down with a fluffy towel to get that blue-tinged skin nice and rosy, powdered her thighs so they wouldn't chafe, and got her into her footed flannel jammies in time for *The Original Ten O'clock News*.

"Now, Simon has to go out for an hour or so, but if you're good, and you don't get into any mischief, I have a very special present for you."

There weren't many words that could induce Missy to tear her eyes away from the screen when Dennis Richmond was on, but *present* was one of them. "What, what?"

"You'll never guess in a million years."

"Will too."

"*Hmmmmm.* Lemmee see now. What's little . . . and yellow . . . and has feathers . . ." Over the years, Simon had learned how to string the hints out so that Missy had the thrill of interrupting him in midquestion, which always made her feel smart. ". . . and wings . . . and Sylvester the Cat's always trying to—"

"Tweety Bird! A Tweety Bird!"

"*If* you're very good and don't get into any what?"

"Mischief."

"Exactly."

"I promise."

Missy was as good as her word, and so was Simon. He drove all the way out to Walnut Creek, surreptitiously dropped off the feathered menagerie outside the Lindsay Wildlife Museum, which specialized in rescuing injured birds, and got back to Berkeley in time to give Missy her present—the healthiest and singingest canary in the whole batch—before tucking her in.

"I love her," said Missy. Simon had put the cage right next to her bed.

"What are you going to call her?"

"Tweety, silly."

"Tweety Silly?" teased Simon. "That's a funny name."

"Brat," said Missy.

"Brat," replied Simon. As he bent over the bed to kiss her on the forehead, the canary began to sing. Simon turned out the light, but left the hall light on and the door ajar.

"Good night, sis."

"Good night," Missy called. "Sweet dreams."

"Let's hope so," muttered Simon, as the canary fell silent. "God, let's hope so."

III

Manie Sans Délire

1

The morning after Pender's retirement party, the spookily efficient Miss Pool made a single phone call, and in nothing less than a Bureau-cratic miracle, twenty minutes later two burly men in white coveralls showed up to haul away Pender's files.

Linda then tackled the task of cleaning out Pender's desk and discovered the bottle of Jim Beam he'd left behind for her. She thought about throwing it into the wastebasket, but reconsidered: according to rumor, Counterintelligence was going through FBI trash now on a regular basis, trying to find the mole who had tipped off a major operation—the tunnel under the Russian Embassy, again according to rumor.

Two hours later, while Linda was on-line, scrolling through the phobia.com chat room archives, the same two men in coveralls, accompanied by Special Agent Steve Maheu, returned with dolly-load upon dolly-load of white cardboard file boxes. Maheu, a crew-cut member of the FBI's Mormon Mafia, wearing a gray suit especially tailored to hide the umbrella up his ass (according to Pender), informed Linda that she'd been loaned to Counterintelligence.

"Actually, I'm working on something kind of promising at—"

He cut her off in midsentence. *"Actually,* you're working on whatever I say you're working on, Abruzzi. Unless you are physically unable to perform the duties to which you are assigned, in which case I suggest you hand in your badge and let's get this charade over with before you embarrass the Bureau any further."

Lucky for you they took my gun away, Linda felt like saying. But what she did say, quietly, after counting to ten in Italian (a trick her mother, from the Sicilian side of the family, the side with the temper, had learned from *her* mother when she was a little girl), was, "Good lord, you really believe that, don't you? That I'm embarrassing the Bureau."

"These boxes," he continued, as if she hadn't spoken, "contain computer printouts of every transaction in every known bank account keyed to the social security number of any agent, clerk, or charwoman with knowledge of a recent operation which may have been compromised from the inside."

"You mean the tun—"

Maheu cut her off again. "Excuse me? I didn't hear that," he said pointedly.

"I said, what fun."

"That's better. I don't know how you did things in San Antonio, Abruzzi, but here in Washington we don't deal in gossip, especially in matters of security."

"Sorry." Linda, a born wiseass, refrained with difficulty from pointing out that technically they weren't in Washington, they were in Virginia.

"Your job is to go through these transaction records one account at a time. The names have been redacted and code numbers substituted. If you find any unusual deposits, or pattern of deposits, write the code number down on a sheet of paper."

"That's it?"

"That's it."

"Do you really think somebody who's spying for the Russians is going to deposit the payoffs into his *checking* account, for crying out loud?"

"No. If I thought there was a chance in Hades of that, I'd assign a real agent to the job. And who said anything about Russians?"

Uno, due, tre, quattro . . .

2

Eight miles high, somewhere over Kansas, Pender turned to Sid Dolitz. "Well?"

Sid polished off the last of his crab cocktail, took another sip of complimentary champagne, and patted his lips with a linen napkin—he always flew first class. "You're kidding, right?"

"Why would I be kidding? I'm sitting next to the man who *invented* profiling."

"I think Brussel, Teten, and Mullany, among others, might have something to say about that."

"But they're not here," Pender pointed out.

"If they were, they'd tell you only an idiot would try to come up with a psychological profile based on such flimsy data."

"Give me a flimsy profile, then."

"I don't *do* flimsy," said Sid.

Pender waited him out.

"Okay, okay. Assuming it's the same perp, assuming all the alleged suicides are really homicides, and with a caveat the size of your enormous ass, here's a shot in the dark: antisocial personality disorder, more commonly known as psychopathy, but *compounded* by a phobia disorder, manifesting counterphobically."

"And now for the English translation . . . ?"

"Here's my theory: As a psychopath, our man's biggest problem is boredom." They were taking the killer's gender for granted: serial poisoners aside, at a conservative estimate, ninety-seven out of a hundred serial killers are male. "Psychopaths characteristically demonstrate abnormally low cortical arousal levels, so they're constantly in search of stimulation. Extreme stimulation: in order to reach the same level of satisfaction and enjoyment you or I might achieve from watching a good movie, your average psychopath has to torture a cat or get into a fistfight. And as for reaching the levels of cortical arousal the normal person gets from any activity they're passionate about, like sex, or at our age, golf—"

"Speak for yourself," said Pender.

"—the psychopath might have to actually murder somebody. But here's where it gets interesting: given that the victims all had different specific phobia disorders, and taking into account the manner of their respective deaths, I think it's highly probable that our man is a phobophobe."

"What's that?"

"Fear of fear: a phobophobe is afraid of fear itself. But this subject's phobia would seem to be manifesting counterphobically—in other words, he seeks out that which he's afraid of—which in turn fits hand in glove with the psychopathy: he fights his boredom by feeding on fear."

"Sounds like one scary sonofabitch," said Pender.

"He'd probably be very gratified to hear you say that."

"I don't want to gratify him, I want to catch him."

"You're retired."

"Not technically."

"You're not on active duty."

"A mere technicality."

"You're really going to go through with this?"

"Bet your ass."

"A word of advice, then: Don't underestimate this man. The original name for psychopathy was *manie sans délire,* which means 'mania without delusion.' He may be crazy as a shithouse rat, to use the technical term, but his mind is at least as clear and focused as yours. Probably more so, considering the amount of booze you've been putting away lately."

"You think I'm drinking too much?" Pender was genuinely surprised.

"For a small county in Ireland, no. For one man, yes."

3

On Wednesday morning, Simon Childs attempted to soften the blow by taking his sister to the Denny's in Emeryville for a breakfast that would have felled a lumberjack, before breaking the news that he had to go away again for a little while.

"How long?" she asked, as morosely as she could with a mouth full of hash browns.

Simon leaned across the table and wiped the corner of her mouth—she hated for him to do that in public, but was too depressed to protest. "It's just for a day or two—tops. And here's the good news: I talked to Ganny Wilson this morning—if you want, you can stay with her until I get back."

Missy brightened. "Peachy keen. I love Ganny."

"And Ganny loves you, too. But she's pretty old, you know." At least eighty by now. "You're gonna have to be good, not give her any trouble."

"No mischief," Missy promised solemnly. But inside, she was giggling. Ganny Wilson didn't care about mischief, only matches. "Just so long as you don't burn the house down, Princess," she used to say. "Everything else, Ganny can fix."

Two hours later, after helping Missy pack her pink valise and dropping her—and Tweety—off at Ganny Wilson's little cottage in the West Berkeley flats, Simon had to upwardly revise his estimate of their former housekeeper's age: the doddering old black woman looked to be closer to ninety.

It was worrisome, no denying that—sometimes Missy could be a handful, even for a caretaker in her prime—but as the Mercedes rolled across the Bay Bridge, top down, radio blasting Vivaldi's ubiquitous *Four Seasons* from all eight speakers, Simon reminded himself that Dorie hadn't left him much choice. He had to get to her before she talked to the FBI—or to anybody else, for that matter.

At the thought of Dorie, Simon's pulse quickened again for the first time since Wayne Summers's death. Ever since their first meeting at the convention, he had been so looking forward to playing the fear game with her—saving the best for last, so to speak. Would it be better, he wondered, to buy several masks at one store, or one mask at several stores? And if so, where?

He was still mulling that one over when the classical station cut to a commercial. Simon pushed the *seek* button, heard Tab Hunter crooning about young love, first love on the oldies station, and quickly punched *seek* again. He didn't want to hear anybody romanticizing about young love, because *his* first affair, with Nervous Nellie Carpenter, had resulted in the worst beating of his life.

On the other hand, if it hadn't been for his involvement with Nellie, Simon might never have discovered his life's path, his obsession, the only sure cure for the blind rat, and, except for Missy, his only reason for living, so perhaps old Tab wasn't so far off after all.

4

Ed Pender was not a religious man, but the feeling of awe and wonder that overtook him as he stepped up to the eighteenth tee at Pebble Beach was nearly overwhelming. The deep green of the fairway, the roundness and whiteness of the ball, the orange sun poised at the edge of Carmel Bay—it was a moment of perfection in an imperfect world.

And Pender, jet-lagged, two months shy of fifty-six years old, fifty pounds overweight, and twenty-three strokes over par up to that point, was Jack, was Arnie, was Tiger, facing one of the greatest character tests in the wide world of golf. Play it safe, lay up right, take a makeable bogey, shoot a hundred. Or take a chance—a big chance, with his tired legs and duck hook—blast it over the water, go for the par, break a hundred.

He had to go for it, of course. *Just don't hook,* he ordered the ball as he went into his backswing. *Don't hook, don't hook, don't—*

Whack, quack, splash.

"Take a mulligan, kid," urged Sid, who was far enough ahead to be magnanimous. "Nobody has to know."

"I'd know," said Pender, as his caddy sadly handed him a new ball—he'd placed a side bet on the bigger, younger guy with his fellow caddy.

Dorie Bell—who despised golf in general and the exclusionary, land-grabbing, prodevelopment, water-wasting bastards at Pebble Beach in particular—was putting the last touches on her painting of the sunset around the time Pender was hooking his drive at eighteen into it.

She worked with her palette in her lap, brush in her left hand, cloth in her right hand, and a stout walking stick leaning against her easel, with which to keep the dogs away. It wasn't the best sunset she'd ever done—got the water, got the sun, missed the pearl-pink blush of the abalone sky by a mile. Sunsets were difficult—you had to work fast and capture the color values on the fly—but they sold well, at least for Dorie, whose plein air oils sold for between five hundred and five thousand dollars each, depending on the size of the piece. *When* they sold, that is—but Dorie couldn't complain. She wasn't making a fortune, but she was making a living, which was more than most artists could say.

Dorie painted until the light was gone, then slipped the canvas into the slotted box she used to transport wet paintings; it took two trips to load her gear into the back of her old Buick Roadmaster station wagon. She drove straight home, grabbed a bite to eat, and was upstairs changing when the doorbell rang. Musical clothes, she liked to call it: she'd start trying on outfits at least an hour before a social occasion, and whatever she had on when her date arrived or when she absolutely positively had to be out the door was what she'd end up wearing.

Tonight's winning entry was a simple but elegant ensemble: man's blue denim shirt (top two buttons open; no, three; no, two), tucked into a pair of Wranglers as soft as chamois and older than dirt, held up by a wide leather belt with a silver rodeo buckle a sweet young cowboy had given her, back in her sweet young cowboyin' days.

"Be right down," Dorie called, checking herself out in the full-length mirror behind the bedroom door. Not bad, she decided, then asked herself why she was even fussing. It wasn't like this was a date or anything—not by a long shot.

To tin—flash a badge—or not to tin, that was the question for Pender. It felt so weird, so unbalanced, to be standing on a stranger's doorstep without a badge case in his hand. He had transferred his old DOJ shield—eagle, scales, blindfolded Justice in a pageboy haircut—to his wallet, to be used in the event of emergencies, such as getting pulled over for speeding, but he knew he had no business flashing it here. This wasn't an official visit, just a favor for a friend.

As soon as the door opened, Pender knew he'd made the right decision. Dorie Bell was tall, striking, and buxom, with cornflower blue eyes, and although her long braided hair was a youthful brown, he could tell by the deep-scored laugh lines at the corners of her eyes that she was close enough to him in age that if things seemed to be tending in that direction, he could make a pass at her without feeling like a dirty old man. Not that that had ever stopped him before. And a pass would definitely have been out of the question if he *had* tinned her.

"Ms. Bell?"

"Agent Pender. Come on in."

"Maybe you'd better call me Ed—I'm not here in an official capacity." Out of habit, he started to take off his hat, a brown Basque beret, as he entered the vestibule, then changed his mind and left it on—he was still a little self-conscious, not about his skin head (he'd started going bald at eighteen), but about the ragged, trident-shaped scar transecting his scalp—a souvenir from an earlier serial killer investigation.

"In that case, call me Dorie." She remembered to lock the door behind them; for a Carmel native, locking up was something that took a little getting used to. "And what exactly does that mean, anyway—'not here in an official capacity'?"

"Like I told you on the phone, I'm more or less retired—Agent Abruzzi's taking over the investigation. But when I mentioned to her last night that I was going to be here, she asked me to stop by and check in on you."

"Check in, or check up?"

"Both," Pender admitted readily—the woman still might turn out to be crazy, but she was clearly no dummy.

"It's all right, I don't mind. I'm just glad *anybody*'s willing to listen to me at this point. Where should we do this?"

"Wherever you'll be most comfortable."

"How about the kitchen?"

"Ideal," said Pender. "My mother always said the kitchen was the most important room in the house."

"Where did you grow up?"

"I'm an Appleknocker," he replied; then, receiving a blank look: "Cortland. Upstate New York. And you?"

"Right here."

"You mean Carmel?"

"I mean right here, this house."

"No kidding? That's unusual, this day and age."

"Tell me about it," said Dorie. "My friend Simon, in Berkeley, is the only other person over fifty I know who still lives in the house he was brought up in."

As he followed Dorie down the hallway toward the kitchen, Pender found himself mentally humming the first few bars of "Something in the Way She Moves." Over fifty, he said to himself: you'd never know it from this angle.

5

Like his sister, Simon Childs was almost always ravenous. Unlike Missy, however, Simon had his looks to consider. And he liked to maintain that hungry edge: satiety led to boredom; boredom led to the blind rat.

Sometimes he overdid it, though—his lean belly was rumbling by the time he reached Monterey. With nearly an hour to kill before nightfall, he decided to treat himself to a crab feast on Fisherman's Wharf. Window table at Domenico's, otters, seals, and sea lions providing the entertainment, dramatic lighting courtesy of the setting sun.

It didn't come cheap—fortunately money had never been a consideration for the heir to the Childs Electronics fortune, especially after his trust fund kicked in at age twenty-one, leaving him enough money to smoke, snort, pop, tweak, and inject himself half to death in a vain attempt to stave off the blind rat.

But again, Simon was lucky: unlike most addicts, he figured out it wasn't working before it killed him. And luckier still, he had something that did work— the fear game. He still enjoyed weed, whites, and wine, as well as the occasional milder psychedelics such as MDA or Ecstasy, and a rainbow array of downers and sleeping pills that were as necessary to him as oxygen, but for the most part, fear was Simon's drug of choice. Other people's fear, that is—he liked to think of himself as fearless.

Simon lingered over coffee and dessert until the last of the color was gone from the sky. He tipped his waiter well, but not lavishly enough to make himself memorable, and stopped into the Wharf's General Store on his way back to the car to buy a cute little sea otter for Missy's stuffie collection.

Then it was time to get to work. Simon drove south to Carmel and parked the Mercedes down-town, where it would be less conspicuous, leaving himself a ten or fifteen minute walk uphill to Dorie's house, where he and Missy had stayed when they came down for a visit in late June. The three of them had explored the Aquarium in Monterey, driven down the coast to Big Sur, and on their last day, toured the lighthouse in Pacific Grove, where the docent had given Missy the honor of striking the big bell with a wooden mallet—seventh heaven for the old girl. She had earned it, though: the trip was her reward for having been left alone with her attendant for a week while Simon was in Chicago.

All the excitement and exertion, however, had nearly proved fatal to Missy. No more road trips, her doctors had ordered when she was released from the cardiac unit at Alta Bates. Only by putting her on a regimen of quiet and diet, they said, could Simon count on another year or so of his sister's company. And as always, they assured him that a heart transplant was out of the question—Down syndromers her age weren't even on the protocol.

Four months later, it still made Simon furious to think that a donor heart would go into the garbage before they'd put it into Missy's chest. But this was no time for anger, he reminded himself as the roof motor whined and the top of the Mercedes closed out the stars. With forced calm he hung the temporary handicapped placard (obtained after Missy's heart attack) from the mirror post so he wouldn't get any tickets that might be used as evidence against him, then locked up the car and set off at an unhurried pace through the quaint streets of Carmel-by-the-Sea; just another tourist, dressed in black, with a shopping bag over his arm.

As he strolled, Simon went over the layout of Dorie's house in his mind. Two bedrooms upstairs. Living room, first floor front; kitchen back left, studio back right. Look for the lighted room—the frugal Ms. Bell never left a bulb burning in an empty one. Easiest access would be through the studio door on the right side of the house—he'd noticed the broken lock on his previous visit.

Almost there. One more steep uphill block. Simon pulled the hood of his sweatshirt up over his head as he turned the corner. Second house in. Casual glance to the right as he strolled by. Housefront dark, curtains drawn in the living room, blinds drawn in the front bedroom, her bedroom.

He cut across the lawn, sauntered around the side of the house as if he belonged there. The kitchen lights were on; Simon raised himself up on his tiptoes and peered over the high windowsill. Dorie was there, all right, but she wasn't alone. Big bald guy in a brown beret and baby blue Pebble Beach sweatshirt sitting across the kitchen table from her—if the man had chosen that moment to look up, their eyes would have met.

Simon ducked back down, squatting behind the ceanothus bush below the kitchen window. His heart was racing, and his stomach felt the way it had back in his high-risk, rock-climbing, Harley-riding, skydiving days, when he'd sought out physical danger as an antidote to the blind rat and learned that the effects of adrenaline, like those of drugs, were only temporary; the rat inevitably returned, ten times hungrier than before.

If he'd had a gun, of course, he could have solved the problem with two shots and been back in Berkeley by midnight, but he'd thrown away his short-barreled .38 in horror six weeks earlier after coming within a whisker of using it to end a particularly virulent siege by the rat. Only the knowledge that Missy still needed him had kept him from putting a bullet through his brain; it wasn't until he found himself kneeling by her bedside as she slept, trying to work up the courage to kill her first, that he'd come to his senses.

So: no gun. He'd have to wait the bald guy out, hope he left soon. If so, the game was on. If not—and it was entirely possible that Dorie was sleeping with the guy, she'd all but thrown herself at Simon back in June—

Simon would have to wait until they were asleep, then bash and run, which was not his style at all.

But then again, being on the wrong end of a lethal injection wasn't exactly his style either.

6

A cozy kitchen, a fresh-brewed pot of red Typhoo tea that contained enough caffeine to give a meth freak the jitters, good conversation with a fine-looking woman— there are worse ways to spend an evening, thought Pender.

"Why masks?" was his first question.

Dorie shrugged. *"Quien sabe?* I've been hypnotized, I've been regressed, I've had my past lives done—yeah, I know, welcome to California—and I still don't have any idea. Ask a dozen shrinks, you get a dozen different stories. One says change or loss is the trigger, another one says trauma, another says there doesn't have to be any trigger. Some say genetics, some say brain chemistry. There's some evidence for that—phobics have greater blood flow on the right side of the brain, and an overactive amygdala."

"What do *you* think? What does your gut tell you?"

"That it doesn't matter why. Origin: irrelevant. All that matters is that I know that if I see a mask, I'm going to have these terrible feelings. I'm going to feel like I've slipped into a nightmare, like anything that's possible in a nightmare is possible now. My heart will start pounding; I'll get short of breath, hyperventilate. I'll feel like I'm dying, or paralyzed, and I'll *know* I'm going to make a spectacle of myself, maybe pass out and break my nose, which I've already done twice, as you may have guessed from the zigzag." Dorie rubbed her nose ruefully.

"It's not the masks I'm afraid of, mind you: it's the anxiety attack, and the idea it could be triggered at any moment. One speaker at the convention described it as going around with a cocked gun; somebody else said a phobia is like a hole in your life that you could fall through at any time."

"Tell me about the convention," said Pender.

"Like I said in the letter, it was fantastic. Amazing. We had shrinks, we had symposiums, we had day trips. Everybody stayed in the Olde Chicago—it was luxe, Ed—first class all the way."

"Must have been expensive."

"That was the best part—it was sort of pay-what-you-can, and the PWSPD Association picked up the rest."

"And the association is supported how? On dues?"

"Just contributions."

"Must be some awfully wealthy phobics out there."

"Between you, me, and the lamppost . . ." Dorie leaned forward; by dint of sheer willpower, Pender managed to keep his eyes from straying cleavage-ward. ". . . most of the expenses for the convention were underwritten by my friend Simon—the one who lives in the house he was raised in?"

"In Berkeley." Pender just wanted to show her he'd been paying attention.

"Right. That's Simon Childs, as in Childs Electronics.

His grandfather started the company—I guess he's got a trust or something. But he's very cool about having all that money—nobody's supposed to know he's supporting the association. He just wants to be treated like everybody else."

"Admirable. How long have you two known each other?"

"We met at the convention, kind of stayed in touch. He and his sister came down for a weekend around the end of June. She has Down syndrome—it's so sweet the way he dotes on her."

"Not to pry," said Pender, "but were you two . . . say, more than just friends?"

"No, just friends."

The reply was quick enough, but registered on Pender's finely calibrated bullshitometer nonetheless. Maybe a spurned overture on either side? "You sure about that?"

Her eyebrows arched, her eyes turned a slightly darker shade of blue. Pender raised both hands in a gesture of surrender. "All right, all right. But there's something you need to understand. There's a rule of thumb in my business: If you want to find the predator, first find the herd. The herd was in Vegas, which means, assuming we have a serial killer on our hands—and right or wrong, at this point we'd be fools to assume otherwise—the chances are, oh, say about ninety-nine out of a hundred that he was at that convention, and about ninety-five out of a hundred that he was one of the attendees—otherwise he'd have stood out more."

"So what you're saying is, I already know the killer."

"More than likely."

"God, that's spooky."

"It's also how we're gonna catch him. And we *are* going to catch him—as these investigations go, this is going to be a slam dunk. It'll take some manpower—we'll have to interview each of the attendees, narrow the pool down to anybody who hasn't got an alibi for . . . what were the dates again?"

"April twelfth, June fifteenth, and August seventeenth," said Dorie without hesitation.

"Slam dunk, then," said Pender, glancing at his watch. Eight-forty-five—he and Sid had a nine o'clock dinner reservation at Club XIX, the four-star restaurant at the Lodge that Sid had been salivating over all day. When Pender took out his cell phone to call a cab, though, Dorie wouldn't hear of it; she insisted on driving him back to Pebble Beach herself.

"It's the least I can do," she told him, as she cleared two weeks' worth of water bottles, sandwich wrappers, rags, old brushes, and empty paint tubes off the passenger seat of the old Roadmaster. "I don't know how I'll ever be able to thank you."

"I haven't done anything yet," replied Pender.

"You listened, you gave me hope. That's a lot." Dorie slid behind the wheel, engaged in her usual struggle with the seat belt—they just didn't make shoulder harnesses to fit tall gals with big boobs—and turned the key in the ignition. "C'mon, Mary—you can do it," she urged. And Mary did it, turned right over. "Attagirl."

"You named your car Mary?" As they drove through the dark wooded streets of residential Carmel, Pender finally managed to get his seat belt buckled—they didn't exactly build them for somebody his size and shape, either.

"After Mary Cassatt. You know—the Impressionist painter. She's so old now, though, I'm thinking about renaming her Grandma Moses."

"Don't do it," said Pender. "Never rename a car— it's supposed to be bad luck."

"I thought that was boats."

"Cars, too. My ex-wife got my old T-Bird in the divorce. Changed her name from Lola to Daisy—the car, that is. Totaled it three weeks later."

"Was she hurt?"

"I told you, she was totaled."

"Your wife, I meant." Then Dorie glanced over, saw him grinning; she couldn't help but notice that he wasn't half as homely when he smiled.

They had to stop at the Pebble Beach gate and tell the guard their business in order to avoid the seven-dollar riffraff tariff. "God, I hate this place," muttered Dorie through clenched teeth.

"I take it you're not a golfer."

"No, I'm a painter. And these bastards think they own some of the greatest views in the world. Did you see the Lone Cypress today?"

"Magnificent," said Pender.

"Did you know it's against the law to sell any images of it? You even hang a painting of that tree in a gallery, Pebble Beach Corporation takes you to court."

They pulled up in front of the Lodge a few minutes after nine. Dorie had to get out and walk around the car to let Pender out—the passenger door didn't open from the inside.

"I'm not sure of the protocol," she said. "Is it okay to hug an FBI agent?"

"Normally you need to fill out a few forms in triplicate and submit them to—"

But she'd already thrown her arms around him. "Thank you."

"My pleasure." It was, too: she gave him a good full-body hug—none of that tentative, shoulder-hunching, stingy-chested nonsense. And she was tall enough that they fit nicely together. "You take care now—and try not to worry too much. These guys have cycles. The intervals tend to shorten, but judging by what you've told me, we probably have another two months before he kills again. That'll probably be more than enough time to catch him."

"That's good to know," said Dorie. "In a twisted kind of way. But you'll stay in touch, right?"

"I'll call you tomorrow."

"I'll be home all day."

That was the plan, anyway. Dorie had a show coming up in February, at the Plein Air Gallery in Carmel. She already had plenty of product for the wall space, but she knew herself well enough to foresee the inevitable panic as the opening approached: the paintings she'd already selected would start looking like crap to her, at which point it would be good for her peace of mind to have some backups ready. And with her oils requiring a minimum of three months to dry, it was time to get cracking.

Tomorrow, then, she would spend putting the finishing touches on Wayne's sunset, gessoing canvases, and psyching herself up for a painting marathon. Five commercial plein airs in five days, starting with the bell tower over at Carmel Mission, the closest thing there was to a guaranteed sale, now that the Lone Cypress was off limits.

The problem was, Dorie had already painted the damn tower from every conceivable angle in every season—which was why she needed another day to psych herself up. Making a living through her painting, a dream of Dorie's from childhood, had turned out to be a trade-off after all—but then, what hadn't?

Returning to a dark house, fumbling her key into the lock, Dorie began to have second thoughts about her lights-off policy. It would be oh so easy for someone to lie in wait in the bushes and jump her on the dark doorstep. Perhaps she could have one of those motion-sensor floods installed—then the light would only come on when she needed it. Of course, any real security measures would have to start with fixing the lock on the studio door, which had been broken for three, four years.

Once inside, though, Dorie was comfortable with the familiar darkness of the house she'd grown up in. She didn't have to turn on the hall light to find her way back to the kitchen, where she put the kettle on to boil in the dark, not to save electricity, but to watch the blue gas flame dancing. Dorie was an intensely visual person; as a child, she had once mentioned to her father that the blue of the gas flame was the most beautiful blue in the world.

"No, sweetheart, I'm afraid I have to disagree with you there," he'd replied thoughtfully, his sibilants coming out wet and juicy around the stem of his pipe.

"The most beautiful blue in the world is the blue of my little girl's eyes."

Oh, Daddy, she thought now, what a great thing to say. He'd been dead twelve years and she still missed him. Mom, too—he'd only outlived her by six months. Just kind of gave up without her. They were buried together in the old Monterey cemetery out by El Estero, next to Dennis the Menace Park; that second funeral, the orphan-maker, had been a gut-wrenching experience even for the forty-year-old Dorie.

For some reason, the blue flame didn't seem quite so enchanting tonight—it looked cold to Dorie, like the light from a distant star. Then she switched on the low-hanging chandelier over the kitchen table and her nightmare began.

At first, she thought it *was* a nightmare, the mask-in-the-window nightmare. Because there was the window, high in the wall, and there was the mask, a white Lone Ranger–type mask, and the eye-holes were empty, the way they always were in the dream.

But she wasn't screaming, the way she always did in the dream, nor did she wake up, the way she always did. Instead she felt her scalp prickling and saw the familiar multicolored fireflies swimming in front of her eyes as she tumbled through the darkness.

7

In her seven years with the Bureau, Linda Abruzzi
had worked more than her share of shit jobs and
shuffled more than her share of paper—federal
employment background checks, interstate car theft
investigations that involved comparing VIN numbers
on computer printouts that were longer than she was
tall, follow-the-money RICO probes—but nothing as
soul-deadeningly, eye-strainingly, sleep-inducingly
boring as going through fourteen file boxes of slop-
pily photostatted bank records.

Her initial inclination had been to blow it off.
She'd finger-walked through the first few boxes, jotted down a few code numbers at random, then
buzzed Miss Pool and asked her if she could come up
with a number for the Chicago PD's homicide division.

"I'll be right in," was the somewhat puzzling response.

"No, I just need—"

A moment later, Miss Pool appeared in Linda's
doorway. She had taken off her suit jacket; she was
wearing a sleeveless black jersey under it. Good upper
arms for a woman her age, thought Linda; no wob-
ble—she must work out.

"You didn't have to get up—I only wanted a phone
number."

"I know, hon—but don't you want to finish going
through those boxes first?"

"Why would I want to do that? You know as well as I do it's busywork."

"Because Maheu obviously doesn't want you to."

"Now you've lost me entirely," said Linda. "Why doesn't Maheu want me to go through the records he asked me to go through?"

"Because he doesn't want you to find something."

"But there's nothing there to find!"

"Oh?" said Pool mysteriously, raising her left hand with a flourish and tapping the rather masculine onyx band she wore on her ring finger before going back to her desk.

"Oh." A ringer—of course. Pool had just warned her that neither Maheu nor the counterspooks were above planting a deliberately doctored record somewhere in the files. Something so obvious that a diligent investigator could not have missed it, and so suspicious that only a double agent would have failed to report it.

Linda had ended up working on the floor all day—it was easier than hauling the boxes onto the desk—and by quitting time she had pains shooting up her legs to her butt, and her legs were so stiff she had to haul herself up using the corner of the desk for leverage. Miss Pool, who'd popped her head into the doorway to say good night, hurried over to help her.

"Don't let the bastards wear you down," whispered Pool, who proved to be even stronger than Linda had suspected, as she helped Linda to her chair.

"Never," Linda said, swiveling her chair around to

face her computer, intending to log back on to phobia.com—she was on her own time now.

Pool shook her head regretfully. "Sorry, no overtime."

"I won't put in for it."

"Maheu wants me to log your hours. I'd fudge it, but your ID logs you in and out every time you go through a door. Then there are the gate logs and the—"

"It's okay, I understand. And thanks for the tip about the, you know . . ." Linda tapped her own bare ring finger.

"Don't mention it."

"No, I—"

"I mean that literally," said Pool. "Don't mention it."

The drive back to Georgetown was a typical Beltway nightmare. At the 66/495 maze, an SUV cut over into Linda's lane, nearly clipping the Geo's front bumper, and when she hit the horn, the driver gave her the finger. Linda thought about flashing her shield at him, just to give him a scare, then remembered that the days when you could cow somebody with a badge were long gone—nowadays you had to have a weapon to back it up.

Not that she would have drawn her weapon on a civilian over a traffic dispute even if she had been packing. But Linda had learned over the years that being armed changed the way a woman, especially a small woman, thought about herself in relation to the world. And now that she was no longer strong enough or steady enough on her feet to make use of the martial arts training she'd received at the Academy, it seemed to Linda that the Bureau should have *insisted* she carry a gun, at least until or unless she developed any optical or cognitive symptoms.

But there was no sense letting her mind wander down that path, Linda reminded herself. The FBI wasn't fair, the disease wasn't fair, and life wasn't fair—big hairy deal, film at eleven. Better to concentrate on her job. Because she still had a job to do, an important one—the only hang-up was that until God in his infinite fucking wisdom decided to get Maheu off her ass, she'd have to do it on her own time.

The Georgetown brownstone was dark when Linda got home, which was not unusual: Jim and Gloria Gee were both attorneys, dinkies (double income, no kids) who dined out more often than in. Gloria had left a note for Linda—"dinner and a movie, back late"—on the kitchen table, along with the classifieds, which she had thoughtfully opened to the apartment rentals. Not a particularly subtle hint, thought Linda—somehow things had gone from the *stay-as-long-as-you-need-to* stage to the *don't-let-the-door-hit-you-in-the-ass-on-your-way-out* stage without any intermediary steps.

Linda glanced through the listings while her pot pie nuked, but without much hope. She already knew what she'd find in her price range—diddly—and wondered again whether she ought to take Pender up on the offer he'd made toward the end of the party last night (Linda hadn't split early after all) of a spare room in the old house above the canal. Be nice and peaceful out there—unless of course Pender had ulterior motives. Then she looked down at herself and laughed. Yeah, right—you're a fucking femme fatale. It's the ankle braces—they drive men wild.

After dinner Linda went into the living room and logged on to the Gees' computer, set up a phony Netscape user profile for an alter ego, then accessed phobia.com, the PWSPD Association web site, and signed into the chat room, selecting a user name of *Skairdykat* and a password of *boo*. The chat room counter went from 0 to 1—Linda was alone. She clicked onto the archives, read back a few weeks until she had the feel of the lingo, then began typing her first entry into the dialogue box:

> Hi everybody. Skairdykat here. Pleez dont flame me if I screw up, I've never done this before. Mostly cuz I never saw a chat room I wanted to join before. But reading you guys stories is like reading about my own life. It feels like coming home. Anyway, heres my story: I am . . .

(No need to narrow the age or sex down yet; if he bites, we can set up a meeting and have our choice of decoys in place.)

> single, and I have been deathly afraid of . . .

(Might as well use the snakes—it'll sound more believable than if you make something up.)

> snakes since as long as I can remember. Thats ophidiophobia, as most of you probably know. The worst part is, I live . . .

(Keep it vague—if you get any nibbles, you can improvise something later.)

> by myself, and sometimes I get so obsessed there might be a snake outside I cant even bring myself to leave the house. I am eager to chat with and maybe someday meet someone who knows how I feel. So if anybody . . .

(How to put this? Don't want to be too obvious, but if the killer is using the PWSPD web site for trolling, he's going to want to take it private as soon as possible.)

> wants to contact me directly, my e-mail address is skairdykat@netscape.com. . . .

(Anything else? Not yet. After all, you're trolling, too. Graceful exit.)

> Anyway, thanks for being there, all of you brave PWSPDs. Hope to hear from somebody soon. TT4N, Skairdy

After reading her entry over and making a few minor corrections, Linda positioned the cursor on the *SUBMIT* box, took a deep breath, then with a single click of her mouse turned poor Skairdy into a piece of bait dangling from a hook somewhere in cyberspace.

8

Dorie opened her eyes and took stock. Her forehead hurt, and there was a little knot—she must have hit the floor with her head, or the corner of the table on her way down—but there was no blood and no egg, just a tender spot above the hairline. At least you didn't break your nose again, she told herself—it's already got all the character it can stand.

Shaken, she sat up slowly, careful to keep her back to the window. Dorie had been dreaming about masks, avoiding them, and fainting at the sight of them for as long as she could remember. But having hallucinations, fainting over masks that aren't even there—that would be a new and disturbing development.

Unless of course there really *was* a mask in the window. But the only way to tell for sure would be to turn around, and she wasn't ready for that, not with her head still pounding and her heart racing and the room spinning and her stomach . . .

Whoops, here it comes. Dorie turned her head to the side just in time to save her clothes. When she finished vomiting, she crawled a few feet away and collapsed full length onto her side, one arm extended like Adam's on the ceiling of the Sistine Chapel.

Then she remembered reading someplace that headache, nausea, and dizziness were all symptoms of concussion, and that the last thing you should do was give in to the urge to sleep. She tried to raise herself up onto her hands and knees, but it felt as if she were fighting gravity on Jupiter—somehow the planet itself had grown impossibly heavy under her and was pulling her down toward that dreamless darkness.

Fight it, she told herself as she sank back down to the kitchen floor, her head pillowed on her folded arms. Got to fight it. But by then she could no longer remember what she was supposed to be fighting against, or why. Still, she felt vaguely guilty.

"Later, Mom," she murmured as the darkness closed around her again. "I promise I'll clean it up later."

Later.

Still on the floor, but on her back now, with her head pillowed on someone's lap. Cool damp cloth on her forehead, the rim of a glass touching her lips. She smelled the musty-sharp, cough-medicine smell of brandy, sipped, swallowed, coughed feebly. Then her eyes fluttered open, a man's hand came over her mouth to stifle her scream, and although the shock to her system was so profound it jarred her down to her soul, Dorie was not terribly surprised to see that the face leaning over her, hovering upside down only inches above her own, was wearing a leering Kabuki mask. Somehow, in fact, it seemed almost inevitable.

IV

Just Another Naked Body

1

Missy opened her eyes early Thursday morning and found herself lying in a strange room, in a bed not her own. Frightened and disoriented, she started to call out for Simon, then remembered that she was on the fold-out sofa in Ganny Wilson's living room, and that Ganny had promised her pancakes for breakfast. Only Ganny called them hoecakes—sometimes different people had different words for the same thing.

But as soon as she started thinking about food, Missy became aware of trouble inside her tummy and realized that that was what had awakened her in the first place. All that good Ganny cooking: pan-fried smothered chicken, corn fritters, southern-fried okra (Missy only ate the southern-fried part, not the okra itself), sweet potato pie, and after supper, all the little sesame seed cookies she could eat. Benni cakes, Ganny called them. And now it all wanted out all at once.

"Uh-oh," Missy told Tweety, who was rustling around in her little square cage on top of the TV. "This is gonna be a stinky." Then another *uh-oh* occurred to her as she sat up and swung her legs over the side of the sofa bed: she couldn't remember where the potty was.

"Ganny! Ganny, I hafta make!" No answer. The cramps were getting worse. She pressed her palms tightly against the sides of her temple to make herself remember. Think, you silly—you went potty last night. Only Ganny calls it the toe-lit. Different people, different—

Then it came to her: you had to go through Ganny's bedroom. Missy shuffled across the room, doubled over from the cramps, clutching the waistband of her pajama bottoms to keep them from falling down. Please don't lemme make in my jammies, she begged Jesus. In her own house you couldn't ask Jesus for things, because Simon said he didn't *exist* there, but in Ganny's house it was okay to ask him for help because he *existed* all over the place here: there were pictures and statues of him in every room—baby Jesus in the cradle, grown-up Jesus on the cross, and lying asleep in his mommy's lap. Missy mostly didn't remember their mommy, but Simon did.

Missy's prayer was answered. She tiptoed through Ganny's room without waking her up, did her stinky, and felt much better. When she came out of the bathroom, Ganny was still asleep under the covers, lying on her side with her face to the wall.

"Spoons?" asked Missy. Taking Ganny's silence for assent, she crawled into Ganny's bed and snuggled up against her back. But something was wrong—Ganny was so stiff it felt like cuddling up against a wooden chair.

"Are you sick?" Missy asked her, reaching around to feel Ganny's forehead, the way Ganny used to feel hers when she was sick. "Nope, cool as a coocummer. C'mon, Ganny, wake up."

But Ganny would not wake up. Gently, Missy tugged the neck of her nightgown. "Ganny, I'm hungry." No response. Missy pulled the covers back, saw that a watery coffee-colored stain had spread across the seat of Ganny's long white nightgown. "Uh-oh." Now she understood—it was *Ganny* who had made in *her* bed and was so embarrassed she was pretending to be asleep. Missy had done that once herself, when she was little, and Ganny had gone along with it, stripped her jammies off, carried her into the bathroom, cleaned her up, changed the bedding, tucked her back in, never said another word about it.

Missy decided to handle this situation the same way—sort of. She crawled out of bed, pulled the covers back up over Ganny's accident, and left the room to give Ganny a chance to clean herself up in private.

But when Missy returned to the bedroom, after what seemed to her to be a *very* long time—long enough to polish off a six-pack of little powdered doughnuts—Ganny still hadn't moved. Quietly—somehow Missy understood she was in the presence of something solemn, though she wasn't quite sure what—she walked around the side of the bed and saw that one side of Ganny's face, the side she was lying on, was black and swollen, and that although Ganny's eyes were open, she wasn't looking out from inside them.

Horrified, fascinated, not quite ready to let herself understand yet, Missy edged a little closer and saw that Ganny's slightly parted lips were crisscrossed with cobweb-thin threads of cottony white dried spittle, as if little fairies had been trying to sew them back together.

"Poor Ganny," she said, as softly as she could—Simon was always telling Missy that she talked too loud. She knew she had to do something—but what? She couldn't call the police even though she knew how to dial 911: Simon had drummed it into her head that if the police ever came to the house, they would end up taking her away from him or him away from her, and in either event, she was bound to end up in an institution for the feebleminded.

Feebleminded: that was the exact word he used, every time he gave her the speech, and Missy had come to fear the speech so much that she'd often be crying by the time he got to "in either event." Then he'd stop, and dry her eyes, and promise to always be there for her, and she in turn would promise him that she'd never, ever call the police.

Nine-one-one was out, then. But she wasn't supposed to talk to strangers, either. At times like this, there was only one person Missy could turn to—only one person she was *allowed* to turn to: Simon.

The first thing to do was get dressed. No, undressed first. Missy stripped off her jammies, then dumped the contents of her valise onto the sofa bed. Picking out undies was easy—they were all white and the label went in the back. Socks were also easy—it didn't matter what foot you put them on, so long as you picked out two of the same color.

As for pants and shirt, Missy knew you had to match them with the weather if you were going outside that day. With some difficulty she managed to unbolt the kitchen door, then stepped out into Ganny's sunlit backyard wearing only her socks and panties, and felt the warmth of the autumn sunshine on her bare skin. Shorts and T-shirt weather for sure—sunglasses, too.

Always grateful for a chance to wear her sunglasses—which not only were pretty, with thick pink rims and lenses shaped like sideways teardrops, but hid her eyes so strangers couldn't tell right off that she was a Downser (or so she sometimes thought)—Missy padded back inside, leaving the door open. She picked out a pair of plaid Bermuda shorts and a Special Olympics T-shirt from the pile on the sofa bed and took them back into the kitchen so she could look at the flowers in Ganny's garden while she finished dressing. There were purple morning glories climbing the back fence, glowing in the sunlight, and golden sunflowers taller than Missy, just starting to go to seed.

It took a few tries to get her Deedees—white Adidas cross-trainers—on the correct feet, with the tongues pulled up smooth instead of crumpled and the Velcro straps tight but not too tight. When she had finished, she slung her pink plastic purse that matched her sunglasses over her arm, picked up Tweety's cage, and left the house via the front door, grim-faced and determined.

"You stay here, Ganny," she called on her way out. "I'll go get Simon."

2

Alluring as she'd been in the late afternoon, Pebble Beach was somehow even more bewitching in the early morning, with the fog drifting in wisps and tatters across moss-green fairways glistening with dew. And as if to make up to Pender for her behavior the day before—or perhaps, beautiful bitch that she was, just to keep him on the hook a little longer—she showered him with favors. The damp air kept his booming drives from flying too far, the breeze blowing in from the bay kept them dry, and the dewy greens saved more than one overmuscled putt from slipping past the hole and rolling all the way to Maui.

The fog burned off a little before ten, leaving the sky a fresh-scrubbed blue. Pender stepped up to the eighteenth tee shooting eighty-four, laid up right, reached the green in three, and two-putted for a glorious, unashamed bogey: he'd broken ninety.

After their round, and an elegant lunch at Roy's, over in Spanish Bay—a Kobe beef carpaccio carved so exquisitely thin that the slices were almost transparent—Pender and Dolitz repaired to their two-bedroom suite at the Lodge. Naptime for Sid; time to get down to business for Pender. His first call was to Linda Abruzzi.

"Linda, it's Pender."

"Hi, Ed—how's the vacation going?"

"Good, pretty good. Weather's great—and I broke ninety at Pebble this morning."

"Is that good?"

"It is if your handicap's higher than the drinking age."

"Have you talked to Dorie Bell yet?"

"At her house last night."

"MDF?"

"Negative on that—I think this one's for real." He started to lay out the plan of action he'd sketched in for Dorie last night.

Linda interrupted him to explain about Maheu and the bank records.

"What an extraordinary asshole," said Pender when she'd finished. "Let me try to get in touch with McDougal. Liaison Support's been his baby from the beginning—maybe he'll let us have this one last hurrah."

"I haven't had my first hurrah yet," said Linda.

"Yeah, well, stick with me, kid."

Pender's next call was to McDougal's office. He was informed that the deputy director would be in conference all afternoon—with Agents Driver, Woods, Irons, and Putter, Pender suspected. He left a message, then phoned Dorie, who wasn't there either.

"It's Ed Pender," he told her machine. Not "Agent Pender"—he had made up his mind to ask her out. "Give me a ring as soon as you can."

He left her his room number at the Lodge along with his cell phone number. By the time he'd finished, the jet lag he'd been trying to ignore all day finally caught up with him. Quick nap, he promised himself, climbing into bed in his boxers and sleeveless wife-beater strap undershirt, and while waiting for sleep to overtake him, he thought about Dorie Bell. Smart, funny, doing her best to get through a hard time, but constitutionally incapable of cruising in neutral. Handsome woman, too, even with that busted nose. Not to mention that certain something in the way she moved.

3

Simon Childs retired to his bedroom at dawn. Exhausted as he was from the evening's exertions, he knew that sleep would not come easily. It never had: he'd been a fretful baby and a restless toddler even before his mother's departure, and a full-blown insomniac afterward. His sleep disorder manifested in both multiple dyssomnias—difficulty falling asleep, difficulty staying asleep—and parasomnias—night terrors and somnambulism. Medications helped: a triurnal rotation of chloral hydrate, Seconal, and Nembutal prescribed by his grandfather's tame physicians had seen him through adolescence, while as an adult he'd kept up with every pharmacological advance, legal or otherwise.

His current favorite was Halwane, an experimental, short-acting benzodiazepine that had not yet been approved for the marketplace. Simon had learned about it on the Net, where it was nicknamed Halloween, and convinced his doctor to put him on the protocol, promising to eschew all other drugs for the three months of the FDA-monitored trial. He'd had no intention of keeping his promise, but the drug more than kept its promise: fifteen minutes, then *bam,* you were out; three hours later, *bam,* you were awake.

If only they'd come up with anything half as effective for the blind rat syndrome, thought Simon—what a simple, ordinary life I might have led. For a rich man, anyway.

But without the looming presence of the blind rat, he reminded himself, he'd never have known the highs of the fear game, never have experienced a moment of such radiant perfection as last night, when Dorie looked up from his lap and their eyes met through the mask. Darkness and light, cruelty and tenderness, fear and hope, all in perfect equipoise for once—how in heaven had the world managed to keep turning, Simon wondered.

Realizing he was still far too excited to sleep, even with the benefit of Halwane, Simon decided to approach Morpheus obliquely. First he treated himself to a long hot shower, then smoked a fat doobie of B.C. super-sinsemilla (what the FDA didn't know wouldn't hurt them) out on the deck adjoining the suite Grandfather Childs had occupied from 1924, when the house was built, until a few days after he'd cut his own throat, at which time Simon, age fourteen, moved in for keeps.

Best not to think about the old man, though, Simon told himself—not compatible with relaxation. Think about the positives instead: this fine weed, the million-dollar view (more like ten million, these days) of the San Francisco Bay at dawn, and last but certainly not least, having the house all to himself for once—no Missy bleating mo hah, mo hah from the bathroom.

Whoops—not so relaxing, that thought. He wondered how Missy and Ganny were getting along—was she too much for the old woman? Was it too early to call her? Old people rarely slept late.

No, God bless it! If ever a man was owed a day off, it was Simon Childs. Besides, they were probably as happy as pigs at a trough, those two—if there'd been a problem, Ganny would have called. She wasn't so decrepit she couldn't use the telephone.

Having satisfied what he knew to be his cheap slut of a conscience, Simon finished the joint and tossed the roach into the open urn that had originally contained his grandfather's ashes, washed down a blue Halwane tablet with a shot of Hennessy's (again, what the FDA didn't know . . .). He set his alarm for 10 A.M., then stripped off his robe and climbed into bed naked, sighing with pleasure at the feel of the cool pearl-gray sheets against his bare skin. To relax himself while waiting for the Halwane to take effect, he cast his thoughts backward through time and hooked a juicy plum of a memory.

Summer, 1959. A new family is going to be moving in next door, Grandfather Childs announces at the dinner table. "The boy looks to be about your age, Simp." That's short for Simple, which in turn is short for Simple Simon. "Maybe you can make friends with him—although I doubt it."

That's a sore point for the ten-year-old Simon—he doesn't make friends easily. But a few weeks later, when the moving van pulls up next door, Ganny bakes a welcome-to-the-neighborhood cake, and Simon is deputized to deliver it. Mr. and Mrs.

Carpenter remind Simon of Ozzie and Harriet. They call Nelson down; turns out he's a year younger than Simon. In eighth grade, when Simon reads *Great Expectations,* the description of the pale young gentleman will resonate for him—in his mind's eye he will picture Nelson Carpenter, his nervous mannerisms; his indoor complexion, so doughy white it looked as though if you poked him with your finger, it would leave an impression; his red-rimmed eyes; and his longish straw-colored hair.

Mrs. C., a hovering, overprotective mother, cuts them each a thick slice of Ganny's cake, unpacks the kitchen stools, the milk glasses, and the chocolate crazy straws, then flutters away reluctantly to supervise the movers. When they're done eating, Simon announces that they're going to go play at his house now, then hops off the stool and starts for the back door. He doesn't turn to see if Nelson is following him—somehow he just knows it.

He takes Nelson to meet Ganny and Missy; luckily for the skittish younger boy, Grandfather Childs is at the office. And the pale young gentleman definitely passes the Missy test: he doesn't make fun of her or— it's a big word, but Simon knows what it means— patronize her. In fact, Nelson and Missy get along almost too well; Simon takes Nelson up to his room so he can have his new friend all to himself.

"Wanna see Skinny?" Simon asks.

"Who's Skinny?"

"My pet."

"Is it a dog or a cat? I'm kind of scared of dogs and cats."

"Nope."

"Bird?"

"Nope."

"Fish?"

"BZZZZ." Simon sounds the imaginary game-show buzzer. "You're outta guesses." He hauls Skinny's cage out from under the bed.

"A snake!" Nelson mouths the words.

"Yup. Genuine striped mamba, most poisonous snake in the whole world. One bite and your dick falls off and you die."

Skinny is a common garter, of course—Simon's venomous snake days are still in the future—but Nelson obviously doesn't know that. He goes stiff and still, only he's kind of quivering too, like Daffy Duck at the North Pole, like if you whacked him he'd break into a million tiny pieces. Simon feels himself getting a stiffy. He unzips his khaki shorts and works it through the fly of his whities until it's poking out.

"Kiss it," he tells Nelson. "Just once. If you kiss it, I won't let him get you."

"You promise?" asks little Nelson, still frozen, still quivering.

"Trust me," little Simon replies.

Three hours after taking the Halwane, Simon awoke feeling as refreshed as if he'd enjoyed a full night's sleep and sporting a wake-up erection. *Haven't had one like this in years,* he thought, admiring his uncharacteristic arousal in the bedroom mirror. *Good stuff, that Halwane—have to save a few for the getaway bag.*

Or maybe it wasn't the Halwane that was responsible for the erection. Maybe it was thinking about

Nelson before he went to sleep. Have to look old Nellie up again, one of these days. Last time Simon had checked, he still lived in Concord, in the house he'd bought after his parents died. And the statute of limitations had probably already run out on the whole Grandfather Childs thing—manslaughter, at worst—which meant the delicate balance, the two-way blackmail that had kept them apart all these years, no longer applied.

Or maybe it wasn't Nelson or the Halwane—maybe it was the prospect of the morning's game that had Simon so excited. In which case, he had been right to save the best for last, he told himself. Or at least for later—with the blind rat lurking about, Simon knew there could never really be a last.

4

Headache. The kind of headache with roots so deep you feel it in your gut. And sore all over, like after a car wreck. Like that time she wrecked Daddy's car.

I'm sorry. Daddy, I'm so sorry.

And Daddy says, *As long as you're safe, sweetheart— that's all that matters.*

But the Chrysler—it's totaled.

That's why we have insurance, sweetheart. You rest now. Okay, Daddy.

A few minutes—or a few seconds, or a few hours— later, Dorie opened her eyes to blackness, true, impenetrable blackness. As a painter, she knew what a rare thing that was. You didn't often find it in nature, not aboveground, anyway.

The mattress smelled of bleach. She sat up slowly, taking inventory. Headache, cotton mouth. Bruised and battered. Cold. No clothes, where are my—

Two masks appeared. They weren't there, and then, impossibly, they were. Tragedy and comedy, a frown and a grin, glowing in midair, surrounded by darkness. Dorie moaned and covered her eyes, which would not close of their own accord, then counted to ten and spread her fingers apart, peeked through the cracks into the darkness, and saw only the darkness. No grin, no frown—had they even been there in the first place?

Dorie drew her knees up and crossed her arms over her breasts, hugging herself for warmth. Got to figure this out. Last thing—what's the last thing you remember? Musical clothes. Upstairs trying on clothes. Blue shirt—my blue denim. But why? Going out? No, somebody coming over. Who? Her memory inched forward. Doorbell rings. Big bald guy on the doorstep. Brown beret, easy grin, Pebble Beach sweatshirt, tragic plaid pants. And his name, his name is, his name is Pender, and he's here because he's here because he's here because . . .

Then she had it, all of it. Carl, Kim, Mara, Wayne. A psychopath who preys on phobics, feeds on fear. Carl, Kim, Mara, Wayne, and now me. She moaned again and hugged herself tighter, tried to tell herself that this wasn't happening, that it couldn't be happening, because things like this just didn't happen. Dreams happened, though—wake up, you big turkey. You know how to wake up—you just open your . . .

But her eyes *were* open. And people weren't cold like this in dreams, all goose bumps and puckered nipples, and they weren't sore, and they didn't have pounding headaches. There was terror in dreams, but no pain—that's what made them bearable. That and the fact that you could wake up from them.

Still cushioned by a lingering sense of disbelief, Dorie was trying to remember what had come next, after Pender, when she heard a click somewhere off in the darkness, and the masks appeared again, comedy and tragedy, white with a violet tinge, six or seven feet off the ground. Then another click, and an instant later they were gone. Black light, Dorie thought: he's doing it with black light and Day-Glo. And instead of terror, she felt a surge of anger. He feeds off fear, does he? Well, fuck him, let him starve.

It didn't take Simon long to figure out that the click of the wall switch controlling the black light was giving him away. Clad head to toe in black, silk socks to lightweight balaclava, like a stagehand in a Noh play, he'd been taking it slow, determined to avoid making the same mistakes he'd made with Wayne. Instead, of course, he found himself making all new mistakes. He'd used the black light setup only once before, for a sixty-three-year-old ailurophobe named Constance, and that had been nearly ten years ago; the basement had been crawling with cats (most of which had been dipped into a solution of fluorescent dye a few hours earlier and were still spitting mad), and Constance had been screaming bloody murder the whole time.

Dorie, though—Dorie hadn't made a sound. Which didn't make her initial reaction any less electrifying. Her sense of shock and horror was almost palpable; it touched someplace deep inside Simon, someplace deep and holy. He'd felt it in his mind, his bones, his bowels, his heart, and most of all he'd felt it in that mystery kundalini spot somewhere between the base of his cock and the base of his spine. The sensation was so intense, so exquisite, that it was almost painful, like being in love.

But the second time he'd clicked the black light on and off, her head had jerked to the right, following the sound of the wall switch. He was startled for a moment—she seemed to be staring right at him, her eyes glowing a pale, panther green in the infrared light of the night-vision goggles. He flipped up the eyepiece just to be sure—nope, black as pitch. She couldn't see him, but she had definitely sensed his presence.

Pity, thought Simon. Still, we had ourselves a moment there, didn't we, babe? Pure, intense, virginal fear—fleeting as it may be, there's nothing to match it. But like virginity itself, when it's gone, it's gone.

Still, it might be possible to at least reclaim the element of surprise. Keeping the goggles trained on Dorie, sitting now with her knees drawn up and pressed together and her arms crossed over her breasts (modesty, thought Simon: how touching; how irrelevant), he flipped the wall switch on. She quivered, closed her eyes, ducked her head. He tiptoed across the room, silent on stockinged feet, knelt down (slowly, carefully, wary of the capricious creaking and popping to which his fifty-something joints were liable), and quietly unplugged the extension cord. Now all he had to do was wait for Dorie to raise her head, then plug the cord back in. No more clicks, no more warning.

He didn't have to wait long. Up came her chin, up, up, up. Slowly she turned her head to the right, where she'd heard the click of the wall switch, then slowly, deliberately, she turned her head back until she was staring straight ahead, with those panther eyes wide, unblinking—it was almost as if she were daring him to try it again.

You got it, babe, thought Simon, slipping the plug noiselessly into the socket. The masks glowed to life, but he kept the goggles fixed on Dorie. Her entire body shuddered; her eyes rolled back in her head until only the whites were showing, eerily green, blank as marbles in the night-vision glow.

Simon stifled a groan, crept closer, closer, until he was close enough to smell her fear. She was squatting now, rocking on her heels, modesty abandoned. He wanted to throw his arms around her, hug her, strike her, suckle at her breast, bite her breast, own her fear. He wanted everything and at the same time he wanted nothing—nothing but this moment, frozen in time. . . .

Now that she'd had a little more time to think, Dorie had changed her mind. Pender had said it was the fear he was after. If it's fear he wants, she'd reasoned, then fear he gets. Don't starve him, feed him; give him a little incentive to keep you alive, anyway. And sooner or later he's bound to slip up. Then he'll find out what a big, strong woman can—

Sooner: it was to be sooner. The masks appeared; she let the terror wash over her, let her eyes roll back in her head, fought the syncope by squatting, rocking on her heels, clenching and unclenching her fists. She sensed him drawing closer—he was a whisper of breath, a rustle of cloth in the silence, a warm, human-size hole in the blackness. A fragment of lyric started going through her mind: Closer. Come a little bit closer. Let me whisper—

Now: she sprang forward, flailing with both fists, swinging, missing, swinging again and again, striking something soft, then something hard and metallic. Her fingers closed around a . . . a camera . . . ? he was wearing a camera on his—

No, goggles. Night vision. Of course. She yanked them off, swung them where his head had been. He ducked under the blow, came at her low, drove his head into her belly, knocking her backward. She drew her legs up, tried to kick him away, but he was too close, she didn't have the leverage. She swung at him again; he grabbed her wrists and pinned her to the mattress.

Now he was on top of her, lying on her, his body pressed against her and his face only inches from hers. She sensed him lowering his head; she knew that he meant to kiss her. She willed herself to go limp, waited until she could feel his breath warm and coppery against her face, then brought her head up and forward with all the strength she could muster.

5

"He must have been a tiny little guy," commented Pender. He and Sid were standing before the altar of the Mission San Carlos Borroméo del Rio Carmelo, better known as the Carmel Mission, looking down at the sarcophagus of Father Junípero Serra, which was barely five feet long.

"And yet this simple, humble monk, this 'tiny little guy,' as you so eloquently phrased it, was responsible for the genocide of tens of thousands of California Indians."

A family of tourists had entered the cool stone chapel and were gathering around the sarcophagus; Pender decided to egg Sid on. "Now, now, Sidney. Surely that's a tad harsh."

"One of the greatest mass murderers in the history of the Catholic Church," said Sid. "Which is no mean company to keep. And now they're talking about beatifying the evil little dwarf. I'm sorry, it just pisses me off."

After the chapel, the Moorish bell tower. Pender took advantage of the elevation to call Dorie's number; he tried it again as they strolled through the gardens behind the church. "I don't understand it—she said she'd be home all day."

"So you keep saying."

"Maybe her phone's out of order."

"Maybe. Or maybe she took one look at you, decided to head for the hills."

"You've always been jealous of my success with the ladies," said Pender.

"Yeah, that and your wardrobe. Look, if you want to drive by her house, see if she's okay, quit nudging and just say so."

"Good idea," said Pender, as if he hadn't been dropping hints to that effect since they'd left Pebble Beach an hour earlier.

"Where's Mary?" asked Pender, as they pulled into Dorie's driveway, Sid behind the wheel of their rented car.

"*Who's* Mary?"

"Mary Cassatt—Dorie's car. Roadmaster wagon. Should be in the carport."

"Let's review, shall we?" Sid shifted into park, but did not cut the engine. "Lady's not answering her phone and her car's not in the driveway. What does that tell us, pard?"

But Pender had already unbuckled his seat belt. "Be right back."

"It tells us the lady is *out*," Sid explained to the now empty passenger seat, as he switched off the ignition. "It tells us the lady is not at home."

Pender rang the bell, tried the front door, which was locked, then checked the windows for signs of forced entry as he walked around the side of the house. The back door was also locked. Okay, so maybe she flaked, he told himself. Or maybe it's me, maybe I read too much into it when she said she'd be home all day.

But as he continued past the studio (once a sleeping porch, now glassed in and shuttered) and around the far side of the house, where a narrow, musty-smelling cement walkway was hedged in by a high board fence overgrown with ivy, keeping his eyes trained on the ground for blood spatters, footprints, whatever, he almost walked smack into the studio door, which had swung open, blocking the walkway.

Pender stuck his head through the doorway. Dim light, shutters closed, smell of paint, turpentine, linseed oil. "Dorie?"

No answer. He entered the studio, glanced around. Everything looked about the same as it had last night, when she'd given him the grand tour. The canvases she had intended to gesso today were still stacked against her workbench, and her plein air gear— portable easel, folding stool, walking stick—was leaning against the wall, just inside the door.

"Dorie?" he called again, mostly for form's sake. He was pretty sure she wasn't home—the house just *felt* empty—but he continued across the hall into the kitchen anyway, and as soon as he saw the puddle of dried vomit on the parquet floor, Pender understood, with a certainty inaccessible to anyone who hadn't spent his entire adult life in law enforcement, that he had just half-assed his way into the middle of a crime scene.

6

The climate inside the DOJ-AOB was so oppressively perfect that toward the end of her second day closeted with the mountain of redacted transaction records, Linda Abruzzi would have killed for a little fresh air or sunlight—even a rainstorm—and was beginning to entertain Count of Monte Cristo fantasies. I could tap on the wall in Morse, she thought, make contact with some other poor office-bound wretch—maybe we could tunnel to freedom together.

Around four o'clock, as she was washing her hands in the ladies' room after using the facilities, Linda asked her reflection in the stainless steel mirror over the sink (for security reasons, there were no glass mirrors in the building) to remind her again why she was putting herself through this, when she could have been kicking back at her parents' new house out on Long Island, being waited on hand and foot by her mother.

But all she got out of the haggard brunette in the mirror, who appeared to be trying to disprove the second half of the old saw about how you couldn't be too rich or too thin—alarmingly prominent Neapolitan nose and a chin you could have opened a beer bottle on—was a beats-the-crap-outta-me shrug.

"Okay, back to work," she ordered herself. "There's only another hour left—then you can go *home* and feel sorry for yourself."

Forty-five minutes later, she felt like celebrating instead, having stumbled across a federal credit union account so bogus it was a wonder it hadn't stunk up the whole office. Some GS-13, judging by the size of the paycheck automatically deposited into his or her account every month, had also made several large cash deposits spread out over a period of thirty months.

"Bingo," she called to Miss Pool in the outer office. "I've either found our you-know-what or uncovered the dumbest double agent in the history of espionage."

"Congratulations." Pool appeared in the doorway; she already had her coat on.

"Should I call Maheu now, or wait until tomorrow morning?"

"Neither."

"When, then?"

"Two weeks from yesterday."

"How come?"

"Because that's how much time they've budgeted for the job."

"And if I finish early, he's only going to come up with some more shit work?"

"I believe that's the plan."

"Thanks, Pool. What would I do without you?"

"Hon, you don't *ever* want to find out."

The brownstone in Georgetown was empty again when Linda got home a few minutes after six. Instead of a note on the kitchen table, there was a pink Post-it on the computer in the living room: *"L: Prefer you not use this machine. Thanks, G."*

Fine, thought Linda—I can take a hint. Still, as she reached into her purse for her cell phone, she was surprised at how badly the rejection hurt. Tears in her eyes, lump in her throat, empty feeling in the pit of her stomach. Oh, grow up, Abrootz, she ordered herself. Just grow the fuck up.

"Pender."

"Ed, it's Linda. I—"

"Linda! Good work—thanks for getting back to me so quickly. Here's what I need: First of all, forget Maheu.

Rule number one for getting along in the Bureau: Better to ask forgiveness than permission. Okay?"

"Yes, but I—"

"Good. Now, what I want you to do: I want you to log on to that web site . . ."

"Ed."

". . . and see if you can contact the webmaster or the system administrator, whatever they call it, find out whether—"

"Ed!"

"What?"

"I'm not in the office, and I haven't gotten any messages from you. I was just calling to ask you if your offer of a spare room is still open."

"Absolutely. There's a key under the stone Buddha on the back porch. Pick out any bedroom but the first—that one's mine—help yourself to anything you need."

"Thanks so much. Now, what were you—"

"Dorie Bell's disappeared."

"Oh, shit."

"My sentiments ex—" He broke off in midsyllable. Linda heard someone yelling in the background, then Pender shouting, "FBI! I'm FBI, don't shoot!"

"Ed? Ed, what's going on?"

"Linda? Still there?"

"I'm here, Ed."

"Barney Fife just showed up—looks like I'm going to have to get back to you."

"Ed, wait—"

"Gotta go."

More shouting in the background, then the line went dead.

7

They say when you've been shot or stabbed you don't feel the pain right away. Not so with a broken nose, as Dorie could have testified even before this most recent fracture. The agony is immediate—sharp and centralized at first, then spreading outward from its locus, swelling and blossoming until it envelops your entire head, which feels as big as a float in the Thanksgiving Day parade. Then, just when you think it can't get any worse, the throbbing begins—slow, rolling waves with barely enough time between ebb and flood, between dread and pain, to form a wordless prayer, much less a coherent thought.

And yet, as she lay on her back in the darkness, vaguely aware that she was drowning in her own blood, a stray thought did manage to insinuate itself into Dorie's consciousness, complete, discrete, in a disembodied voice that was somehow familiar, though not her own: *There are worse things in life than bleeding to death.*

Yeah, or drowning, she answered quickly, before the tide could pull her under again.

Thank heaven for pure dumb luck, thought Simon, ruefully rubbing his brow, just below the hairline to the left of the widow's peak. He knew it was only an accident of timing that he'd ducked *his* head to go titty-diving just as Dorie had brought *her* head up to butt him, so that instead of catching him in the nose with her forehead, she'd caught him in the forehead with her nose. Broke it again, too, judging by the amount of blood.

He crawled toward the sound of her moaning—an eerie, bubbling sound. The closer he got, the more blood there was—his palms were sticky from crawling through it, the knees of his trousers were damp by the time he reached her, and when he rolled her onto her side to prevent her from drowning, her bare skin was wet and slick with warm blood.

Not as unpleasant a sensation as he might have thought. In fact, it reminded him a little of bathing Missy—the feel of soft, cushiony flesh beneath slippery-smooth wet skin—only without the attendant taboos, of course. Unlike Missy's, Dorie's body was Simon's to do as he pleased with, for as long as he could keep her alive—and contingent, as always, upon the amount of fear they could generate together.

Because without the fear, dead or alive, it was just another naked body, and naked bodies, per se, had never held all that much fascination for Simon. Which brought him back to the question of the moment: what to do about *this* one. Stop the bleeding, of course. Clean her up a little. Hog-tie her, hands to ankles, keep her out of mischief. And no gag: the poor thing'd be breathing through her mouth for days, if she lasted that long. Maybe throw a spare mattress up against the side door leading to the garage: that was the weak spot for the soundproofing.

But after that, there would be no sense in hanging around. Something that Simon had learned over the years, something most people would never know, was that while anticipation of physical suffering produced fear, the actual pain was itself anodyne. For several more hours, while her agony was in full bloom, Dorie would be incapable of experiencing any viable fear.

Inconvenient, sure, but Simon was only mildly disappointed. Because the ejaculatio praecox that had plagued him since early adolescence rendered penile insertion problematical and extended intercourse all but impossible, he was incapable of enjoying prolonged sexual gratification, but when it came to the fear game, Simon Childs was an all-night, do-right, sixty-minute man. The longer he could make a game last, the better he felt about himself.

And since Dorie's broken nose was going to force him to delay his gratification for another twelve to twenty-four hours, Simon realized as he crawled off into the darkness to find his goggles, by this time tomorrow, barring complications, he could expect to be feeling very, very good about himself.

8

"I *said,* put your hands *up!*"

Pender hit the kill switch on his flip phone, then turned slowly. The young Carmel cop was in a textbook two-handed firing crouch, his feet spread shoulder-width apart, his knees slightly bent.

"And *I* said FBI," replied Pender in his best command tone. "Which letter didn't you understand?"

But the kid was starting to tremble from the strain

of the position, so Pender adjusted his approach from authoritarian to folksy.

"Listen, son, we both know you're not gonna shoot me," he said in the possum-eatin' drawl he'd learned in Arkansas as a rookie agent working out of the Little Rock field office. "The paperwork alone'd take you a month to complete, not to mention the hearings. Then, assumin' you get to keep your job, the counselin' starts; you're gonna be tellin' some shrink all about how you shot that friendly ol' FBI man because Daddy didn't give you that red wagon for Christmas when you were five. So why don't you just back them sights offa my chest, I'll show you my tin, we'll whistle in the fire, piss on the dogs, and get back to shootin' the bad guys 'stead a each other."

A bit much? Maybe, but it worked—to a degree. "Okay, nice and slow," said the cop. "Open your coat, let's see your badge." He still had his sights centered in on Pender's chest—the kill grid, on the firing range—but they both knew it was more to save face than because he seriously believed Pender was a threat.

Pender played out the scene for all he was worth anyway, slowly opening his plaid jacket, lifting his wallet out of his inside pocket gingerly, with two fingers, and letting it fall open to reveal the old DOJ shield that only two days ago, he'd have bet he'd never be using again. "Okay?"

"Yeah, sorry." The kid flipped the safety back on and slid the Glock into its holster. "You know how it is."

"Sure I do," said Pender soothingly. "What's your name, son?"

"Mackey. Wynn Mackey." Clean-cut, soft-spoken,

nicely trimmed 'stash, well-tailored uni—just shaking hands with him made Pender feel old and tired.

"Ed Pender. Pleased to meet you."

"Pender! Sure, sure—you were down here in July, that serial killer who broke out of County. I thought I recognized you from someplace—I just figured it was a wanted poster or a BOLO."

"Yeah, I guess I have that kind of face." Pender nodded toward Mackey's holster. "Now, don't forget you have a round chambered there." Then something occurred to him. "Hey, what happened to Sid?"

"Who's Sid?"

"The old guy, sitting in the car?"

"There wasn't any old guy in the—"

He stopped—they'd both heard the studio door slam. A moment later, Sid appeared in the kitchen doorway.

"Where the hell were you?" snapped Pender.

"I had to take a leak."

"I nearly got my ass blown off."

"It'd take at least a shotgun to cover *that* spread," said Dolitz, glancing pointedly from the holstered gun to Pender's rear.

Mackey checked out the new arrival from the ground up: white bucks, beige slacks, white Ralph Lauren Polo with the collar turned up in back, jaunty toupee. "Don't tell me you're FBI, too."

"Retired. Very retired. What's going on?"

"I was just about to ask Agent Pender here the same question."

"Ms. Bell contacted us a few weeks ago," said Pender, then paused. The idea was to get as much information as possible, while releasing as little as possible. But Mackey waited him out. He was young and he was local, but apparently he wasn't stupid, so rather than waste any more time, Pender gave him the rundown—everything up to, but not including, the fact that he, too, was retired, at least technically. It would only have muddied the water, Pender told himself, especially since he'd already tinned Mackey.

And to Pender's surprise, before he'd even finished explaining the significance of the vomit stain on the parquet floor, how extremely unlikely it was that Dorie would have simply left it there and gone off for the day, Mackey was talking into the two-way radio clipped to the front of his uniform, near his left collarbone.

"This is Mackey. Patch me over to Smitty. . . . Al, it's Wynn. You know that Buick wagon you tagged down on Ocean . . . ? Yeah, well, *don't* tow it. Don't even touch it; it might be a crime scene. . . . No, I'm not shitting you. . . . Look, just tape it off, I'll get right back to you."

He thumbed off the walkie-talkie and turned back to Pender. "Dorie Bell's car has been parked in a metered space collecting tickets since sometime last night. I've known her since I was a kid—she used to baby-sit me. I figured maybe the old heap broke down, thought I'd come up here, give her a shout before it was towed. There was a strange car in the driveway, the side door was open . . ."

"It was open when we got here," said Pender. "I almost walked into it."

"Did you touch anything else?"

"I didn't even touch the door."

"How about you?" Mackey asked Sid.

"Took a whiz over in the bushes."

Mackey looked disgusted. "You FBI guys usually go around pissing on crime scenes?"

Dolitz shrugged. "At my age, I'm lucky to be able to piss at all."

9

The kitchen—the whole mansion, for that matter— seemed empty and enormous without Missy around. In the past it had always been Simon who went off and Missy who stayed behind. He tried to tell himself he was enjoying having the place to himself, but he couldn't help worrying about Missy. At least when *he* was away, he knew she was safe, in familiar surroundings, with an attendant she liked and he trusted.

With Dorie safely installed in the basement and the game on hold, however, there was really no reason not to bring Missy home. Simon called Ganny's number from the kitchen—no answer. He finished his lunch, went upstairs, called again from the office adjoining the bedroom. Still no luck. Maybe they went out for *IiiKee*—ice cream.

Simon logged on to the computer, which was on a DSL hookup and was rarely, if ever, turned off. From force of habit he found himself browsing the PWSPD-sponsored phobia.com chat room. The new kid, Skairdykat, sounded awfully tempting. Simon immediately fired off an e-mail to Zap Strum, the far-from-reformed South of Market hacker–drug dealer who had designed and still administered the site, ask-ing him to poke around behind the screen for Skairdy's real-world name and address.

But as he logged off the computer and called Ganny's number again—still no answer—it crossed Simon's mind that he might already have gone to that well once too often. Dorie had been in touch with the FBI before Wayne's disappearance, then again after his death. Now she was missing, too—that would make five PWSPD deaths in six months. Cops were dumb, but they weren't that dumb.

And the more he thought about it, the more Simon appreciated the magnitude of the risks he'd been taking lately. He hadn't pursued his dicey hobby for thirty years without a cross word from law enforcement by being this careless. Maybe he was starting to slip, he told himself—maybe the pressure of arranging a game every few months instead of once a year was starting to get to him. But the alternative was the rat—which was no alternative at all.

Simon sighed—the PWSPD Association was his masterwork, but there was no denying the fact that it had outlived its usefulness—and picked up the phone again.

Zap's machine picked up after two rings: *"Do the message thing,"* it demanded curtly.

"It's Simon. I know you're screening. Pick up—it's important."

"Zup, dude?" An intermittent Ridgemont High surfer drawl was one of the MIT graduate's more annoying affectations.

"Remember when we set up the PWSPD, you said you could make it disappear when the time came?"

"Yeah?"

"The time has come."

"Web site, archives, bank records, the whole schmear?"

"Like they never existed. Can you do it?"

"Never ask the Zap-man if he *can* do something. Ask only how much and how long."

"How much and how long?"

"The usual hourly, and as long as it takes. Shouldn't be too hard—the Zap-man built it, the Zap-man can disappear it. Anything else?"

"Not at the moment. Just let me know when you're done."

"Log on in a couple hours, dude. If it ain't there, I'm done."

Though the Berkeley hills were a world away from the Berkeley flats, it was only a short drive from one to the other. After spending the next hour trying unsuccessfully to contact Ganny, and working himself up to the point where he was envisioning God knows what, blood on the walls and bodies hacked to pieces, Simon made the trip in five minutes. He parked the Mercedes on the street outside Ganny's little cottage and set the antitheft, but left the top down—they'd only have slashed it, otherwise.

He rang the front doorbell—no answer. He tried the door—it wasn't locked. Simon let himself in, saw Missy's pink valise lying open on the fold-out sofa, its contents scattered across the unmade bed. It was like a waking nightmare—Simon found himself drawn almost against his will toward the bedroom, and the sound of buzzing flies.

What he found there—Ganny's mummified-look-ing corpse lying on its side in the darkened room, with the covers pulled up to its neck as if someone had lovingly tucked it in—seemed even more night-marish than the scenes of *Helter Skelter* Simon had been picturing on the ride over.

Numb as a sleepwalker, his mind filled with images of Missy lost or kidnapped, sick or injured, frightened and alone, Simon wandered distractedly into the kitchen, which looked like an explosion in a cocaine factory. There was white powder everywhere, and an empty packet of Hostess mini-doughnuts on the table.

That about tore it, that stupid cellophane dough-nut wrapper. Simon sank down onto one of the kitchen chairs, buried his face in his hands, and let out a wrenching sob, the kind that comes from so deep inside you feel as if your guts are coming up with it. Just one sob—then he looked up, and through the open back door he saw Missy curled up over by the fence in the far corner of the backyard. Above her, gangly sunflowers hung their golden heads.

10

Packing was no problem—Linda had more or less been living out of her suitcase since she got to Washington. She knew it would have made more sense to move up to Pender's on the weekend, but she wanted to avoid her former dear friend Gloria—she wasn't sure she could count high enough in Italian to keep from saying things she'd regret later.

As it was, she confined herself to a terse Post-it note with her new address. She had considered playing a computer prank on them that the boys in San Antone had once played on her—changing the default address on their browser from Yahoo to the SSN, the Scat Sex Network, which would plaster coprophagous images all over their screen when they logged on—but decided against it at the last minute.

Lock the front door, drop the key through the mail slot, haul the suitcase out to the Geo. Linda's legs were pretty much gone, this late in the day: she nearly overbalanced as she lifted the suitcase into the trunk, and her thigh muscles were quivering as she drove away with her left shoe poised over the brake in case she needed to make a sudden stop. Eventually, she knew, she'd be reduced to driving with hand controls—if she was lucky.

Linda was halfway to Pender's when her cell phone began chirping. She fished it out of her purse without taking her eyes off the road.

"Abruzzi."

"It's Pender."

"Are you all right?"

"Little misunderstanding—we're all on the same page now."

"What happened to Dorie Bell?"

"All we know for sure is that she's gone. The concern is, if it *is* our man that's got her, his cycle has shortened from one victim every two months to two victims in one week. What we need to do—what *you* need to do—is see if you can get hold of somebody at the PWSPD Association, get them to fax you a copy of the membership roster, which at this point is beginning to look like a list of potential victims, then find out who their webmaster is, see if you can get a warning posted on the site."

"I'll get on it first thing tomorrow morning," said Linda.

"Now would be better. I'll give you Thom Davies's number. He's with the CJIS over in Clarksburg—he ought to be able to help you."

Linda parked behind Pender's Barracuda, which was shrouded beneath a form-fitting tarpaulin, left her suitcase by the front door, and followed the grassy flagstone path around back.

"Up the wooden mountain," she told herself dubiously, eyeing not only the rickety steps leading up to the porch, but the haphazard maze of timbers, struts, and cross braces that supported the railed platform itself. She shuddered, thinking back to the party. At one point, late in the evening, there must have been two dozen of them out there singing oldies—it was a wonder the whole thing hadn't come down.

Fortunately, the steps were also railed and the railings close enough together to use as parallel bars. If they can take Pender's weight, they can take mine, Linda told herself. She felt like planting a flag when she got to the top.

Linda remembered the Buddha from the party. It was Tibetan, the first scowling Buddha she'd ever seen, and couldn't have resembled Pender more closely if he'd sat for the sculptor. "It was the only thing my ex didn't get after the divorce," he'd explained. "And that was only because she didn't want it."

By the time she'd retrieved the key, descended the wooden mountain, walked back around the house, and dragged her suitcase inside, she was ready to collapse onto the orange sofa.

But Pender was right—now *would* be better. Back at the Academy, Linda had been taught that serial killers were characteristically divided into two types, organized and disorganized offenders. The phobia killer, as she'd come to think of him (they'd have to come up with a more colorful name when they took the investigation public—unless, of course, they had a suspect by then), was obviously organized, and one particularly bothersome characteristic of organized serial killers, the instructor from the Behavioral Sciences Unit had explained to the trainees, was that they got better at it as they went along. They selected their victims more carefully, planned their attacks more meticulously, and, especially alarming from the law-enforcement point of view, they tended to learn from their mistakes.

But the fact that the phobia killer was organized didn't mean his personality wasn't subject to deterioration, and the evidence that his homicidal cycle was shortening could be taken as an indication of a downward spiral. More active meant crazier; crazier meant more active—literally a vicious cycle.

So she compromised—she took her phone out of her purse, dialed the number Pender had given her, and *then* collapsed onto the sofa by the living room fireplace.

"Davies here." British accent.

"Mr. Davies, this is Linda Abruzzi. I believe we met

at Ed Pender's retirement party. He suggested I—"

"Sorry, Thom's gone home for the evening. This is a recording, actually. Leave a message at the beep, he'll get back to you in the morning. Beep."

"Please, it's a matter of—"

"If you say 'life and death,' I shall positively *hurl.*"

"I was going to say extreme urgency. But as a matter of fact . . ."

"Linda, darling, the night I got home from E. L. Pender's retirement party, I gathered my little family round the hearth. 'From now on,' I told them, 'Daddy will be spending his evenings and weekends at home. He'll be able to help you with your homework, attend your dance recitals and your Little League games— he'll even have time to learn all your names.' My dear wife wept for joy, Linda—she literally wept for joy."

"So what are you doing in the office, this time of night?"

"With six children, it's the only place I can get any fucking peace and quiet."

"Excellent. First rate. Here's what we're looking for . . ."

11

By the fifth or sixth time Dorie awoke that day—or evening, or night—the swelling had gone down enough to enable her to open her eyes. Not that it made any difference—you can't get blacker than black. It was also slightly easier to breathe, but otherwise nothing had changed, except in degree—she was thirstier than ever, and needed to pee even more desperately. If she hadn't been hog-tied, she might have been tempted to solve both problems at once by sipping her own urine—Dorie knew a famous photographer down in Big Sur who claimed to drink a glassful every morning—but as it was, even that unpleasant expedient was denied her.

Dorie had read or seen enough hostage and POW stories to know what she had to do to survive. Keep alert, stay oriented, maintain a positive attitude. Yeah, sure. Ha, ha, and ha. But difficult as she was finding it to keep awake, much less alert, or to stay oriented in total darkness and virtual silence, the real challenge was to avoid giving in to despair.

You can lie here feeling sorry for yourself, waiting to die, she told herself, or you can use every waking minute and every ounce of energy figuring out how to get out of this . . . *predicament* was the second word that came to mind; the first had been *nightmare*. But since for the moment words were the only thing Dorie had any degree of control over, she chose the less charged one. *Predicament* was a good word, the kind of word you could use to stave off panic. Because predicaments, after all, were things you figured your way out of, she told herself, closing her eyes again. All you could do with a nightmare was wake up from it.

Or not.

V

Warm Water, No Pain

1

"Ed, you up?" Sid rapped on Pender's door, then let himself in. "Come on, wake up and smell the coffee."

"Eat the shit and die." Pender didn't bother opening his eyes—he had no intention of getting out of bed, then or ever. It was the worst kind of hangover, the kind that comes, not from having been too drunk, but from having been unable to get drunk enough, no matter how hard you tried. And Pender, despondent over Dorie, *had* tried—he'd tried his heart out, and a lobe or two of his liver, but he couldn't get her out of his mind. That laugh, that hug, those cornflower blue eyes—even that zigzag nose.

Nor was there enough Jim Beam in the world to help him forget their last conversation. We'll get him, says the famous G-man. Don't worry about a thing, says the famous G-man—be another two months before he kills again. You sure called that one, famous G-man. Fidelity, Bravery, Integrity? Fumbling Bumbling Idiot is more like it. Probably forced the killer's hand just by showing up.

"Let's move it, Sparky." Sid crossed the room, parted the curtains, opened the jalousies. "Plane leaves in an hour."

That got Pender's attention. "I thought we said we were going to stick around for a few days, try and make ourselves useful."

"No, *you* said we were going to stick around and make ourselves useful. I said we were flying to San Francisco, as scheduled, changing planes, as scheduled, and that as soon as we got home I was going to recommend a good therapist to help you work through the grieving and the denial."

"What the hell are you talking about, grieving?" Pender, who'd fallen asleep in his underwear, sat up reluctantly, belched swamp gas. "I hardly knew her— she was an interview."

"That's not what I was referring to—although it is interesting that that's what came up for you."

"Don't play the shrink with me, Dolitz."

"I'm telling you this as your friend, Ed." Sid smoothed the crumpled coverlet with his neat little hand and sat down on the foot of the bed. "You're retired. The purpose of this trip—in addition to using up some frequent flyer miles before they expired— was to put a period—no, a big, fat exclamation mark—at the end of your career. To make it easier for you to accept the fact that you are no longer an officer of the law, and that catching every serial killer that comes down the pike is no longer your responsibility. Which is just as well, frankly, because you are obviously not up to the job."

"Now you're just trying to piss me off." Pender swung his legs over the side of the bed, sat there for a moment with his shoulders slumped and his heavy head hanging. When he realized that his nausea was *not* going to subside, and that the next belch was likely to contain more than swamp gas, he made a desperate dash for the bathroom, where he knelt to assume the position known as driving the porcelain bus.

"You said as much yourself, last night," Sid called after him. "In Jim Beam-o, *veritas*. Ten years ago—hell, five years ago—would you have just left her alone like that, somebody who fits the victim profile for an active serial killer? At the very least you'd have contacted the locals, let them know what was going on so they could keep an eye on her. Instead, you acted like a lovestruck teenager. '*Sid, whaddaya think, should I ask her out? I think I'm gonna ask her out, Sid. Sid, should I ask her out?*'"

Pender, chalk-faced, reappeared in the bathroom doorway. Beard stubble, bags under his eyes, strap undershirt, pendulous gut, rumpled boxers, one sock. "You think *I* don't know I fucked up, Sid? You think I don't know it's my fault she's probably dead now? If she's lucky? And now I'm supposed to pack it up and go home? Oops, mea culpa, so sorry, so long."

"Precisely. You've already accomplished everything you came out here to do. Let the pros handle it from here."

"But—"

"Ed, you can't be half a cop and half a civilian. People get themselves killed that way—themselves and others."

Pender couldn't think of an answer. He turned and went back into the bathroom to brush his teeth.

"You look like shit," he told the old, fat, bald guy in the mirror. "Didn't you used to be a famous G-man or something?"

"Used to be," said the o.f.b.g. "I'm retired now."

2

"Simon?"

Simon awoke, stiff and sore from a night in the uncomfortable burnt-orange side chair, and looked up at the clock on the wall. Quarter to six. He pushed himself up from the chair, stretched, crossed the room to Missy's bedside, stroked the broad forehead tenderly, patted the back of her swollen wrist. She was badly sunburned, except for the elongated bluish white circles around her eyes, where her sunglasses had protected her.

"How you feeling, sis?"

"Thirsty."

Simon glanced around. Every hospital room he'd ever seen had a pitcher of ice water on the bedside table. Not this one, though. What's the matter with these people? he thought angrily, snatching up the call button and mashing it repeatedly with his thumb like a frustrated *Jeopardy* contestant. A thousand bucks a day and they can't afford a glass of water?

"Yes?" A few minutes later the elderly night nurse popped her head through the doorway.

"My sister's thirsty—could we get some ice water in here?"

"Sorry, no can do."

As the old bat brushed by him to check Missy's vitals and plump her pillow—all the little as-long-as-I'm-here-anyway nursing attentions—Simon caught a whiff of stale sweat. It didn't seem right, somehow—nurses weren't supposed to smell. He rose and pushed his chair back. "What do you mean, 'no can do'?"

"Fluid retention. Doctor has her on a diuretic—the orders are no liquids by mouth until we get the edema down."

Simon grabbed her by the arm, just above the elbow. She glared up at him; he glared back until he saw a flicker of fear, then released her. "Look here, I won't have my sister suffering."

"I'll . . . I'll bring some ice chips for her to suck on and some glycerine for her lips."

"Would you?" said Simon, as pleasantly as an alcoholic who's just had a much-needed nip. "We'd *really* appreciate it." He turned back to Missy. "Ice chippos coming right upski."

"Simon, I want to go home."

"I'm going to be talking to Dr. Yo later this morning. Let's see what she has to say, first." The nurse returned; Simon took the carafe from her, held a sliver to Missy's sunburned lips.

Missy didn't have the strength to throw a tantrum—pitching a royal, Simon called it—but there were other approaches; when it came to getting her way, Missy's

IQ was in the genius range. Much as she wanted that ice, she turned her head away. "Home."

"Honey, your poor lips, they're all cracked and—"

"Home."

"I'll talk to Dr. Yo as soon as—"

"Home."

Home. It took a few hours to work out the details, sign the waivers Dr. Yo required before she would discharge her patient, arrange for round-the-clock private nursing, then rush home to be there before the Home-Med techs arrived to set up the hospital bed in the living room (no stairs for Missy—Dr. Yo had been quite insistent on that point). None of it came cheap, but it was worth every penny—by noon, Missy and her day-shift nurse were playing Candy Land in the living room, and Simon, at long last, was free to visit the basement. By his reckoning, close to twenty-four hours had passed since Dorie had broken her nose. She ought to be ready for a game by now, Simon told himself. He certainly was.

3

Linda Abruzzi was a city girl, born and raised. Several times during the night she had awakened with the sense that something was terribly wrong; eventually she figured out that it was the quiet that was bothering her. It seemed unnatural, somehow—it wasn't until the birds began singing in the gray faux-dawn light that she was able to get a few hours of uninterrupted sleep.

Unfortunately, the metallic burr of her windup Baby Ben alarm clock was among the noises that failed to interrupt Linda's sleep, so she ended up racing through a truncated version of her morning routine, skipping her PT exercises and chasing her vitamins and supplements with instant coffee instead of a smoothie. Luckily, it wasn't one of her Betaseron mornings (self-administered subcutaneous injection of .25 mg every other day), so she was spared that painful and time-consuming task.

She made it to the office on time. Pool handed her an old-fashioned pink while-you-were-out slip. It was the first such slip Linda had ever seen with every blank filled in—date, time, caller, reason for call, action requested, message taker's initials—even though according to the time entered, the call, from Thom Davies, at the Criminal Justice Information System, had come in only two or three minutes ago.

"Great," said Linda. Having struck out in her own attempts to locate someone from the PWSPD Association by phone, she was anxious to see what Thom had come up with. "I'll call him right back."

"I'll get him for you."

"No, that's okay; I'll call him myself."

Fat chance—Davies was on the line by the time Linda reached her desk. "Thank you, Cynthia," Linda called.

"No problem," was the reply from the anteroom.

"But please, call me Pool." Then, before Linda had a chance to examine her feelings to see how badly they were bruised: "All my friends do."

Linda felt absurdly better. "Thank you, Pool. Hi, Thom—whaddaya got?"

"Nuttin'—and plenty of it. Are you quite sure you haven't hallucinated this entire PWSPD Association business?"

"Sure I'm sure—I was logged on to their web site just the other day. Phobia-dot-com."

"Try it now—I'll wait."

Linda logged on. "I got a No URL."

"Try a search engine—any search engine."

She tried Yahoo, then Google. "No hits either way—not even cached pages."

"Precisely. And I have access to some databases you've never heard of—and if you had, I'd have to kill you—that could tell me who your date was at the Junior Prom."

"Tony Guglielmino. No wonder I struck out with four-one-one."

"Whoever did this is a real wizard. So what we need now is a wizard of our own. The best one I know of is Ben Wing, with the Nerd Squad in San Jose. I left a message for him to call me when he gets in. That'll probably be around noon, our time—if you'd like, we can make it a three-way."

"Yes, please, a thr— I mean, a conference call would be great."

"Oh, you're no fun," said Davies.

"You'd be surprised," said Linda.

4

"Here's to the hair of the dog." Pender raised his recently refilled glass.

"Ed, the fucking dog is bald by now." Two o'clock in the afternoon, and by Sid's count it was Pender's fourth drink of the day—one Jim Beam on the rocks at the airport bar in Monterey, a Bloody Mary on the connecting flight to San Francisco, and now, after receiving the call from Linda about the disappearing PWSPD Association, another Jim Beam at the airport bar in SFO.

"Don't nag me, man—I'm feeling very vulnerable."

"I know."

"I was being facetious."

"The hell you were." Sid reached across the too-high, too-small round pedestal table, the kind you find only in airport bars, to give Pender's beret a sharp sideways tug. "There, much better."

"What was that all about?"

"If you insist on wearing a brown beret with a plaid sport jacket, the least you can do is adjust it properly."

"I was going for jaunty." Pender glanced at his drink and seemed surprised to find it half empty. "You know what doesn't make sense?"

"I can think of a few things. What did you have in mind?"

"Your whole life, they tell you clean up after your mistakes. You break it, you fix it. Then you reach a certain age, you screw up, and now it's 'Get the hell outta here, pops. Go home, grab a nap, we'll take it from here.' "

"I believe that's covered in the book of Ecclesiastes," said Sid. "To everything there is a season. One generation passeth away, and another generation cometh. It's the way of the world, Sparky—you might as well get used to it."

Pender made a well-I'll-be-damned face. "Since when did *you* start reading the Bible?"

"Since right after Esther died."

"Did it help?"

"Turns out there's a lot of good stuff in there—you ought to try it sometime."

"You know, I just might," mused Pender, looking down at his glass, which had somehow emptied itself again. "I just goddamn might."

"Excuse me, sir?" It was the female flight attendant—all legs and smile.

Sid took off his reading glasses and looked up from the in-flight magazine; there were still five minutes remaining before takeoff and he'd already read everything in it that wasn't about shopping. "Yes, dear?"

"Your friend asked me to give you this." A brown paper bag from the gift shop.

"My friend?" As far as Sid knew, Pender had excused himself to use the terminal rest room before boarding—the airplane toilet was yet another modern invention that hadn't been designed for men his size. "Are you sure you have the right guy?"

The stewardess looked around the first-class compartment to see if there were any other little old men wearing blue blazers and gray toupees. Seeing none, she nodded. "He said he marked a passage for you. He also asked could you please pick up his clubs in baggage claim when we get to Dulles?"

Sid reached into the paper bag and pulled out a leather-covered, pocket-sized Holy Bible. It was black, with gilt-edged pages and a gold silk ribbon sewn into the binding. He opened it to the page marked by the ribbon and saw that Pender had circled a passage in Ecclesiastes; the print, however, was too small for Sid to make out, even with his glasses on.

"Would you mind reading that for me?" he asked, handing the Good Book back to the stewardess.

"Of course." This *was* first class, after all. "It's Ecclesiastes . . . chapter, lemme see, looks like chapter nine, verse ten:

"Whatsoever thy hand findeth to do, do it with thy might; for there is no work, nor device, nor knowledge, nor wisdom, in the grave, whither thou goest."

5

You lie in the dark long enough, you start to make your peace with loss, with loneliness, with pain and regret and the shame of having wet yourself and the fear of knowing you're about to die. You make your peace with all that and it's like a headache after a couple of aspirin: you know it's in there, it just doesn't hurt anymore.

What Dorie missed most of all was her house. She

wasn't proud of that, and she definitely didn't want to examine the meaning of it too closely, but that's what it boiled down to for her. Not her friends, not her painting, and not even her on-again-off-again lover Rafael (a fine-looking Big Sur carpenter who would have made a great poster boy for Peter Pan syndrome), but rather a fifty-five-year-old frame house nestled under a live oak at least twice its age. In her mind, she went through it room by room, stood like a ghost in every doorway, looked out from every window in every season. It was hard to imagine a stranger living in it after she was gone. I should have made a will, she thought. Left it to some starving painter.

It took a few seconds for her eyes to adjust when the lights finally came on. The room was obviously a basement; a tall man dressed all in black was padding across the cement floor. Dorie, still on her side, still hog-tied, avoided looking up at his face, instead keeping her eyes trained on his black-slippered feet as he approached. When her glance did begin traveling upward involuntarily, there was something disturbingly familiar in his easy, Clint Eastwood, backward-leaning slouching walk and the way his long-fingered hands dangled loosely at his sides.

Who *are* you? was Dorie's last thought before a glimpse of the Kabuki mask covering his face propelled her into an alternate universe where there were no thoughts, only wordless terror welling up from somewhere deep inside, in the dark region of the brain stem where the lizard-self still ruled, and the human mind never ventured.

* * *

When it worked, when it all came together, there was a rare quality to the fear displayed by a phobic confronted with the object of his or her phobia, a purity and intensity to which your average Joe or Josie could never aspire. At such moments, the emotional closeness between Simon and his victim/partner made him feel the way other people seemed to feel when making love, even when his victim/partner was a male; when it was a naked female, any naked female, his sense of involvement was so acute as to be almost unbearable.

With Dorie, however, the relationship was both enhanced and skewed by the unfamiliar presence of a third party—the lurid Kabuki mask. Wearing it took Simon outside himself, somehow. It was as if he were seeing himself approach through *her* eyes and hearing the whispery rasp of his slippers on the rough cement, the buzz of the overhead fluorescents, and her own shallow panting through *her* ears. He felt the shock down to his bones when she saw the mask; when her terror peaked, when her thoughts shut down, he knew, and understood.

He was even glad for her when her vasovagal reflex kicked in, causing her to lose consciousness. He was glad for himself as well—the connection was too intense to be endured for extended periods, and it wasn't until it had been broken that Simon realized he was in a state of extreme arousal.

And with that realization came the release. As always, the premature climax was unsatisfying and anticlimactic—a shameful, irrelevant spasm, a dribble and a blush instead of a gush and a roar.

Simon's shame quickly transmuted itself into anger. Dorie was awakened by a series of open-handed slaps. Hog-tied, all she could do was tuck her chin tight into her chest and wait it out. It didn't hurt much, anyway—or at any rate, it didn't hurt any worse than the pain from the broken nose, cramped limbs, and parched lips that it had supplanted.

The mild beating also helped take her mind off the mask—that seemed important. And afterward he was gentle. He loosened her bonds, rolled her onto her back, and retied her wrists in front of her. Her legs were left free; it wasn't until he slipped his hands between her knees and urged them open that she realized he hadn't left her ankles untied as a mercy.

But her captor apparently changed his mind about molesting her sexually when he caught the scent of urine.

"I think *somebody* needs a bath," he said, patiently but firmly. It was the first time he'd spoken in her presence.

Simon Childs, thought Dorie. Our founder. Of course, of course: the fox starts a support group for the geese. Which makes me the biggest goose of all.

Though her eyes were closed again, she sensed that he had moved away; then she heard water running. Not a gentle plashing, but loud and violent, the sound of water falling from a height into a big, empty, metal tub. It made her want to pee again, but she decided to save it up this time. Having a name to put to the monster, and even more important, a face to put behind the mask, had sent Dorie back into survivor mode: she had remembered the antirape measures she and her girlfriends used to recommend to each other. Act crazy. Laugh, don't cry. Howl, gibber. If you can pee, pee; if you can shit, shit your pants;

and if you can't do either, stick your finger down your throat and puke all over him. Anything to kill desire, buy time, stay alive. Where there's life, there's hope—isn't that what everybody always said?

Then Dorie remembered something else, a parable her father once told her when she hadn't sold a painting in a year and was thinking about giving up and taking a straight job. It was about a man sentenced to death who promised the king that if his life was spared, within a year he would teach the king's favorite horse to talk. His friends told him he was crazy, that he'd set himself an impossible task. But a year is a long time, he told them. A lot of things can happen in a year. The king could die. The horse could die. Or maybe—who knows?—maybe the horse will actually learn to talk.

Stranger things have happened, thought Dorie. Miracles have happened—you just have to stay alive long enough to be there when they do.

6

According to the Karma Kagyu school of Tibetan Buddhism, a Down syndrome reincarnation is meant to be a reward, in the form of a short, restful, and relatively stress-free lifetime, for good karma accrued during a meritorious previous incarnation. DSers, or at least well cared for DSers, tend to have loving, caring natures and sunny dispositions, and for the most part spend less time worrying about matters beyond their control than the more able-minded general public—not a bad description of an enlightened being, according to the Tibetans.

From that point of view, Missy Childs, sheltered, pampered, and privately tutored, must have been a veritable saint in her previous lifetime. Saintliness, however, is not exactly a survival skill in the Berkeley flats, and enlightened or not, as a mentally disabled white female, Missy could be said to have been on borrowed time, statistically, from the moment she stepped through Ganny's front door.

The boys had probably seen her coming a block away. There were three of them, hanging out in front of a mom-and-pop liquor store, decked out in Blood summer wear in honor of the unseasonably warm weather: backward Raiders caps, oversize black polo shirts, baggy-saggy black Ben Davis cutoffs, high black socks, red-trimmed Airs; they also wore red bandannas tucked discreetly into their back pockets—any more obvious gang styling might have gotten them picked up by the Berkeley cops on a loitering-with-intent-to-associate rap.

The two twelve-year-old baby gangstas were cutting school; the thirteen-year-old had already been expelled. They were bored, they were broke, and Missy must have looked like a godsend, waddling up the street in her pigeon-toed gait, with her pink plastic purse over one arm and a birdcage dangling from the other. Simultaneously, as if at some undiscernible signal, the three boys hopped off the low concrete retaining wall next to the sidewalk outside the mom-and-pop (the entrance to which was not only barred, but protected by a pair of concrete pylons to prevent drive-through break-ins) and fell into step behind Missy. "Hey, you a retard?"

"Sticks and stones," said Missy, without turning around. She was dog-tired already, her feet hurt, she had sweated through her T-shirt, and the cage weighed a ton (she knew by now that it had been a mistake to bring it along—all the water had already sloshed out of the little dish clipped to the bars, and Tweety herself was clinging desperately to her little trapeze as it swung to and fro), but Missy's instinct told her to keep walking. "Go away. Leave me alone."

"Hoo hoo ha ha." The oldest boy mocked her speech. "And what you doin' wearin' 'Didas 'round here?" Only Crips and Crip satellites wore Adidas.

The maneuver, when it came, was so slickly executed that to an observer—and fortunately for Missy, there had been an observer—it looked like one of those nature documentaries where a pack of wolves cut off a lame caribou from the herd. As they passed a boarded-up vacant lot, one of the boys darted around to get in front of Missy, slowing his pace to block her way, while the second closed up behind her and the boy to her left eased her to the right, through a gap in the board fence.

And before Missy could even call out, one boy was behind her with one hand pinning both wrists against the small of her back and the other hand across her mouth, the second boy had her purse, and the third had begun twirling the birdcage over his head, preparing to launch it across the weed-strewn lot like an Olympic hammer thrower.

Afterward, she would remember everything about

that moment: the heat, the distant traffic, the weeds, the broken glass, the sunbaked earth of the vacant lot, the whirling cage, the crows on the telephone line, the buzzing blue sky, the sweat running down her face, the boy's tense little body pressing up against her from behind, the salt taste of his hot little hand covering her mouth—it all seemed terribly real and so terribly important that she almost forgot to be afraid.

"Stall it out right there, youngbloods." A man's voice, from the other side of the fence.

"Oh, shit, it's Obie," whispered the boy holding Missy. The boy holding her purse quickly shifted it behind his back, while the boy swinging Tweety's cage over his head lurched comically around the lot trying to arrest its momentum as the biggest, second-hand-somest black man Missy had ever seen squeezed himself sideways through the gap in the fence.

"Let her go, Jerome." He was wearing a black sweat suit, his gray hair was cut short and curly like Dennis Richmond's, and his skin was a deep chocolate brown.

"Yeah, lemme go, you brat," said Missy, when the hand came off her mouth; her arms were still pinned behind her.

"Naw, Obie, naw, we—"

"Answer up, blood." The way the man said it— patiently, without raising his voice—reminded Missy of Simon: the quieter he said something, the quicker you'd better mind.

And sure enough, the boy released her. Missy tugged angrily at the neck of her T-shirt, which was all rucked up and twisted around. "Gimme."

The boys started laughing as she reached for the cage; the man silenced them with a glare. "You heard the lady."

"I heard *humma humma,*" said the boy holding the cage. "Thass what *I* heard."

A moment later the cage was on the ground and the soles of the boy's Airs were dangling a foot above the weeds and the dirt and the broken glass.

"Work the mind before you work the mouth, baby g." The old lion gave the cub an admonitory shake, then set him down gently.

"We was just—"

"I know what you was just. You a got-damn disgrace to the race, all a you." He handed the cage to Missy. "You okay, honey?"

Dazed by all the sudden twists and turns her day had been taking, Missy managed a nod. She didn't feel very okay, though. She couldn't catch her breath and her heart was beating fast and fluttery in her chest, like Tweety's heart.

"Okay, you run along, then," said the man. "I'll watch your back."

Missy wasn't sure why he'd want to watch her back, but she didn't wait around to ask. She ducked through the hole in the fence and started walking. She walked and walked and walked, and by the time she realized that the nasty little boys had taken her purse—the purse containing not just her twenty-dollar bill and her lucky penny from Cannery Row that Dorie had given her, the one with the otter stamped on it, but also the card she was supposed to show strangers if she was ever lost, the card with her address and her phone number, neither of which she had ever quite managed to commit to memory—she had no idea how to make it back to the vacant lot.

Or to Ganny's, for that matter. Missy had no idea how long she wandered with that heavy cage before she found herself passing a familiar-looking fence overgrown with purple morning glories. Two, three hours? Missy wasn't real good with time—but then, she'd never had to be. There'd always been someone to tell her when it was time to do something, or stop doing it. All she knew was that she was tired and sunburned and hungry and thirsty and her feet hurt, but she couldn't bring herself to go inside that house again and be all alone with Ganny.

She did make it as far as the kitchen, where she leaned over the sink and tilted her head and drank water directly out of the faucet until her tummy felt as if it were going to burst. But when she turned the water off, she heard, or thought she could hear, the flies buzzing in the bedroom, and decided it would be better to take Tweety, who'd been lying motionless on the paper in the bottom of the cage ever since the vacant lot, and go back outside to wait for Simon in the garden. She'd fallen asleep in the shade of the fence, under the sunflowers, and awakened to find Simon kneeling over her, crying with joy.

"I knew you'd come," she'd whispered through her cracked lips.

And now, she was home again, with sunlight pouring in like gold through the tall windows of the living room. From her nifty new hospital bed she could see most all of Berkeley and, beyond it, the dark, sparkling waters of the bay; that city of white towers gleaming in the distance was San Francisco. It looked like a toy city from way up here; it looked like a whole toy world.

As for the new day nurse, Missy could take her or leave her. She was pretty and she had a funny name—Missy liked that about her—but she was mean about food. When Missy wanted an after-lunch snack, Nurse Apple said she'd already *had* lunch. Well, duh!

Something else Nurse Apple was mean about: she wanted to get rid of poor Tweety's empty cage—she said it was full of germs. And because of Missy's speech problems it would have been impossible for Missy to explain to her why she wanted the cage nearby for a while, even if she'd fully understood it herself. As it was, all she knew was that when things die, you have to have something to remember them by, something to touch and smell, or else they disappear and you can't remember what they were like even if you have a picture—you can only remember the picture.

Like with her mother: all Missy had of her was her hairbrush. It was slender and dainty and had a few silky-soft hairs caught in the bristles, and when Missy held it next to her cheek, even though Simon said it was impossible because she was too little when their mother went away, she remembered not just that Mommy looked like Audrey Hepburn, but that she smelled like powder and her hair was soft and her touch so gentle that when she held Missy in her arms, Missy felt as if she were floating.

And all Missy had left of Tweety was the cage. Even though its emptiness made her a little sad, it helped Missy remember how yellow Tweety had been, and how prettily she sang, and the way she crooked her head sometimes as though she were asking Missy if she still loved her. Which was why, when Nurse Apple tried to take it away, Missy had to throw a royal until they came to what Nurse Apple called an arrangement: Missy could keep the cage by her bed if she let Nurse Apple wash it down real good first.

A few minutes after Nurse Apple took the cage into the downstairs bathroom, the doorbell rang. Missy knew she wasn't supposed to get out of bed, but she didn't get to answer the door very often and wasn't about to let an opportunity like this pass her by. She slipped on her pink chenille robe; the bell rang again as she padded barefoot into the foyer.

"Hold your horses," she called, fumbling with the lock. "Just hold your horses."

7

After Pender's last physical, his doctor had suggested he take up smoking. Why would I want to do that? Pender asked. You're a dangerously obese, hypertensive, fifty-five-year-old man with a drinking problem, the doctor had replied—I just thought you might want to go for the perfecta.

Six weeks later, trudging up a steep blacktop driveway on a warm autumn day, Pender had occasion to remember those words. By the time he reached the

top, his yellow Ban Lon polo shirt was clinging like a
damp second skin, he could feel his heart pounding,
and if a genie had popped out of the azalea bushes
lining the driveway and offered him three wishes, the
first one would have been for an oxygen mask.

Not that he regretted his decision to ditch Sid at
the airport, impulsive though it may have seemed.
The trigger had been the telephone call from Linda
Abruzzi. Without access to the PWSPD Association,
Pender knew, the investigation was back to square
one. He'd had a few suggestions for Linda—surely
the hotel where the convention had been held would
have, if not a list of attendees, then at least a roster of
hotel guests for the weekend in question. And with
the phobia.com address currently unoccupied, perhaps she could get Thom to arrange some sort of
pop-up that would alert visitors or redirect them to
an FBI site, while she herself worked the Las Vegas,
Fresno, and Chicago police departments to get them
to reopen their investigations in light of recent
events.

But that was about all Pender could come up
with—nothing case-breaking, nothing she wouldn't
have figured out on her own eventually. No, at this
point, if the case was going to be broken, it was going
to be broken by good old-fashioned police work. The
Bureau already had an Evidence Response Team with
a good criminalist going over Dorie's house in
Carmel—so the question Pender had asked himself,
as he and Sid were waiting in the bar for their flight to
be called, was what, if anything, could he bring to the
party?

The answer wasn't long in coming. He'd interviewed Dorie Bell—he had the name of at least one living PWSPD convention attendee. And according to Dorie, that same attendee who lived in nearby Berkeley had helped finance the convention—he had to know more about the PWSPD Association than Dorie had.

Unless of course the association was nothing but an Internet dummy, something the killer had set up in order to provide himself with a pool of victims. Which, Pender realized, would make the man who was financing the operation either a complete sucker, an accomplice, or the killer himself. Which meant in turn that it was high time somebody interviewed Mr. Simon Childs, of Berkeley. Somebody cautious enough to show up on Mr. Childs's doorstep without advance notice, somebody experienced enough to ascertain what Mr. Childs knew without alerting him to the fact that he was under suspicion.

Pender had nominated himself, of course—and there were no other candidates.

The address had been in the phone book: 2500 Grizzly Rock Road, Berkeley. The house was built of weathered stone and dark timbers. The front door, rough-planed black oak, was opened by a short, fat, balding woman wearing footed pink pajamas under a pink robe. Her complexion was mottled, white as a chronic shut-in around the eyes, brick-red, ointment-smeared patches of sunburn on her cheeks and brow, and she appeared to be almost as out of breath as Pender.

"Heyyo." Deep voice, unmodulated. Down Syndromer—this would be the sister Dorie had mentioned. Older than Pender had pictured—but then, DSers tended to live a lot longer nowadays. "Hi. Is Simon home?"

And although he couldn't comprehend all that she said next, thanks to the time he'd spent with his sister Ida's son, Stan, who'd also survived to middle age but had passed away a few years ago, Pender understood enough of it that when she concluded by pointing downward, he understood. "Simon's in the basement?"

An enthusiastic nod, a delighted grin—she was clearly tickled to have made herself understood.

"Could you get him for me?"

"Ohhh no." The nod turned to a shake. There was a wary quality to her grin now; it no longer lit up her eyes. Pender, who read nonverbal responses the way poetry lovers read verse, was immediately intrigued. *Something* was making the woman uncomfortable— the basement? interrupting Simon? interrupting Simon *in* the basement?—and whatever it was had set off his cop radar.

"Why not?" After spending his entire adult life in law enforcement, although Pender still couldn't have said for sure whether cop radar was something old FBI agents developed or whether they just didn't get to be old FBI agents without it, he had definitely learned to trust it.

"Gary," said the woman.

"Somebody named Gary's down there?"

Her shoulders slumped. A lifetime of not being understood, thought Pender. He slapped himself on the forehead comically. "I'm such a stupidhead. Give me one more chance?"

"Gary, gary." She hugged herself and pantomimed a mock shudder.

"Scary—it's scary down there."

"Yeah."

"I know what you mean—basements can be scary places. If you'd like, I could go down there with you."

The shudder was genuine this time.

"Or I could go down by myself—you wouldn't even have to go."

She said something he couldn't quite make out—I hate him? I'll get him?—and turned away, leaving the door ajar. Pender thought about it for a good two, two and half seconds (since she lacked the mental capacity to give informed consent, it wouldn't exactly have been a kosher entry even if she'd invited him in, which she hadn't), then followed her inside.

8

Warm water, no pain. Strawberry bubble bath—Missy's favorite, as Dorie recalled. She leaned back, rounding her shoulders to fit the curving metal sides of the tub.

"Feeling better?" asked the now unmasked Simon. He was sitting on an overturned milk carton next to the tub with his knees drawn up and his chin cradled in his palm like Rodin's *Thinker*.

"Much better." True enough: even knowing she

was going to die soon, this was paradise compared to her last thirty-six hours—or however long it had been. Simon had given her a Percodan for her pain, and equally important, a glass of water to wash it down with, and though he'd immediately retied her ankles after helping her into the tub, he'd subsequently untied her wrists so she could wash herself. It felt good to have her hands free again; she'd almost forgotten what it was like. And as for the trade-off—the Percodan, in addition to taking away her pain, had also taken all the fight out of her—she was scarcely aware of it.

Simon, however, for all his languid posing, was dialed in dead center, acutely attuned to every nuance of Dorie's mood, every fluctuation of her spirit. He knew they didn't have much time left together, but he was hoping to make the most of it. First, though, he had to get her relaxed and off her guard again—not an easy task, given the circumstances.

"Are you sure you're not hungry?"

"I was a few hours ago. I don't think I could eat anything now."

"Well, just let me know."

"I will."

Dense silence, broken only by the sound of the bathwater lapping hollowly against the sides of the tub when Dorie shifted her position and the whistle of air through her broken nose on the tail end of each exhale. The term *awkward pause* didn't begin to cover it. Simon tried once more to get a conversation going. "I like your hair up like that." Absent a comb or hairpin, she had twisted her brown braid into a precariously balanced bun.

Dorie closed her eyes. The painkiller had given her a new kind of courage—the courage not to care.

He tried again: "What do you think of this Y2K deal?"

"Doesn't matter to me—I'm not going to be around for it, am I?"

"That depends," said Simon. Over the years he had learned the importance of leaving his victims with a little hope. Without hope, there was no fear. But he could tell she didn't believe him—she didn't even ask the almost automatic question: depends on what? Instead she turned away, picked up the bath sponge, squeezed it over her head. Her eyes were closed just long enough for him to slip on the Kabuki mask he'd been holding on his lap, out of her line of sight. It must have seemed to her as if it had appeared out of nowhere. Again he felt the shock pass between them like an electric current. Then her eyelids fluttered, her eyeballs rolled back in her head, and her head drooped forward onto her chest.

Now, he thought—do it now, don't be greedy. All he had to do was put his hand on top of her head, shove her down under the water, and hold her there. She might not even wake up—so much the better for her. And if she did wake up, if she struggled a little, so much the better for him.

9

"*Page* him—you're *paging* him." The penny hadn't dropped for Pender until Childs's sister pushed the button on the two-way pager clipped to the railing of the hospital bed set up by the tall, arched windows at the far end of the high-ceilinged, oak-beamed living room.

She held up the device in one hand, pointed to it with the other, pursed her lips, and shook her head sadly—it was a *duh* face if Pender had ever seen one.

"Is this *your* bed?" he asked her.

She nodded.

"Are you ill?"

She tapped her chest. "Ticker."

Just like his nephew, Stan. "I bet you're supposed to be *in* bed."

A sly grin. "'Posed to."

"C'mon, in you go." Pender helped her back up onto the bed, pulled the covers up to her rib cage, and was tucking in the corners when he realized they were no longer alone. He turned slowly, saw a slender man in black slouched casually in the archway next to the massive fieldstone fireplace, arms folded at his chest, weight on one leg, one slippered foot crossed nonchalantly over the other as if he were modeling clothes in a magazine ad.

Pender let the details register: white male, early fifties, approximately six foot one, approximately one hundred and sixty pounds. Cleft chin, trim gray mustache, sleepy eyes, silver hair, prominent widow's

peak. Black slippers, black pleated slacks; the cuffs of
his blousy black shirt were turned up.

"Mr. Childs?"

A nod—barely perceptible.

"Special Agent Pender, Federal Bureau of Investigation."

"Nice to meet you," said Childs. He crossed the
room, held out his hand. His handshake was surprisingly firm, given his languid manner; his palm was
cold and damp, as if he'd only just dried it. "I see
you've met Missy."

"I'm afraid I got her out of bed."

"Not your fault—she's supposed to have a nurse
with her at all times." Childs turned to Missy, asked
where the nurse was. The reply was unintelligible, at
least to Pender.

"Mr. Childs, is there someplace we can talk privately?"

"Sure, follow me. And Missy—no more getting out
of bed. If you need anything, just holler—we'll be in
the kitchen."

"Peachy keen," replied Missy.

Simon's beeper had gone off just as he was bending
over the tub. He'd given the other unit, Missy's unit,
to the nurse, with instructions to beep him only in the
event of an emergency, so when the summons came
he'd rushed upstairs, expecting to find Nurse Apple
performing CPR on Missy—or pulling the sheet up
over her face: that was the first, unacceptable image
that had crossed his mind.

When instead he found Pender tenderly tucking
Missy into bed, recognized him as the man he'd last

seen talking to Dorie over her kitchen table, then learned that he was an FBI agent, a flood of conflicting emotions washed over Simon—relief over Missy, then panic, then the rage that invariably followed panic. He knew better than to act on it, though, and by the time Pender turned around, Simon had mastered his emotions well enough to deliver an I'd-like-to-thank-the-Academy performance. And now it was Pender who was off *his* guard. Turning his back.

If only I had some kind of weapon, thought Simon. The knives were all stowed away in a high, Missy-proof cabinet on the far side of the room. Nearer to hand, however, suspended from the rack above the central butcher-block workspace, hung Ganny Wilson's three cast-iron skillets. Papa Bear, Mama Bear, Baby Bear, Little Simon used to call them. Papa Bear would be too heavy to swing, Baby too light to do much damage, but Mama Bear—Mama Bear would be just right. Somehow Simon knew in advance exactly what it would feel like: the blow would be cushioned by the thin wool fabric of Pender's beret; the shock would travel all the way up Simon's arm to his shoulder.

First, though, he needed to find out what Pender already knew. It couldn't be too much, or he'd never have shown up alone like this. Would he have time to break out Plan B, which involved grabbing Missy and the getaway bag and heading south of the border, to Dr. Andrew Keene's secure condo in Puerto Vallarta? Simon had to know—Mama Bear would just have to wait.

Simon adopted what he hoped was an appropriately concerned, mildly puzzled John-Q.-Citizendealing-with-the-fuzz expression: "So, what can I do for you, Agent Pender?"

"Do you know Dorie Bell?"

"Yes—she's a friend of mine."

"Where did you meet?" With a suspect, as opposed to a witness, you always ask a few questions you already know the answer to first—give them a chance to lie early, save everybody some time.

"We met at the PWSPD convention in Las Vegas."

"When was the last time you were in Carmel?"

"Missy and I were down there around the end of June. We had a wonderful time—visited the Aquarium, drove down to—"

Oh-ho, thought Pender. The first two answers had been unequivocal; this one sounded more as if Childs was trying to lead the conversation away from the question. "Excuse me, Mr. Childs? Are you saying that was the *last* time you were in Carmel. In June?" Polite, but dubious enough to draw Childs out—if the guy was dirty, he'd start tap-dancing anytime now.

And sure enough: "Are *you* saying it *wasn't*?"

"How would *I* know?"

"Agent Pender, what's this all about?"

Tap dancing? The guy was turning into fucking Bojangles. "Mr. Childs, we have reason to believe Miss Bell has been kidnapped."

And Childs followed his lead fluidly: "No! Oh, my God, poor Dorie. What do they want?"

"Who?"

"The kidnappers. If it's money, I could—"

"It's not money, Mr. Childs. When was the last time you spoke to Ms. Bell?"

Simon saw his chance, and took it. "Yesterday

morning. She was planning to drive down to Los Angeles with some guy she'd met."

By now, Pender was feeling the chill he'd told Linda always to trust. If he'd had his SIG Sauer with him, he'd have pulled it now, held Childs at gunpoint until the tac squad arrived, then claimed that Childs had attacked him so the entry and search would be kosher.

Of course, Pender knew there was also a possibility that both he and his hunch were entirely full of shit, and that either Dorie had changed her mind or he had misunderstood her when she told him she'd be around all day Thursday, and that the chill he was feeling was only the sweat drying on his Ban Lon shirt—Lord knows he'd been wrong before. But what he wasn't going to do at this point, right or wrong, gun or no gun, was leave Childs alone long enough to kill Dorie—if she wasn't dead yet—then make a run for it.

Which meant he'd have to do a little fancy dancing himself. "Really! Los Angeles, you say." He started to reach for his trusty notebook, then remembered that he was no longer carrying it. "This man she'd just met—did she happen to give you a name?"

"I'm afraid not," said Childs, edging to his left.

It seemed to Pender that the man was trying to ease around behind him. Like a fighter trying to avoid being cornered, Pender edged to his own left. "Did she tell you anything at all about him?"

"Excuse me?"

That was a bad sign—if Childs was no longer paying attention to the questions, he was probably preparing to make his move.

"Never mind." They had casually circled each other; one more quick step, and Childs was no longer between Pender and the doorway. Whatever he's planning, he won't want to do it in front of Missy, thought Pender, turning suddenly and starting back down the hallway toward the living room.

Childs caught up, grabbed Pender's elbow. Stronger than he looks, thought Pender. He kept going, towing Childs impersonally in his wake like a big dog straining at its leash. Just as they reached the living room, a middle-aged nurse wearing a cardigan sweater over her uniform appeared in the archway on the far side of the room, holding an empty bird-cage aloft like a brakeman's lantern.

10

There had been a moment of surrender, no denying that. The second time Dorie faked a syncope, it wasn't to lull Simon, like the first time, it was to lull herself. Close your eyes, let go. It's not real anyway—you've dreamed it a thousand times. Maybe not exactly like this, in a metal tub in a basement, the mask face leaning over you, the surprisingly gentle hand pressed against your forehead, urging you down, down, under the warm, soapy, strawberry-scented water—but you knew it would be *something* like this.

Just let go, she told herself—either you wake up or you don't. And if you don't, maybe you see the light at the end of the tunnel. Dorie found it easy to believe in the light—she just wasn't so sure what came after. But whatever it is, she thought, sooner or later we all find out.

Just let go.

No light, no tunnel. No hand over her face, no mask looming over her. Just the rapidly cooling water and a sense that she was alone in the dark again. So much for surrender; so much for letting go.

But the darkness was different this time around. Dorie knew its shape, its dimensions, knew where the light switch was, where the stairs were. And her hands were free—unaccountably, he'd left her hands free. Was it a trap? Only one way to find out: Dorie grabbed the rim of the tub and hauled herself up into a sitting position, sat shivering for a moment, hunched over, waiting for . . .

For what? For Simon to come back and finish her off? Quickly she leaned forward, untied the nylon cord looped around her ankles, tried to stand up, fell backward with a splash. On her second try she pulled herself up to a squatting position and climbed out of the tub crouched over, holding on to the rim tightly with both hands.

Even after Dorie regained her balance, it took an effort of will to let go of that rim—it was like pushing off into deep space. She became aware of the bathwater in her ears, tilted her head to the side, and began hopping from one foot to the other, arms crossed over her chest to minimize the flop factor. Once her ears were clear, she realized that she'd been all but deaf. Simon could have been sitting next to her in the dark all along; he could have been whistling "Dixie" for all she'd have known.

Dorie shuddered, forced herself to take that first step into the dark.

Missy screamed. Pender wheeled, threw up his right arm, caught the blow on the back of his forearm, just below the elbow. A cast-iron pan—a fucking frying pan. The nurse dropped the cage with a clatter. Pender found himself on the floor. The pain was blinding—the whole room seemed to be on fire with pain. He watched through the flames as Childs strode purposefully across the room to the fireplace and snatched up a gleaming brass poker.

Much better, thought Simon, slashing the air with the poker as if it were a rapier as he turned back to Pender. Mama Bear was too heavy, too slow, too awkward.

"Simon, no." Missy trotted toward him, slippers flopping, hands flapping at her sides as if she were trying to take off. "Stop it, Simon."

"Missy, you stay out of this." Simon brandished the poker at her.

Missy flinched, but kept coming. "He's nice, don't hurt him." She threw herself at her brother, wrapped her short arms around him, and held on for dear life as Pender lumbered to his feet, right arm hanging limply, gathering himself for a charge.

Simon shoved Missy roughly aside and flailed wildly with the poker as Pender came at him. Pender, a pretty fair two-way guard for the Cortland High Purple Tigers in his day, ducked under the awkward swing and caught Simon in the midsection with his left shoulder, hit him head up, ass down, and legs driving, just the way his coaches had taught him forty years earlier.

The poker went flying; they hit the floor together. Pender landed on his broken arm. He blacked out, or rather, whited out momentarily from the pain; when he regained his senses, Missy was lying on top of him, arms spread wide, shielding him with her body. Childs stood over them, brandishing the poker wildly, shouting at his sister to get off, to get out of the way.

Dorie walked slowly through the blackness, arms outstretched like a somnambulist. When she touched the wall, she turned left and felt her way along until she reached the newel post at the bottom of the steps. She felt around, found a light switch. She closed her eyes before turning on the lights, so as not to blind herself; when she opened them again, the first thing she noticed was Simon's night-vision goggles hanging on a nail, only inches from her face.

Seeing them, it occurred to Dorie that even with the lights on, Simon would still have the upper hand; in the dark, however, the advantage would belong to whoever wore those goggles. She slipped them over her head carefully, mindful of her nose, adjusted the strap, flipped the power switch. Everything turned a hideous, bright, oobleck green. Quickly she turned off the basement lights. The intensity of the color faded; still, as a plein air painter, an aficionado of natural light, Dorie found the artificial, monochrome world of the goggles extremely unsettling, almost nauseating.

She left them on, though—the darkness was now

her ally. To ensure the alliance, she flipped up the goggles, turned the light switch on, and circled the basement unscrewing every bulb she could find, until the room was black again. Then she flipped the goggles back down and went exploring, in search of two things. The first was a way out that didn't involve following Simon Childs through the door at the top of the stairs; the second was a weapon of some sort, in case the first didn't exist.

11

". . . twenty-five hundred Grizzly Rock Road. And an ambulance. Hurry, please."

Nurse Apple's voice, cutting through the red-hot rage, brought Simon back to his senses. He found himself standing over Missy and Pender with the poker raised; he didn't want to think about how close he'd come to smashing her fat, stupid skull with it. Thank God he hadn't—but now there was no time to deal with Pender. Nine-one-one, once called, could not be uncalled. Five minutes. Wild, improbable schemes sprang into his head—kill them all, stab myself—intruders, bikers, a black gang. Four and a half minutes. Just grab Missy and run. But Missy was still hanging on to Pender with a death grip. Four minutes. Maybe just grab Missy and the getaway bag and run. Or maybe just the getaway bag. He who fights and runs away . . .

* * *

It was a little like being underwater, this all-green, nightscope world, a little like exploring a cave, a little like being inside one of those camera's-eye scenes in a horror movie, and nothing at all like the brightly col-ored, safe, sunny life Dorie had constructed for her-self over the years to keep the mask-monsters at bay.

The basement itself, save for the big room with the mattress and the tub, was a series of chambered cav-erns joined by low, thick-walled archways. It reminded Dorie of something out of Poe—*The Cask of Amontillado,* perhaps—but by now she was so far beyond being moved by imaginary fears that she never even flinched when she found the cardboard box containing Simon's cache of masks near the bottom of the stairs.

Kabuki, its white glare and red frown even more lurid in shades of green, was on top. Dorie reached into the box, lifted it out with a sense of wonder, held it up like Hamlet holding Yorick's skull. Plaster—could it be that it was only paint and plaster and a droopy little rubber band cord? Strange as it felt to actually be hold-ing a mask in her hands, the little tug of regret she experienced as she tossed it back into the box seemed even stranger. Dorie's phobia had been an essential part of her identity, her sense of self, for so long that like a newly freed slave, she found herself wondering what life was going to be like without her chains.

Probably short, if you don't get your ass in gear, she reminded herself, kicking the box under the stairs and turning away.

With Missy on top of him—and there wasn't a doubt in his mind that she had saved his life—Pender couldn't see where Childs had gone. It was enough, for the moment, that he had gone—then Pender remembered that Dorie might still be alive, might be somewhere in the house.

"It's okay, honey—you can get off now," he whispered urgently—whispered because her two hundred, two hundred fifty pounds were crushing the breath out of him. She felt like dead weight. He started to extricate himself one-handed, saw the nurse standing openmouthed, still holding the receiver. "Little help here," he gasped.

She was terrified, hugely undecided. Pender couldn't blame her—for all she knew he was a crazed intruder whom her employer had been trying to fend off with that frying pan.

"FBI," he called.

She was either unconvinced or frozen with fear.

"Please, I think she's stopped breathing."

That brought her out of it. Leaving the phone off the hook, Nurse Apple bustled over to help Pender roll Missy off him. He staggered to his feet, cradling his injured arm. There was no time to break anything gently. Letting the arm dangle—fuck, that hurt—he pulled his wallet out of his hip pocket with his left hand, flipped it open to show her his badge.

"Pender, FBI. Simon Childs is a serial killer. There may be another victim still alive in the house—when the police get here, tell them I've gone after him."

Nurse Apple was already bending over Missy, preparing to begin CPR—she waved him away impatiently, half-listening. Then it dawned on her: serial killer, gone after him. "No, don't—"

Too late—he was gone. "No more private gigs," she

muttered, turning back to her patient. *Pender, FBI,* had just bugged out, leaving her alone with a serial killer who ran around bashing people with frying pans. "This time I mean it."

Dorie's hope died with the battery that had powered the night-vision goggles; along with hope went courage; along with courage went the last of her strength. Wet, naked, thoroughly disoriented, she threw the goggles aside and sank down onto her haunches, shivering as much from despair as from the cold.

Sooner or later, she told herself, Simon would come looking for her. It wouldn't take him long to figure out that she'd unscrewed the lightbulbs—after that it would only be a matter of time. She remembered how peaceful she'd felt in that warm tub, how easy drowning had seemed back then. Now the universe had turned so ugly that she no longer believed in the light at the end of the tunnel—in any light, for that matter. Part of her wanted to go primal, to howl and tear out her hair, but she was too tired and beaten even for silent grieving.

Never mind, she thought, leaning her bare back against the cold concrete wall—let him come. But even that weak note of defiance deserted her when she heard footsteps descending the wooden stairs; she covered her ears with her hands to block out the sound and shut her eyes against the sudden brightness of the flashlight beam shining down on her from above.

And that was how Pender found her, squatting against the wall in the far corner of what had once been Grandfather Childs's wine cellar, her hands pressed tightly over her ears.

"Dorie," he said gently, then, louder: "Dorie, it's Ed Pender."

When there was still no response, he sat down beside her and waited. After thirty seconds or so she opened her eyes. "It *is* you," she said. "I was afraid maybe I was dreaming."

"I know what you mean," said Pender. "I know exactly what you mean."

VI
Dead Man Whispering

1

Simon Childs was no fool. He'd always understood that the fear game was inherently risky and, moreover, that the risk was potentially fatal, not because California was a death-penalty state, but because for Simon, imprisonment was simply not an option. For years he'd kept the huge leather satchel he called his getaway bag packed and ready, stuffed with cash, drugs, prescription and otherwise, fake ID and credit cards, and in the event it all went south, a little blue capsule that, Zap Strum had assured him, was the same formulation issued by the CIA to its operatives. Just bite down, Zap promised Simon—an instantaneous death is guaranteed.

"What's in it?" he'd asked.

"Dunno."

"Will it be painless?"

"Hard to say: nobody who's actually taken one has ever lived long enough to tell anybody."

Despite Simon's precautions, it wasn't until he was in the Mercedes, driving north on Grizzly Rock with the satchel beside him on the passenger's seat and what seemed like every emergency vehicle in Alameda County passing him in the opposite direction, lights flashing and sirens blaring, that it began to sink in: this is actually happening, buckaroo—this is Plan B for real.

But not Plan B as he'd envisioned it. It was all happening too fast. Forget Mexico—they'd have a description of the Mercedes out before he made it to South San Francisco, much less south of the border. Which meant he had to get it off the road pronto. But where? And then what? And what about—

No. He couldn't allow himself to start thinking about Missy just yet. He felt so guilty about leaving her. Not that Pender had left him with any choice. Hiding behind her like that—what a coward. And of course if Pender hadn't taken advantage of Missy's disability by tricking her into letting him into the house, where he had no right to be, or if Pender hadn't stuck his nose in where it didn't belong in the first place . . .

Pender, Pender, Pender—it all came down to Pender, didn't it?

For Simon, it was a calming revelation, even comforting somehow; he turned his attention back to his more immediate concern: getting this red-hot, highly conspicuous car off the road as soon as possible.

2

According to the *Farmer's Almanac,* which Nelson
Carpenter consulted every morning of his life, adjust-
ing as always for a latitude of 37°50′ and allowing for
daylight saving time, which still had another week to
run, the sun would be setting at 6:23 P.M. on Friday,
October 22.

Nelson, once known as Nervous Nellie (a sobri-
quet that, given his first name, the cruelty of children,
and the severity of his polyphobia, was probably
inevitable), needed at least an hour to complete his
preparations for nightfall. It wasn't a large house, just
a standard suburban colonial in Concord, California,
the kind of place where horror movies (at least the
horror movies Nelson and his former best friend
Simon had been addicted to as adolescents) were
never set, but still it took time to ready it for darkness.
There were lights to be turned on (two in every room,
in case a bulb burned out in one), blinds and curtains
to be drawn, doors and windows to be locked. He also
had to inspect and lock every closet, then look under
every bed and examine every corner of the house
where an intruder might conceivably be hiding, both
before and after all entrances had been secured.

So as soon as Nelson's watch went off at 4:00 to
remind him to watch *Oprah,* he reset the alarm for
5:23 and eagerly turned on the television. Phobias
were the theme of today's show; it was Dr. Phil's con-
tention that whatever the specific phobia, all phobics
were afraid of the same thing: loss of control.

"Yeah, tell me about it," muttered Nelson. Just then the front doorbell rang, throwing him into an agony of indecision. There was no chance he'd be opening the door, of course—he didn't have many friends, but the few he did have would have known better than to show up at his doorstep without calling first. Nelson's dilemma, rather, was whether to get up and look through the Securit-Eye peephole or simply hole up in the living room with Dr. Phil and wait for whoever it was to go away.

Both options had their downsides. On the one hand, the prospect of peering through the peephole at an unannounced visitor was an intimidating one for a man with as overactive an imagination as Nelson Carpenter's. On the other hand, it might be important—a police officer going door to door to warn residents about a chemical spill or an escaped convict, for instance. But on the other, other hand, it might be the convict himself.

Nelson understood from years of behavioral therapy that what he needed to do at this point was evaluate the prospective threats. It was probably only a Witness or a kid selling magazine subscriptions—in which case there was nothing to be afraid of. And of the other possibilities, the prospect of a toxic cloud from a refinery fire was more realistic than the possibility of finding an escaped convict on the doorstep.

So Nelson gathered up his courage (and it would be a mistake to think that severe phobics are lacking in courage: it took more nerve for Nelson to leave his house once a week than it would for most of us to bungee-jump off the Golden Gate Bridge), muted the

television, tiptoed over to the door, and put his eye to
the peephole.

Oh, Mama! He gasped and drew his head back
sharply. Toxic clouds, escaped convicts? Bring 'em
on—there was nothing Nelson wouldn't rather have
seen through the fish-eye lens than what he saw, no
monster that wouldn't have been more welcome at
his door than the one standing there now. He tried to
tell himself he might have been mistaken—after all,
he hadn't seen his childhood companion since the
sixties—but in his bones, and by the fluttering of his
heart and the tightening of his scrotum, Nelson knew
better. *This* was it, *this* was what he'd *really* been afraid
of all these years, *this* was the worst-case scenario.

"Open the door, Nellie," called Simon, when he saw
the peephole darken. "Open the door, ol' buddy."

"Go away."

"Is that any way to treat an old friend?" Nice and
calm, Simon told himself—you owned the boy, you
own the man.

"We had a deal."

"Circumstances have changed."

"I'll call the police. I'll tell them about your grandfather—I'll tell them everything."

"Yesterday's news."

"There's no statute of limitations on murder."

Manslaughter, thought Simon—then it occurred to
him he could turn Nelson's misconception to his
own advantage. "There's no bail, either—perhaps
they'll let us share a cell."

Simon waited for the click of a lock or the snick of
a bolt, and was faintly surprised not to hear one. That

should have done it, he thought; and maybe it had—although it had been quite a few years since he'd last seen Nelson paralyzed by fear, Simon had never forgotten what a moving sight it was.

"Nellie . . . ? Nellie, we both know you're going to open this door; let's just get it—"

And for the first time in thirty years, the childhood friends were face-to-face. The pale young gentleman had aged, but his hair was still the same shade of washed-out blond, still too long—he'd always been afraid of barbers. "How did you find me?" he asked dully.

"My spies are everywhere," said Simon, slipping past him into the house. He glanced around disapprovingly at the avocado walls and beige carpeting, track lighting, built-in knickknack crannies, faux-white-brick facing on the fireplace; Julia Morgan would have puked. "We'll catch up later—right now we need to get my car out of your driveway before anybody notices it."

"There's no room in the garage."

"Make room."

"Are you in some kind of trouble?" Nelson locked the front door behind him.

Simon slipped his arm around Nelson companionably. "Buddy, I'm in all *kinds* of trouble."

"If I help you, will you leave me alone?"

"It doesn't work that way, Nellie," Simon whispered into his ear; his breath was warm and moist, his tone unbearably intimate. "Not for you and me."

3

Emergency rooms, with their gurneys, sparsely furnished cubicles, rolling carts, folding screens, and curtained-off beds, had always seemed to Pender to have a sort of makeshift feel about them, as if they were temporary, and not very well suited, accommodations to be utilized until permanent quarters were ready. He couldn't wait to get out; as soon as his cast was dry and his arm in a sling, he went searching for Dorie.

She wasn't hard to find—a uniformed cop was stationed on a folding chair outside the door of her cubicle. He recognized Pender, tipped him a little salute, then leaned over without getting up, and opened the door for him.

"Helluva job," said the cop.

"Sure is," Pender replied pleasantly.

"No, I mean *you* did a helluva job."

"Oh. Thanks." Pender was slightly taken aback—locals weren't usually all that appreciative of federal help. Still, it *was* a good job, he thought, closing the door behind him. And there before him was the proof, sitting up in bed, her dark hair fanned out across the pillow, looking surprisingly good for a woman with a broken nose and two black eyes.

Dorie was equally glad to see Pender. There had been times, sitting next to him in the basement, or upstairs, wrapped in a blanket, waiting for the ambulance, or in the ER before they were wheeled off to separate cubicles, when she'd wanted to express her gratitude to this man who hadn't given up on her, who'd risked his life to save hers. But every time she looked at him, the feelings just welled up inside, threatening to overwhelm her. And above all, Dorie did not want to be overwhelmed by anything right now; she was having a hard enough time holding it together as it was.

Now she looked up shyly. "How's the arm?"

"Good as new in six weeks. I had 'em put the cast on with my elbow in putting position. How about you?"

Dorie shrugged. "They tried to talk me into a nose job, till I told them I didn't have any insurance. They still want to keep me overnight—somebody came by from admissions to ask me if I had a credit card with me. I told her the guy who kidnapped me forgot to bring my purse along."

"Have they taken your statement?"

"Repeatedly," said Dorie. "Berkeley cops, your FBI guys, detectives from San Francisco—I even talked to Wayne's uncle. He sounded, I don't know, almost *relieved* Wayne had been murdered, instead of having killed himself."

"I've seen that before. *Are* you staying overnight?"

"Not if I have a choice."

"Think you can drive?"

"Absolutely."

"Wanna blow this pop stand?"

"I thought you'd never ask."

4

After the initial shock had worn off, Nelson Carpenter was pleasantly surprised to discover how easy it was to surrender, and how simple it made his life. Instead of being afraid of everything, he only had to be afraid of Simon Childs, and instead of being ruled by the scrupulous and demanding (his shrink said obsessive-compulsive) daily routine he had developed to keep fear at bay, all he had to do was play Simon Says; everybody knows how to play Simon Says.

Of course, not having to worry about darkness or intruders anymore, or fire or food poisoning or spiders or spooks, would have come as more of a relief to Nelson had it not been for the nagging certainty that Simon planned to kill him as soon as he was done with him. Dead man walking, he whispered to himself; dead man whispering to himself.

Fortunately, Simon had neither demanded nor welcomed conversation at first. Once they had the Mercedes safely stowed in the garage (there was plenty of room, Simon had pointed out: it was only a matter of clearing out Nelson's junk), Simon announced that he was famished. Nelson cooked dinner—boned chicken breasts, broccoli, and Rice-A-Roni—while Simon brooded at the kitchen table; they ate in the dining room. Click of silverware, the unpleasant sounds of mastication, intensified by the ambient suburban silence.

Simon cleaned his plate, then pushed it away.

"My compliments to the chef. Love that Rice-A-Roni."

"It's the San Francisco treat," said Nelson—what else was there to say about Rice-A-Roni?

"What time do you have?" Simon had left his wristwatch back in the basement of 2500—he'd taken it off to bathe Dorie.

Nelson glanced at his Rolex, which was the only timepiece in the house. Chronomentrophobia—fear of clocks. "Almost six."

"Time for the news."

"I never watch the news."

"That's all right, just come keep me company," replied Simon pleasantly. It was easy for him to be pleasant about the matter under discussion—he'd never had any intention of allowing Nelson to watch the news in the first place. It was going to be hard enough to keep his old pal from flipping out prematurely—Simon certainly didn't want him finding out how far the fear game had advanced since the comparatively innocent days of the Horror Club, at least not until Simon was good and ready for him to find out.

"But how will I—"

"Nellie," Simon said quietly. That was his warning tone; after all these years Nelson still recognized it.

"Yes, Simon?"

"Trust me."

"Yes, Simon."

5

Twenty-five hundred Grizzly Rock Road had been transformed into a crime scene. Floodlit, yellow-taped, crawling with cops, besieged by reporters and mobile uplink news vans, the grand old dame was being accorded no more privacy than the corpse of a murder victim when Pender and Dorie arrived from the hospital in the back of a squad car, accompanied by a preppy-looking Berkeley homicide detective.

Special Agent Eddie Erickson, from the San Francisco field office, offered them a walk-through. Dorie, dressed in a set of borrowed pink scrubs, declined with a shudder, preferring to wait for Pender in his rented Toyota, which was still parked on the street near the bottom of the steep driveway, where he'd left it only—it hardly seemed possible—six hours earlier.

Every inch of the basement was brightly illuminated; Erickson led Pender through the maze to a chamber where a tech from the Evidence Response Team was using what looked like an alien-technology metal detector to sweep the smooth, level cement floor, which was higher by several inches than the rest of the basement, while another tech monitored a computer readout—they were employing state-of-the-art infrared heat-sensing technology to look for bodies.

"What's the count so far?" asked Erickson.

"Just the one—but the wet cement's throwing off my calibration—and of course if a skeleton's clean enough, it won't put out enough heat for us to pick it up." The second tech turned to Pender. "The top layer of cement was put down pretty recently. It's only about two centimeters thick except over in that corner, where it goes down almost two meters. I have a hunch that once we take 'er down to there, we're gonna be in business."

After a quick stop-off in a chamber that housed a jackhammer, kidney belt, protective eyewear, shovel, spade, and several bags of lime and Quik-Dry cement, Erickson led Pender back upstairs. The living room was still being dusted for prints; up in the master bedroom, Special Agent Ben Wing, from the San Jose resident agency, was seated at Childs's computer terminal.

"Any luck?" Erickson asked him.

"Yes, sir," said Wing. "All bad. One of the local yokels—" He glanced at the Berkeley detective trailing along behind Erickson and Pender. "Whoops, sorry. I mean, one of the indigenous experts up here tried to access it without checking for booby traps. The first key he pressed trashed the hard drive—what I'm doing now is the cyber equivalent of sifting through the ashes."

"Could Childs have rigged it himself?"

"He'd almost have had to. Or hired some gunslinger—no reputable security consultant would install a fail-safe device to nuke the client's system in the event of a breach."

"That gunslinger idea—that might be worth following up," suggested Pender.

"You think?" said Wing, archly.

"Us local yokels are already on it," explained the detective, as Wing turned back to the machine. "By tomorrow we'll have his bank records, and take it from there."

Pender followed Agent Erickson back downstairs. "Looks like you guys are all over it," he said—he felt as if he were expected to say *something*.

"Yeah—yeah, I think our chances are pretty good. It's not like he has much experience, rich fucker on the run. Take good care of Miss Bell, though—if there's any trouble with the warrant, I at least want to be able to put him away for kidnapping with special circumstances and bodily harm."

"Don't forget assault," Pender reminded Erickson, nodding toward his broken right arm, which had begun to throb as the anesthetic started to wear off. *"With* intent," he added—after all, if Childs's blow had been an inch or two to the right, there would have been three more bodies under two meters of Quik-Dry cement in that last chamber: his, Dorie's, and Nurse Apple's.

6

Simon, sitting in the comfy chair, had watched the news. Nelson, lying at Simon's feet with his back to the TV, head pillowed on his arms and his ears stuffed with cotton balls, had watched Simon—for fifty-five boring, soul-deadening minutes, though it had been obvious that Simon had stopped paying any attention after the lead story.

Around seven o'clock, Nelson tried clearing his throat—no reaction. He sat up, half expecting a blow or a kick, but Simon didn't seem to notice. He removed the cotton from his ears, then took the remote from Simon's unresisting fingers, pointed it behind him, and switched off the TV without turning around. (Nelson's viewing was always carefully planned, and he *never* surfed: sometimes it seemed to him as if there were an unwritten rule that in any given time slot, there had to be at least one channel showing a program about deadly snakes.)

Simon shook his head like a man coming out of a trance; he seemed to notice Nelson for the first time. "You think there's an afterlife, Nellie?"

"Are you talking about heaven and hell, or about . . ." Nelson couldn't bring himself to say the word *ghosts.* He never said *witches,* either, or *ghouls* or *spooks* or *vampires,* lest he somehow call them into being. He knew it was only foolish superstition; he also knew that superstition was mankind's only defense against the supernatural.

"Heaven and hell."

"Heaven, I'm hoping for; hell I'm sure about. I've been living there most of my life. Why?"

"Missy's dead."

"I'm *so* sorry," said Nelson. He'd liked Missy, spoiled brat though she was. But he wasn't surprised—the way Simon always talked about her, she'd been dying since Nelson had met her. "Her heart?"

"That's what they're saying."

"It was on the news?"

Simon ignored the question. "Where's the nearest phone?"

"Upstairs—there's only the one."

"In the entire house?"

Nelson explained his reasoning as he led Simon up to the bedroom. Originally there'd been a wall phone in the kitchen, but the very first night he'd moved in, Nelson found himself lying awake thinking about a story Simon had told him at one of the earliest Horror Club meetings, the one about the woman who gets a call from a slasher, and the police tell her if he calls again, keep him on the phone and we'll trace it. He does, and they do—the story ends with the woman learning that the call is coming from her own house, from the downstairs extension. Run, the cop screams over the phone, get out of the house—but of course it's too late. Next morning, Nelson told Simon, he'd called Pac Bell to have the kitchen phone removed, jack and all.

"I'm extremely flattered," said Simon, sitting on the edge of the bed. "Did it ever occur to you to buy a cordless?"

"You kidding? Those things give you cancer."

"Nellie, your continued survival is living proof that Darwin was wrong. Put that cotton back in your ears and wait in the bathroom . . . No—leave the door open so I can see what you're up to."

"Zap, it's Simon. . . .

"Yes, I know I'm all over the news. Don't believe everything you hear. . . .

"Yes, well, I hope you understand that if they do, I'll flip you like a half-cooked hamburger. . . .

"I thought you would. Now, here's what I need. This FBI man, this E. L. Pender—I want all the information you can get for me. . . .

"Like where he *lives* to start with, who his *friends* are, is he *married?* does he have a *lover?* that sort of thing. Ultimately, I'd like to find out what he fears, but I know that's not likely to be—

"No, not *feels, fears*—what he's afraid of . . .

"Okay, just Google him to start with. If I need you to hack the FBI site, I'll let you—

"That's *your* problem, Strummy old boy. *My* problem is, he killed my sister, and—

"Of course that's not what they're saying. Trust me on this, though—Missy's dead and Pender's to blame," asserted Simon, with utter conviction. He then went on to embellish what he knew in his heart to be the righteous truth, in order to sound more convincing: Pender had tricked Missy into letting him into the house without a warrant, then attacked Simon; Missy tried to stop him, and there was a scuffle; Simon was forced to flee, but Missy had been alive when he left the house; the struggle with Pender had probably overtaxed her poor heart. By the time Simon had finished, the details of the embellishment had been imbued with the authority of his emotional investment: for a sociopath, there *was* no other truth.

"So how long and how much?" he concluded.

"No, *I'll* call *you*. And don't even *think* about—

"I know you wouldn't. But a man in my position can't be too—

"Okay, I'll call you later."

As he replaced the receiver in the cradle and turned back to Nelson, Simon felt more like himself again. Except for the unaccustomed pangs of grief, of course, but it didn't take Simon long to discover that grief, unlike guilt or self-doubt or boredom, was bearable, even welcome. It sharpened the senses and focused the mind.

And suddenly Simon realized why he'd been drawn *here,* of all places, in his time of grief.

"Nelson?" he called.

Nelson stuck his head out of the bathroom. "Yes, Simon?"

"I think it's time for a game."

7

They had no business driving, no business operating any heavy machinery, according to the caution labels on their respective pain medications, but neither of them felt right suggesting a motel.

Instead they drank bad road coffee and harmonized on oldies to keep themselves awake—Pender sang a high, sweet tenor and Dorie a ballsy alto—and took turns behind the wheel of the rented Toyota, with Dorie manipulating the automatic gearshift for the one-armed Pender.

Dorie drove the last leg of the two-and-a-half-hour journey. Rounding the Seaside curve on Highway 1 and seeing the twinkling lights of the peninsula circling the great black sweep of Monterey Bay put a coming-home lump in her throat. Pender's, too, though he'd only been here twice before. Of course, the buzz from the two Vicodins he'd taken before they left might have had something to do with that.

They continued on past Monterey, Pacific Grove, and Pebble Beach; Dorie took the Ocean Avenue exit into Carmel, then a right on San Carlos and a quick left on Fifth; she pulled over into the first available parking space. "I'll just be a minute," she told Pender; "there's something I have to do."

Dorie was halfway up the block before the big man managed to extricate himself from the little car; Pender caught up to her in front of a women's clothing store. "What—"

Dorie put a finger to her lips, then pointed to the mannequin in the shop window. It was dressed in a black-and-white-checked hooded robe; a simple black mask covered its eyes.

"Oh," said Pender, moving back a step.

She stood there for a few minutes, staring at the mask in the window, still as the mannequin save for the gentle rise and fall of her chest; when she turned away, there were tears in her eyes.

"You okay?" Pender asked.

"I think so," replied Dorie. "It's just gonna take some getting used to, you know?"

"I can imagine," said Pender, crooking his good elbow. Dorie slipped her hand through it, and they walked back to the car arm in arm.

Mary Cassatt was parked in Dorie's driveway when they pulled up to the house. Half a dozen parking citations were stuck under the windshield wiper, along with a note from Wynn Mackey telling Dorie not to worry about them.

"Nice kid," said Pender.

"Yeah, he turned out pretty good," Dorie allowed

grudgingly. "He was a handful when he was little, though—you never saw such a brat. Last kid in the world you'd figure would have grown up to be a cop. When he was eight, the little bastard rolled a lit firecracker under the bathroom door while I was on the throne."

"When I was eight, I dropped a cherry bomb down my parents' chimney," Pender offered. "Damn near set the house on fire."

"You were a brat, too?"

"And dumb. I wanted to see it go off, so I stuck my head over the edge of the chimney to watch. Blew off both eyebrows—I spent the worst two weeks of my life with my eyes all bandaged up, waiting to find out whether I'd get my sight back. I'll tell you, it was the worst fear *I've* ever known."

The front door was locked, with yellow crime-scene tape across the doorway. Pender followed Dorie around the side of the house. They entered through the studio—the door had been closed and sealed with crisscrossed yellow tape, but the lock still didn't function. Inside, the doorknobs and windowsills still bore traces of the gray carbon dust used to lift latent fingerprints; Dorie winced when she flipped the wall switch in the kitchen and saw the dried vomit on the parquet floor.

"Oh, hell," she muttered, dropping to her knees. "Now I'll have to strip all the . . . all the . . . Oh, hell." To her surprise, Dorie found herself weeping uncontrollably, big old honking, snot-snorkling, gut-wrenching sobs.

Pender knelt beside her and began patting her back awkwardly. "It's okay, it's only a little stain," he told her, though they both knew that it wasn't the parquet she was crying about. "It'll come right out."

"You think?" she asked, between hiccups as he helped her to her feet.

"Sure," said Pender confidently. He was no expert on housecleaning, as Linda Abruzzi would soon discover, but as hard a drinker as he was, he did know a thing or two about vomit stains.

8

Seven words were all it took. Seven words to dispel any illusions Nelson might have had about how easy it would be to surrender, to play Simon Says until it was time for Simon to go. Seven words to prove to him that they'd all lied—his parents, his shrinks, his support groups—when they'd assured him that his fears were phantoms and his phobias the products of disordered emotions, not a malevolent universe.

Seven words: *I think it's time for a game.*

"Game? What kind of game?"

Simon, rummaging through his getaway satchel, ignored the question. "C'mon, it'll be like old times."

"That's what I'm afraid of," said Nelson.

Simon looked up sharply. "Why, Nellie, was that a joke? I didn't think you had it in you."

Nelson tried another tack. "I'm afraid I wouldn't be very . . . These medications I'm taking . . . I'm afraid

they're not exactly conducive to . . . you know. . . ."
His voice trailed off miserably.

"Not a problem," Simon reassured him. "The
game's evolved way beyond that—it's not about sex
anymore."

Nelson didn't like the sound of that at all—if the
game wasn't about sex, what *was* it about?—but he'd
as soon have sawed off one of his own fingers with a
rusty nail file as ask for clarification. "I really don't
think my psychiatrist would—"

"Nellie?"

"Yes?"

"Hush now."

Nelson hushed.

The game began in the dark for Nelson, blindfolded
with one of his own bandannas and locked in his
walk-in bedroom closet with his hands tied behind
his back. The irony of the situation did not escape
him: Nelson had installed external locks on every
closet door in the house to allay his own childhood
fear of closets as potential hiding places for bogeymen
and burglars.

He had no way of telling how long he'd been in
there before Simon came for him again. Long enough
for two anxiety attacks, the first more acute, the second of longer duration. Pounding heart, vertigo,
shortness of breath, hysterical paresis, feelings of
dread so intense that a vasovagal syncope would have
come as a blessing—unfortunately, Nelson wasn't
subject to syncopes.

During the paretic phase of the second attack, as he
lay on the floor of the closet with his hands tied

behind him, the muscles of his legs so weak and trembly he might as well have been paralyzed, Nelson's ears registered the snick of the closet door being unlocked.

"Come out, come out, wherever you are," called Simon, cheerfully.

No fucking way. His legs still too weak to propel him, Nelson dragged himself in the opposite direction, away from the door, away from the voice, humping like an inchworm until he could hump no farther, and curled up hyperventilating in the far corner of the closet, waiting to learn what fresh hell Simon had in store for him.

He would have to wait a little longer, though—the door never opened. Instead he heard footsteps padding across the bedroom carpet—retreating footsteps.

"Come out, come out, wherever you are," Simon called again, from the hallway this time, and again Nelson told himself no fucking way. But they both knew he'd be coming out eventually—his claustrophobia would see to that.

If there was a more terrifying, more vulnerable feeling than tottering forward through total darkness with your hands tied behind you, Nelson told himself, he'd just as soon not know about it. Every few steps he'd stop, listen. The only sounds in the bedroom were Nelson's own ragged breathing and the furious pounding of his heart.

All the silence meant, of course, was that Simon was waiting for him elsewhere in the house. But if so, Nelson began to realize, even if Simon was standing right outside the bedroom door, then his old friend had miscalculated for once. Simon must have failed to notice that the bedroom door was reinforced with steel to make it fireproof and furnished with a dead bolt, in the unlikely event an intruder ever succeeded in breaking into the house.

Suddenly Nelson couldn't get enough air; he felt as if his heart were about to burst inside him, spattering the inside of his chest cavity with blood and shredded muscle. Another panic attack? No—it was hope, a sensation far less familiar to Nelson. All he had to do, he told himself, was get that stout door between himself and Simon, throw the bolt, and there'd be no way Simon could get to him.

Easier said than done. Shuffling out of the closet in what he desperately hoped was the direction of the door, Nelson tried to remember whether the dead bolt was set low enough for him to be able to reach it with his hands tied behind him. There wouldn't be time to fumble around for it in any case, he realized—he'd have to locate, slam, and bolt the door all in one motion if he was to have any hope of keeping Simon on the other side. Which meant he needed to turn around and back toward it.

Again, easier said than done. As Nelson executed a tentative about-face (turn too far or not far enough, he knew, and he'd be wandering around the bedroom, disoriented, until Simon came to fetch him) and began to inch backward toward the door, it occurred to him that at least he had learned the answer to his earlier question: there was indeed a more terrifying, more vulnerable feeling than tottering *forward* into the darkness.

Nelson's ciliary radar—the tiny hairs on the back of his arms and neck—whispered a warning just before his bound hands bumped against the back of the bedroom door. It was already closed, he realized, hope surging again—and again, the sensation was nearly indistinguishable from panic. He slid his hands up and down along the crack of the door; at the apex of his reach his fingers brushed the cold iron of the dead-bolt fixture, but the bolt itself was too high for him to grasp. He hunched forward, wrenching his arms higher and higher up his back until his shoulders felt as if they were about to dislocate, until at last he was holding the little round knurl of the bolt between the thumb and forefinger of his right hand.

Working backward with his hands crossed behind him at the wrists was doubly disorienting; with his arms torqued painfully and his shoulders wrenched in their sockets until the shoulder blades felt as if they were sticking out like angel wings, Nelson finally managed to rotate the bolt upward, slide it into its socket, and rotate it down again, then collapsed on the floor, simultaneously exhausted and exhilarated. You did it, he started to tell himself, you—

Then he knew. Nothing had moved in the bedroom, not a scrape, not a rustle, but all the same, he knew. "You're in here, aren't you?"

"Oh, yes," said a voice in the darkness.

9

Drought be damned, conservation be damned—
Dorie wanted a shower, she wanted it hot, hot, hot,
and she wanted it to last forever. She stripped off the
pink scrubs one of the ER nurses had filched for her,
stepped into the shower, and let 'er rip.

It took ten minutes and several relatherings to rid
herself of the stink, which was compounded by the
reek of Missy's cheap strawberry-scented bubble
bath. Poor Missy, thought Dorie. The nurse had still
been performing CPR on her when Dorie and Pender
emerged from the basement; by the time the paramedics arrived to take over, Nurse Apple had nearly
passed out from hyperventilation, and although the
ambulance docs had kept the CPR going all the way
to Alta Bates, nobody seemed surprised when she was
declared DOA.

It was just as well, though, Dorie decided—from
what she had gathered about their relationship, Missy
would probably have preferred death to being separated from her big brother for any length of time.

The hot water ran out as Dorie finished rinsing the
conditioner out of her hair. She stepped out of the
shower, wrapped her hair in a bath-towel turban,
dried herself off, dusted herself liberally with L'Air du
Temps scented talcum powder—one of her few personal extravagances—and returned to the bedroom to
begin a round of musical clothes. Dear *Cosmo:* What
does a gal wear for an informal tête-à-tête with the
man who saved her life, whom she might want to get

involved with someday, but definitely not tonight, thank you very much, even though she's already invited him to sleep over?

Then she reminded herself that Pender had already seen her in the buff, under the least flattering conditions imaginable; after those hideous pink scrubs, could it really make any difference what she chose to wear now? She threw on some comfort clothes—roomy fleece sweatpants and an oversize Carmel Padres sweatshirt—and went down to the kitchen, where Pender was on his knees, scrubbing one-handed at the parquet.

"What'd I tell you," he said, climbing to his feet. His outfit—beret, rumpled polo, and plaid slacks that made his rear end look like a slip-covered sofa—reminded her that clothes really didn't make the man—or the woman. "Good as new. Didn't even strip the wax."

"Pender, you're a prince."

"So I've been told."

"Are you hungry?"

"To put it mildly."

"How do you like your eggs?"

"Sunny side up—like my personality."

"How 'bout a beer?"

"They say it's the perfect food."

"Glass?"

"Naah."

"Man after my own heart."

The beer was Tree Frog dark ale, not a brand with which Pender was familiar. The food was perfect, the eggs neither dry nor runny, the bacon neither crisp nor burned. Pender told Dorie she could make breakfast for him whenever she'd a mind to.

"And you can clean my kitchen floor whenever you want." Dorie took a swig of Tree Frog—out of the bottle, of course. "Where do you think Simon is?"

"Ain't that the sixty-four-thousand-dollar question?" Pender sopped up yolk with a corner of toast. "You've known him for a while. Did he ever mention the names of any close friends, relatives, anybody who might hide him out? My guess is it'll be someplace in the Bay Area—he'd have to have gotten that car off the road pretty quick."

"Nothing comes to mind. But they're gonna catch him, right?"

"What? Oh, sure. You bet."

"You don't sound very convinced."

Pender looked up from his plate. "Scout, I've been chasing monsters for a long time." There was a seen-it-all sadness in his soft brown eyes. "You tell me how much you want to hear."

"I've been hiding from monsters for a long time," replied Dorie. "You tell me what you think I ought to know."

10

While Nelson had been in the bedroom closet facing his demons, Simon had been in Nelson's bathroom preparing to face his demon—singular. With every pass of Nelson's electric clippers another piece of it had appeared in the mirror. *Bzzz,* there went the widow's peak and the rest of the wavy silver hair. That much had been part of Plan B all along—Simon had come to identify so strongly with his handsome head of silver hair that cutting it off was the first thing that came to mind when he thought about disguising himself.

But then, *bzzz,* there went the two-day stubble and *bzzz,* there went the mustache, and Simon was reminded that it had been in order to disguise the long, cruel upper lip he'd inherited from the Childs side of the family that he'd grown the stash in the first place.

But a shaven head and face did not a demon make. It wasn't until the eyebrows were gone that it really started to take shape. Even then the transformation into Grandfather Childs, who as a boy had suffered from an attack of scarlet fever so virulent it left him without a hair on his body, wasn't complete until he'd finished the difficult task of clipping back the lashes.

Luckily Nelson had a pair of safety-tipped (what else?) nail scissors. Leaning over the sink until his face was within inches of the mirror, his eyes tearing like a soap opera queen, Simon clipped the lashes as close to the lids as possible, then leaned back, and voilà, the pièce de résistance. While he'd never thought of his pale blue eyes as cold, once the lashes were gone, they were positively reptilian.

Which would come in handy even after he finally left the shelter of Nelson's house, Simon knew: not only wouldn't the authorities be looking for a bald scalp, but no one would ever peer too long or too hard at the face under this chrome dome, not with eyes like these staring back at them.

They even made Simon uncomfortable. He turned away from the mirror, bending down to rummage through the catchall storage space under the sink until he found some witch hazel to use as aftershave—he didn't want to spoil the effect by dousing himself with Nelson's Old Spice.

He wasn't surprised when Nelson refused to come out of the closet at first. Hey, the longer the better, thought Simon. Delayed gratification and all that. And once he saw that Nelson had fallen for the heavy-footsteps-down-the-hall-then-tiptoe-back-to-the-room ploy, he waited, still as a spider, to see if Nellie would actually try to lock the door.

What did surprise him was that Nelson had figured it out so quickly, before Simon could spring his own surprise. But Simon was nothing if not resourceful when it came to the game. He helped Nelson up, led him over to the bed, and let him weep for a few minutes, until Nelson had a few endorphins pumping.

Then, when he judged the time was right, he arranged the lighting and removed Nelson's blindfold.

11

"I'm afraid that in this case, identifying Simon as our suspect was the easy part," explained Pender, over another round of Tree Frogs. "His mistake was making your PWSPD Association disappear. As long as we thought it was legit, he'd have been just another member of the potential victim pool—at least until he'd been interviewed and his alibis checked out."

"Which wouldn't have been nearly in time to save me," said Dorie, who was at the sink washing the dishes. Couple of beers and another Vicodin, she was feeling no pain. "You know I owe you my life. Have I thanked you yet?"

"Don't get sentimental," said the secret sentimentalist. "Like I said, that was the easy part. Now that he's on the run, this thing could go flying off in any one of a dozen different directions, and I don't just mean geographically. Personality like that, no telling what's going to happen. Especially with his sister gone—God, I felt terrible about that."

"Her doctor said it could have happened any time."

"Yes, well, *she* saved *my* life—and she's not even around for me to thank. Were they as close as they seemed?"

"Closer."

"Think there was anything . . ." Pender put down his bottle and waggled his good hand iffily.

Dorie shuddered. "I don't know and I don't want to know."

"Doesn't matter—we can assume news of her death will come as quite a blow to a man who's already stressed-out to the max just from the strain of being a fugitive, and probably wasn't that stable to begin with. So on the one hand, we might be dealing with a disorganized psychotic serial killer on the edge of snapping. Most likely outcome there is either suicide or suicide by cop. Soon, if it hasn't happened already.

"On the other hand, we might be dealing with a cunning, organized psychotic serial killer, now in a white-hot rage, with considerable resources, who has a plan, a false identity, some money stashed away, maybe a hideout someplace where they don't ask too many questions. If that's the case, there are so many ways this can go, I couldn't handicap it if I tried. I *can* tell you that very few serial killers ever quit voluntarily. So if they haven't caught him or found his body by the time we wake up tomorrow morning, we could be in for a long, bumpy ride."

"Do you think he might come after either of us?" asked Dorie, sitting across from Pender again.

"Probably not. I can't remember a case where an organized serial killer came after a victim a second time, unless they were related. As for him coming after me, that's even less likely. Serial killers choose victims they can dominate and control. Cop killers are different. They have the assassin mentality, and as a rule of thumb, they generally don't care which cop they kill. It's rarely personal."

The plates were clean by now, the bottles empty. Dorie stifled a yawn. "Getting to be that time," she said.

"Definitely getting to be that time," Pender agreed.

"I aired out the guest bedroom. Nobody's used it since . . . Good lord, since Simon and Missy stayed here."

"In June, right?"

"In June. He was taking Missy on vacation to make

up for having been away on some kind of . . . of . . ."
She finished the sentence with a moan.

"What?"

"Some kind of business trip. It must have been
Chicago—he must have just come back from killing
the Rosen girl." She shuddered. "I hope you don't
mind sleeping up there—I changed the linen."

"The guest bedroom'll be fine," said Pender. He
had, of course, been entertaining fantasies about
sleeping with Dorie tonight, but he didn't think there
was much of a chance Dorie would want to sleep with
him, banged up, exhausted, and traumatized as she
was. For that matter, he wasn't entirely sure *he* really
wanted sex tonight either, banged up, exhausted, and
traumatized as he was. Still, nothing ventured, nothing gained—and what a tragedy it would have been if
it turned out that she was willin' and only waiting for
him to make the first move. "In the absence of any
other offers, of course," he added.

Dorie, mildly flustered, ignored the tender. Men,
she thought. As far as she knew, and despite the
warm, golden, pain-free glow from the Vicodin and
beer, she had most definitely *not* been waiting for
Pender to make the first move, not with her face
looking like Rocky Balboa's after the Apollo Creed
fight. Although she had to admit that tonight of all
nights, it would have been nice to have somebody
bigger and stronger than her to cuddle with—bigger
and stronger and with a badge. But she was too wise
in the ways of men, and too considerate to expect a
grown man to settle for cuddling—a grown *straight*
man, anyway.

"There are clean towels in the bathroom," she told him on the way up the stairs. "If you get hungry in the middle of the night, help yourself to anything in the kitchen. I don't usually turn the furnace on until November, but if you get cold, there are extra blankets in the— Oh, the hell with it. Do you snore?"

"Like a freight train."

"Me too—my room's this way."

"Is this the offer I was hoping for?"

"I'm not promising anything," Dorie replied. "Let's just put the bodies together and see what happens."

"Maybe we oughtta try a kiss first," Pender suggested.

"Careful of the nose," said Dorie.

"Careful of the arm," said Pender.

12

Nelson wept. Someone with strong hands, someone smelling of witch hazel, helped him to his feet and led him over to the bed, where he sat with his legs outstretched, his arms still tied behind his back, resting his sore shoulders against the walnut headboard.

The blindfold was removed. Nelson opened his eyes and was blinded by a fierce white light; as he looked away, he caught a silhouetted glimpse of a hooded figure seated on the edge of the bed, training the beam from a six-volt lantern directly into his eyes.

Courage, Nelson resolved; for once in your life, courage. "Simon? Is that you?"

"Yes and no."

"What's *that* supposed to mean?" As Nelson's eyes grew accustomed to the penumbra effect, he realized that Simon had borrowed one of his sweatshirts and pulled the hood up, covering his head and throwing his face into shadow.

"All part of the game, Nellie, all part of the game."

"I'm not *playing* your goddamn game," said Nelson, too loudly, sounding more doubtful than defiant even to his own ears; he could feel his courage, or at least his resolve to be courageous, draining away.

"Aren't you?" said a harsh new voice, both familiar and unfamiliar, more nasal than Simon's normal speaking voice, with a hint of a quaver in it. Nelson recognized it immediately, though he hadn't heard it since he was a boy.

And as the figure let fall the hood and slowly turned the lantern that had been shining into Nelson's eyes upon himself, Nelson felt as if he were passing through a sort of prism—the kind where beams of light converge and condense themselves into a single point before emerging on the other side with their spectrums all reversed.

No, he whispered, trying to close his eyes again, trying to unsee what he told himself he couldn't possibly have seen, but it was too late. Nelson had already crossed over to the other side of the prism, where he found himself staring into the lashless, browless, reptilian eyes of the bald old man whom he'd last seen over thirty-five years ago, lying in a pool of blood on the floor of a smoke-filled bathroom, with his throat cut from ear to ear, and a straight razor still clutched in his lifeless hand.

VII

A Good Shaking

1

Pender's cell phone woke him a little after six o'clock on Saturday morning, chirping the first two bars of "Moon River" from somewhere in his pants, which were on the floor next to Dorie's bed. Retirement or no retirement, after twenty-seven years with the Bureau, it never occurred to him not to answer it. He grabbed the pants and took them into the hall, shook the phone out just before it kicked over to the message center.

It was Steve McDougal, Pender's longtime boss and longer-time friend. "Jesus H. Christ, Pender, did I or did I not attend your retirement party earlier this week?"

"I was poking around a little, doing a favor for Abruzzi—it got personal."

"And what the screaming fuck possessed you to enter a suspect's home without a warrant or backup?"

"The sister invited me in."

"Ed, she was a fucking mongoloid idiot! And what were you doing on his doorstep in the first place?"

"That's Down syndrome. And Dorie had mentioned Childs's name the night before. When she disappeared, I became concerned for his safety as well." That was the story Pender had been giving out since the first cops arrived on the scene yesterday afternoon. Might as well stick with it—it would make things go more smoothly for all concerned. "I decided to drop in and check on him—not as a suspect but as a potential victim. The sister invited me in, he attacked me. It'll stand up. And by the way—I did try to get in touch with you Thursday afternoon, but you never returned my call."

Irrelevant as the reason for Thursday's call had been to the matter under discussion, Pender had decided to throw it in anyway—when you're low on ammunition, you toss anything you can find into the cannon: grapeshot, scrap metal, whatever. And sometimes you even hit something.

"All right, all right," said McDougal. "You're talking to me *now,* and I want your word, both as your friend and as your boss, that from this day on, the word *retirement* will mean more to you than putting a new set of Michelins on the Barracuda. No poking around, no favors for Abruzzi, no nothing. Agreed?"

"You bet. Word up, as the kids say." Pender decided there was no point bringing up the fact that he had just launched an affair with one of the victims in the case. "Speaking of Abruzzi, can you get Maheu off her ass?"

"Why, what's going on?"

Pender told him. "And the worst part of it is, if there was ever a case where Liaison Support could be useful, this is it. Childs is wealthy, he's slick, he's mobile, there are probably victims we don't know about scattered all over the country, and unless I miss my guess, he's going to be leaving a trail of new ones. Plus Abruzzi's had some bad breaks lately—why not give her a chance?"

"I'll think about it. We do have a personnel drain, what with this Y2K flap on. But if I give her the point on this one, I want it understood, I'm giving it to her, not you. You're still out."

"I'm out, I'm out. One more favor, though—do you still have that cane I gave you after your knee operation . . . ?"

2

Zap Strum, who was not a morning person—he wasn't even a daylight person—surprised Simon by answering the phone on the first ring.

"Duude, saw you on the news again," he said, even before Simon had identified himself. "You're famous. And how are you enjoying your visit with Mr. Nelson Carpenter of 1211 Baja Way in scenic Concord?"

"How did you know that?" demanded Simon.

"Dude, please." Strum sounded vaguely offended, as if somebody had asked Houdini how he'd worked the got-your-nose trick on a toddler. "You have nothing to worry about, though—if I was going to turn you in, I'd have done it last night."

"Did you get the information I asked you for?"

"Sure thing. It's going to cost you a little more than we discussed, though—you being a fugitive from justice and all."

"No problem," said Simon. *You being a dead man and all.*

Before leaving, Simon popped in on Nelson, who had spent the latter half of the night naked in the bathtub, not out of choice, but because Simon had superglued him to the porcelain after the game.

"I have to go out for a little while," Simon told him pleasantly. "I'll be borrowing your car—try to stay out of mischief while I'm gone."

There was no response, which was not surprising, since Nelson's lips had been superglued as well. The idea had come from a recurring childhood nightmare of Nelson's that Simon had kept in mind all these years. Young Nellie used to have dreams in which he'd been captured by witches who erased his mouth as cleanly as if he'd been a cartoon figure, to keep him from crying out; in real life the effect, the panicked jerking and stretching of the seamed lips, would have been more satisfying to Simon had it not been for the unmistakable madness in Nelson's eyes.

Fear stimulated Simon, but insanity only repelled him—when he returned, he decided, if he returned, he would seal those eyes as well.

3

Linda Abruzzi awoke Saturday morning to the pleasant sound of a gentle rain pattering against the crumbling shingles of the old house by the canal. It sounded sweet—Linda didn't remember much gentle rain in San Antonio, where it had sometimes seemed to her as if the relentless drought was broken only by the occasional murderous gully washer.

She stayed under the covers another half hour or so, luxuriating in the idea of having the house to herself on her day off. (The last she'd heard from Pender, he'd called her back yesterday afternoon to tell her he'd canceled his flight after all, and was going to "poke around" a little; the events at Grizzly Rock Road had taken place after she'd left the office.) But when at length she climbed out of bed to visit the bathroom across the hall, it was with a vague sense that she was forgetting something; a moment later she found herself facedown on Pender's hard plank floor.

It was the drop foot, of course—she'd forgotten about the paresis in her anterior tibial muscles that caused her to trip over her own toes unless she had her braces on.

Linda knew, lying there, that her whole day, perhaps the entire weekend, hung in the balance, and forced herself to laugh. "I give it a nine point five," she announced as she picked herself up, hanging on to the end of the bed for support. "High degree of difficulty, but the landing was a *leetle* rough."

The rain had stopped by the time Linda got out of

the shower. After her Betaseron, which raised a nasty red blotch at the injection site, and a breakfast of coffee, vitamins and supplements, and a smoothie she drank out on the back porch, she explored the house a little more thoroughly. Because the place had been built on a hillside that sloped down toward the canal, the front door was at ground level, while the back porch was fifteen feet above the sloping hillside.

To the left of the living room, as you faced the back of the house, was the bedroom wing. Pender's room, the largest of the seven, was at the near end of the long corridor; Linda had selected the third bedroom, which was the smallest, but located directly across the hall from the guest bathroom.

To the right of the living room was another corridor, ending in a small kitchen that might have seemed homey if it hadn't been quite so filthy. Getting it cleaned up to code would be a project, but Linda knew that if she was going to live here for any length of time, it would have to be done.

First, though, she desperately needed some clean clothes. Searching for a laundry room, Linda opened the door on the far side of the kitchen, and with her laundry bag over her shoulder, limped carefully down a dark narrow staircase with a railing on the right and a sheer drop to the left.

The cellar was also dark and narrow, a combination laundry room, storage area, obstacle course, which ran the length, but not the breadth, of the house. There were gaps in the red-brick facing of the walls, the concrete floor appeared never to have been swept, and the crossbeams supporting the plank flooring overhead were in turn supported by a haphazard forest of timbers varying in shape, size, age, and provenance; some rough-hewn and primitive, with clumsily beveled corners; some massive as debarked tree trunks; some gray, rounded, and splintery like telephone poles; some so new that they might have been borrowed from construction sites by midnight salvagers.

Not the place you'd want to be during an earthquake, thought Linda—but she did find a venerable Kenmore washer-dryer combo, and a sagging clothesline had been strung between two of the support beams. She decided there would be no point in hauling herself up and down that steep staircase between loads, so after getting the coloreds started, she dragged a legless, rump-sprung armchair over by the furnace, and began thumbing through a boxful of old *National Geographic*s. Half an hour later, whites in the washer, coloreds in the dryer, and Linda herself deep in the Kalahari with a tribe of underdressed Bushmen, she heard a telephone ringing directly above her head. Pender's answering machine picked up, and surprisingly, or perhaps not surprisingly, given the architectural eccentricities of the old dump, she found she could hear every word.

The real surprise was that it was Deputy Director Stephen P. McDougal, and he was calling for her. She hadn't a prayer of intercepting the machine—he'd left his private number and hung up before she'd even managed to push herself up from her stumpy chair. A moment later she heard a familiar chirping sound, also overhead, but much farther to her right, and realized with a sinking feeling that she'd left her cell phone in the bedroom.

This is not a good thing, Linda told herself as she

hurried (a relative term) upstairs. FBI agents were supposed to be on call at all times—it was part of the job description—and although she was technically no longer a special agent, she knew that missing a call from a deputy director was not exactly a terrific career move.

Sure enough, the number blinking on the screen of Linda's cell phone was the same one McDougal had left on Pender's machine. He didn't seem put out, though. Quite the opposite: he thanked her politely for getting back to him, then asked her if she'd spoken to Pender recently.

"Not since yesterday afternoon."

"You haven't heard, then?"

"Heard what?"

"How long will it take you to get to my office?"

"You're in Edgar?"

"Edgar." He sounded amused. "Yes, I'm in Edgar."

"It depends on the traffic. It's Saturday, though, so—"

"See you in an hour."

"But—"

Too late—the connection had already been broken.

4

In the fall of 1999, with the dotcom bubble distended to the bursting point and the prick of the first market corrections still in the future, the SoMa area, south of San Francisco's Market Street, was *the* location for cyber-entrepreneurs. Spiking rents had driven most of SoMa's previous population of struggling artists and leather-clad bondage-and-discipline aficionados from their lofts and warehouses, and every storefront big enough to hold a few PCs, a server cabinet, and an espresso machine now housed an IPO *in posse*.

Kenny Strum, nicknamed Zap by admiring fellow hackers for his ability to reduce your hard drive to an expensive Frisbee if you pissed him off or if he just happened to be in the mood, had occupied his Brannan Street loft for three years; his five-year, pre-dotcom lease was the envy of his neighbors and the despair of his Indian landlords. He had made some improvements to the place, though—if your idea of improvement includes the installation of case-hardened steel grilles on the windows and a double-doored airlock-type front entrance complete with a security camera.

It wasn't that Strum was paranoid, just realistic: since his return from Amsterdam in the early nineties, he'd been involved with some awfully shady characters. Ironically enough, setting up and hosting phobia.com for one of those shady characters, Simon Childs, was one of Strum's legitimate operations, providing him with enough declarable income to keep the IRS off his back. Their connection would have been entirely legitimate if he hadn't also been Simon's most versatile and reliable supplier of illicit substances, including, but not limited to, super-sinsemilla by the ounce, solubilized Rohypnol by the bottle, and one lonely little blue suicide capsule.

Strum, a pudgy, pungent thirty-year-old with unhygienic-looking blond dreadlocks, had been hitting the bong hard all morning while he awaited Childs's arrival. If only half the things he'd heard on the news were true, Simon Childs was a dangerous fugitive—but a dangerous fugitive who needed Zap's cooperation. He told himself not to worry, but when the door buzzer sounded, he had to take one last billowing toke to allay his nerves as he checked the security cam. Quick double-take: the change in Simon's appearance was so startling that Zap almost didn't recognize him at first.

"Love the new 'do, dude," he drawled from his state-of-the-art Aeron desk chair, as Simon climbed the open staircase leading up to the loft, carrying a big leather satchel. "I ever start to lose this—" He patted his tawny dreadlocks affectionately. "—that's how I'm going, too. Much classier than a comb-over."

"Oh, shut up," said Simon. "It's a disguise."

"Just yanking your chain, dude."

"Well, don't. I've had a hard couple of days." He looked around for a place to light, settled for the saddle-shaped footstool next to Strum's chair. "And quit calling me dude."

"Sorry, dude." Zap offered the bong to Simon. "Want a hit?"

"Maybe later. What do you have for me?"

"Plenty—what do you have for me?"

"What you asked for." Simon patted the satchel on his lap.

"Bitchin'." Strum reached behind him, twisting in his chair so as not to break eye contact with Simon. There was something almost hypnotic about those eyes, those lashless, browless, naked eyes: you didn't want to stare into them, but you didn't want to look away either. He removed a ten-page printout from his printer tray.

"I started with your basic Google, got three, four hundred hits. News stories, FBI press releases, conspiracy theories, the usual crap—I saved you a couple highlights. But there was one item caught my eye—a press release in *Publishers Weekly* on-line, that St. Swithin's Press had bought the rights to Pender's autobiography, and he'd be working with a freelancer named Arthur Bellcock.

"Now, to tell you the truth, dude, when I sat down last night I didn't think there was a chance in hell I'd be coming up with much. Kind of data you're looking for, the real personal shit, you're just not gonna find on-line, unless the guy's some kind of freak or something. But I figured what the fuck, a name like Bellcock's unique enough to be worth a shot.

"Sure enough, I found his e-mail address, went in through the usual Microsoft Swiss cheese firewall, and downloaded his hard drive. He doesn't appear to have started writing anything yet, or if he has, it isn't on his computer—there aren't even any notes.

"What there is, though—bada-bing, bada-boom!— is a complete list of contacts Bellcock had to have gotten from Pender himself, dating back all the way to his childhood. Friends, family, names, addresses, phone numbers—" Strum waved the printout over his head. "—it's all in here. I were you, I'd start with the sister."

"I appreciate the advice," said Simon. "This Bellcock—would there be any way for him to tell he's been hacked?"

"Guy with a system like that? He wouldn't even know he's got mail, the little bell didn't go ding-dong.

Oh, yeah, I almost forgot—I also have that other address you wanted."

"What other address?"

"Skairdykat at Netscape?"

"Right, right. It slipped my mind, what with everything else going on."

"I can dig it," said Strum. "Here you go, free of charge, as promised. Now, where did I— Oh, yeah." Zap reached behind him, unpinned a rainbow Post-it from the corkboard on the wall behind his desk, and handed it to Simon. "The name on the account is the same as the screen name, but according to the ISP file, the phone line is registered to somebody named Gee— the address is on there."

"Thanks." Simon slipped the Post-it into his pocket without looking at it. "Now, about that printout?"

The two men were sitting face-to-face, almost knee-to-knee. Strum gave Simon the printout with one hand, took the satchel with the other, opened it, glanced in, nodded decisively. "Mercy buckets—a pleasure doing business with you, dude."

"Likewise," said Simon. "I do need the bag back."

"Sure thing." Zap twisted around in his chair again; as he started to dump Simon's getaway money—ten thousand dollars in rubber-band-bound stacks of worn, nonsequential twenties—out onto his desk, he felt something hit him in the right side, just below the rib cage.

Zap's first thought was that Simon had punched him. "Dude!" he murmured reprovingly. Then he raised his right arm and looked down past his armpit to see what looked like a piece of dark wood protruding from his side. Confused—it had felt like a dull blow at first—he tried to lift his shirt for a closer look, but it wouldn't lift; the fabric was pinned against his side by what he now realized was a wooden-handled steak knife. "Fuck, dude!"

Simon, torn between drawing back so as not to get any blood on himself or the printout, or drawing closer so as not to miss anything, settled for shielding the printout with his arms as he leaned in to search Strum's eyes for the first traces of fear. Instead there was only hurt and confusion.

"Nothing personal," Simon explained, as Strum clawed awkwardly at the serrated knife lodged in his liver; it must have been extremely painful, thought Simon. "I just can't take the chance. You know what I look like, you know where I'm staying, and you know where I'm going. And I will be needing that cash—you did get greedy there, you have to admit that."

"I'm sorry," Zap gasped, truthfully; he hadn't a drop of irony left—just regret. He was sorry about having been greedy, sorry about dying, sorry about the whole bloody business, but most of all, he was sorry about the pain, which was so all-enveloping by now, so much larger than himself, that it was like being sorry for all the pain in the world, not just his own, but everybody's.

"It's okay," replied Simon. He watched Strum sag in the chair, heard the wet fart and saw the stain spreading across the crotch of Zap's orange cotton drawstring pants as the sphincters relaxed in death; he'd turned away in disgust even before the light had finished fading from those stoned, red-rimmed eyes.

"I think I will take that hit now, though," he added, reaching for the bong. "Dude."

5

"Abruzzi. Have a seat."

For a man with no real power base left, and just over two months to go before retirement, Deputy Director Steven P. McDougal had himself one sweet office, thought Linda, doing her best to minimize her exhausted drop-foot shuffle as she crossed the expanse of the blue-gray carpet with the FBI logo in the middle and eased herself down into the handsome yellow wing chair set squarely in front of McDougal's aircraft carrier of a desk.

On the far side of the flight deck, McDougal, in shirtsleeves and a gorgeous blue shot-silk necktie, was canted back in his leather executive chair with his legs crossed casually at the ankle, reading a newspaper. "How are you feeling?" he asked without looking up.

Once upon a time that would have been mere conversation; now Linda felt she had to sell the answer. "Fine, sir," she said firmly. "Just fine."

The deputy director glanced at Linda for the first time, lowering his chin and peering over the half-glasses he wore balanced on the end of his patrician nose. "Pool tells me you're settling in nicely."

"Settled, sir—I'm settled."

"Catch that spy yet?"

Linda thought she saw a glint of amusement in those cool gray alpha-male eyes. "Yes, sir, I believe so."

He folded the newspaper smartly in half and handed it across the desk. It was the *San Francisco Chronicle,* Saturday, October 23. FBI FOILS KIDNAP

ATTEMPT, screamed the banner headline, SERIAL KILLER IN BERKELEY? and ELECTRONICS HEIR SOUGHT were the subheads, and straddling the fold was a captioned photograph of Pender, beret comically askew, right arm in an air-cast and sling, being helped out of an ambulance. "Recognize anybody?"

Linda raced through the article *(Simon Childs, heir to the Childs Electronics fortune . . . brief struggle . . . authorities believe more victims . . .)* until she found what she was looking for: *fractured arm . . . treated and released*—Pender was okay. She was more relieved than she would have expected, considering she'd only met the big galoot twice in her life. "I guess he had a hunch," she said.

"And it nearly got him killed," McDougal snapped. "He was lucky. So were we—as you may be aware, lately the Bureau hasn't exactly been getting the kind of press it once enjoyed. The director called me from home this morning—he said this is the first article in any newspaper in over a month that mentions the FBI without also including the words *Waco* or *bungled.*"

"First rate," replied Linda, though it seemed to her that the director of the Federal Bureau of Investigation ought to have *something* better to do with his time.

"There's a problem, though."

Linda waited; then she realized that McDougal wanted her to state the nature of the problem. "Childs is still at large."

"Which is where Liaison Support comes in. You're on point—you'll be coordinating the investigation. I want you on it from now until Mr. Simon Childs is either dead or in custody. Because if he starts killing people again, this thing can go south fast, and we'll lose all the ground we've gained."

"Not to mention all the people he kills will be, like, *dead,*" said Linda.

McDougal lowered his chin again and peered at her over the rim of his reading glasses for what seemed like an eternity. "Know who you remind me of?" he asked eventually.

"No, sir."

"Pender—you remind me of Pender."

"Thank you, sir, I—"

"He's a major pain in the ass, too. Which is another reason I want you working this case—to keep him off it. When it comes to serial killers, Pender's like nature—he abhors a vacuum."

"I understand."

Linda started to hand the newspaper back; McDougal gave her a little *keep-it* wave. "Tell Ed it's for his scrapbook. And one more thing . . ." He reached under the desk and came up with a handsome blackthorn walking stick with an ivory handle and a ferrule of thin, beaten gold. "This is his—I gave it to him in seventy-five, that time he took a bullet for me. He loaned it back to me last year, when I had my old football knee replaced. I haven't used it in months, though—would you give it back to him, thank him for me?"

"Sure," said Linda, taking the cane. It was both lighter and stronger than it looked, and the ivory grip was delicately mottled, like mutton-fat jade. "I didn't know Pender'd been shot."

"It's a good story—you ought to get him to tell it to you sometime. If he offers to show you his scar, though, I'd respectfully decline."

Linda, stubborn to the end, deliberately avoided

using the cane when she pushed herself up from her chair after McDougal dismissed her, or taking advantage of it as she left the office, but on her way back to the car she found herself leaning more and more heavily on it. And although it was a little too tall for her, it made enough of a difference—she felt so much more stable, and was better able to clear the ground with her toes—that when she reached the DOJ-AOB, she didn't think twice about using it on the short walk to the first elevator, or the long walk from the second elevator to her office.

By then it was a done deal—Linda was hooked. The first time she tried to make it to the ladies' room unaided, she had to go back for the cane—walking without it now felt like tottering along a tightrope in a high wind—and by the end of the day, Linda and her cane were inseparable.

Which, Linda realized belatedly, was probably why McDougal had given it to her in the first place. Still, she couldn't help thinking that Pender and/or Dolitz might have had something to do with it as well. Sneaky bastards that they were.

6

Lying on his back, glued to the bottom of the tub from the back of his shaved scalp to the skin of his ass and testicles, with his arms and legs splayed out and glued to the sides of the tub, even the slightest shift of position is excruciatingly painful for Nelson. He can't move, he can't sleep, and worst of all, if there is a worst, with his lips sealed, he can't even scream.

And unlike Wayne Summers, Nelson Carpenter has no imaginary cello to play, no Bach suites committed to memory. For most of his life he has focused his attention and his energies so intently on his phobias that he has no other real interests, no driving passions, no inner resources to draw upon in order to distract himself from this waking nightmare. His only respites come during the spells of panic-and-sleep-deprivation-induced psychosis that overtake him for ever-lengthening periods of time, at ever-shortening intervals.

Small wonder, then, that by late morning Nelson is spending most of his time in a long hallucinatory doze, reliving the death of Simon's grandfather over and over again. It doesn't get any easier, either, starting with the shame of being caught in flagrante when the old man walks in on the boys during a meeting of the Horror Club.

Meeting—that's what they still call it, anyway, though by this point in their adolescent development an observer would be hard put to distinguish the game they play at every session from a good old-fashioned homosexual tryst. Nelson, in fact, would be just as happy to skip the horror phase entirely, but Simon seems, not just to enjoy it, but to *need* it: no horror, no sex, Nelson has learned, and wearing as it is on his psyche, he is willing to put up with the former for the sake of the latter.

So here he is in Simon's room late one Friday afternoon in December of 1963, a few weeks after his thirteenth birthday. It's dusk, the curtains are drawn, the room is dark except for the conical beam of Simon's eight-millimeter Bell and Howell projector and the flickering black-and-white images of *The Cabinet of Dr. Caligari* unspooling against the back of Simon's bedroom door, and the only sounds are the crepitating whirr of the projector and the muffled, rhythmic grunting of the boys humping on the floor so the squeaking bedsprings don't give them away.

And that's how the old man finds them. Once again, lying glued to his bathtub, Nelson hears the film clicking through the Bell and Howell, smells the characteristic projector odor of hot bulb, warm celluloid, and burnt dust, sees Grandfather Childs standing in the shockingly open doorway with an appalled expression as the images from the film flicker, wavy and distorted, against his white shirt front, his ashen face, his glabrous scalp.

The worst beating of Simon's life begins then and there, as Nelson scrambles for his clothes and dashes out of the house half-naked, past an openmouthed Missy and a frowning Ganny Wilson. Not that old man Childs would dare lay a finger on *him*—*his* father's a lawyer and none too fond of his neighbor. Nelson is barred from the premises forever, though, and Simon is forbidden to contact him—also forever.

Forever lasts two days, which is how long it takes for Simon to recover enough from the beating to be able to leave his bedroom. They meet in Nelson's old tree house; Simon shows him his bruises and makes him swear an oath of revenge. It's all very dramatic, but a little hard for Nelson to take seriously.

Not Simon, though: Simon is deadly serious—*and*

he has a plan. Everybody has a weakness, he tells Nelson, a crack in their armor; everybody's afraid of something. In the old man's case, it's fire: Grandfather Childs is deathly afraid of fire. They'll have to be very, very patient, though, Simon informs him—they'll have to wait two whole weeks, until Missy goes home with Ganny for her pre-Christmas sleepover.

Lying in the bathtub thirty-six years later, Nelson relives it one last time. He's in his own bedroom, waiting for Simon's call. He's trying to study, but his eyes skim the print of his American history textbook uncomprehendingly. The phone rings; he snatches it up before his parents can answer. "Hurry up," says Simon—that's all, just the two words and the click of the receiver in Nelson's ear.

The onset of Nelson's acrophobia is still a few years off; he has no trouble climbing out his bedroom window, cutting through the backyard and across the patio to Simon, waiting at the back door.

"He's in the shower," Simon whispers urgently. Everything's ready—they've dry-run it a dozen times in the last two weeks, when the house was empty. As they race through the kitchen, Simon grabs the box of safety matches from the drawer next to the stove; Nelson grabs the big turkey-roaster pan from the cabinet under the counter and the newspaper from the kitchen table, and races up the wide stairs after Simon, who's already emerging from his room carrying his straight-backed metal desk chair. They hurry down the hall and through the open door of the master suite. The moment is electric; even Nelson is more excited than afraid as he helps Simon jam the chair under the knob of the bathroom door; on the other side of the door he can hear the shower running.

"Care to do the honors?" Simon whispers. Nelson shakes his head. Simon gives him a suit-yourself shrug and takes the newspaper from him, rolls it into a cone, lights it, and as it begins to catch, carries it over to the wall socket where Grandfather Childs's prize Tiffany lamp is plugged in. After unplugging the lamp, scorching the plug, the wallpaper under the socket, and the socket itself, Simon retraces his steps, scorching the carpet until he reaches the bathroom door again. He holds the torch to the crack under the door until the fire threatens to burn his hand, then, with a conjuror's flourish, drops the flaming *Chronicle* into the roasting pan.

And as the sound of the running water stops abruptly and the room begins to fill with smoke, Simon backs away to join Nelson over by the doorway. Together they watch, wide-eyed with excitement as the doorknob begins to turn as if by magic, then rattles frantically. A moment later—bam!—the door shudders, the chair wobbles. Bam, bam, bam again; Nelson pictures the old man throwing himself against it. A shiver of fear runs through him, but the door holds, the chair holds. Nelson can hear the old man screaming now: *eeee, eeee, eeee*—a high-pitched, keening sort of sound.

"Listen," giggles Simon, putting his arm around Nelson's waist, giving his love handle a little squeeze; "listen, he's squealing like an old woman."

"An old woman," Nelson agrees. "C'mon, let's—"

But before they can carry out the rest of the plan (ditch the ashes, put the matches, the baking pan, and the chair back where they belong, then take a powder before the old fart figures out the bathroom door is no longer mysteriously jammed; old fart, old lamp, old wiring, electric fire—hey, it happens, you know?), the door stops shuddering, the sound of the old-womanly keening dies away, and they hear a heavy, meaty thump, followed by a breathy, gasping gurgling, followed in turn by . . .

By nothing. By the soft crackling of the newspaper in the roasting pan. But from inside the bathroom, not another sound, until they are standing together in the bathroom doorway a few minutes later, looking down at a bald old man lying in a pool of blood, his throat cut from ear to ear, and a straight razor clutched in his lifeless hand, at which point Simon turns to Nelson, and in a voice filled more with awe than with fear, guilt, or rancor, says, "Sometimes you get lucky, Nellie—sometimes you just get lucky."

And sometimes you don't. Something drags Nelson out of his hypnotic doze. Pain—it's pain: his right leg, glued slightly higher to the side of the tub than the left, is beginning to work itself loose. He is encouraged briefly—then the pain begins to build. It's a whole new order of misery, exfoliation by gravity, the fine hairs on the side of his calf being ripped out in agonizing slow-mo. He tenses the leg, holds it up against the pull of gravity for as long as he can, breathing shallowly through his nostrils. Eventually, though, the muscles tire, the leg sags, the torture begins again. Tears swim in his eyes, blurring the midnight blue wall tiles, but even the release of a good cry is denied to Nelson—if his nose stops up, he will surely suffocate.

Finally he can bear it no longer. Summoning all his courage, and the strength of despair, with one convulsive effort Nelson manages to yank the leg free of the porcelain, leaving a patch of hairy, bloody skin the approximate size and shape of a Dr. Scholl's insert adhering to the inside of the tub. But the pain, at its flood stage, is worse than he could have imagined, and even after it begins to ebb, he knows he will never be able to summon either the courage or the strength to face it again.

And with the departure of that last, forlorn hope—that he might somehow be able to free himself, a limb at a time—comes a sudden clarity. But even though Nelson knows what comes next, the life force is still surprisingly strong within him—if it hadn't been, he'd have ended his own life years ago, ended it a hundred times over. So as he uses his free heel to kick down the lever that closes the drain, then to nudge open first the right-hand tap, then the left, he tells himself he's only running a bath. For the warmth. And maybe the water will melt the glue before . . .

The running water is the first sound Nelson has heard since Simon left, except, of course, for the high-pitched squeal of his own stifled screams. He closes his eyes. The water rises, rises; it covers his ears, muffling its own roar. It sounds like a distant cataract now, and Nelson is floating downstream toward it. It's all very peaceful, in a hallucinatory sort of way, until the first trickle of water tickles his upper lip. He tries to raise his head, is almost surprised to find it held fast.

Not like this, he thinks. Death, yes: being dead meant you didn't have to be afraid anymore. Funny that hadn't occurred to him before. And drowning, sure: there was supposed to be some kind of reflex that kicked in after your lungs filled with water, that made it a much more peaceful way to go than most people thought. But not slowly, not like this, not a trickle at a time. Then the trickle becomes a steady flow, and the flow a warm, choking flood; Nelson flails wildly with his free foot, trying to find the taps again, trying to find the drain lever as the warm water begins to close over his head.

7

Say what you will about the inconvenience of being hunted for capital crimes, it not only kept the blind rat at bay almost as efficiently as the most elaborately planned session of the fear game, but was a liberating experience as well. There was no need for Simon to dispose of Zap Strum's body, or even hide his own culpability—they could only execute you once, only incarcerate you for a single lifetime.

On the other hand, it was Simon's understanding that every web site or e-mail address, every keystroke recently accessed on a computer, could somehow be recovered from the hard drive. Which meant that somewhere in this rat's nest of a loft was information that could not only tell the cops (and when Simon thought of cops now, it was Pender's face that came to mind) where Simon had been, but might also tip them off as to where he was heading.

"Can't have that," Simon explained to Zap, still slumped in his expensive chair, as he rolled the Aeron out from in front of the command post and tipped it forward to empty it. The dreadlocked corpse hit the floor with a meaty, tumbling thud—a gratuitous discourtesy on Simon's part, as it turned out, the blood-soaked seat back and cushion rendering the chair unsittable.

Undeterred, Simon dragged the saddle-shaped leather footstool over to the desk, straddled it, and began tapping the keyboard randomly—he assumed Zap's own system had a poison pill or fail-safe device similar to the one Zap had installed on Simon's. Sure enough, the screensaver—a blond woman with breasts larger than her head, performing an endless striptease—fragmented into hundreds of tiny ASCII characters; a few seconds later the screen went dark.

Just to be on the safe side, though, Simon decided to go low-tech for backup. He ducked under the desk, unplugged the CPU box from the surge protector, and proceeded to dismantle, not just that CPU, but every computer and Zip drive in the apartment, then take a ball peen hammer to every silvery disk he found. There was also a small box of floppy disks— these he incinerated in Zap's toaster oven, along with a videocassette he'd ejected from a deck that looked as if it might be connected to the security camera monitoring the vestibule.

Fifteen minutes later, just as the first wisps of oily, pungent, probably toxic, black smoke had begun to issue from the countertop oven, Simon located Zap's stash in a false-front bookcase, behind a dummy set of vintage *Encyclopaedia Britannica*s. "Mercy buckets,

dude," he muttered, as he stuffed a few prebagged
ounces of sinsemilla into his satchel, along with an
eclectic, rainbow assortment of uppers, downers, and
the milder psychedelics he preferred.

Then, after a short wait in the downstairs vestibule
until the sidewalk was clear, it was sayonara Zap, sayonara SoMa, and sayonara San Francisco as Simon,
his getaway satchel bulging with cash, drugs, and most
important, the Pender printout, pointed Nelson's
Volvo toward the shadowy lower deck of the Bay
Bridge, in the direction of Concord, sanctuary, and
one final reunion with a bathtub-bound childhood
friend—his last surviving friend, it occurred to Simon.

It was a bittersweet realization, a little sad, a little
lonely, and as intensely liberating as being hunted for
murder. With Missy and Ganny gone, once Nelson
was out of the way, Simon would be alone on this
earth. Except, of course, for the old woman in Atlantic
City who called herself Rosie Delamour, but she
didn't really count. Screw her and the horse she rode
out on, was Simon's motto.

But even thinking about *her* could degrade a bittersweet mood down to just plain bitter. And bitter was
no way to be when you were about to bid farewell to
your oldest friend, thought Simon as he pulled into
Nelson's driveway and used the remote clipped to the
Volvo's sun visor to open the garage door, then close
it behind him.

Inside the garage, all was peaceful again—at least
after Simon had treated himself to a few tokes of Zap
Strum's finest. Dim gray light, smell of old oil stains
and cement dust; the only sounds were the hum of
the water heater inside its cozy blanket of insulation

and the distant, homey gurgle of water through overhead pipes, which reminded Simon of Missy and her endless bath. A little catch of a sob caught in his throat, even as the memory brought a smile: the bittersweet feeling was back.

Not for long, though. As he let himself into the house, it suddenly dawned on Simon that there shouldn't have been any water-heater hum or homey gurgle in the pipes—there shouldn't have been any water running anywhere in that house, unless a pipe had burst or Nelson had somehow—

But no, that was impossible. Had to be a pipe, he thought, stepping back as a drop of water fell past him and hit the already saturated hall carpet with a fat plop, then looking up to see the dark, continent-shaped water stain spreading across the underside of the ceiling, a nipple-shaped drop gathering at its center. Simon hurried down the hall into the living room, saw that the flood in the hallway was relatively minor compared to the cataract sluicing down the narrow enclosed stairway from the second-floor landing, as if the staircase were a salmon ladder cut into the side of a dam. He splashed up the stairs two at a time, careened around the corner, raced through Nelson's bedroom, and skidded to a halt at the bathroom door, the heels of the hard-soled black loafers he'd borrowed from Nelson that morning kicking up tiny rooster tails in his wake.

And although Simon had not knowingly been afraid of water since Grandfather Childs had cured him of his fear of drowning nearly half a century ago, he found himself frozen in the doorway, unable to move, watching helplessly as the torrent poured full-throated from the tap, noisily churning the surface of the bath and overflowing the side of the tub like a miniature Niagara. All he could see of Nelson were a few strands of blond hair waving like tendrils of sea-weed in the roiling water.

"Coward," he screamed, as much at himself as at Nelson; Simon could forgive himself anything except cowardice. "You yellow coward." The shoes were soaked, his feet wet to the ankle, but the pho-bia had him in its grip, and he knew that until he had mastered it again, he would be unable to either retreat or advance.

You can do it, he told himself. You've done harder things than this in your lifetime; you've overcome more than this. You can do it, you can do it, you can do it. And if he concentrated, if he listened hard, in the human-voiced burble of the running water he could hear Missy singing to encourage him, singing that song she sometimes sang to encourage herself: *"Cinderelly, Cinderelly, you can do it, Cinderelly."*

And call it foolish, even infantile, but slowly his feet began to move, shuffling through the water, one step at a time, but one foot following the other, until he'd reached the tub.

Afterward Simon couldn't remember turning off the water; all he knew was that it was quiet again, except for the sound of the water still dripping down the staircase, and he was leaning over the tub looking down at poor drowned Nelson.

My last surviving friend on earth, he thought sadly—then it was time to go.

8

The next time Pender's cell phone rang, Dorie rolled over sleepily and patted his cast. "It's okay, I'm up."

More or less—she dozed, drifting in and out of a pleasant Vicodin haze, comforted by the sound of Pender's voice and the solid, grounding presence of his big body beside her in the bed. They hadn't made love yet. Once they were actually in bed together last night, broken-boned, drugged, and exhausted, common sense had kicked in—or was it maturity? It *was* going to happen, though, maybe soon—Dorie was as sure of that as she'd ever been about anything.

"Who was that on the phone?"

"First call was McDougal, my boss. He's putting Linda Abruzzi in charge of coordinating the investigation. Second call was Pool."

"Who's Pool?"

"She runs the FBI. I figured Abruzzi could probably use a few pointers getting this thing off the ground. But to get McDougal to put her in charge, I had to promise to stay out of it."

"But what if you'd stayed out of it before? Where would . . . Where would that . . ." *Where would that leave me?* Dorie couldn't bring herself to finish the question, probably because she knew the answer: in Simon's basement.

"Sid Dolitz says there's an old Yiddish expression that translates: 'In the land of What-If, all travelers are unhappy.' Of course, being Sid, he might have made it up. How's your nose?"

"I think it probably hurts something awful, but I took a Vicodin when I woke up and another one when I woke up the second time, so the pain ain't reaching the brain. How's your arm feeling?"

"Like it got whacked with a frying pan."

"May I recommend a Vicodin?"

"I already took one."

"Take another."

"You think?"

"Hey, it worked for me."

9

Excited as Linda was about finally having something useful to do, she also wondered whether she might be in over her head. After all, she asked herself as the afternoon wore on, what did she know about coordinating an investigation of this size and complexity, involving five separate investigations in five separate jurisdictions and almost certainly more to come, in addition to an interstate manhunt and a growing media interest that was rapidly threatening to turn into a feeding frenzy?

Precious little, came the answer. And she didn't feel right asking Pender for advice on how to conduct the rest of the investigation, not after McDougal had specifically informed her that part of her assignment was to keep him as far away from it as possible.

Once again, it was Pool to the rescue. She showed

up out of nowhere around three-thirty—Linda certainly hadn't called her—dressed, not for success, but for raking leaves on a Saturday afternoon, hit the phones, called in a few favors or engaged in a little blackmail, and by six o'clock (miraculous as Pool's earlier Bureau-cratic machinations had been, this one was on the order of parting the Red Sea), the bogus bank records were gone, and Linda's little office in the DOJ-AOB had been turned into a mini-SIOC (Strategic Information and Operations Center) command post, complete with additional phone and data lines and a cork-backed map of the U.S. that took up the entire wall behind Linda's desk, along with tiny color-coded flag pins with which to track Childs sightings—white for *reported*, red for *confirmed*.

And while the map was going up, Pool, as per Pender's suggestion, transferred a copy of the database program Thom Davies had devised for Pender a few years ago—a cascading boilerplate calendar, year tiles opening up into months, months into days, days into hours—onto Linda's computer and, under the pretext of showing Linda how to use the program, gently reminded her of the importance of establishing a time line for her suspect: If you want to know where somebody's going, first you have to know where they've been.

Linda didn't need a second hint. She set to work, culling data on Simon Childs from every available source, starting with Dorie Bell's letter and ending with the preliminary findings of the Evidence Response Team still combing through the house on Grizzly Rock Road, and entering it into the database herself. Three hours later, not only did she have a preliminary time line, admittedly with more gaps than entries, tracking Simon Childs from birth through yesterday, but through a sort of immersion therapy, she had begun the unpleasant but necessary process of trying to get into the killer's mind by first letting him into her mind.

The way it worked, you absorbed and memorized every shred of information about your suspect, until you were as conscious of his tendencies, his likes and dislikes, as you were of your own; when things were really cooking, a stimulus would be almost as likely to bring up one of the suspect's mnemonic associations as it would one of your own. That way (at least theoretically; Linda had never done this sort of thing before), when the time came, you'd not only know which way your suspect was going to jump, but when, and how high.

Early as it was in the process, then, it was no accident that on her way home that night, when Linda stopped at the Safeway in Potomac to get what passed for a deli sandwich this far from the Bronx and saw a teenage girl with Down syndrome in the parking lot, she thought immediately of Missy Childs.

And later that night, as she lay in bed trying to get to sleep, instead of having her thoughts dwelling morbidly on her MS, as they had almost every night since her diagnosis, Linda found herself thinking about something that Kim Rosen had posted on the PWSPD web site less than a week before she died.

> I know how people think. They think your doing
> it on purpose, or your doing it for attention, and
> that if only somebody would grab you by the
> collar and give you a good shaking, maybe slap

you around a little and tell you its all in your
head, you idiot, its only in your head, that you'd
be cured. And what they don't understand is
that life has already shook us dizzy and slapped
us silly. And knowing that the fear is in your
head doesn't make it easier to bear, it makes it
harder. Because you can protect yourself from
something outside, you can run away or lock
your door or get a gun. But there's no place to
run when the fear is inside you, and even if you
do run, there's no place to hide.

Ain't that the truth, thought Linda. She opened an
eye. It was nearly one A.M., according to the glowing
green hands on her alarm clock, and something was
nagging at her. Not Kim, not Simon—something
closer to home. Something she'd left undone? Half
done? Never mind: if it was important, she'd—

Then it came to her: the laundry. She'd left one
load wet in the washer this morning, one load damp
in the dryer. Abrootz old girl, she told herself, you're
gonna have some serious ironing to do tomorrow.

10

Not yet, thinks Simon, swimming up through the
darkness toward consciousness. Not just yet. He's
been dreaming; Missy was there; he doesn't want to
lose her again quite so soon.

But it's too late—he's awake now, surrounded by blackness. For a moment his mind is a delicious blank—he can't quite place himself in time or space. He might be anywhere, any age, a child in his own bed, awakening from an afternoon nap, or an eighteen-year-old nodded out in a crash pad in the Haight. Then he opens his eyes, turns his head, sees the glowing red numbers on the cheap clock radio next to the bed. Three A.M. Figures; he'd dropped the Halwane around midnight.

He sits up, fumbles for a light switch. The motel room materializes around him. Pastel walls, TV on the dresser, still life on the wall: this is where the blind rat lives, he thinks—in a generic, three-in-the-morning motel room outside Winnemucca, Nevada. At least it's a smoking room, he tells himself, firing up the half-smoked joint he's left in the ashtray against just such a contingency.

And as he waits for the weed to take effect, he finds himself wondering where Missy is spending the night. On a roll-out slab in a pitch-black drawer in the coroner's basement, most likely. Don't be afraid, he wants to tell her—you don't ever have to be afraid again.

He spreads his map out on the bed and, using his thumb and forefinger as calipers, measures out how far he's come on 80, then doubles that, pivoting the thumb and forefinger around twice to calculate how far he's likely to get tomorrow. The second time, his forefinger lands on Ogallala, Nebraska. Two more digital pirouettes, and his forefinger is poised over La Farge, Wisconsin, where Pender's sister lives.

Monday night, then: at his current pace, he can

expect to reach La Farge sometime Monday night. Tomorrow he'll make the initial overtures. If the real Arthur Bellcock hasn't already been in touch with her, he'll set up an interview—have to get a tape recorder on the way, or maybe just a notebook— arrive early, scope out the scene, look for signs of surveillance.

If the coast is clear, he shows up as Bellcock. If it's not, he moves on to one of the other names on the—

No! If there are any signs of surveillance or even suspicion, it dawns on Simon, that would mean the whole Arthur Bellcock scenario is blown. Which would mean in turn that Pender knows he is being stalked—Simon would have lost the element of surprise.

So the question he has to ask himself at this point is, Is it worth it? Is finding out what Pender's afraid of worth the risk of putting him on his guard?

Simon fires up the roach again, takes a serious hit, and waits for the answer to come to him.

VIII

The Widow Bird

1

"Thank you for another day, O Lord; may I use it to your everlasting glory."

And it did look to be a glorious Indian summer Sunday. Sunny, once those high clouds burned off, with highs in the low seventies—about ten degrees higher than normal for Wisconsin, this time of year, but Ida Day would have started her morning with the same prayer of thanks if it had been fifty and raining, or twenty below and snowing. When you were seventy and still had all your faculties and most of your teeth, every day was a good day.

Mind you, Ida's idea of how to use a Sunday to the Lord's glory was not the same as most folks, especially around La Farge. For one thing, it didn't include church. She and Walt had always distrusted organized religion; the more organized it was, the more they distrusted it. If she wanted the word of God, Ida had only to look up at the sampler hanging over the bureau.

Deuteronomy 31:8: "The Lord Himself goes before you and will be with you; He will never leave you nor forsake you. Do not be afraid; do not be discouraged."

She had stitched it herself, for Walt, to encourage him during those last difficult days. Throat cancer—no goddamn way to go. Ida still had Walt's old army Colt in the bottom drawer of her bureau; if and when she found herself in a similar situation, she was reasonably confident she'd have the right combination of courage and cowardice to use it.

But today was not a day for morbid thoughts. Today was a day for, let's see . . . for apples! She still had a few bushels left over from the Gays Mills Applefest. Oh, yes—Ida could almost smell it already, the sweet, faintly winey bouquet of autumn apples being cidered.

Although, come to think of it, cidering was best left for a cool day; not only were you less likely to draw wasps, but you could mull the first gallon to warm you.

Then Ida remembered the pumpkins sitting on the front porch. She'd told herself she wasn't going to carve jack-o'-lanterns this year, but yesterday the little Steinmuller boy had come trudging up the sidewalk hauling a rusty red wagon piled high with pumpkins he'd grown himself, a dollar for the big ones, fifty cents for the little ones, two bits for the gourds. It was right off the cover of a *Saturday Evening Post;* how could she resist?

Pumpkins, then. After breakfast—two eggs and a rasher of bacon, black coffee, and her first Pall Mall of the day (don't bother lecturing her: she's already buried two doctors; three, if you count Walt)—Ida sharpened her carving knife on a Washita stone dampened with vinegar, spread newspapers out on the porch, turned the likeliest looking pumpkin around and around until she discovered its natural face, and had just finished sawing off its cap when the phone rang.

"It never fails," she grumbled, hauling herself up from the overturned milk crate she'd been sitting on and hurrying into the house to pick up the phone in the living room before the answering machine in the kitchen got into the act. There was nothing Ida hated more than shouting *hold on* into the receiver while her own flat Appleknocker voice bleated *I'm not here now, leave a message at the tone* into her ear.

"Hello?" She'd made it.

"Ida Day?"

"Yes?"

"Ida Pender Day?"

"Yes?"

"Mrs. Day, this is Arthur Bellcock."

"The man who's writing the book about Eddie?"

"One of the only advantages to a name like mine, Mrs. Day, is you never get confused with any other Arthur Bellcocks."

"Yes, I suppose that's true. Eddie told me he'd given you my name and that you'd probably be in touch, but I thought it wasn't going to be for another month or so."

"That *was* the plan, but due to a scheduling conflict, I've had to push things up a few weeks. I was wondering, and I understand if it's an inconvenience, but I'm actually down in Madison winding up another project, and it would be so helpful if I could drive up tomorrow evening."

"Oh, I think I can manage to clear my schedule, Mr. Bellcock. And Eddie did encourage me to tell you anything you wanted to know."

"Good. Because I definitely want to capture him, warts and all."

"I'll do the best I can. But you understand, Mr. Bellcock, I was fourteen when Eddie was born, and I moved away from Cortland when he was ten."

"I understand. At this early stage, everything I can learn about your brother will be a great help. By the way, will Mr. Day be around?"

"Only in spirit," said Ida. "Dr. Day passed away ten years ago."

"I'm so sorry. You live alone, then?"

"Alone, but not lonely, as I like to say."

"A laudable attitude. Until tomorrow then, Mrs. Day."

"Until tomorrow, Mr. Bellcock."

2

On Sunday, Linda was up at dawn. From her bedroom window she could see the mist rising placidly from the domesticated water of the canal, like steam from a bowl of soup. The autumn colors of the surrounding woods were muted, drenched in the morning dew.

It occurred to Linda, as she made her way sleepily across the hall to the bathroom, that nobody had told her what hours she was expected to keep. Like today, for instance. Was she supposed to come into the office on Sunday? If so, to do what? Answer the phone? Call forwarding could take care of that. Work on her time line? The Visa and Pac Bell printouts detailing Childs's credit card purchases and telephone calls wouldn't be coming in until tomorrow at the earliest. So why go into the office?

The answer came to her after breakfast, as she was down in the cellar ironing, with the second load of yesterday's laundry now spinning in the dryer. The BOLO, she thought: a "Be On the Lookout" for Simon Childs was undoubtedly being sent out to every law enforcement agency in the United States. But then, so were dozens of other BOLOs, every day of the week. Go-getters memorized them, doughnut dunkers ignored them, but what about your average cop, overworked, overBOLOed, drowning in a sea of red tape and paperwork? Wouldn't a call or a fax or a heads-up of some kind from a genuine (well, almost genuine) FBI special agent go a long way toward raising his or her consciousness as to the importance of Being On the Lookout for a particular suspect, at least until the Ten Most Wanted List had been updated to include him?

More than likely, thought Linda, holding her favorite blouse up to the unshaded bulb hanging from a crossbeam, to examine the results of her ironing. Still a little wrinkled after twenty-four hours in the dryer, but close enough for guvmint work, as they used to say in San Antone; or at any rate, close enough for guvmint work in an empty office on a Sunday morning.

3

For Pender and Dorie, Saturday had been a day of rest and recuperation. They never made it out of the house—they barely made it out of bed. Canned soup—Dorie's cupboard had more Campbell's than a gathering of the Scottish clans—and sleep had sustained them. For Dorie, who had never married, or even shacked up with a man for an extended stretch, this nonsexual bed sharing was something new. Pender, having endured a twenty-year marriage that had gone sour after the first five, was, of course, familiar with it.

By Sunday morning, Pender had had two nights to learn that Dorie hadn't been kidding about her snoring—she was indeed a window rattler. He didn't mind, though—at least when she was snoring, she wasn't thrashing, moaning, or crying out in her sleep.

Not that he blamed her. After what she'd been through, Dorie would be lucky if sleep disturbances were the worst, or last, of her problems. And awake, despite all she must have gone through in that basement in Berkeley, she never complained, which Pender found extraordinary in a day and age when everybody who'd ever had their fanny patted as a kid called themselves a sexual-abuse survivor, and feeling sorry for yourself was practically a cottage industry. Pender was impressed—he only wished he could somehow rescue her from the psychological and emotional shitstorm as successfully as he had from physical danger.

He knew, of course, that it was a risky game, this white knight business. The relationship burying ground was littered with the corpses of failed white-knight/damsel-in-distress romances; nowadays they even warned recruits in the Academy about the syndrome.

But what was a secret sentimentalist to do? Pender was a goner long before the relationship was consummated late Sunday morning. The consummation itself was necessarily gentle. Due to their injuries, they were forced to make love, in Pender's phrase, like porcupines—very carefully—but perhaps because of the time they'd already spent in bed together, there was little of the awkwardness, emotional discomfort, or uncertainty that so often marked first sexual encounters, even at their age.

Afterward, Dorie went back to sleep; soon she was tossing and whimpering again. Pender reached across his body with his good arm, patted her shoulder, stroked her side all the way to the swell of her hip, then back again, murmuring that it was all right, that everything was okay now.

Which was a lie—everything was not okay. Simon Childs, the man who'd done this to Dorie, was still out there somewhere. And if this case had been personal before, it was doubly so now. Pender tiptoed out of bed without waking Dorie this time, and took his cell into the bathroom with him.

4

The call came in just as Linda was thinking about knocking off for the day. There had been no developments in the investigation, no Childs sightings, either reported or confirmed. He'd probably gone to ground, was the consensus; if the pressure was kept on, sooner or later he'd have to surface, if only to change holes.

In the meantime, she'd made her calls, exchanged a little small talk on the order of *sucks catchin' a Sunday shift, whaddaya gonna do?* and gotten a few BOLOs posted that might have languished in somebody's in box. When the phone rang around quarter to three, she thought it might be one of the callbacks she'd left. Instead it was Pender. She tried, she really did: she told him McDougal had handed her the investigation on the express condition that she keep Pender out of it.

He didn't sound very impressed. "How long have you been with the Bureau?"

"Seven years."

"And you still can't tell when your boss is just covering his ass?"

"He didn't sound like he was just covering his ass. He sounded concerned."

"Yes, kiddo—he's concerned about covering his ass. Let me ask you two questions. One: What's the priority here—what's the job?"

"That's a no-brainer. The job is apprehending Childs as quickly as possible. What's the second question?"

"Can you do a better job apprehending Childs as quickly as possible with or without the benefit of my twenty years of experience?"

"Well, with it. But McDougal told me—"

"Linda, I don't care what McDougal told you—his priorities are exactly the same as yours. And mine. And anybody else in law enforcement who hasn't got his head so far up his ass he can count his own fillings. Agreed?" Then, without waiting for an answer: "Attagirl. Now, the first thing you have to understand . . ."

So much for McDougal and the hierarchy; so much for going home early. According to the Book of Pender, the first thing Linda had to understand was that the cops on the street, both local and federal, weren't going to need any help from her when it came to the usual avenues of investigation. With or without Liaison Support, the evidence response techs would hoover up every shred of gross or trace evidence; the Berkeley cops would comb all of Childs's reported haunts; the so-called suicides in Vegas, Fresno, and Chicago would be reopened as homicide investigations; and every friend, neighbor, or casual acquaintance Childs had ever called or been seen with in public or visited or written a check to in the last year or so would receive at least cursory attention from law enforcement.

Now, the time line Linda was working on would be lots of help there, Pender assured her (as soon as he mentioned the time line, Linda realized how it had happened that Pool had just sort of magically turned up at the office Saturday afternoon), and sooner or later events would start dictating her course of action. For instance, he could almost promise her more work than she could handle as the ERT in Berkeley continued to unearth the corpses in Childs's basement.

But until then, he explained, Linda could basically expect law enforcement to be all over Simon Childs's recent past and foreseeable future like Yogi Bear on a picnic basket. So what Pender suggested was that as soon as the time line was done, Linda turn her efforts to probing a little deeper into Childs's past. Were there any childhood friends whom he hadn't seen in a long time, whom he might be desperate enough to seek out as a fugitive? How about medical records? Not just his current physicians—investigators would be lined up five deep at their doors—but his former doctors, all the way back to his pediatrician. If in addition to being a psychopath, Childs was also a counterphobic phobic, as Sid had suggested, perhaps he'd seen a shrink as a child. That'd really give the profilers something to work with.

Encouraged and energized, even inspired by Pender's call, Linda worked what was left of her ass off for the rest of the afternoon (of the twenty pounds she'd lost this year, at least ten had to have come off her rear end), but by eight o'clock, five on the West Coast, everything was done that was going to get done on a Sunday evening, so an exhausted Linda packed it in.

Basta, as her mother used to say to her father when he worked on Sunday—enough is enough, even God rested on the seventh day. Then, of course, Mom Abruzzi would do a load of ironing, maybe vacuum the curtains, cook a five-course Italian dinner, and mend clothes all through *60 Minutes*. After all these years, Mom still had no idea what Mike Wallace looked like, went the family joke, because she never looked up from her sewing basket.

Thinking about home always made Linda hungry. When she got back to Pender's, she went straight to the kitchen and opened the fridge before she even took off her coat. The freezer compartment was well stocked—sort of: if somebody had gone through the frozen food section of the supermarket and selected TV dinners solely on the basis of fat grams, the higher the better, they'd have ended up with something very like the contents of Pender's freezer.

Linda opted for the Marie Callender's spaghetti carbonara (what a concept, she thought: some twisted guinea genius had actually looked at a bowl of pasta and said to himself, you know what this needs?— white gravy and bacon), and while it was heating, she made her traditional, not to say mandatory, Sunday night phone call. It went well—Mom didn't nag her about moving back home. She *mentioned* it three or four times, but by Italian-mother standards that didn't count as nagging. Then she'd handed the phone to Dad, who told Linda he couldn't talk long because *The Sopranos* was coming on.

Oh, Dad, she wanted to moan, not you, too. Linda had tried to watch the show once—it was the episode where the bumbling FBI agents tried to plant a bug in Tony's basement; she'd felt like throwing her shoe through the screen. And Charlie Abruzzi, of all people, should have known better—you didn't run an Italian butcher shop in the Bronx for forty years without learning what the mob was really like; Big Pussy my ass!

But at least the Sunday call helped clear the nostalgia out of Linda's system. After all, she told herself as she climbed into bed that night, home is where you make it. And life is what you make of it. She understood how blessed she was to have a job where she could make a difference.

It was like her dad said when she told him she wanted to change careers and apply to the FBI. The secret to happiness, he told her, was to be able to go to bed Sunday night looking forward to getting up and going to work Monday morning.

"Do you?" she'd asked.

"Hell no," he replied. "By the time I figured that out, I already had a wife and three kids to feed."

5

"And how would you like to pay for this tonight, Dr. Keene?" asked the desk clerk at the Holiday Inn Express in Ogallala on Sunday night. (Several of his false identities were doctors—if things had turned out differently, Simon had often thought, he'd have liked to have been a doctor. Of course, he'd have had to finish high school first, but if he had, he could have gone on to specialize in treating Down syndromers—*then* Missy would have received that heart transplant.)

Simon was ready for the question—the clerk at the Holiday Inn Express in Winnemucca had phrased it in exactly the same words the night before. "I'd *like* to pay in peanut shells," he replied drolly, "but I suppose you had something more like this in mind." And he slid Andrew Keene's Visa across the counter.

The clerk glanced at the card before running it through the machine. Simon experienced a moment of delicious suspense—not quite fear, but definitely a sense of heightened alert until the card was approved. Which it always was—Dr. Keene was Simon's most reliable alter ego. The condo in Puerto Vallarta was in his name; the bills were paid electronically through a double-blind offshore account in the Caymans that Zap had helped Simon set up years earlier.

"Thank you, Dr. Keene. This is your room number—" The clerk jotted down 318 on the cardboard envelope containing the room key, then turned the envelope around for Simon to read. Desk clerks never spoke room numbers aloud nowadays, even if there was nobody else within thirty feet of the desk; Simon wondered if at some point in the past there'd been a crime wave involving eavesdropping burglars with supernatural hearing. "—and the elevator's right around the corner. Enjoy your stay."

Enjoy your stay. Not bloody likely: after sixteen hours in the womblike Volvo with nothing but the scenery and Zap's weed for entertainment (reception was sketchy in the mountains—for some reason only country music stations were able to overcome the topography), Simon now found himself looking at essentially the same motel room he'd checked out of that morning.

So now what? Sleep would be nice, sleep would be delightful, but Simon had been drinking road coffee

all day, plus he'd ingested a few Mexican crosstops—
ten milligrams of dexedrine apiece—when he'd started
nodding out somewhere east of Salt Lake City, so he
wasn't sure he'd be able to knock himself out even
with a Halwane.

Still, he had to do something—he could sense the
blind rat lurking. It seemed as though the rat was
always lurking lately. Once, Simon had been able to
go a year or two between rounds of the fear game;
more recently the cycle had shortened to a month or
two; and now it seemed to be spiraling in on itself
even more drastically. Three games so far this month
(Wayne, Dorie, and Nelson; Zap didn't count, but
Dorie did: the game wasn't about murder, Simon
always told himself—that was just something you had
to do afterward if you didn't want to end up in jail),
and October wasn't even over, yet here he was again,
twitchy as a weekend tweaker on a Friday morning,
reduced to making a tent of the bedclothes, firing up
a joint as thick as his pinky under the covers, and like
a baseball fan in January, replaying the glory days in
his head. Thinking about the game was better than
no game at all.

Tonight, probably because of the time of year,
Simon found himself remembering that scrawny little
coke whore from La Honda. For the life of him he
couldn't recall her name at the moment, yet without
her, there might not have been any game at all.

The year was 1969, the month was October, the
drug of choice was Peruvian marching powder, and
Simon had recently come into his majority—if it
weren't for bad companions, he wouldn't have had
any companions at all. Except of course for the blind

rat, which had been gnawing at him since Nellie had gone back into the loony bin. There didn't seem to be enough coke in the world to keep the rat at bay and he couldn't work up much interest in sex, plentiful as opportunities were in the circles he frequented. Compared to the ecstasy of the fear game with Nellie, there just wasn't any point, especially in light of his ejaculatio praecox problem.

And although in retrospect the solution to Simon's anhedonia seems obvious, even inevitable, it wasn't until the incident with—Corky! that was it, her name was Corky—that he'd begun to put two and two together.

Corky What's-her-name. White girl, rib-counting skinny. Used to hang around Ugly George's Harley ranch in La Honda trading blow jobs for blow, when she could get any takers, and being used as a piñata by the bikers the rest of the time.

Talk was going around, though, that Corky was about to be upgraded from piñata to feature player in an eight-millimeter snuff film, so when she popped up from the rear floorboards of Simon's first Mercedes saloon somewhere around Daly City (Simon had recently dumped his Hog, which was being repaired out at the ranch), Simon resisted his first impulse, which was to take her back to La Honda to be there in person and watch movie magic being made.

Who knows, perhaps Simon had a touch of the white knight syndrome himself—he certainly hadn't done it for the free head. But although she may have been in distress, Corky was no fair damsel. She hoovered up vast quantities of Simon's newly pur-chased flake, proved to be horny as a she-goat and mean as a snake once she'd finally had an elegant sufficiency, and was foulmouthed to boot, making the next-to-last mistake of her sorry life by teasing him for his lack of interest in sex, calling him a faggot, then telling him even a queer ought to be able to enjoy a good blow job.

But she'd changed her tune pretty quickly when Simon told her that he'd had enough, that he'd just as soon stick it into a cesspool as into that sewer of a mouth, and that as soon as he was able to drive, he would be taking her back to the ranch to make her film debut. That was when things got interesting. First she cajoled, then she begged, and then, after he'd tied her up and stuffed his handkerchief into her mouth, she made her last mistake—she let the terror show in her eyes.

The effect on Simon was as immediate, electric, and profound as that of the fear game at its most intense. Thirty years later, almost to the day, huddled under the smoke-filled covers in room 318 of the Holiday Inn Express in Ogallala, Nebraska, he could still remember the shock of recognition: he wasn't a queer, it wasn't Nellie, or men, or even sex in general that turned him on, it was *this,* all *this,* the sudden quiescence, the pupils gone dark and vulnerable, the mouth forced open, the trembling lips nearly as white as the handkerchief stuffed between them. It wasn't so much Corky's fear as it was the way the fear had transformed her, stripped her more naked than naked, until her soul was as bare as her sad, pale, skinny little body.

Simon was so moved by the experience that he even thought about letting her go, really he did. And although it hadn't worked out that way in the end, by the time Ugly George's snuff film was in the can, Simon had learned another important lesson, the one about pain being anodyne to fear.

Over time, Simon would further define his needs and desires; by specializing only in true phobics he would, in effect, transform himself from a gourmand to a gourmet, an aficionado of fear. But as much as he'd refined the game over the years, from crude targets-of-opportunity abductions to the apotheosis of the fear game, the late lamented PWSPD Association, it all had its roots in just two people, Nelson Carpenter and Corky What's-her-name, and to those two, both gone now, Simon Childs knew that he would be forever grateful.

6

On her fourth night in the country, Linda managed to sleep through the worst of the quiet, awakening Monday morning to the racket of songbirds. And although she still found herself looking forward to going to work, after her Betaseron injection she brought her soy-protein smoothie out onto the porch and took her time drinking it—she had figured out by now that until Simon Childs was in custody, these early breakfasts were probably going to be her only chance to enjoy the fabulous autumn foliage in the daylight.

And she was right—things did start heating up Monday. At six in the morning, Pacific time, federal agents, armed with search warrants obtained on the basis of Simon Childs's bank records, raided Kenneth "Zap" Strum's SoMa loft. The discovery of Zap's body, the medical examiner's estimation of the time of death, and the fact that Childs's fingerprints were not only all over the loft, but on the murder weapon as well, put Childs in San Francisco no later than Saturday.

Meanwhile, the evidence response techs were hard at work digging up the cellar of the Childs mansion. The corpses, in varying states of decay, were all buried at the same depth, four to six feet, not stacked vertically, but evidently Childs had laid a thin layer of cement over the entire floor of the chamber every time he buried one, either to minimize the odor or disguise the fresh patch. Only four corpses had been uncovered so far, three female, one male, but there were a dozen thin strata of cement. As per Pender's suggestion, Linda asked Thom Davies at the CJIS in Clarksburg to massage the appropriate databases for possible matches between missing persons and found bodies.

She also asked Thom to have copies of all reports of new so-called "stranger" homicides (assailant believed to have been unknown to the victim) received by the NCIC (National Crime Information Center) forwarded to her as they came in. Any patterns, or any correspondence of victims to names or locations that had or would come up in the Childs investigation, would not go unnoticed for long.

Something else hadn't gone unnoticed by Linda:

all this, all she had done, all she was doing, she could do from her office chair. And all across the country, she knew, there were FBI agents performing jobs no more physically demanding than this. The only difference was that they were special agents and she was an investigative specialist. It shouldn't have mattered to her, of course, but somehow it did. The proudest day of her life had been the day she earned the right to call herself Special Agent Abruzzi. You shouldn't take something like that away from somebody without an awful good reason, thought Linda.

She didn't have much time to brood, though. At the crack of noon—opening of business on the West Coast—Linda initiated contact with the venerable San Francisco law firm of Bobbeck, Pflueger, and Morrison, which had been administering the Childs Trust since the death of Marcus Childs, Simon's grandfather, in 1963. One switchboard operator, two secretaries, and a paralegal later, she found herself speaking with an actual Pflueger, Hearst Pflueger IV, Esq., who was, he told her during a surprisingly pleasant conversation, the third of his line to grace the firm's letterhead. She had been prepared for a lot more resistance, but when she told him why she was calling, and what she was looking for, Pflueger was unexpectedly forthcoming, for a big-shot attorney.

He'd been expecting a call ever since he'd read the newspaper Saturday morning, he told her. "I wish I could say I was more surprised, but my father, who was Marcus Childs's personal attorney, always said there was more to the old man's death than met the eye."

"That would have been Hearst Pflueger the third?"

"Trey—everybody called him Trey. He thought there was something *off* about the grandson—unsound, I believe was the word he used."

"Have you ever met Simon personally?"

"I did. I was fresh out of law school—"

"Which one?"

"Boalt, of course."

"I went to Fordham." Might as well establish a little common ground, let him know she was a lawyer, too.

"Yes, I thought I detected a New York accent in there somewhere. As I was saying, I was fresh out of Boalt, just passed the bar, Trey put me in charge of the trust. Basically, I controlled Simon's money from 1967 until 1969, when he turned twenty-one, and during that period he must have called me at least every six weeks asking me to release funds above and beyond his monthly allowance, which was considerable.

"He even showed up at the office a few times, obviously under the influence of drugs—our interactions were not at all pleasant, Agent Abruzzi. He used to refer to me as—forgive me—fuckface. Whenever somebody called the switchboard and asked for Mr. Fuckface, the switchboard operator always put him straight through."

"The fact that you're alive and talking to me now, Mr. Fuh— Oh, God."

"Quite all right."

"I'll try that again. The fact that you're alive and talking to me now, Mr. *Pflueger,* tells me they could have been a whole lot more unpleasant. How long will it take you to get those records to me?"

"I'll make you a deal. As an attorney yourself, you

understand I can't just release a client's confidential documents. What I *can* do, though, is have my people dig out the old files and start Xeroxing them while your people obtain a subpoena for them. We won't contest it—as soon as the subpoena arrives, I'll have the files overnighted to you."

"Thank you so much, Mr. Pflueger."

"I'm on the board of the San Francisco Symphony, Agent Abruzzi. You can thank me by catching that monster before he kills any more promising young cellists."

"We're doing our best, sir."

"I know you are."

The mail arrived while Linda was on the phone asking Eddie Erickson, the case agent in San Francisco, to obtain the subpoena for the Childs Trust files. Along with a manila envelope from the Fresno Police Department, there was a box containing a videotape from the Las Vegas PD.

Instead of going down to the DOJ-AOB cafeteria for lunch, Linda ate at her desk while running, reversing, rerunning, and rereversing an edited dub of a grainy, jerky, stop-motion security video showing two men getting into an elevator at 23:57 hours on 04/11/99.

Simon Childs and Carl Polander, of course, in the lobby of the Olde Chicago Hotel and Casino, where the PWSPD convention had taken place. Sunday night—the convention was over, most of the attendees had checked out and gone home. Linda, who'd only seen Childs's DMV photo, couldn't take her eyes off him. Sitting at her desk, using the remote to oper-

ate the VCR in the corner of the room, she watched
the loop over and over, until his slouching posture,
his air of calm self-assurance, the way he smoothed
his palm across his widow's peak as he stepped into
the elevator (probably caught a glimpse of himself in
one of those convex elevator mirrors), was part of her,
as familiar as her dad's sore-footed butcher's walk or
the little moue her mom made into the mirror when
she was putting on her lipstick.

"That's him, eh?"

Linda looked up, startled—Pool was in the doorway. "That's him." She stopped the tape, rewound it,
switched off the VCR. "Something occurred to me
while I was watching: I'll probably never see him."

"In the flesh, you mean?"

"Yeah. By the time this is over, I'll know more
about that man than I knew about my first boyfriend,
but I'll never actually see him in person," mused
Linda, opening the envelope from the Fresno PD and
placing a stack of color photographs on her desk.

"Unlike that poor gal," said Pool, pointing to the
print on the top of the stack. Taken from a bathroom doorway, it showed a nude woman sitting up
in a bathtub, her heavy breasts lolling to the sides,
her head thrown back so far that her long dark hair
cascaded over the back of the tub; her eyes were
closed and her lips parted in what might have been
ecstasy.

Mara Agajanian, of course—and despite appearances, the picture was not soft-core porn, but evidence, as the rest of the photos (the pink-tinged
water, the close-ups of the slashed wrists) made clear.
But as she shuffled through them, Linda kept coming

back to that first one. It was the old *what's-wrong-with-this-picture?* game—she got it on the third pass.

"Look at that," she said to Pool, pointing to the long dark spill of hair draped over the back of the tub. "Wouldja look at that."

Pool, to her credit, got it right away. "He brushed her hair," she said. "The s.o.b. brushed her hair."

7

Say this about the upper Midwest: they had some terrific classical music stations. Nebraska, Iowa, Minnesota—as one station faded out, another would kick in down at the bottom of the dial where public radio lived. And not just the usual suspects either, Vivaldi, Mozart, the three Bs, but a smorgasbord of off-brand baroque composers, the Albinonis and Stradellas and Guerrieris of the world. It was a musical education for Simon—as he drove, he kept making mental notes of CDs he'd be wanting to order for his collection, next time he was on-line.

Except, of course, that he didn't have a computer any longer—or a CD collection, or an address. It was a strange dual state of mind Simon found himself in, as the Volvo rolled across the great iron bridge spanning the Mississippi above La Crosse. He was an intelligent man, and as Sid Dolitz had pointed out to Pender only five days earlier, his *manie* was decidedly *sans délire:* on one level, he understood that life as he'd known it was over. He was a fugitive now, condemned to a short, harried existence and a violent end, either at his own hands or those of law enforcement.

But on another, deeper level, down where the personality takes root, Simon's grandiose sense of himself, the preternatural confidence of the psychopath, and the inability to empathize with others (Missy didn't count, Sid would have said; psychologically, pathologically, to Simon she was not an *other*, but an extension of his *self*) or to appreciate that others lived on the same plane of consciousness as himself, with the same interior life, all combined to render Simon constitutionally incapable of imagining the universe continuing after his death. In this regard, for all his intelligence and awareness, Simon was like an infant, unable to establish any boundaries between itself and the outside world, to say this is where I end and the world begins. Simon was the universe and the universe was Simon, unable to comprehend the inevitability of its own nonexistence.

And yet here he was, hurtling toward a certain bloody death.

Instinctively, without being consciously aware of the problem, Simon knew the solution: purpose, focus, concentration. Whenever he found his thoughts drifting as he drove (and he'd been driving since 6 A.M.), whenever the riotous autumn colors, the lush music, or the elemental joy of highway speed failed to hold his interest, he turned his thoughts to Pender.

Pender, who was responsible for Missy's death. Pender, who was responsible for Simon's own exile. Pender, Pender, Pender: Simon kept the image of that bald, scarred melon of a head, those ridiculous clothes, that fatuous grin, in front of him always as a lodestar. Every mile he put behind him, he told himself, brought him another five thousand two hundred and eighty feet closer to wiping the smirk right off that fat face, and replacing the dull, self-satisfied expression with one of pure, sweet fear.

8

"Don't move," called Dorie when Pender opened his eyes.

"Why not?" He'd been dozing on a picnic blanket spread out under a wind-sculpted cypress tree at Lovers Point while Dorie painted; now he opened the other eye and saw that she'd moved back another fifteen yards or so and had swung her chair and easel around to face him.

"You're in the picture now."

"Wait." Pender, feeling the breeze on his scalp, assumed his beret must have slipped off. He started to look around for it. Dorie called to him not to move again. "But my hat, I need my—"

"It's over here." She was seated behind and slightly to the right of her easel, glancing back and forth between subject and canvas, painting rapidly with her left hand. Even at this time of day, the light was constantly changing; take too long and you find yourself finishing a different painting than the one you'd started. "I had to take it off."

"What do you mean you 'had to take it off'?"

"The brown just bled. Into the tree trunk. Behind you," she called between brushstrokes. "I needed the splash. Of pink. For the composition. Now quit. Fidgeting."

"I want my hat."

"Think of it. As a sacrifice. To art." But much as she hated to interrupt her work, Dorie could sense from the growing tension in the reclining figure that a little TLC oil was going to have to be applied to the subject. She put down her brush and crossed the lush green lawn, knelt on the edge of the blanket. Pender, lying on his left side, his right arm suspended in a clean sling (a trapezoidal patch of white in the painting; another reason why she needed the whitish-pink of the scalp for balance), started to sit up. She touched his shoulder lightly. "Pen, please—this is important to me." Pen was her own private nickname for him; somehow, he just didn't feel like an *Ed* to her. "It's been years since I last tried putting a human figure into one of my paintings."

"The mask thing?"

She nodded. "The faces—I couldn't finish a face and I couldn't leave one blank."

"Well, you picked a hell of a one to start with."

"It's only this big." She held her thumb and forefinger about a quarter of an inch apart. "Please, Pen? I'll make it up to you, I promise."

And after a brief, whispered lovers' conference, during which they discussed just *how* she might make it up to him, Dorie returned triumphantly to her easel and Pender to his nap. When she'd finished, she packed up her gear, crossed the green again, slipped his beret over his scarred scalp, and lay down next to him.

"When do you have to be back in Washington?" Much as she treasured both her independence and her privacy, with Simon still on the loose Dorie wasn't exactly looking forward to sleeping alone again.

"I have a meeting with my ghostwriter on Friday. I'm supposed to be taping my memoirs for him. Funny little guy named Bellcock—you'd like him. He says he's cowritten so many books his friends think his first name is As Told To. He loaned me a Dictaphone, told me just start talking, tape is cheap, he'll sort it out later. Then he said don't censor myself, he's heard it all. And I'm thinking, my friend, you have no idea." Pender shook his head sharply, as if to clear it of a quarter century of serial killers—the rippers, ghouls, collectors, and necrophiles that comprised his *all*.

"So Thursday?" asked Dorie, nestling close against him.

"At the latest. Abruzzi could probably use a helping hand, too." He slipped his good arm under her head for a pillow, and they lay together listening to the raucous seagulls, the barking seals, the waves breaking gently against the rocks at the tip of the point. "I could sure get used to this, though," he added after a few minutes.

Oh, *do,* thought Dorie.

"Say, you want to come with?" Pender asked her casually, as if the idea had just occurred to him. He'd been thinking about it for a while, though—with Childs still at large, he wasn't real thrilled about the prospect of leaving Dorie alone.

"You mean, like, come home with you? To Washington?"

"Maryland, actually. Just for a little while—at least until Childs is behind bars."

"You don't think—"

Pender quickly backtracked. "No, no. Of course not—there's no reason to think he'd be coming back for you. He's not that stupid. I just thought you might enjoy a little vacation. I could show you around, you could do some painting."

"No can do." Dorie was tempted—but there was no sense getting all worked up over an impossibility.

"Why not?"

"Aviophobia."

"What's that?"

"Fear of flying."

"Maybe it's time to deal with it."

Dorie sat up, annoyed. "What are you, my shrink now?"

"No," replied Pender. "But I know enough about fear to know that it makes a useful servant and a lousy master."

"Oh, swell," muttered Dorie. "First he's a shrink, now he's Yoda."

"Think it over, scout. Do me a favor, just think it over. I'll be there holding your hand every inch of the way."

"It's not just the fear of flying," Dorie temporized—phobics were good at temporizing. "I have too much work to do here—I have to get another half-dozen paintings done in time for my show."

"Why, that's perfect, then. The trees around Tinsman's Lock are a knockout this time of year. Box elder, white ash, sugar maple, sycamore, hickory, elm—I bet you'd have to buy a whole new box of crayons."

"Hey, Pender."

"What?"

"Give it a break, would you?"

"You bet," said Pender, making a mental note to pick up a ticket for Dorie when he called for reservations. He had a first-class ticket to turn in—it would more than cover two coach fares.

9

Scarlet fever, thought Ida, the moment she clapped eyes on Arthur Bellcock. You didn't spend thirty years as a small-town GP's wife without learning to recognize a scarlet fever victim.

"Mrs. Day?"

"Mr. Bellcock—come in."

Bellcock had arrived around six, an hour earlier than scheduled. No problem, though: on Monday there was still plenty of meat left on the widow bird she had just taken out of the refrigerator (a *widow bird* was the local name for a chicken a single woman would roast on Sunday for a whole week's worth of suppers), so she invited him for supper.

She wasn't sure what to expect, having never met a ghostwriter before, but for some reason she'd been picturing a little guy with glasses and a tape recorder, and was therefore unprepared to find this tall, rather creepy looking, entirely hairless fellow with the arrogant slouch and the hypnotic eyes standing empty-handed on her doorstep.

But Ida Day was not one to judge a man by his appearance—Walt had been no Ronald Colman, either. And once he turned the charm on, Arthur Bellcock made it easy to forget his looks. He complimented her cooking, he flattered her about her appearance—if she'd been ten years younger or he'd been ten years older, she might even have suspected that he was making a pass at her.

After supper, though, when they retired to the parlor and the talk turned to Eddie, Bellcock was all business, jotting down her answers in a little spiral-bound pocket notebook. But again he surprised her—the questions weren't at all what she'd been expecting. He seemed to be less interested in facts than in generalities. What was Eddie like as a boy? What were his interests, his likes and dislikes, his favorite and least favorite pastimes? He appeared to be leading up to something, but to save herself, Ida couldn't figure out what.

"As I told you on the phone yesterday, Mr. Bellcock," she explained, bending over the brick hearth to light the fire, "I left Cortland when Eddie was only ten, so I never got to know him as well as I'd have liked to."

"When was the last time you spoke with your brother?" said Bellcock, leaning back, draping his long arms over the back of the sofa, his pose of studied casualness betrayed only by a nervous twitch in his left thigh that set his heel to tapping.

"A few weeks ago—when he called me about you."
Your motor's running, Ida wanted to tell him—that's
what Walt always said to Stan, whose leg also used to
vibrate annoyingly like that when he was anxious or
excited.

Almost there, thought Simon. But before he asked
the only question that really mattered, he had to find
out for sure whether she knew anything about
Pender's recent exploits. If, say, she'd been following
the case in the news, a direct question about fear
would be bound to arouse her suspicions—he'd have
to find a way to fit the question within that context.
"I've been out of touch for a few weeks. Any idea what
Ed's working on lately?"

"Now that he's retired, you mean? His golf game, I
should imagine—he told me he and his friend Sid
were going to be flying out to California. He was all
excited about playing Pebble Beach, as I recall."

"Right, right." Retired! That's why Pender never
pulled a gun on me, thought Simon—because he
didn't have one. If Pender was retired, though, then
what was he doing nosing around Carmel? And what
had Dorie told him that sent him to Berkeley? And
what, for that matter, did it say about Simon, that he
had allowed his life (and Missy's—don't forget about
Missy) to be destroyed by some retired old poop.

But never mind all that now, Simon told himself,
tamping down his growing rage as best he could.
Those were all peripheral issues; the time had come
to get down to the meat of the matter. He flipped
through the pages of his notebook, pretending to
have lost his place.

"Let's see now, where were we? Likes, dislikes, favorite sport, blah blah blah, first girlfriend . . . Oh, yes, here we are. Next question is: Did Eddie have any phobias when he was a boy?"

"Phobias?"

"Yes—was there anything in particular that he feared?"

"I know what the word means, Mr. Bellcock—I was trying to remember. There *was* an episode, when Eddie was . . . let's see, I was in my senior year at Ithaca when our mom called and told me to come right home . . . so Eddie would have been around eight or nine. He and his friend were fooling around with firecrackers. They dropped one down our chimney to see what would happen—it blew up in Eddie's face. It was touch and go for a couple of weeks whether he'd even regain his sight."

"Firecrackers, then?" asked Simon, cutting to the chase. "He's afraid of firecrackers?"

"No, no," said Ida. "Blindness. Terrified of it. As a boy, you could never get him to play pin the tail on the donkey. And as an adult . . . Let's see, it was Stanley's birthday, Eddie had just graduated from FBI Academy, so it must have been 1972, we had a piñata, and Eddie absolutely refused to put on the blindfold, even after Stanley begged him. And Eddie adored Stanley—he'd have done anything for him."

But although Arthur Bellcock was busily scribbling in his notebook, Simon Childs was no longer paying any attention. Blindness, is it? he thought. That's a good one, that's a juicy one—we can make a game out of that, Eddie-boy; we can definitely make a game out of that one.

And with that out of the way, there was only one more question remaining to be asked: "Just out of curiosity, Mrs. Day, as long as we're on the subject—is there anything in particular that *you're* afraid of?"

"There was," said Ida, putting the emphasis on the past tense. And then, probably because Mr. Bellcock was such an extraordinary listener, hanging on her every word, his lips parted and his strangely naked eyes aglow with the reflected light from the fire, Ida found herself telling him what it was—or rather, what it had been.

IX

Micrurus Fulvius Fulvius

1

The wooded hillside below Pender's house sloped down to a narrow strip of lawn abutting the eastern bank of the C&O; a tall windbreak of mixed white ash, box elder, hawthorne, sycamore, and sugar maple lined the towpath along the western bank. From the porch, Linda saw the broad silver ribbon of the Potomac winding lazily in the distance through the Froot-Loopy autumn countryside.

She also saw her breath. Enjoy the view while you can, Linda told herself—in a few weeks those trees will all be bare.

Linda glanced at her watch—6:30—washed down a handful of vitamins with the dregs of her breakfast smoothie, grabbed her cane, and pushed herself up from her chair. Then it was heigh-ho, heigh-ho, down the River Road we go, to the DOJ-AOB in suburban Virginia, where she received a familiar howdy from the gate guard, who examined the backseat, trunk, and undercarriage of the Geo anyway. The daily security code for the underground garage was 1220, which also happened to be her mom's birthday; Linda told herself that meant it would be a lucky day for her.

It was a busy one, at any rate. Two more corpses—well, skeletons—had been unearthed in Simon Childs's basement, so Linda spent the entire morning reviewing the missing persons printouts for the western states that Thom Davies had culled from the NCIC database over the weekend. Some went back as far as 1968. Where there seemed to be at least a possibility of a match, Linda would fax the preliminary forensic data to the appropriate local authorities.

Around one o'clock, the eleven cartons of records arrived from Bobbeck, Pflueger, and Morrison—Mr. Pflueger had been as good as his word. She enlisted Pool's help in cataloguing the contents, which took most of the afternoon. *What'd you do in the FBI, Mommy?* she imagined her kids asking her someday in the distant future. *Darlings, I shuffled paper like nobody's business.*

Then she remembered that she wasn't going to be having any kids—or, most likely, any distant future. And although the realization wasn't exactly news, it did rattle her a little, sucker punching her like that. Too bad, so sad, get over it, she ordered herself, and went back to her paper shuffling.

2

With amphetamines, there comes a point where a dosage sufficient to keep you awake is also large enough to cause optical field disturbances similar to hallucinations. Flashing lights in the periphery of your vision, trails and prismatic distortions—you don't see things that aren't there, but you *almost* see things that weren't there a second ago, and aren't there when you look again.

Simon reached that point late Tuesday afternoon. He'd fled La Farge profoundly shaken by how deeply the old woman had gotten under his skin, and though he'd driven blindly through the night and into the dawn, he couldn't seem to drive fast enough or far enough to get her out of his mind—the fond look in her eyes when she told him about her Down child, her Stanley; the sincere anger in her voice when she recounted how the doctors had told her the best thing she could do for all of them, Stanley, her husband, and herself, was put the child away in an institution before they all got too used to each other; the shame when she told him how close she'd come to listening to them.

"They wouldn't let me breast-feed him—they told me I'd get too attached. When he was three weeks old, we put him in his little basket and drove him to the state home down by Madison. The papers were signed—all I had to do was turn around and walk away, but do you know what, Mr. Bellcock? It was as if my legs had turned to stone. To this day—to this *day,* Mr. Bellcock, I still can't understand how any mother could do it, *physically* do it, is what I mean, walk away and leave her baby behind."

There's an old woman in Atlantic City I'd like to ask that same question, thought Simon. And suddenly, although he couldn't have put a name to the disquieting sensation welling up inside him—it was a strange amalgam of self-pity and empathy—he realized he couldn't stand to hear much more about how it felt to be Ida Day in particular, or a mother in general, or how it felt to be anybody else at all other than Simon Childs. All *he'd* ever asked her about, he told himself, all *he'd* ever wanted to know was what she was afraid of, so they could get on with the game.

The irony of the situation was that when she finally got around to telling him, it only made things worse. Simon had known, of course, that there were other Down children in the world, tens of thousands of them, and if he'd bothered to think about it, he'd have understood that their parents had some of the same problems that he'd had, loco-parenting Missy—and probably with a lot fewer resources. But it wasn't until Ida turned from the mantelpiece holding a photograph of Stanley in a filigreed silver frame, and told him how every night for the three years between Walt's death and Stanley's, she had lain awake in terror at the thought of dying first, of leaving Stanley behind, helpless, alone, afraid, that she really started getting under his skin.

Because every time she said "Stanley," he heard *Missy,* and the nameless, unfamiliar, disquieting sensation worsened; when she told him how sometimes she even thought about using the revolver in her dresser drawer on both of them if her health started to fail, Simon could scarcely bear it. He fled La Farge at midnight, needing a game more desperately than he had when he'd arrived; by the time he finally pulled off the interstate somewhere in the middle of Pennsylvania on Tuesday afternoon, to look for a motel before he drove the Volvo off the road while swerving to avoid something that wasn't there, the need had turned to a craving.

Yes, and people in hell crave ice water, as Grandfather Childs was fond of saying. Simon should have remembered that when he saw the sign for *Graham Graham's Reptilarium, Route 15, Allenwood* at the bottom of the off-ramp and was immediately reminded of the ophidiophobe who called herself (or himself, though the majority of ophidiophobes were female) Skairdykat, the last fruit of the PWSPD tree. According to Zap Strum's information, Skairdy lived in George-town, which was not far from Pender's home in Maryland. He should also have remembered what Grandfather sometimes used to add: if those folks in hell ever get their ice water, they usually find the devil has salted it first.

Graham Graham's Reptilarium! Simon, whose inter-est in snakes went back to his boyhood pet Skinny and whose subsequent hobby had involved him with ophidiophobes more than once (it was one of the most common specific phobias), had often seen Graham on television and had wanted to visit the place for years, but it wasn't until this afternoon that fate had brought him anywhere near Allenwood, Pennsylvania.

The reptilarium looked fairly crummy from the

outside—it shared a strip mall with a hoagie shop—
but once inside, Simon was not disappointed.
Mambas, cobras, pythons, vipers, a twelve-foot gator,
giant tortoises, exotic frogs and lizards—Simon even
saw Graham Graham himself, in safari khakis, leading
a group of schoolchildren on a tour. In other circumstances, he told himself, he'd have liked to shake the
man's hand, buy him a drink, talk reptiles. But it
would have been indiscreet—after all, Simon *was*
planning to rip the place off right after closing.

3

"Who was it said, beware of any venture that requires
new clothes?" Pender wanted to know. Dorie had
half-dragged him to Khaki's, an upscale men's cloth-
ier in Carmel's Barnyard shopping center.

"It wasn't a woman, I'll tell you that," she replied.
The only clothes he had were the ones he'd packed in
his carry-on for what was supposed to have been a
two-day trip. If she saw that yellow Ban Lon shirt one
more time, she'd announced Tuesday morning, she
was going to upchuck.

Her choice of emporiums backfired on her, though.
Khaki's advertised itself as a classy, post-preppy kind
of store, but Pender had made a beeline for a rack of
Hawaiian shirts and picked out a couple of doozies; he
was trying on Panama hats when his cell phone began
chirping.

Weird, thought Dorie, watching Pender as he wandered over to the doorway of the shop for better reception. She'd never fallen for a homely man before—it took some getting used to. Not in bed, oddly enough—she was surprised to learn how little looks seemed to matter when you were making love—but in broad daylight those eyes, under that scarred expanse of scalp, seemed much too small, and that putty nose and those LBJ ears much too big; only the full-lipped mouth was just about right, but somehow when it broke into that easy grin, it made the rest of the face seem just about right, too.

Still, she couldn't help comparing him to Rafael, her Big Sur carpenter. Walk into a joint on Rafe's arm, and you could sense every other woman in the place curling up with jealousy like the wicked witch's toes after the ruby slippers were removed. And when Rafe was working, with his muscles rippling beneath his sweat-stained T-shirt like Brando's in *Streetcar* and the heavy suede carpenter's toolbelt slung diagonally athwart his narrow hips—

"Hey, Dorie!" Pender waved her over, his hand covering the mouthpiece of the phone. "Have you ever heard of a shrink named Luka—Janos Luka?"

"Janos Luka? Sure, who hasn't?"

"Me and Abruzzi, for two."

"He's a famous gestalt therapist—he worked with Perls and Maslow, all those guys. He must be about a million years old by now—he still runs the Lethe Institute, down in Big Sur. Why?"

"Apparently he was Simon Childs's psychiatrist at one time." Then, into the phone again: "Linda? Yes, Dorie knows him."

"Hey! I didn't say I—"

Pender put a forefinger to his lips, gave Dorie a wink. "Yeah, he's an old friend of hers. She says he's pretty reclusive, though—maybe you ought to let us make the first contact. . . . Right, right, somebody from the resident agency should definitely do the interview itself. . . . Of course I will. . . . Okay, talk to you later."

"What was that all about?" asked Dorie.

"Just a little Bureau-cratic gamesmanship. How long a drive is it?"

"How long a drive is what?"

"From here to Big Sur," said Pender—and here came that grin again, lighting up his whole face, chasing away all the ugly.

4

Linda Abruzzi was no fool—she understood that Pender's promise to have somebody from the FBI's resident agency in Monterey conduct the formal interview with Dr. Luka was probably bogus. But if the priority here was catching Childs, then having a Bureau legend like E. L. Pender doing your background interviews was like having Derek Jeter for a pinch hitter: you'd be a fool if you *didn't* bring him off the bench. And as a law school graduate, Linda was quite familiar with the concept of plausible deniability—as was Deputy Director Steven P. McDougal, she was reasonably certain.

Besides, Linda had other fish to fry. In the same carton as the medical records—actually just the bills—she had found both Simon's and Melissa's birth certificates, so as soon as she got off the phone with Pender, she called Thom Davies and asked him to perform a little of his database wizardry.

A few minutes later, as she was lifting the latest forensic report from Berkeley off the fax tray—middle-aged female with a titanium screw in the left femur, a type of screw that had only been in use since 1992, the medical examiner had assured Linda—Davies called back to report that Simon Childs's long lost mother was lost no longer.

"Good work," Linda told him.

"Piece of piss," said the expat Brit. "According to social security records, she's been living at the same address in Atlantic City for over fifteen years. If you consider four hundred and fifty dollars a month living, that is."

"Kimberly Rosen would," said Linda grimly, glancing up to the two photographs from the Chicago PD she'd posted on her victims' bulletin board. The first was a perky three-quarter head shot of Kim from the New Trier yearbook, class of '95; the second was a full-face shot from the Cook County morgue, class of '99.

"Hello?"

"Hello, Miss Delamour?"

"Not *Dela*more, it's Dela-*moor, comme le français.*"

"Sorry, Miss Dela-*moor.*"

"*Aah,* call me Rosie, ever'body else does."

Plastered, Linda told herself—four o'clock in the afternoon and she's plastered. Interviewing drunks was like fishing—you let them ramble a bit, then you reel them in, let them ramble, reel them in. "Rosie, I'm calling about your son."

"Got no son." The way she said it, though, it was less a denial than it was a renunciation. "Tried to explain, he didn't wanna hear."

"Explain what, Rosie?"

"Why."

"Because I'm trying to get in touch with him."

"No, why—explain why. Why I left."

Oh, swell, thought Linda: it's turning into an Abbott and Costello routine. "When was this, Rosie?"

"Too late. It was too late. Guess I waited too long. To call."

Linda tried again—this could be the break they were looking for. "Rosie, I need to know when you last spoke to Simon." Elementary psycholinguistics: "I" statements often elicited responses where questions failed.

"I dunno, this year, last year—no, wait, I remember. It was February—February fourth. Missy's birthday. He wouldn't lemme . . . said it would only . . . wouldn't lemme . . ."

Not recent, then, thought Linda, as Rosie began sobbing on the other end of the line—so much for our big break. "February fourth of this year?"

A drawn-out, drunken wail that under other circumstances might have been almost farcical, followed by an extended silence broken by the clink of ice in a thin-walled glass. "Rosie?"

"Who is this?"

"Linda Abruzzi." Linda decided not to identify herself as an FBI agent just yet—she didn't want to

arouse any maternal protective instincts. "I'm trying
to get hold of Simon—it's very important."

"S'matter, he knock you up or something?"

"No, I—"

"Listen, Bootsie honey, I haven't seen my children
since nineteen fifty-one. That's, uh— That's almost—
That's a helluva long time. He don't know where I
am, and if he ain't home, I don't know where he is. So
unless you get some kind of weird kick out of making
old ladies cry, why don't you let me get back to my
shows and I'll let you get back to whatever you were
doing."

"Rosie, there's something you should—"

Click. Linda redialed, but the phone was now off
the hook. Fuck it, she thought, putting down the
phone and picking up the fax from the medical examiner in Berkeley again. Let somebody else tell Rosie
her daughter's dead and her son's a monster—there
must be people who get paid for that.

5

Simon hid in a utility closet off the snake exhibit area
until the last employee had left the reptilarium a little
after seven-thirty. When he emerged with his pencil
flashlight (the Volvo, having belonged to Nelson, was
well-stocked with flashlights, flares, and even a first-
aid kit), the snake room was pitch-dark save for the
red glow of the exit lights over the doors.

The glass fronts of the snake cages were set flush into a curved wall ringed by a sloping carpeted ramp from which the public could view the snakes in safety. Simon circled the ramp all the way around to the back, until he reached the door marked *Staff Only—No Public Access,* which led, he had learned that afternoon, to the workroom in the center of the circle of cages. It was locked, but a hard kick sprang it; a moment later Simon found himself inside the workroom, surrounded by cages containing a veritable who's who of the world's most venomous snakes.

The flashlight beam darted around the circular walls. Here a black mamba (which was actually kind of gray), there a spitting viper, a hooded cobra, an eight-foot python, a Florida cottonmouth, a Texas diamondback rattler. He hadn't come for any of these, though. The mambas were too fast and agile, the rattlers too noisy, the cobras, cottonmouths, and vipers too venomous, and the constrictors not venomous at all.

No, what Simon had come for was the humble eastern coral snake, *Micrurus fulvius fulvius,* a red-, yellow-, and black-banded member of the Elapidae family, which, with its small mouth, short fangs, and delayed-action, borderline-lethal neurotoxic venom, was perfect for his purposes. Even better, for educational reasons, the three coral snakes were housed with members of various mimic species—nonvenomous, look-alike milk snakes, scarlet snakes, and scarlet king snakes. Surely the reptilarium staff wouldn't miss just one coral and one scarlet king out of that whole tangle.

Simon grabbed a leather gauntlet and a snake hook, which was basically a golf club with a hook on the business end instead of a club head, and dragged a plastic garbage can over to the cage. Carefully he opened the trapdoor in the back, and holding the flashlight in his mouth, the garbage can lid in his bare hand, and the snake hook in the gloved hand, he gingerly extended the hook into the pen and positioned it under the neck of one of the corals, which accommodatingly wrapped itself around the shaft.

This was the most dangerous part of the transfer— for a few seconds, as he lifted the snake-on-a-stick out of the cage, there were only two feet of haft between his gloved hand and the deadly reptile curled around the base of the hook, with nothing at all to prevent it from slithering up the shaft and past the gauntlet, and sinking its stubby fangs into his upper arm. But the coral knew the drill—lazily it unwound itself and dropped into the garbage can. Simon quickly clapped the lid on—*fait accompli.*

Half *accompli,* anyway. The nearest scarlet king snake to the hatch proved equally cooperative; the only danger in this second transfer would have come if the coral had made a break for it when Simon raised the lid to drop the king in. But luckily the coral, having recently been fed, was already fast asleep again, curled peacefully in the bottom of the can, dreaming, no doubt, of fat rats and juicy, slow-moving mice.

6

"We should have called first," Dorie had said repeatedly, from behind the wheel of Pender's rented Toyota—the winding, cliff-hugging, two-lane stretch of Highway 1 between Carmel and Big Sur was definitely not a drive for a one-armed man.

"You should have called first," announced the young neohippie who greeted them at the door of the Lethe Institute Retreat Center of Hot Springs. Behind her, a great empty cathedral of a room—vaulted ceiling, redwood beams, and through a picture-window western wall of rose-tinted glass, nothing but ocean and sky. The smell of incense hung in the air; New Age space Muzak filled the room, where half a dozen figures in white meditation pajamas were either performing yoga exercises or training for jobs as circus contortionists.

"So I've been told." But Pender, who was wearing one of his new hula shirts and his glorious new wide-brimmed white Panama, had learned over the years that it was more difficult for somebody to turn him away from their door than it was for them to refuse him an interview over the phone. And having parked the Toyota at the top of what seemed like a sheer cliff and descended a flagstone path so steep it would have given a Grand Canyon donkey second thoughts, he was not going to be dismissed by some flunky quite so easily. "Why is that, exactly?"

"Because Dr. Luka won't see anybody without an appointment," said the young woman.

"I see. And what's your name?"

"I'm Lakshmi."

"Lakshmi, I need you to do something for me." Linda Abruzzi wasn't the only one who knew psycholinguistics. "I need you to tell Dr. Luka that Special Agent E. L. Pender of the Federal Bureau of Investigation wants to speak with him briefly about a former patient of his, by the name of Simon Childs. We'll wait here," he added—it was all about seizing the initiative.

"Hell of a view," Pender whispered to Dorie, as Lakshmi left the room via a side door.

"Dramatic, anyway," she replied. "But you could paint it with a roller."

Lakshmi reappeared, beckoned from the side door, and led Pender and Dorie down another fearfully steep path to the famous Lethe baths, a series of recessed natural hot tubs carved into the side of the cliff over eons by a mineral spring, and canopied by a great granitic overhang that gave the baths the feel and echo of a shallow cavern or grotto. Alone in the hottest and deepest tub, the one nearest the mouth of the spring, sat the hairiest old man Dorie had ever seen naked, or wanted to—white hair to his shoulders, bushy Santa beard, and the matted white pelt covering his chest and arms would have made a yeti reach for the Nair.

"Come on in, the water's fine." His accent was a strange hybrid of hip and cultured, of Berkeley and Budapest.

Pender shrugged, pointed to his cast, and sat down on a backless marble bench, facing the tub, with his back to the ocean. He could hear the surf crashing below; silvery reflections from the light playing off the steaming surface of the baths danced on the shiny granite walls of the cliff like hundreds of manic Tinkerbells.

"And you, dear?"

Dorie shuddered as she sat down beside Pender. "I may never take another bath again."

"Ablutophobia?"

"Simon Childs–ophobia."

"Oh?"

Dorie looked over at Pender, who nodded. He suspected her story would make a more eloquent argument for Luka's cooperation than anything he could say. As she spoke, the damp walls of the shallow cavern gradually took on a pinkish glow from the western sky. When she'd finished, Luka asked Pender to give them a moment alone. Pender walked a few dozen paces up the flagstone path and watched the sun hovering twice its width above the curved horizon—he'd never seen anything as vast as that horizon.

Dorie appeared around a bend in the path. "He wants to talk to you now."

"What did he tell you?"

"He just wanted to make sure I had a good therapist. Said he could give me a couple of names if I needed."

She told Pender she'd wait for him up at the house. Pender retraced his steps. The light back at the baths was now a refulgent primrose pink—it was like being inside a Tiffany lamp.

"Tell me, Agent Pender," said Dr. Luka, "is it FBI policy now to schlep victims around on interviews?"

"No, I—"

"Your relationship with Miss Bell is more of a personal nature then, I take it."

"Yes, we—"

"In that case, let me give you a little professional advice, free of charge: Either Miss Bell has one of the best-integrated psyches in the western world—which her history of severe phobias would tend to argue against—or she's heading for a psychological blowup of Hindenburgian proportions."

"But isn't it possible that it could be kind of, what's the word, *empowering* for her—helping put Childs behind bars?"

"I suppose so—but if she were my patient, and I were thirty years younger, I'd kick your ass down that cliff there. Now, what is it you think I can do for you, Agent Pender?"

"Tell me everything you can about Simon Childs—the more we know, the more likely we'll be able to catch him before anybody else has to go through what Dorie went through. And worse."

"Oh, my, I have been out of touch, haven't I? And when was it, precisely, that the privilege of doctor-patient confidentiality was revoked?"

"Come off it, Doc—you know perfectly well that a physician is not only permitted, but *required* to breach confidentiality when lives are endangered. You can't testify in court without a waiver from Childs, but neither can you withhold information that may help us capture him."

"It's been thirty-five years, Agent Pender, and my memory isn't what it once was."

"Mine either," said Pender. "I can't remember what

I had for breakfast this morning. But I can give you chapter and verse of every case I ever worked, and I'm willing to bet you can, too."

Luka sank down until he was chin deep in the steaming water, with his long white hair fanning out around his head. "Agent Pender, are you familiar with the old joke about the gay man who tells his friend that his mother made him a homosexual?"

" 'If I buy her the yarn, will she make me one, too?' "

"Precisely. And Simon Childs's mother and grand-father couldn't have done a better job of making a counterphobic phobic if they'd knitted one from a pattern. The way Simon tells it—or at least the way he told me, back in 1963 (I remember the year, because it was right around the time my friend Jack Kennedy was assassinated)—he was already suffering from multiple specific phobias by the time he and his sister were abandoned by their mother at their paternal grandfather's proverbial doorstep after their father died—drowned drunk after driving his car into the bay, if I remember correctly.

"First and foremost, understandably enough, little Simon was afraid of drowning. So his grandfather took it upon himself to cure him of his weakness by beating him, holding his head under water, then alter-nating beatings and dunkings, until Simon had learned to master his terror. Next came fear of the dark, which the grandfather cured by beating him, then locking him in the basement, then beating him some more. After nyctophobia, however, came cyno-phobia, the fear of dogs (specifically, his grandfather's two attack-trained Dobermans, as I recall), which the grandfather cured by making him sleep in the kennel—and beating him, of course.

"Subsequent phobias, including the fear of heights, spiders, and mirrors, were cured along similar homeopathic principles, until by the time he reached puberty, Simon told me, he wasn't afraid of anything. He was equally in denial about his feelings toward his sister, whom his grandfather obviously adored—or indulged, at any rate. But Simon had so internalized his sibling rivalry that he had, in a sense, internalized his sister. It's a syndrome that's seen more often with identical twins—not at all healthy, needless to say."

"Is that why he was in therapy?"

"No—apparently he and a neighbor boy had been caught in flagrante, so to speak, by the grandfather. According to Simon, the two boys had formed something they called the Horror Club. Obviously it was related to the entire gestalt of Simon's polyphobia and compensatory counterphobia. The boys used to watch horror movies on late-night television, then masturbate together. Of all the reasons for Simon Childs to go into treatment, this adolescent experimentation with homosexuality was about the least important. Except of course to the grandfather. Who killed himself a few weeks after Simon began therapy—I never saw young Childs again after that."

"Do you happen to remember the other boy's name? From the Horror Club?"

"I'm afraid not—why?"

"Childs has probably gone to ground somewhere in the Bay Area. We want to cover all the bases."

"All I can tell you is that his family lived next door to the Childs house in the autumn of 1963, and . . .

No, wait—it's coming to me. Simon called him—there's an expression for a timid soul . . . nervous something? Nervous Norman?"

"Nervous Nellie."

"Yes, that's it—Nervous Nellie. Short for Nelson, if memory serves."

"I don't suppose you have a last name for me?"

The old psychiatrist sighed. "Now I know how Jesus felt. The more miracles you perform, the more they want."

7

For the first Tuesday evening in nearly a month, Jim and Gloria Gee had their house, and equally important, their computer, to themselves.

Inviting her old college roommate to stay with them had been a mistake—Gloria admitted that freely. (Gloria and Linda had roomed together as undergraduates at Stony Brook, before going on to different law schools, Linda to Fordham, Gloria to Georgetown.) But by the time the Gees realized how much the sessions of the Swingin' Tuesdays Club had come to mean to them, Linda was already installed in the spare room. Although they considered themselves quite the liberated couple—flat-out wild, by Chinese-American standards—neither of them felt liberated enough to participate in a cyber-orgy with Linda just down the hall.

So this evening, they were eager to make up for lost time. Gloria, an attorney for a consortium of Taiwanese exporters, was already out of the shower by ten, squeaky clean, oiled and depilated, when Jim, who was well advanced on the partner track at a powerhouse D.C. law firm, arrived with the tabs of Ecstasy he'd picked up from one of the mail-room boys. While they waited in their living room for it to take effect, Gloria brushed the glossy, ass-length black hair that was her pride and joy; Jim, already stripped down to his red bikini briefs, set up the web-cam and logged on to the STC web site.

The session was already well under way. Five of the six segments of the split screen displayed photo-icons of the five couples logged on (including a promising pair of newbies who went by the screen names Hot and Hotter). As the Gees' own photo-icon appeared in the upper left portion of the split screen, the bottom portion of the screen filled with welcoming chatter.

Hi our friends of the mysterious Orient, typed Plumpie, of Piers and Plumpie, the dedicated fiftyish couple who hosted the site—they had to be dedicated: it was three in the morning in Amsterdam. **We missed you**.

We missed you too, typed Gloria, aka Dragon-Girl—for some reason, it always seemed to be the women who did the typing.

How touching, typed the female half of the couple known as Wolfman and Wolfwoman. **Let the games begin**.

Like many other cyber-sexuals, the Gees were a predominantly male-voyeur–female-exhibitionist couple. Gloria was turned on by the presence of the camera and often made love with her eyes closed, while Jim usually kept one eye on the screen, even when he was having an orgasm. Gloria didn't mind— it made her extra hot to think of other men watching Jim making love to her with the same hunger that Jim felt, watching them screwing their wives.

Tonight was good for both of them. Not only had they built up a head of steam during their three-week hiatus, but the new kids were indeed hot and hotter— mixed race, he hung, she stacked. The sense of connection between the two couples was immediate and undeniable; each couple had selected the other's video stream for viewing—it was almost like a private fourway, especially under the influence of the Ecstasy.

Around one in the morning, however, just as two couples, presumably from the West Coast, were logging on to fill the slots vacated by the easterners and Europeans, Jim froze in mid-hump.

"No," Gloria ordered him, thinking he was about to ejaculate prematurely—or at least prematurely as far as she was concerned. "Not yet, I'm not there yet."

"Did you hear that?" he whispered into her ear, shrinking inside her.

"What?"

"I think somebody's breaking in. You call nine-one-one; I'm going to get the gun." He rolled off her, sprang to his feet, stuffed himself back into his red bikini briefs, adjusted his package self-importantly, then dashed out of the living room, bent double in a ridiculous commando crouch.

A moment later he was back with his hands in the air and the front of his trunks flat as a Ken doll;

behind him, a tall skinheaded white man with a long-barreled revolver had stopped in the doorway, out of range of the camera.

"Turn it off," the stranger said quietly.

Gloria, tripping on Ecstasy, dazed by the sudden turn of events, her system flooded with dozens, maybe hundreds, of conflicting hormones and neurotransmitters, was too bewildered to respond at first. On screen, Hot and Hotter were laughing. **Looks like somebody dropped in unexpectedly**, Hotter typed with one finger. Gloria rose, fumbling at her see-through peignoir, and with her eyes trained on the computer screen, she watched herself crossing to the desk in an awkward modesty crouch, covering her breasts with one hand and her crotch with the other. It was disorienting, watching herself cut obliquely across the screen while walking straight ahead, but she couldn't tear her eyes from the screen, or bring herself to switch the computer off once she reached it—it was as if she wanted to see how the show was going to come out.

"I said, turn it off!"

Gloria was still frozen. Jim stumbled into the picture on the computer screen; an instant later he appeared bodily at the edge of her vision, crawling on his hands and knees toward the surge protector strip. There was a popping, staticky sound; the screen flared white, then black; reluctantly, Gloria turned back to the room.

"If you want money . . ." Jim was saying. Having unplugged the computer, he'd climbed out from under the desk and positioned himself in front of Gloria, shielding her with his body as he crossed the living room toward the man, who took one long stride toward him, grabbed his arm, spun him around, and clubbed him over the top of the head with the barrel of the revolver.

"Sorry about that, Skairdykat," said the intruder, stepping over Jim's twitching body. "But you shouldn't have lied about living alone."

8

Stoked on Mexican crosstops and anticipation, Simon had driven straight from Allenwood to Georgetown with only a single stop to gas up and purchase a street guide for the District of Columbia and a cheap canvas travel bag, into which he transferred the snakes. He'd parked the Volvo down on M Street and walked up to Conroy Circle, effecting an entry by the simple expedient of using the leather snake gauntlet to punch through a pane of glass in the back door.

As soon as he had the woman secured—Simon was operating on the assumption that the female was Skairdykat—he went off to explore the premises, with mixed results.

On the one hand, the house was hideously furnished. American Moderne in a neo-Georgian brownstone: oh, *please!* On the other hand Simon was extremely gratified not to find any little Chinese Rugrats tucked into their beddy-byes. In the thirty-odd years he'd been playing the game, it was a point of pride for Simon that he had never harmed or even frightened a child. Tempting as it might have been to taste *that* fruit, Simon had taken his self-imposed stricture to such extremes that the only thing his victims had in common was that they were all childless. Having been deprived of both his parents, he just couldn't bring himself to do that to a kid.

When he returned to the living room, Skairdykat was wriggling around on the chrome and leather couch, rolling her eyes, and making those *mmmff, mmmff* sounds that meant she was ready for him to take the gag out.

"Are you sure?" he asked her, stroking her forehead, smoothing back that glorious head of jet-black hair.

An eager nod.

"Because if I take it off and then you try to scream again, you're going to regret it deeply."

She nodded that she understood. He walked around behind the couch and untied the gag—a terry-cloth bathrobe belt. She spat it out, turned, and followed him with her eyes as he came back around the couch and sat beside her. "Now, is there something you wanted to tell me, Skairdykat?"

"Why do you keep calling me that?"

"Skairdykat? You chose the name, not me."

"I don't . . . Please, I don't—I have no idea what you're talking about. You have to believe me; there's been some kind of mistake."

He held her face lightly by the chin, tilted her head up toward him, looked into her eyes. She was his first Oriental—there was something particularly appealing, almost childlike, about the smooth curve of the upper eyelid. They weren't slanted at all, these brown eyes, but sweetly elliptical, like Missy's. And he could finally see the fear in them, now that the shock and anger had passed. "You're telling the truth, aren't you?"

"Yes."

"I believe you, but I want to run a little test, a little experiment, just to be on the safe side," Simon explained, gagging her again. "I'll be right back."

He stepped over the man's body and strolled down the hall to the back door. He brushed the glittering glass dust off the leather gauntlet, unzipped the canvas travel bag lying next to the getaway satchel, and used the pencil flashlight to peer inside. The snakes were asleep again. Simon recited to himself the mnemonic used to distinguish between the venomous coral and its various look-alikes (*if red touches yellow, it kills a fellow; snout of black, bad for Jack*) as he reached into the bag and grabbed the scarlet king (that was the one with the red snout and the black rings intervening between the red and yellow ones) just behind the head.

When Simon returned to the living room with the scarlet king, he knew within seconds that Skairdykat, or rather, Gloria, had been telling the truth. She was frightened half to death—who wouldn't be?—but she was no ophidiophobe. He couldn't provoke a syncope, or anything resembling a true panic attack, even when he jabbed the king's head directly toward her eyes, though the terrified snake did its part by baring its harmless teeth and flicking its narrow forked tongue out to smell her.

He left the room, returned the king to the travel

bag; the coral glanced up disinterestedly. Simon tip-toed back, stuck his head around the archway. Gloria was staring at the man on the floor. When she saw Simon, she quickly looked away, but it was too late. Simon had followed her glance, seen the smeared blood trail on the carpet, realized that the man was feigning unconsciousness: he had managed to drag himself a few inches closer to the desk, to the tele-phone. Simon wasn't worried—he still had a long way to go. And the poor fellow might even come in hand-ier, awake.

"Is it *him?*" he asked Gloria, sitting down beside her. "Is he the one who's afraid of snakes?"

"Not so far as I know."

He knew she was telling him the truth. Most of them did, once they'd gotten past their resentment and realized that in addition to being the man who was going to kill them, Simon was also the only one who could spare them. He liked this phase of the game.

"Think real hard then, Gloria. Think as if your life depended on it. Is there anyone else who had access to your computer last week?"

She didn't have to say anything—he could read the answer in her eyes. "Who was it, Gloria?" he asked gently.

"Linda."

"Linda who?"

"Linda Abruzzi."

"And who's Linda Abruzzi."

"An FBI agent."

A decoy, then—Skairdykat was only a decoy, Simon realized with a start. Which meant this was all a trap. Was it about to snap shut on him? "You're not, are you?"

"What?"

"An FBI agent."

"No. No, I swear. I swear to God. She was my roommate at college. She was staying with us until she found her own place. I told her—goddammit, God *damn* the bitch, I told her not to—"

Simon cuffed her lightly across the side of the head. "Watch your language."

"I'm sorry."

"You're forgiven." He never felt more magnanimous than when he was totally in control. "Go on."

"Just, I told her not to use the computer. She moved out last Thursday. That's all."

"I bet she left a forwarding address, though, your old roomie?"

Gloria didn't hesitate. "There's a yellow Post-it on the side of the computer hutch."

On his way across the room, Simon stopped briefly to check on the superfluous Mr. Gee; he seemed to be coming around a little. Have to remember to tie that puppy down, thought Simon as he glanced at the address on the Post-it: *"Care of E. L. Pender"* was as far as he got.

"Well, I'll be blessed," he murmured, thunderstruck, as he slipped the yellow square of paper into his trouser pocket.

Not that he needed it—he already had Pender's address on Zap's printout, along with driving instructions Pender had so thoughtfully provided to the invaluable Mr. Bellcock.

9

Okay, so Gloria wasn't Skairdykat—Simon hadn't always restricted himself to pure phobics. But try as he might, he couldn't seem to get the game off the ground—there was something wrong, something missing. Then he spotted the pill bottle on the floor beside the couch, next to the goody box of sex toys and lubricants. The label had been removed from the bottle, which was a red flag for an old doper such as himself, and an *X* drawn on the lid; inside were two hand-milled tablets. Simon knew the code.

"*X* for Ecstasy," he said aloud. "Why, Gloria, you raver, you. And you haven't even offered one to your guest."

"Please—they're yours."

"As are you, Mrs. Gee—as are you."

It was true, however, that without a pure phobic at its center, the game could never be at its best. But Simon, who took another crosstop while waiting for the Ecstasy to kick in, was happy to improvise. When he wasn't able to provoke a satisfactory reaction by threatening Gloria directly, he tried to reach her through her husband, using him as a sort of dress rehearsal for the upcoming game with Pender.

But just about the time things were starting to go purple around the edges from the Ecstasy, Gloria turned away in horror—maybe even disgust. That had given Simon the clue he needed. Her hair alone should have told me, he thought. All the time and trouble it must cost her. A grown woman with hair down to her ass *has* to be vain. And the flip side of vanity is . . . ? Fear of disfigurement. But of course.

In order to get Gloria away from the mess he'd made of her husband, Simon brought her, along with his luggage, up to the second-floor bedroom. Leaving Gloria bound and gagged on the bed, he went into the bathroom to answer nature's call, which, probably due to the speed, turned out to be what Missy used to call a stinky. And the whole time he was in there, Simon found himself unable to shake the feeling that he was not alone.

That kind of paranoia, he told himself, had to stem from an imbalance—too much speed or not enough Ecstasy. So since he couldn't take less speed, he popped the last tablet from the bottle marked *X,* and was at the sink filling the bathroom glass with tap water when he happened to glance up, and suddenly the mystery about not feeling alone was solved.

"It's you," he said to the grim-visaged old man in the mirror.

"It's you," Grandfather Childs replied.

It shouldn't have jarred Simon as badly as it did—after all, he'd been seeing the creepy old face in the mirror for four days now. But not on a double dose of crosstops and phenylethylamine-based psychedelics: this time the entity on the far side of the looking glass seemed to have taken on a life of its own. It wasn't exactly a hallucination, more like the little girl old Senor Wences used to paint on the side of his hand: you knew she wasn't real, but you couldn't help suspending your disbelief anyway.

Simon decided to have some fun with it.

"S'awright," said Simon, just like Senor Wences.

"S'awright," said Grandfather Childs simultaneously.

"Shitfuckpisscuntsuck," said Simon, who never swore.

"Shitfuckpisscuntsuck," said Grandfather Childs, who never swore either.

"You deserved it, you know," said Simon.

"You deserved it, you know," said Grandfather Childs.

"I hate you."

"I hate you."

"I love you."

"I love you."

"You're not capable of love."

"*You're* not capable of love."

"I loved Missy," said Simon.

"*I* loved Missy," said Grandfather Childs. "You k—"

Simon knew what his grandfather was about to say; he snatched up a man's hairbrush from a basket next to the sink and smashed the pewter handle straight into the old man's face, shattering the mirror. "It was *Pender* who killed Missy, and don't you forget it," he said.

"It was Pender who killed Missy, and don't *you* forget it," said Grandfather Childs, though his face lay in shards all over the marble counter.

Upon returning to the bedroom, Simon untied Gloria, sat her down in front of her chromed-steel mirrored vanity, and made her watch as Grandfather Childs began to give the pretty looking-glass Gloria a clumsy haircut. From the way both Glorias shuddered when the scissors bit in, Simon knew he was on the right track. He also knew it wasn't *really* Grandfather Childs in the mirror—Ecstasy didn't cause hallucinations—but he was starting to learn that sometimes it was a whole lot easier to suspend disbelief than it was to *unsuspend* it.

First pass, they only took a few inches off the bottom. Gloria seemed more angry than frightened, and both emotions were blurred by drugs and trauma—but then, she still didn't know where he was going with all this. That was a discovery he wanted her to make on her own; he wanted to see the realization dawning in her eyes before he so much as nicked her. And who knows, he told himself: if her initial reaction proved to be intense enough, pure enough, he might not have to mess up that pretty face at all.

In any event, Simon was aware that the longer he stalled, the better. Once he cut her skin—if indeed he even had to—the race for her soul, the race between fear, shock, and pain, would be under way. So he proceeded slowly on the hair, a few snips here and a few snips there, until at last Gloria was shorn like Ingrid Bergman in *For Whom the Bell Tolls*.

"There you go." He rubbed her scalp affectionately—the black stubble was surprisingly soft, like one of Missy's stuffed animals—and tenderly dabbed away the tears trickling down her cheeks. Or at least, he *felt* affectionate and tender, but when the old man in the mirror did the same for his gal, it looked smirky, and insincere as all get out.

"It'll grow back," Simon whispered, helping Gloria to her feet and leading her over to the bed—to tell the truth, he was getting a little tired of seeing his dead grandfather in the looking glass. "Hair grows back."

Then he'd repeated it, with a slight change of emphasis. *"Hair* grows back."

Still no reaction—so much for subtlety. "As opposed to lips or noses, that is."

Bingo. There was no need to disfigure Gloria beyond a few shallow scratches for effect—Simon soon discovered that he had only to bring the single-edged blade of the box cutter he'd found in a kitchen drawer anywhere near Gloria to provoke the fear he craved.

Once he realized that, all that remained was the fine tuning: finding the perfect rhythm, knowing when to press and how hard, when to back off and for how long, learning when a mere threat or feint would suffice to get her attention and when an actual thrust was required: the game might not be about sex, thought Simon, but when it was good, it was an awful lot like making love—or the way making love was supposed to be, for those who didn't suffer from ejaculatio praecox.

X

Lhermitte's Sign

1

When she found herself feeling kind of punk at breakfast on Wednesday morning, Linda decided to blame it on the Betaseron. Flu-like symptoms were not an uncommon side effect. And if it was more than a Betaseron reaction, if her T-cells *had* decided to go off on another myelin-munching spree, there wasn't much she could do about it anyway. In the multiple sclerosis sweepstakes, Linda Abruzzi had drawn the booby prize. Unlike relapsing-remitting MS, in which the effects of each episode are only temporary, or secondary progressive MS, in which the symptoms are permanent, but which typically doesn't develop until a good fifteen years after the onset of the relapsing-remitting course, in the primary-progressive course of the disease, with which she had been diagnosed, the effects of each attack are permanent from the get-go.

Linda's first episode, nearly six months earlier,

had been presaged by a weird, electric tingling in her lower extremities, followed by near-paralytic weakness in her calves and ankles. Still, she knew she was one of the lucky ones. Thanks to an early diagnosis by her doctor in San Antonio, she had been put on a course of Betaseron almost immediately, and to date had suffered no subsequent attacks. Her vision was good, her mind and memory sharp as ever, her pain was bearable, her fatigue generally surmountable, and now that she had her cane to lean on, she was getting around like shit on a wheel—no sense giving in to the bastard now.

Unless— What if—

She tried to stop her mind from finishing the thought, but it was already formed: What if she had an attack while she was driving? Or in the office, or at lunch? Wouldn't it be better to stay home, make sure of what she was dealing with, rather than risk—

Then it struck her: this was what classic agoraphobia was like, this was what her poor phobics (and she thought of them as hers now, a week and a half into the investigation) went through every day of their lives. It wasn't going out to the market or the mall or the office that they feared, it was having an anxiety attack while they were out there. Isn't it better to stay home than risk public humiliation?

The answer, of course, was no. You said no—*fuck no,* if you were from Linda's neighborhood—and you dragged yourself out into the arena. Because if you said yes, if you gave in to the fear, there would be no going back. The excuse, the cop-out, would be there again tomorrow, and the day after tomorrow, and the day after the day after tomorrow.

* * *

Something else they used to say in Linda's old neighborhood: I shoulda stood in bed. At first, it seemed as if she might as well have, for all the progress being made in the Childs manhunt. Save for one lonely red pin in San Francisco, representing Zap Strum's apartment, the map on the wall was still embarrassingly blank—no valid Childs sightings to date, though a highway patrolman near Flagstaff had chased and braced a gray-haired attorney driving a silver Mercedes convertible with California plates, who had in turn threatened to hit the state of Arizona with a lawsuit so punishing that its unborn children would die broke.

But a few minutes after ten, Pender called from the coast. "You're up early," she told him.

"Your FBI never sleeps, kiddo. I was down in Big Sur yesterday—Dorie and I stopped in to see her old friend Dr. Luka."

"That'd be the Dr. Luka you promised you weren't going to try to interview yourself."

"No interview—just an informal chat." He gave her the gist of it.

"So where does that leave us?" she asked, when he had finished.

"With a first name and an approximate address for the year 1963. How would you go about nailing that down a little more concretely?"

Swell, a pop quiz. "I guess I'd have somebody check the property records. City of Berkeley or Alameda County."

"That'll give you the owner's name. Nelson was a kid."

"Call me a dreamer, Ed, but I'm guessing he'll have the same last name as his parents."

"Good point. But if you do run into trouble—"

"I'm not a *total* rookie, Chief. In the words of one of my favorite T-shirts, 'quit yanking my ears,' I know what I'm doing."

Pender laughed.

"Call me on my cell when you've got it—I'm going back to bed."

"I thought my FBI never sleeps."

"Who said anything about sleeping?"

2

Drained, energized, empty, full of himself—Simon never knew how he was going to feel after a game.

This morning it was all of the above, plus a polypharmaceutical hangover. He awoke alone in Gloria's shiny bed—the headboard was constructed of stacked, polished aluminum rails—after an hour or two of sleep so unrestful that it was only the act of awakening that told him he'd been asleep in the first place. The satin pillowcase next to him was spattered with blood; when he rolled onto his back, he saw Grandfather Childs staring down at him from the mirror on the ceiling over the bed, and when he sat up, the old monstrosity was looking out from the elliptical mirror of that monstrous Moderne vanity table where he'd given Gloria her haircut last night.

Naked, he tottered into the bathroom to empty his bladder. He had to close the shower curtain to block out the sight of Gloria sitting upright in the tub like Marat in his bath—something about the puffy features and the slanted eyes with their drooping lids reminded him uncomfortably of Missy.

But he couldn't block out the triptych of mirrors set at oblique angles just inside the bathroom door, presumably so the formerly vain Mrs. Gee could view herself from all sides. Spooky as it was to look directly into a mirror and see Grandfather Childs looking back at you, it was spooky cubed to see him out of the corner of your eye, or sense him behind you, then wheel around and see him wheeling around as if to catch you in the act.

Simon hurried out of the bathroom without stopping to wash his hands or brush his teeth at the sink, which in any event was still littered with shards of broken mirror from the night before. Badly rattled—not frightened but rattled (there was a difference, he reminded himself)—he tossed a bedsheet over the oval mirror of the vanity table, brushed Gloria's hair from the chair with his fingers, hauled his getaway satchel onto the chromed steel counter of the vanity, and began going through his pharmacopoeia in search of remedies both for his jangled nerves and his hangover.

The latter was easy—there wasn't a hangover in the world couldn't be cured with a five-hundred milligram Percodan—but the heebie-jeebies, which often presaged a visit by the blind rat, presented more of a challenge. There was Valium of course, in five-, ten-, and fifteen-milligram sizes—on top of the Percodan, though, it might knock him out. There was Xanax—but that sometimes gave him the runs, which after last night's stinky was something he definitely didn't need.

Or perhaps he could go in another direction entirely, he told himself. He had certainly enjoyed Gloria's Ecstasy last night. Surprisingly, it was the first time he'd ever played a game on X—surprising because, now that he thought about it, the empathy drug seemed like a natural fit. The game was all about empathy—fear and empathy.

Ecstasy, then, but at what dosage? He'd taken two last night, and he didn't remember his own X, which came in pink capsules stamped with little hearts, as being any stronger: he decided to start with two. While waiting for the medication to take effect, with trembling fingers he tore two rolling papers to shreds trying to roll a joint at the vanity, and ended up with one of those lumpy, python-digesting-a-gopher numbers, which he smoked down to the roach before going downstairs in search of a more congenial bathroom in which to shower.

When he saw the contorted figure in the red bikini briefs lying in full rigor mortis on the living room couch, Simon was surprised at its savaged condition—he couldn't remember having inflicted that much damage. He hurried past it into the guest bedroom. No bodies here, and no American Moderne—just a single bed, a garage-sale dresser, and a few amateurish still lifes on the walls.

So this austere little maid's room was where the real Skairdykat had slept, according to Gloria. And this little closet of a bathroom was where she had

showered. And her name is Linda, and now she lives
with Pender. Which means another first for the
game: a doubleheader. How convenient, thought
Simon. How very . . . bloody . . . convenient.

3

"Not bad for a one-armed old fat man," declared an
exultant, if exhausted, Pender, after a morning of
extended lovemaking punctuated by endorphin-
drenched naps.

"One-eyed," Dorie murmured, equally satisfied,
but less inclined to crow about it. She did think it was
sort of sweet, how boyishly proud Pender was to have
collaborated with her on that last, noisy multiple O.

"Hunh?"

"One-*eyed* old fat man—it's a line from *True Grit*."

Pender shuddered—small wonder he'd misremem-
bered the quote: the thought of losing even one eye
filled him with horror. Once that happened, he knew,
you were only a sharpened pencil away from total
blindness.

Linda called back while Dorie was in the shower.
"Nelson Carpenter," she announced.

Pender checked his watch. "Just a little over three
hours—couldn't have done better myself. I don't suppose you also came up with a current address?"

"You know where Concord is?"

"Massachusetts."

"Concord, California. North of San Francisco—Contra Costa County, I think. The subdivision's named Rancho del Vista."

"Just give me the street address; I'll find it."

Here we go again, thought Linda. "Ed, sooner or later, McDougal is gonna—"

"—be very, very proud of his little Liaison Support Unit. But I give you my word of honor, if Nervous Nellie has anything at all to tell us about Childs's whereabouts, I will pass the information along to the appropriate authorities."

Linda gave him the address, reminded him of his promise, and wished him luck; it wasn't until another hour had passed that she realized their agreement could have been more precisely worded. She called him back and got his message box.

"Ed, this is Linda. Just to clarify: the term 'appropriate authorities' does *not,* repeat *not,* include yourself. Talk to you soon."

"How far is Concord?" Pender called through the bathroom door, when Dorie had finished her shower.

"Two, three hours. Depends on the traffic and the time of day. You can pretty much bypass San Fran and Oakland entirely, if you swing around on six-eighty. Why?"

"That's where Nervous Nellie lives."

"All right! We should probably leave now, avoid both commutes."

"Whoa. To paraphrase Tonto, what you mean 'we,' white woman?"

"What *you* mean, what I mean?" Dorie came out

wrapped in a bath towel, winding a second towel around her wet hair. "You're not leaving me alone here, buster."

"Luka practically tore me a new one for bringing you along yesterday. Said I could be doing you untold psychological damage."

"In the *first* place: you didn't bring me, I brought you. In the *second* place: Luka is at least ninety, and rumor has it he takes LSD once a month. In the *third* place: the psychological damage has already been done—by Simon. I dream about him, I imagine him popping up every time I turn a corner, and if you're not in the room with me, I can't even bring myself to look at the window, in case his face pops up there. In the *fourth* place: *you're* the one who keeps saying he's probably within driving distance of Berkeley, and in case you've forgotten, this house, my home, which he's already invaded once, is very much within driving distance. Is that enough places for you yet? 'Cause if it's not, I can come up with a whole lot more."

He raised both hands, palms out. "Okay, okay, I surrender." But half an hour later he sneaked out of the house via the studio door while Dorie was on the phone with one of her girlfriends—better to ask forgiveness than permission was as effective a strategy with women as it was with the Bureau.

Some women, anyway: when Pender reached the driveway, he stuck his hand into his pants pocket for his keys and came up empty. He told himself they must have fallen out of his pocket when he took his pants off last night. As he tiptoed into the house and past the kitchen on his way up to the bedroom, though, Pender heard a familiar jingling sound and backed up to see Dorie seated at the kitchen table, telephone in one hand, his key ring dangling from the thumb and forefinger of the other.

"Be with you in a minute there, Lone Ranger," she said, and jingled the keys merrily again.

Just as well, thought Pender—he'd forgotten that he couldn't work the damn shift anyway.

4

Conventional wisdom would argue that Simon Childs's use of powerful pharmaceuticals, on top of all the other stress he was under, could only have served to accelerate the inevitable deterioration of an already unstable personality.

Simon would have disagreed—and a case could well be made that the serotonin-reuptake-inhibiting effects of 3,4-methylenedioxy-N-methylamphetamine, also known as MDMA, Adam, or Ecstasy, in addition to the weed and the Percodan, were indeed having a pacifying effect on him.

But Simon was no pharmacologist. All he knew was that he'd stepped into the little stall shower in the guest bathroom half a jump ahead of the blind rat, and emerged feeling as giddy as a schoolboy and so full of fellow-feeling that on his way upstairs, he took the time to rearrange the body on the chrome and leather couch into as comfortable a position as rigor mortis would allow and cover it with a striped Hudson's Bay blanket from the spare bedroom.

Simon was feeling so mellow, in fact, that upon his return to the bedroom, before sitting down at the vanity to roll another doob, he removed the sheet he'd draped over the mirror earlier, and played a quick round of Senor Wences—"S'awright? S'awright! S'okay? S'okay!"—with Grandfather Childs.

That was pushing it, though: once the joint—a better effort than the last one—was rolled, tempting as it would have been to watch his grandfather toke up, Simon turned his back on the old man. He took a deep drag—his glance fell upon the canvas travel bag on the floor next to him. He unzipped it a few inches to peek in on the king and the coral, sleeping peacefully in the bottom, entwined in each other's arms like an old married couple.

"Except you don't *have* any arms, do you?" giggled Simon, zipping the bag, then unzipping it again. "S'awright . . . ?" "S'awright!" he called in two different voices.

But why this sudden obsession with Senor Wences? he asked himself. Hadn't thought of the old ventriloquist from the *Ed Sullivan Show* in years, and now he was practically channeling him. Eventually it came to him: he missed his sister. Missy had been so taken with Senor Wences that she'd spent most of 1959 with a little face painted on the thumb side of her fist. *"Eassy for you, deefeecul' for meee,"* she used to croon to her hand. Not that anybody but me ever understood her, Simon thought sadly.

But it was a good sadness, a sweet, loving sadness welling up inside him, filling the emptiness like a big warm golden marshmallow. Then he caught a blur of movement in his lower peripheral vision and looked down in time to see a banded snake slithering out of the canvas bag—God *bless* it, he'd left it slightly open. A second serpentine head emerged from the bag, testing the air with its tongue. This second snout was black, thank goodness—Simon snatched up a hairbrush and forced the coral back into the bag.

"No big deal," he muttered to himself, zipping up the bag again—the scarlet king snake was only an enhancement. He'd planned to use it to deliver a few practice bites first—something that was not, of course, feasible with the coral—so he could watch Skairdykat's panic slowly build as she waited for the venom to take effect. And as soon as it began to dawn on her that the king snake was harmless, it would be time to bring out the real deal.

That had been the plan, anyway. But as long as he still had the coral, he reminded himself, Skairdykat's game would not be seriously compromised. And after Skairdykat, Pender: the plans for *that* game had been hatching ever since La Farge, as the eyeless corpse on the living room couch mutely attested.

And yet, under the enforced calm of the Ecstasy, Simon was vaguely aware of a budding anxiety. Somehow it seemed that the closer he got to Pender's game, the less anxious he was to have it over with. That was probably why he'd driven east after La Farge, instead of south to Maryland, he was beginning to understand why he'd detoured through Allenwood and Georgetown, risking life and liberty for a game with Skairdykat. It had been Pender's game that had been driving him ever since Missy died, but thinking about what came after Pender was like speculating on what came after infinity, what lay beyond the borders of the universe.

A fellow could hurt himself, trying to wrap his mind around a paradox like that—especially a fellow as stoned and as constitutionally unable to contemplate the possibility of his impending nonexistence as Simon Childs. So what Simon asked himself instead was whether he had any unfinished business here in the east. And when the answer came up yes, he knew what his next move had to be.

5

Dorie steered the Toyota through the wide, empty suburban streets of Rancho del Vista, past cookie-cutter colonials with wide, empty suburban lawns.

"Speaking as a plein air painter, if I lived around here, I'd starve," she said. "No damn ranchos, no damn vistas."

"Yeah, but at least there's plenty of parking." Pender was navigating with the aid of a point-to-point map Dorie had printed out from MapQuest.com, which had recently been voted one of the top ten "Sites That Don't Suck" on the Internet. "Okay, left on Guerrero . . . right on Oaxaca . . ." The streets were all named for Mexican states—so the gardeners would feel at home, according to the local wits. "And . . . here we go, twelve-eleven Baja Way."

The driveway was empty, but Pender had Dorie drive past and park on the street, two houses down. She started to scoff. "C'mon, Pen. What are the chances he was even here in the first place, much less—?"

He cut her off long before she got to the second place. "You painter, me FBI," he said, unbuckling his seat belt and donning his new Panama, which he had to take off in the car—insufficient headroom. "Until I've established with one hundred percent confidence that he's *not* in there, I'll run the show. Understood?"

"Understood."

"Good. Wait here."

"Yes, sir!" replied Dorie, who was not entirely unfamiliar with the *better-to-ask-forgiveness-than-permission* theory herself.

Mailbox stuffed. Driveway empty. Blinds drawn, upstairs and down. Front door locked; garage door locked. Pender walked around back. The landscaping was minimal, the fences low—not much privacy here at Rancho del Vista, despite the spacious lots. There was a patio, backed by a floor-to-ceiling picture window, but the curtains were drawn. He put his ear to the glass: not a sound inside the house.

Nobody home, thought Pender, trying the patio door, which was also locked. It happens—that's the drawback of dropping by unannounced. But he continued his circumambulation, and when he came around the front of the house again, he saw Dorie at the end of the driveway, chatting with the mailman. She waved him over.

"Ted, tell Special Agent Pender what you just told me."

"FBI, hunh? What I told your partner, I was off Monday, but I come back yesterday, Saturday is still in the box, along with Monday. Now, this guy Carpenter, he's kinda weird, doesn't like to answer the door, keeps it on the chain if I need a signature or something, but I've been on this route five years now, and in all that time he has never *not* emptied his mailbox. I was gonna give it one more day, then report it in. We're supposed to report stuff like that—you'd be surprised how many dead people get found that way."

"A sad comment on our times," said Pender. "Thanks for keeping your eyes open."

"I don't need to report it, then?" asked the letter carrier.

"Not necessary," Pender replied. "My *partner* and I can take it from here."

Pender jimmied the patio door with the lockpick he'd been carrying in his wallet since his days as a Cortland County sheriff's deputy. In another five days, after his retirement had officially taken effect, carrying it would be at least a misdemeanor bust in most states. Not that entering the house on Baja Way without a warrant wasn't, he thought, sliding the door open.

But in a quarter century with the FBI, Pender had never willingly turned his back on a virgin crime scene—if this even *was* a crime scene. If it wasn't, he could be in and out in five minutes, no harm done and nobody the wiser. As for Dorie, if she wasn't going to follow instructions, it would obviously be better to have her where he could keep an eye on her. "Stick close, walk in my footsteps, and don't touch anything."

"Can do." Without being consciously aware of it, until a week ago Dorie had had her life arranged so that she'd rarely had to walk into a strange house or an unfamiliar room until someone had vetted it first (you never know, could be a mask on the wall: booga booga!). Now she was starting to regret her newfound boldness. It wasn't just the musty smell of the soaked carpet that had her spooked, it was Pender's manner, the hushed but commanding tone of his voice, the grim set to his jaw, the wary tilt of his head as he started up the carpeted stairs, which were also squishing underfoot—somehow Dorie's affable, comfortable, slow-moving Pen had turned into an FBI agent before her very eyes.

"Wait here," he told her when he reached the top of the stairs.

"Pen, what's that smell?" Stuffy, as if the rooms hadn't been aired out in months. Or, no, not stuffy, more like sickly sweet, like old melon rinds in the garbage.

But he'd already disappeared into one of the bedrooms. Wait here? thought Dorie. Alone? You'd have to handcuff me to the banister. She followed him through the door, saw him standing in an open doorway on the far side of a bedroom. When he turned around, Dorie could tell from the look on his face that for a moment there, he'd forgotten she was even in the house. She started toward him—he met her in the middle of the room and put his arms around her to stop her from going any farther.

"You don't need to see what's in there," he said softly.

"Is it Nelson?"

"It was."

6

The seventy-six-year-old woman watching her soaps in a studio apartment in a deteriorating, if not blighted, neighborhood on the outskirts of Atlantic City had been born Rose Ella Moore and passed her happiest years as Rosella Childs, so it sometimes seemed strange to her to look back and realize that she'd spent a larger portion of her life as Rosie Delamour, a name she'd adopted half in jest and three-quarters stoned, than she had as Rose Moore and Rosella Childs combined.

Rosie's drug of choice back when she'd first adopted her name was Moroccan hash—which was appropriate, as she was living in Tangier at the time. More recently, her drug of choice had been vodka, the cheaper the better—store brand would do nicely, thank you. If you asked her, she'd have admitted to being, if not a drunk, then a binge drinker; if you pressed her, though, she'd have had to admit that her current binge had begun last February, after the fiasco on Missy's birthday.

The kids' birthdays were always a hard time for Rosie, and when she'd finally worked up the nerve (okay—gotten drunk enough) to actually make the call after all those years and all those halfhearted attempts (calls she'd abandoned in mid-dial or mid-ring; answering machines she'd hung up on), only to have Simon hang up on *her,* there just didn't seem to be much point in sobering up anymore.

But like many alcoholics, it gave Rosie a feeling of control to discipline her drinking. Her allotted intake was determined by her shows. One vodka tonic apiece during the morning soaps, a can of Ensure for lunch, then another vodka tonic with each of the afternoon soaps. In the evening, she would either dine out with one of her gentlemen or dine in with Dinty Moore— the beef stew, not one of her dust bowl relations, she liked to joke. In either case, her nightly allotment was determined not by television but by how much vodka remained in the bottle, because her iron rule was never to open two in one day.

Of course, if one of her gentlemen had the funds to purchase adult beverages with dinner, or bring a flask back to Rosie's apartment afterward, that didn't count against her quota.

Last night had been a Dinty Moore evening. This morning Rosie had awakened with a menacing hang-over and a vague memory of having spoken to some-one about Simon over the phone. The who and the why of it had vanished into the mist of memory, how-ever, and Rosie knew better than to try to go into the mist after them—the only thing she'd ever found there was frustration.

But whether it was the call or something else, Rosie's schedule had definitely been thrown off. By the end of *General Hospital,* the last soap of the day, less than three inches remained in the red-labeled fifth of Select Choice vodka; by the time *Oprah* was over, less than two. That was going to make for a difficult evening, unless of course it was Wednesday. Wednesdays, Rosie could count on Cappy Kaplan springing for a bottle of wine.

And, Rosie told herself, she might even be able to persuade Cappy to stop off at the corner liquor store on the way back to the apartment. True, it was a little late in the month for those on fixed incomes, but Cappy's circumstances weren't as straitened as hers, on account of his VA benefits.

But was it in fact Wednesday? Rosie was working that one out by dead reckoning—she remembered Monday for sure, because Ralph Rosen, her Monday gentleman, had taken her to the buffet at one of the casinos; so if yesterday was Dinty Moore, then today *had* to be Wednesday—when the doorbell rang. Rosie checked the time on the cable box: 5:05. She rolled her eyes: Cappy and his twilight/senior discount dinners.

The intercom hadn't worked for months. Rosie buzzed Cappy up, then unbolted the door and retired to the bathroom to freshen up. Cappy was among the spryest of Rosie's beaux—he even rode a motorcycle—but it still took him a few minutes to climb the four flights of stairs to her fifth-floor walk-up. Sometimes she would wait for her gentlemen in the lobby to save them making the climb twice in an evening, but they certainly couldn't expect that courtesy if they insisted on showing up in the middle of the afternoon.

"You're early," she called from the bathroom when she heard the apartment door open. "I'll be out in a minute."

"Take your time."

It didn't sound like Cappy—maybe he had a cold. Rosie splashed a little water on her face, freshened her lipstick, opened the bathroom door.

Her first reaction was the same as Nelson Carpenter's—or that of anyone who's ever seen a ghost made flesh. If something can't be, but is, then it is the nature of that *is-ness,* of reality, of the universe itself, that will seem to have shifted.

Unless of course it was only the d.t.'s. Rosie snatched at that explanation like a drowning woman at a piece of driftwood. Some people get pink elephants, she tried to tell herself—I get Marcus Childs sitting on my bed.

In her heart, though, she knew he was no hallucination, and when he looked up from the bed with a strange, imploring look, as if he were begging for her to recognize him, it was in her heart that the recognition of his true identity first blossomed.

7

"How are you feeling, hon?" Miss Pool asked from the doorway. She already had her coat on.

"Like death warmed over," replied Linda. The sluggish, leaden feeling had persisted all day. No real symptoms had popped up, which made her think she might indeed be having a Betaseron reaction—but if so, it had lasted longer than it ever had before.

"Why don't we call it a day?"

Linda looked up at the clock: 5:10. "You go on home—I'll lock up." A little joke: the office locked itself, of course.

"What are you working on?"

Linda held up a faxed death certificate. "Elaine Ferry, Petaluma. She was a pharmacophobe—terrified of taking drugs, even prescribed medicine. They found her at the bottom of her swimming pool twelve years ago, wearing an overcoat with the pockets stuffed with rocks."

"Virginia Woolf," said Pool.

"Beg pardon?"

"That's how Virginia Woolf drowned herself."

"Yes, well, the thing is, the SF field office got a call from Elaine Ferry's mother yesterday—she recognized Simon Childs as a friend of her daughter's. They got permission for an exhumation and necropsy, to run some toxicology exams on the bones, teeth, hair if any, for traces of parent drugs or metabolites."

"Are they likely to find anything after all this time?"

Linda shrugged. "It's like that joke about the guy who lost his watch on Forty-second Street but looked for it on Forty-third because the light there was better—you can only do what you can do. And who knows, maybe they'll find a note tucked between her ribs: 'I did it, Love Simon.' "

"Which reminds me," said Pool. "Do you have any plans for Halloween?"

"Is it that time already?"

"This coming Sunday. The reason I asked, we always have a costume party and put together a haunted house for the trick-or-treaters. Why don't you come by—we'd love to have you."

It occurred to Linda that after working with Pool for a week and a half, she still had no idea who that "we" represented. Husband, girlfriend, aged parent? "I don't know—I don't have a costume or anything."

"We'll fix you up—you can be a bloody corpse in the haunted house."

"Somehow, being a bloody corpse has never been one of my ambitions," remarked Linda, as the phone rang. Pool started back to her desk to answer it— Linda gave her a g'wan-g'home-getouttaheah wave and picked it up herself.

It was Pender. "Got any red pins on that map yet, kiddo?"

"Just the one in San Francisco."

"Stick another one in Concord." He told her about finding Nelson Carpenter in the bathtub.

"Homicide?"

"Unless he glued himself to the enamel."

Linda winced. "Any estimate as to the time of death?"

"The M.E. hasn't gotten here yet. From the looks of it, I'd say around a week."

"Oh, jeez."

"Oh, jeez is right." But Pender spared her the worst of the details: the floating, gas-bloated corpse, the sloughed skin. "And guess what we found in the garage?"

"Silver Mercedes convertible."

"And guess what we didn't find?"

"Whatever Carpenter drives."

"Late-model white Volvo sedan, according to the

mailman. I'll call you back as soon as the plate numbers come in from the DMV."

"I'll get the BOLO updated. Do we want to notify
the public?"

"No—hold that back. If he knows we're looking for
the Volvo, there goes any chance of catching him in it.
As it is, we'll probably find it abandoned some—
Whoops, here comes Erickson. Gotta go. I'll call you
back with the plates and the VIN."

Pender broke off the connection. Linda opened
her desk drawer and took out the box of flag pins,
then scooted her chair all the way over to the left of
the big map behind her desk. But when she tried to
insert a red one into the dot marking Concord with
her left hand, it slipped from her fingers, the tips of
which seemed to have fallen asleep.

Must have been leaning on it funny, she told herself, bending to pick it up. Next thing she knew she
was on the floor—the flexion of her neck had sent a
bone-jarring jolt of electricity shooting down her
spine and fanning out across her entire neural network.

It was like being hit by a bolt of lightning, was how
Linda described it to the nurse over the telephone,
when she was able to use the telephone.

"Give me your number," said the nurse. "I'll have
the doctor call you back."

At five o'clock? thought Linda. And do you have a
nice bridge in Brooklyn to sell me? "You promise?"

"I promise. Just stay where you are."

"No problem," said Linda wryly.

8

For Cappy Kaplan, the key to enjoying a successful date with Rosie Delamour—and make no mistake, at seventy-four, Cappy's idea of a successful date was about the same as any male over the age of thirteen and under the age of dead—was to time your move to her consumption.

To begin with, you had to pick her up early—if left to her own devices, by the time the sun was under the yardarm, so, generally, was Rosie. But with dinner, he'd buy a bottle of wine, which Cappy could afford only because the early start enabled him to take advantage of the discounted senior menus offered at the eating establishments frequented by the social security set in Atlantic City. After dinner, back at her place, was where it got tricky. Once Rosie started knocking back the store-brand vodka she favored, there was a very small window of opportunity between hotto and blotto, as they said in Cappy's day.

Like most Navy men, the retired chief petty officer (Cappy was his nickname, not his rank) was prompt. He pulled up in front of Rosie's apartment building in his '68 Harley Electra Glide with the fishtail mufflers and the studded cowboy saddle (he could still ride the Hog, he just couldn't lift it if it spilled), walked it into the vestibule (the bike wasn't entirely secure even there, and sometimes it leaked a little oil, but he'd be damned if he was going to leave it out on the street in this neighborhood), and rang the buzzer to apartment 5-B at precisely five-fifteen. When Rosie failed to buzz him in, his first thought was that she had fallen asleep on the couch watching her soaps. His second thought was that his hopes for a successful date were probably as doomed as his first ship, the escort carrier *Ommaney Bay,* which went down off Luzon in January of '45.

But it never occurred to Cappy to just turn around and go home. Rosie might need him—she might have passed out, fallen, struck her head on something. You could bleed to death from a scalp laceration—that's how Bill Holden kicked it. Like they say, it ain't the fall that kills you, it's what you hit on the way down.

So he mashed all fifteen buttons on the wall with the flat of his big hand, waited by the door, and sure enough, somebody buzzed him through. Intercom must still be fubared, he decided, on his way up the stairs. Somebody oughtta call the super.

A little winded, he stopped to catch his breath at Rosie's door, then rang the bell. No answer, but he could hear it ringing. He knocked anyway. "Rosie, you okay in there?"

The peephole darkened. "Go away." Man's voice.

Cappy knew he wasn't Rosie's only fella. Hell, she wasn't his only gal—or hadn't been, until Helen Breen, Tommy Breen's widow, finally passed. But Wednesday night was their night, Cappy and Rosie's, and had been for years. Something wasn't copacetic around here. "Where's Rosie?"

"You Cappy?"

"Yeah."

"She doesn't want to see you."

"I'd like her to tell me that."

"She told me to tell you."

Cappy drew himself to his full height—once, six-two, still close to six-one—and crossed his arms over his chest. "Either I see Rosie or I call the cops."

The door opened. Cappy found himself face-to-face with one of the creepiest guys he'd ever seen. And balder than Cappy on his worst day, bald right down to his eyeballs. "C'mon in."

Cappy brushed by him—he'd dealt with more desperate characters than this in his thirty years in the Navy; hell, he'd been commanded by more desperate characters than this. Rosie was lying on the Murphy bed, a cold compress over her forehead. She sat up.

"Cappy, this is my son, Simon," she said, weakly, but with an undertone of pride in her voice. "Simon, this is my friend Cappy I told you about."

Simon stuck his right hand out, reached behind him with his left to close the door. "Pleased to meet you."

"Didn't sound that way a minute ago." But Cappy shook the man's hand. He knew how big a deal this was for Rosie—she'd often mentioned the children she'd been forced to abandon as infants. "Rosie baby, why don't we take a rain check on dinner? You probably want to have a little time alone with your boy here."

"Yes, that might be—"

"I wouldn't *think* of it," said Simon quickly. The old guy seemed to be pretty clueless as to Simon's recent notoriety, but you never knew, he could leave here, turn on a radio, pick up a paper, watch the news, make the connection. "I'm the one who came busting in without calling first. Why don't we have dinner together—we'll send for takeout. My treat."

"Very kind of you," said Cappy, trying to work his way around Simon, who was standing with his back almost to the door. "But I couldn't possibly . . ."

"Oh, yes, you could," said Simon, reaching behind his back and drawing the Colt from his waistband. "You really, really, could."

Cappy backed away from the door. Rosie saw the gun for the first time. "Simon, what are you—"

"I'm in a little trouble. Mom." The word sounded strange to Simon, coming out of his own mouth—he hadn't used it as a form of address since he was three. "I can't take a chance on Cappy here dropping the dime on me." He turned back to Cappy. "Why don't you join your girlfriend on the bed—I'm sure you've been there before."

9

To Linda's surprise, the doctor, with whom she'd had only one appointment shortly after her transfer to Washington, returned her call within a few minutes; to her relief, he didn't sound particularly alarmed.

"It's called Lhermitte's sign," he told her. "If you hadn't already been diagnosed with MS, it would be a red flag—as things stand, it just tells us what we already know. The numbness and tingling in your fingers concerns me more. That's a new symptom, is it not?"

"Yes, sir."

"And we have you on a course of Betaseron every other day?"

"Yes, sir."

"Side effects?"

"Just the red blotches at the injection site—and those flu symptoms I told you about."

"Let's stay with it, then, and if necessary we'll think about stepping it up a notch after your next evaluation. When are you scheduled to come in?"

"First of the month—I guess that's Monday."

"I'll see you on Monday, then. And until then, I want you to take it easy. Avoid stress, no strenuous physical activity. And by all means try to avoid any sudden bending or twisting of your neck."

"Yes, sir," said Linda promptly. As far as she was concerned, one Lhermitte's sign per lifetime was plenty.

Linda hung around the office long enough to see the updated BOLO and arrange for its high-priority national distribution to law enforcement only, then left for home. Although the information about the vehicle Childs might be driving was the closest thing to a break in the manhunt thus far, it wasn't the sort of break you'd expect to bring about immediate results.

Nor would it have, if the car had still been in California, or even a neighboring state. But on M Street in Georgetown, a Volvo with California plates might have been conspicuous enough to have been noticed even if hadn't already accumulated two tickets and a tow warning since Tuesday evening.

Linda had left the office by the time the patrol car called it in. She was traveling north on the River Road and had just passed the sign for Piney Meetinghouse Road (she loved that name), which meant she was only a few miles from Tinsman's Lock, when her cell phone started chirping.

"Abruzzi."

"Joe Buchanan, Metro." Washington Metropolitan on Fourth Street was the FBI field office with jurisdiction over the District of Columbia. "Thought you might want to know a patrol car spotted your Volvo in Georgetown."

"Georgetown," echoed Linda dully.

"Yeah. No sign of Childs yet. They pulled off it right away and set up a surveillance perimeter: if he so much as shows his—"

"Joe—what was the location of the car?"

"I don't remember exactly. Somewhere on M, I think—I can get it for you if it matters."

"Please," said Linda so calmly it was hard to believe that her world, and what was left of her career, was crashing around her ears.

"Just a sec."

It was more than a sec, it was an eon, an age, an eternity, during which Linda tried to tell herself that although M Street's retail shops and restaurants were within walking distance, even *her* walking distance, of the Gees' brownstone—it was a long street—this could be a coincidence. But deep down she knew better: even before Buchanan came back on the line to confirm her worst fears—the Volvo was parked only two blocks from Conroy Circle—her mind had already switched into cover-your-ass mode. You don't *have* to tell them, she reminded herself; it *still* could be a coincidence. Or maybe it wasn't Skairdykat at all, maybe he got the address some other way.

Yeah, sure. And maybe God didn't make little

green apples, and maybe Hoover and Tolson were just good friends. "Joe, I've got an address about two blocks north of there that needs to be checked out soonest. Seventeen Conroy Circle, that's one seven C-O-N-R-O-Y. It's a one-family brownstone. I stayed there for a few weeks when I first got to Washington. Should be two residents, James and Gloria Gee— that's G-E-E."

He told her he could have somebody there in five minutes—Metro agents were already converging on Georgetown. And although he did not ask her why the Gees were at risk, or what the connection was to Childs, she knew that before too long, the question would have to be asked.

Along with a few others. Such as what the fuck could you have been thinking, putting civilians in jeopardy like that?

No excuse, sir, she muttered to herself as she switched off the cell phone and slipped it back into the pocket of her black wool car-coat. A glance in the rearview mirror—all clear. She jammed on the brakes and wrenched the wheel to the left, throwing the poor Geo into a screaming, sliding, four-wheel-drift of a U-turn.

As she passed Piney Meetinghouse Road again, this time from the opposite direction, her phone went off in her pocket.

"Terry Marks, Hostage Rescue. We're setting up a perimeter around Seventeen Conroy. There are no signs of movement inside, and nobody's answering the phone, but there's a broken pane of glass in the back door. We want to go in quick, while we still have the element of surprise, but I need to get some more information first. I understand you're familiar with the house?"

"Yes."

"There are two occupants?"

"Yes: Gloria Gee, Chinese-American female, age thirty-seven, height five-two, weight around one-five, one-ten. Jim Gee, Chinese-American male, late thirties, five-seven, around one-forty."

"Short Chinese—that's good; nobody's likely to mistake either of the hostages for the suspect."

"Not unless you have Stevie Wonder going in."

"Any entrances or exits other than the front and back doors?"

"Not that I know of."

"What's the layout inside?"

Linda gave Marks a walk-through, first from the front door, then the back.

"Good job. One more thing, what do they drive?"

"Jim drives one of those new Mercedes SUVs, blue with gold trim. Gloria has a late-model Lexus, that champagne color—I don't know the license numbers."

"The Mercedes is here—we'll get the Lexus plates from motor vehicles, thanks."

Linda wished him luck, which was more than she dared hope for for herself. There were only two ways this could play out that wouldn't mean the end of her career. The first was a complete false alarm, in which case, once the confusion had been cleared up, she might get off with a reprimand and a nasty note from OPR in her personnel file.

The second involved the HRT killing Childs on the way in, then finding two more dead bodies, in which case there would be no need to clear up the confusion. No one but herself would ever have to know that Childs had been drawn to the house by a decoy *she* had set up, a decoy that in the end had succeeded only in drawing the hunter to his prey.

The Gees would still be dead of course, but Linda would be in the clear. And that's what counts, isn't it? she asked herself bitterly.

10

The three of them shared the bed. Cappy and Rosie sat next to each other at the head, framed by the alcove in the wall that hid the old-fashioned, pull-down Murphy bed during the day. Rosie had a newly opened bottle of Select Choice propped between her legs. The hell with measuring it out, she had decided; the hell with the glass, the ice, and the tonic, for that matter.

Simon sat cross-legged at the foot of the bed. Oddly, he wasn't as put out by Cappy's intrusion as he might have been. Things hadn't worked out the way he'd thought they would when he called directory information from the Gees' kitchen and wangled Rosie's address out of the operator with a sob story about how it was his mom's birthday and he had to get some flowers delivered. It was almost too intense, being alone with his mother after all these years—a lifetime, really. But in addition to being mother and son, they were also virtually strangers to each other. The third party changed the equation—Simon found himself playing to the old man as if he were an audience of one.

"I was just telling my mother about a woman named Ida I met in Wisconsin," he explained. "Ida asked me a question that's been rattling around in my head for days now—I was hoping maybe Mom here could answer it for me."

Simon's eyes traveled from Cappy to Rosie. Despite the strain he'd been under, despite the Ecstasy, the sinsemilla, and the dearth of sleep, it seemed to Simon that his mind was clearer than it had been since this whole sorry business had begun. (Although the crosstops he'd been popping like Pez all afternoon might have had something to do with that.) "How about it, Mom? What's the secret? How can a mother bring herself to walk away from a year-old baby girl with Down's and a three-year-old who's just lost his father?"

And at that moment, he realized that it no longer even mattered what her answer was—it was finally getting to ask the question that had made the difference, that had brought him to this place of clarity.

XI

Skairdykat

1

The media was already gathering outside Conroy Circle, which was, as the name suggests, a cul-de-sac. Sawhorses blocked the entrance; Linda flashed her shield, and the D.C. cops manning the barricades let her through.

I think we can probably rule out a false alarm, Linda told herself wryly, as the Geo rolled past the media circus to join the cop circus. Patrol cars, unmarked Bu-cars, ambulances, Hostage Rescue Team in full ninja gear straggling out of number seventeen, Evidence Response Team straggling in, paramedics stowing away their gurneys, coroner's men unfolding theirs, D.C. cops standing around everywhere. Linda parked behind an Animal Control van. As she reached for her cane, an agent wearing a blue windbreaker with the letters *FBI* in yellow across the back approached her.

"You Abruzzi?"

"Yes, sir."

"I'm Joe Buchanan. Thanks for coming down." He opened the door for Linda, helped her out of the car. "We figured since you were familiar with the house, you might be able to spot if anything was missing, anything out of place. You up for a walk-through?"

"Yes, sir," said Linda, surprised at how readily she was able to don a brisk professional demeanor. Maybe feeling numb inside somehow made it easier. If so, she was all for numb. "What have we got?"

Or perhaps she was more transparent than she'd hoped—Buchanan put his hand on her shoulder. "I understand these people were friends of yours?"

Linda nodded warily.

"It's not pretty in there."

"Then let's get it over with," said Linda. Too late to turn squeamish now. She'd played with their lives and was responsible for their deaths—the least she could do was look at their corpses. She felt as if she owed them that much, somehow.

The walk-through, though it was Linda's first "wet" crime scene (not unusual for an FBI agent—the Bureau was rarely the initial responder or lead agency on a fresh homicide), wasn't so bad initially. Not downstairs, anyway, which was both surprising, because they were just removing the blanket covering the body on the couch as she limped into the living room, and predictable, because it was probably the shock of seeing Jim's savagely mutilated corpse that caused Linda's mind to protectively dissociate, to pull back in order to distance itself from the carnage.

Linda's detachment was tested in a different way

when she glanced into the guest bedroom. Nothing gruesome about it—the shocking part was that it looked pretty much the way it had the night she'd moved out. That's what got to her: for a second, she saw her own corpse lying on that bed, the bed she'd slept in for three weeks, the bed she'd have been sleeping in last night if not for sheer undeserved luck.

She shook it off, followed Buchanan up the stairs and into the Gees' bedroom, feeling as if she were seeing and hearing everything from inside a deep-sea-diver's helmet. There were blood spatters on one of the bed pillows; black hair littered the floor around the vanity. Linda turned to Buchanan, asked the question with her eyes.

"She's in the bathroom," he replied. "In the tub."

"Yes, he likes to bathe them," said Linda.

Gloria was not alone.

"I think I found the envenoming point," said Reilly, the forensic technician kneeling beside the tub, when Buchanan and Linda appeared in the doorway. With gloved fingers he tilted Gloria's shorn head up and to the side to show them a small, ragged-edged hole in her neck.

"Not how I pictured a snakebite," said Buchanan, peering over his shoulder.

"Coral snakes have short mouths and stubby fangs—they have to chew their way in."

"How about the facial lacerations?"

"Razor—probably some kind of box cutter or utility knife, with the blade extended a few millimeters."

Coral snakes . . . chew their way . . . razor blade.

Think about something else. "Why are her eyes drooping like that?" asked Linda.

"That's one of the symptoms of a neurotoxin, which would fit with the coral ID. Corals are Elapidae—neurotoxic venom, borderline lethal." Then, to Buchanan: "Did they find it yet?"

"No, they're sending for a dog." He turned to Linda, still in the doorway. "First man up the stairs saw this skinny striped snake coming out of the bedroom. Red, black, and yellow. They think either it got into the walls, or else it's up in the attic."

"I'm rooting for the attic," Linda said weakly.

"Don't worry," said Reilly. "Like I said, coral venom is only borderline lethal, plus there's often a delayed reaction, plus Animal Control's supposed to be on their way over with the specific antivenin."

"When did you become such an expert on venomous snakes, Reilly?" Buchanan asked him.

"Since Herro got the printout from Poison Control about fifteen minutes ago." Reilly nodded toward the fax stuffed into his kit. "You think there's a chance in hell I'd be up here otherwise?"

"Could I see that?" Linda asked.

"Here you go."

. . . reaction to envenomatim may be delayed from four to twelve hours. . . . Clinical manifestations . . . bilateral ptosis, diplopia, anisocoria, myalgia, dyspnea, respiratory paralysis. Death from acute respiratory failure.

Linda handed the sheet back to Reilly. "Translation?" Still all business.

"*Ptosis*—that's the drooping eyelids. *Diplopia* is double vision, *anisocoria* is the different sized pupils, *myalgia* is muscle pain, *dyspnea* is air hunger.

Respiratory paralysis is actually paralysis of the diaphragm. Basically, she suffocated to death. He must have held it right up to her jugular, see . . . ?" Again he tilted Gloria's head up.

"Don't *do* that," snapped Linda, who was still about a million miles away emotionally, but approaching earth at light speed.

"What's *your* problem? I guarantee you *she* doesn't care."

"She was my college roommate," Linda said softly, as Buchanan put his arm around her shoulder again and steered her back into the bedroom.

"I feel like I'm missing something here, Abruzzi. What's the connection with Childs—what was *he* doing here?"

By now, Linda should have been ready for the question. She'd had plenty of time to prepare her answer on the ride down: *Gloria was afraid of snakes. I was researching the case; I told her about phobia.com. She must have gone on-line. Childs got her address somehow.*

Yeah, that'd work, she'd told herself, that'd play. But that was before she'd seen Jim's mangled, eyeless corpse in those ridiculous red bikini briefs; seen Gloria exposed, naked and vulnerable for once. Roomed with her for two years, never once saw her naked *or* vulnerable.

Suddenly Linda felt immensely tired. "It's a long story," she told Buchanan. "Is there someplace I can sit down?"

2

"I left you. That's what he told you?" Rosie took a slug out of the bottle, then offered it around.

Cappy shook his head. Simon refused it, too—thanks to the crosstops, his mind still felt razor sharp, and he wanted to keep it that way. " *'Like Moses among the bulrushes,'* were his exact words. I always pictured us in reed baskets on the doorstep."

"What else did he tell you?" She raised the bottle for another slug—seeing the ghost of Marcus Childs had sobered her up something awful. Simon reached for the bottle, intending to take it away from her before she managed to overcome her unaccustomed state of coherence, but the look she gave him as she clutched it to her chest reminded him so sharply of Missy that he couldn't go through with it.

"That you called us the brats, that you said the brats would cramp your style."

"Nothing about your father, though?"

"He never talked about my father at all. What was he like?" Simon asked eagerly.

"Danny? Sweetest man you'd ever want to meet. A real prince. In fact, that's how we girls referred to him down on the line."

"The 'line'?"

"The assembly line—I started working in the Emeryville plant in 1942. When Danny got out of the Navy in forty-six, your grandfather put him in charge of converting the plant from wartime production.

Everybody thought we'd all get fired when the vets came back, but somehow he kept on every girl who wanted to keep working, and hired back the vets, too. The crown prince, we called him. And it *was* kind of like a fairy tale. He gave me a ride home one night— don't ever let anybody tell you there's no such thing as love at first sight.

"But when your grandfather found out about it, he hit the roof. Said I was beneath Danny—said it to my face. Said I was Okie trash, a gold digger. He gave your father an ultimatum: me or his inheritance. Love or money."

"And he chose love." Simon had meant to sound derisive, but somehow it didn't come out that way.

"We chose love," said Rosie. "We moved to Vallejo. One of Danny's old crew got him a job working in the shipyard. You were born six months later. We were poor but happy. I know that's a cliché, poor-but-happy, but it was true. And even when Missy was born—it was a shock, everybody said put her in a home, but we loved her so dearly—we all did. You did—you were always so sweet to her. Sure, money was a problem, but then the Korean War started up and they converted the shipyard to submarine maintenance. Danny called me one afternoon, said he'd just been promoted to foreman. He was going to have a few beers with the guys to celebrate."

Rosie raised the bottle to her lips and glared at Simon as she took another stiff belt, as if daring him to try to take it away from her again. "A few beers with the guys," she repeated. "On the way home, his car went off the road, ended up in San Pablo Bay. The wreck didn't kill him—they said he'd drowned. I got the call while I was nursing Missy. My milk went dry that night and never let down again."

"And that's when you dumped us off with Grandfather?"

"No, that's when I went to your grandfather to ask him for help. I was penniless, you were still his grandchildren—where else could I turn? And guess what?—he gave me an ultimatum. He was big on ultimatums, your grandfather. He was also big on buying people. He hadn't been able to buy his son, but he could buy his grandchildren. He told me he'd give me fifty thousand dollars and see to it that my children would be raised in the lap of luxury, and that Missy would get the best care available. In return, I had to sign a legal document relinquishing my parental rights and agreeing to drop out of your lives forever."

"That's twenty-five grand per kid. Not bad money in those days."

"Try to put yourself in my shoes, Simon. I was in my mid-twenties, two kids, one with Down syndrome. The only work I'd ever done was on the assembly line at the Childs plant, and nobody was hiring women for that kind of work in 1951. And even if I'd found work, what kind of life would it have been for you and Missy? At best, latchkey kids; at worst *you'd* have ended up in a foster home and Missy in an institution."

"Never," muttered Simon. "We'd have made it somehow."

"That's easy for you to say. Have you ever been poor, Simon? Have you ever gone to bed hungry?

Have you ever wanted for *anything?* Anything at all? I don't know who this Ida was, but she was right about one thing: there's nothing harder in this world than for a mother to give up her children. Even if the choice is to watch them starve. Every day of my life I've had to wonder whether I made the right decision."

Again, that unfamiliar feeling—the tug of empathy. Simon fought against it. "But you must have known—you *had* to have known what kind of a monster he was."

"No, I—"

"He beat me, Mom, he whipped me every night."

"Please, Simon." Rosie covered her ears.

"He locked me in the cellar, *Mom.*" Simon leaned forward, pulled her hands away, put his face against hers, brow to brow. "He held my head under water, *Mom.* He made me sleep with the dogs, *Mom.* He—"

"No, Simon. Please."

But Simon was not about to stop now. This was more like it, he told himself, this was more like what he'd had in mind, coming here in the first place. She was a clever old gal, he had to give her that—she'd nearly gotten to him with her fairy tale, her sob story. But in the end she was no better than Grandfather Childs had painted her. Worse, in a way: she hadn't just abandoned baby Missy and little Simon, she'd *sold* them.

Grownup Simon snatched the vodka bottle from between his mother's legs, thrust it toward her. "Here you go, Mom, have another drink. Then you won't have to think about how Missy used to cry herself to sleep every night, holding your hairbrush in her little hand. It was the only thing she had to remember her mother by; it was—"

"That's enough," Cappy said quietly, as a sobbing Rosie buried her face in her hands. It was the first time he'd opened his mouth since Simon had pulled the gun on him. "Can't you see she's suffered enough?"

Who hasn't? thought Simon, raising the Colt, leveling it directly at the old man's face, and drawing back the heavy hammer. With his new clarity of mind, he could see the next few seconds as if they'd already happened, only in slow motion. The bullet spinning out of the rifled barrel, the impact, dead center, between the eyes, the spray, the sitting body lifting from the bed with the impact, slamming into the wall behind it, sliding down, trailing a smear of blood.

Or was that only something he'd seen in a movie? Of course—how very cheesy of me, Simon thought. In real life, it would be nothing like that. There would be nothing balletic about a forty-five-caliber bullet hitting a face at point-blank range.

On the other hand, there would be nothing left of the face, either.

Rosie continued to sob. Simon tuned her out, but kept the gun trained on Cappy. This wasn't about her, anymore. The question had been asked and answered—she'd had her say. This was about Simon, this was about survival. His plan, insofar as he'd had one when he'd left the Gees, was to finish his unfinished business with Rosie (although just how *that* would play out was something he had not allowed himself to think about), then double back to Maryland for the doubleheader, the game to end all games.

Now, however, with his newfound clarity of mind, Simon realized what a sorry, drug-addled excuse for a plan that was. Pender, Skairdykat—these weren't feeble, neurotic PWSPDs; they were trained FBI agents, even if Skairdykat did have MS, according to Gloria. If Nelson's body had been discovered, if the Volvo had been spotted or the Gees missed at work this morning—if any one of a dozen likely possibilities had occurred, at best Pender and Skairdy would already be on the alert; at worst, they'd have an ambush set up.

But that image, the image of a faceless corpse, was beginning to resonate for Simon. A real plan began to form itself. Vague at first—just a series of short takes, quickly rejected. A faceless corpse and a suicide note—he and Cappy were about the same size. But the body of an old man wouldn't fool the FBI for long. How about a faceless corpse and a fire? Ludicrous: how could a man shoot himself, then set himself on fire? Just a fire, then—but where would he put the note. In the bath? Along with Rosie's body? Yes!

No. The stand-in corpse would still have to be charred beyond recognition. In which case it wouldn't take an FBI agent to smell a setup—who but a Buddhist monk would commit suicide by self-immolation?

So much for Plan A. Cappy and Rosie were still frozen in place. Either they hadn't blinked yet, or time had stopped, or Simon's thoughts were moving at the speed of light as he began working on Plan B. As of this moment, Cappy and Rosie were both still unaware of . . . well, of the nature of Simon's little problem with the police. Could Simon convert them into allies? You didn't play the fear game for thirty years without having learned a thing or two about acting.

Okay, then, say you win them over. Rosie'd be a piece of cake, and also the key to Cappy. But then what? Was there some way to persuade them to cover for him? Mislead his pursuers, stall them somehow, send them off on a wild-goose chase? But once they were in contact with the authorities, they wouldn't be likely to remain unaware of the . . . nature of Simon's problem. Not long enough for Simon's purposes.

Then it came to him: Plan C. *C* for *Combination*. A little of Plan A, a little of Plan B—but not in that order. Slowly Simon lowered the Colt's hammer, then the gun, then his head.

"You're right," he said. "I'm so sorry—and I'm so ashamed. Maybe you *should* turn me in. It doesn't matter to me anymore. Nothing matters to me anymore—not since Missy died."

3

Is there someplace I can sit down? It was not a rhetorical question—you couldn't just plop down in the middle of a crime scene. Buchanan led Linda to the kitchen, which the evidence response techs had vacated after picking up a good set of latents from a dirty glass and sending the thumbprint to IAFIS, the CJIS Division's high-speed Integrated Automated Fingerprint Identification System.

He brought her a glass of water, sat down next to her at the glass-topped tubed-steel kitchen table—not across from her, so it wouldn't seem like an interrogation. Linda appreciated the courtesy. She wasn't sure what to expect when she finished telling him about Skairdykat. Would he turn away from her in disgust? Notify OPR? Ask for her badge?

None of the above. Buchanan was a field agent, and as such, a practical man. He waited, he listened, he nodded, and when she was done, he asked the only question of immediate practical interest: "How much does Childs know?"

For the next twenty minutes, they spitballed all the possible scenarios. Had Childs simply assumed Gloria was Skairdykat and acted accordingly? Both the manner of her death and the fact that Childs had left the coral behind (they were still assuming it was the coral the HRT had spotted on the way in) certainly argued for that scenario, suggested Buchanan.

"I wish I could buy it," Linda said, almost wistfully. "But he could have more than one snake. And it just doesn't make sense that Childs would never have told them what he was doing there, why he'd broken into their house, or that Jim and Gloria, who are both very intelligent people—" She interrupted herself. "—*were* very intelligent people, that neither of them would have figured out how it was that somebody named Skairdykat ended up contacting the PWSPD through their computer."

"Let's take Jim out of the equation," said Buchanan.

"He has a skull fracture you can see gray matter through—let's say he got it in the initial attack. That leaves Gloria. She was your friend—she might have covered for you."

"You think? When did they first tag the Volvo?"

"Ten-thirty."

"And what's her estimated time of death?"

"Reilly says sometime between midnight last night and dawn this morning. What with her in the water and all, they won't be able to narrow it down any further until they get her on the slab."

The slab. Runnels for the blood. They'll open her up right down the middle like a—

No. Not there, Linda ordered herself—don't go there. Stick to your job while you still have one. "Okay, say a minimum of two hours. If it was me, I'd have spilled my guts in two *minutes*."

"And she had your new address?"

"Yeah—I'm staying at Ed Pender's place."

"Out by the canal?"

"Yeah."

"Think he'll come after you?"

"If she told him I was Skairdykat, definitely. If she also told him I was FBI, probably not."

"It might be worth a shot, though," said Buchanan eagerly. "I know that place—it'd be perfect for an ambush. One road in, one road out, plenty of cover for the snipers—he comes after you there, his ass is ours."

Buchanan's excitement was contagious. "He'd probably come around back," Linda offered. "I could be up on the porch. Then when he— What?"

Buchanan was shaking his head. "As my daughter would say, that is *so* not happening."

"C'mon, I could—"

Another agent interrupted them. "Okay if I check the redial now?"

"Did you dust it yet?"

"No, Joe, I'm a complete idiot," the man said, taking the wall phone off the hook. "Of course I dusted it, what do you think?" He pushed a button on the handset, listened for a second or two, then asked whoever had picked up: "Actually, operator, I need to know what city *you're* in. . . . No, this is Special Agent Stroud with the FBI. I'm redialing from a phone at a crime scene—we're trying to ascertain . . . Right, right . . . I'll hold." He turned back to Buchanan with his hand over the mouthpiece. "It's directory assistance for Atlantic City—she's getting a supervisor."

"Atlantic City?" Linda's head jerked around so swiftly she almost gave herself another Lhermitte's.

"Yeah, I—"

"Never mind, I know who he was calling."

"Who?"

"His mother lives in Atlantic City—he was calling his mother."

Buchanan already had his cell phone out; he punched a speed-dial number. "This is Buchanan. Get me the R.A. in Atlantic City. If nobody's there, track 'em down—this is crash priority." He looked over at Buchanan, who was still on hold. "When the supervisor comes back on the line, get a phone number and an address for . . . ?" He looked back to Linda.

"Delamour," said Linda. "Rosie Delamour."

"How much does she know?"

"As of four o'clock yesterday, diddly-squat."

"Well, let's hope she's still blissfully—" Then, into the phone: "Yeah? Yeah, okay . . . LaFeo, this is Buchanan from Washington. We think Simon Childs might be heading your way."

4

After taking care of a few minor housekeeping details (yes, the patio door of 1211 Baja Way had been unlocked; no, Pender hadn't broken in; yes, Pender had had reason to believe Mr. Carpenter might have been in immediate physical danger; no, Miss Bell hadn't intentionally misled the mailman into thinking she was a federal agent—that sort of thing), Pender and Dorie drove back to Carmel.

He didn't offer any details as to what had been in the bathroom; she didn't ask. But that wasn't the real elephant-that-nobody's-talking-about in the car on the drive down; the real elephant for Dorie was that this was going to be their last night together—Pender had booked an eight o'clock flight out of San Francisco tomorrow morning.

So it took her completely by surprise when he asked her, hypothetically speaking of course, how long it would take her to pack.

"For what?" she asked suspiciously.

"Hypothetically? Call it a little vacation."

"How long?"

"I dunno, a week or two—that'd be up to you."

"Leaving when?"

"Tomorrow—with me; I got us two tickets." Then, before she could mount a protest: "Look, scout, the hardest part is the anticipation, right? By not telling you, I've already pared that down to the bare minimum. We pick up a pizza on the way home, you pack, ask Mrs. Whatsername next door, Mrs. Tibsen, to keep an eye on the place. Four-thirty in the morning, bing, we're on the road, and this time tomorrow we're sitting on my back porch eating crab cakes and watching the sun go down over the canal. And your aviophobia's a thing of the past, like your prosophono— your proposono— whatever the hell you—"

"Okay."

"—call it. What?"

"I said okay. I'll do it. I just don't want to talk about it."

"That's my girl," said Pender. "Heart of a lion, guts of a burglar, cornflower blue eyes to die for, and a rack that won't quit."

"Pender."

"What?"

"Shut the hell up before I change my mind."

5

Once again, time demonstrated its essentially elastic nature for Linda, as she and Buchanan waited for the callback from Larry LaFeo. Fifteen minutes, he said—it would take him fifteen minutes to get to Rosie Delamour's apartment. That was at eight-thirty, but the Danish Modern clock in the Gees' kitchen might as well have been a Dalí watch, as slowly as time seemed to be passing.

Guilt, of course, was no stranger to a good Catholic girl like Linda, but even when you're only beating yourself up, you still get to rest between rounds. And being an FBI agent, Buchanan reminded her, was like being a surgeon or an air traffic controller: you make a mistake, sometimes people die. Comes with the territory—you don't like it, maybe you should go into advertising, where the worst that happens, somebody buys a crummy car.

Which didn't mean OPR wasn't going to have her on the griddle—but neither, given the current climate, were they going to be eager to broadcast the fact that one of their agents had endangered two civilians, with fatal results. They'd probably settle for a medical retirement, and there was a provision in her federal health coverage plan that would—

Buchanan's cell phone beeped; they both jumped.

"Buchanan . . . Yeah, that's the one . . . Okay . . . Okay, got it . . . Affirmative, keep me in the loop. . . ." He hit the disconnect, but didn't put the phone back in his pocket.

"Well?" said Linda. "I'm dyin' heah." *Dog Day Afternoon* was one of her favorite movies.

"The Lexus is parked out front of the building. Atlantic City PD is bringing up their tac squad."

More Dalí's-clock watching. Buchanan left the kitchen, returned with two cups of hot coffee from God-knows-where. Linda switched from feeling guilty about the Gees to trying to decide whether she'd been negligent in not having Rosie put under surveillance. But yesterday, she reminded herself, there was no reason to believe Childs was even west of the Mississippi. So maybe she could let herself off on that one.

Or maybe not. The next call came in at nine-fifteen.

"Buchanan . . . No shit? . . . Sounds about right. . . . Let me know." Again the disconnect, followed by the infuriating stage pause.

"C'mon, spit it out." Linda wasn't sure how much more suspense she could take.

"He's there, all right. They have the mother on the phone—she called them while the tac squad was moving into place. She told the negotiator he's holding a gun on her. She says he says he doesn't want to shoot her, but he will if they try to come in. But the situation is currently stable, so as long as they have Childs contained, they want to wait him out, see what develops."

"*If* they have Childs contained. Rosie's his *mother,* Joe. She could be covering for him. He could be miles away by now."

"I'm sure they thought of that," said Buchanan. He

called LaFeo back, though. "Larry, Abruzzi wants to know how you know he's really in there. . . . Check, got it. . . . I'll let her know." He gave Linda the thumbs-up. "Negotiator says you can hear him talking in the background."

"Guess I'm getting paranoid." So much for all our scenarios, thought Linda. You can spitball until you're out of paper and spit, and in the end it plays out the way it plays out. His mother—he wanted to see his mother.

Special Agent Lawrence LaFeo's last call came in at nine-thirty-seven. ACPD officers were in the process of clearing the building floor by floor, and LaFeo himself was on his way up to the fifth floor with Mark Scott, one of the FBI's best hostage negotiators, who'd just arrived from Philadelphia, the field office with jurisdiction over Atlantic City.

Special Agent LaFeo's last words, to Buchanan anyway, were, "I'm getting too old for this shit," apparently in reference to the long climb. He promised, as he'd been promising all night, to call Buchanan back, keep them in the loop, so when ten o'clock had come and gone with no word, Buchanan called him and got a "not-responding" message on his cell screen.

"It must be going down," he told Linda. "God-*damn* I wish I was there."

So did Linda—until the call came in at ten-fifteen from LaFeo's partner, Special Agent Lisa Kingmore, out on the street outside Rosie's apartment building. Buchanan could barely hear her over the roar of the flames and the screaming sirens—not that there was much to tell at that point, other than that there'd been one hell of an explosion, and that the top two floors of the building were fully involved.

Eventually, with both Linda and Buchanan working their phones, they managed to piece an outline of the story together. At nine-forty-six, just around the time LaFeo and Scott would have been reaching the fifth floor, Rosie had mentioned something to the ACPD negotiator about smelling gas. The explosion had followed within seconds (the negotiator was still deaf in one ear from percussion tinnitus), blowing a hole clean through to the kitchen of the adjoining apartment (or so it was believed).

Casualties, in addition to the partially deafened negotiator and a few Atlantic City cops down in the street who'd been slightly injured by falling masonry, included both Childs and Rosie, probably killed in the explosion, as well as LaFeo, Scott, a sergeant from the tac squad, and Mrs. Schantz, Rosie's eighty-year-old next-door neighbor, who had all perished in the fire.

It would take another hour before the fire was brought under control, and yet another forty-five minutes until it was extinguished, and the arson investigators could begin the grisly work of sorting out the bodies. Exhausted as she was, Linda wouldn't allow herself to relax, much less head home, until Agent Kingmore, who had attached herself to the arson boys (always the first ones in after—and sometimes before—the all clear), was standing in what was left of Rosie's kitchen, looking down at two charred corpses, one female, one male.

And yes, the male, though curled up now, had probably been a six-footer in life, according to the arson investigator, who ought to have known, having seen quite a few of what he referred to as the crispy critters.

As for a more definitive identification, Linda was told that would have to wait at least until Simon Childs's dental records were obtained from his dentist, presumably in the Bay Area, for comparison with the corpse's dentition. But at this point nobody doubted it was Childs—certainly not Linda. Why, then, was she so reluctant to give it up and go home that Joe Buchanan practically had to drag her out to her car? Maybe it was because she already knew that this would be her last case.

And not just because of the Lhermitte's sign, or the numbness and tingling spreading up her left arm, but because Joe was right—when you screwed up in this job, people died. First the Gees, then Rosie and all the others. Linda thought back to her conversation with the poor old drunk only yesterday afternoon.

Let somebody else tell her her daughter's dead and her son's a monster—there must be people who get paid for that.

Good call, Abrootz, she told herself, as she climbed into the Geo. Then something else occurred to her: her grand gesture this evening, unburdening herself to Joe Buchanan, had been unnecessary. She'd gotten her wish—no, not wish, never that. What she'd *wished* for on the ride down was a false alarm. Instead, the second scenario: Gloria, Jim, Childs all dead. But as far as she was concerned, the results would have been even better this way—no one would ever have had to know who Skairdykat really was.

But maybe it wasn't too late. She could go back inside, throw herself on Joe's mercy, beg him to keep silent. He was a field agent, he'd understand. And he wouldn't even have to lie—just forget something a fellow agent had told him.

Sure, she would still have to resign, for all the reasons she'd already laid out for herself. But not in disgrace. And she would have spared herself the OPR grilling and all that other unpleasantness.

It all sounded good—so good that even thinking about it helped lift some of the crushing weight from Linda's bony shoulders, as she buckled her seat belt, turned the key in the ignition, and drove off, leaving Conroy Circle, her career, and her professional reputation behind, but bringing away with her the last few tattered shreds of her self-respect.

6

Pyromania, enuresis, cruelty to animals—the homicidal trinity of forensic psychiatry. Sid Dolitz used to have a standing bet with Pender: if Pender ever caught a serial killer who *didn't* have a childhood history of starting fires and/or wetting his bed and/or torturing small animals, Sid would buy him dinner.

Simon Childs had never wet his bed as a boy, and cruelty to small animals per se was anathema to him, although he did get a kick out of feeding white mice to Crusher, the boa constrictor who'd succeeded

Skinny as his boyhood pet. But Simon had certainly started a few fires in his day, and while the thrill wasn't as intensely orgasmic for him as it was for your true pyromaniac, there was a definite erotic charge that accompanied watching the flames and hearing the sirens.

So it was something of a disappointment to him, to have to miss the fire. But otherwise, Plan C had gone so smoothly that by the time he left Atlantic City on Cappy's classy old Harley, he was not only reasonably certain that the explosion and fire would take place as scheduled, but that the fates had given their seal of approval to the entire venture.

The key to the first part of the plan, as Simon had foreseen, was Rosie. The news about Missy had devastated her—but it gave Simon a chance to comfort her, to play the heartbroken, but loving son, which had not only endeared him to Rosie, but to Cappy as well.

With the ground prepared, Simon had then spun the same yarn he'd spun for Zap Strum after learning of Missy's death, once again imbuing the embellishments with the authority of his own emotional investment, as well as making sure that both Rosie and Cappy were kept well-lubricated with Select Choice vodka. And by the time he'd finished telling his rapt audience of two how a crooked FBI agent named Pender had tricked Missy into letting him into the house, then attacked Simon, how Missy tried to stop him and there was a scuffle, how the struggle had overtaxed her heart, and how Pender had then shifted the blame to Simon to cover his own rear end, Rosie didn't need any more convinc-

ing—maternal guilt alone would have been sufficient
motivation for her.

But just to be on the safe side, Simon added a
spoonful of sugar to make sure Cappy's medicine went
down smoothly. He took the old CPO aside and
showed him the satchel filled with cash, then explained
how once he, Simon, had confronted Pender while
wearing a hidden tape recorder and fooled him into
confessing, he wouldn't be needing his getaway money.
In which case, he would be happy—no, honored—to
leave the money behind for Cappy, as a token of his
appreciation for his help in clearing his name and
bringing Missy's killer to justice, not to mention the
loan of the Harley.

From the glitter in the old man's eyes when Simon
dumped half of his remaining stacks of dead presi-
dents on the bed, Simon was reasonably certain that
he had just bought himself a second accomplice. But
it wasn't only the money that had won Cappy over, it
was the prospect of adventure. Judging by the man's
excitement and enthusiasm when they started going
over the next part of the plan, Simon had the feeling
that Cappy would have paid *him* for the opportunity
to be useful again, to do something important for
somebody, something that mattered, to be a participant in life again, and maybe even have a little fun
with the cops in the bargain.

Simon had thought of everything. The two were to
stay in the kitchenette portion of the apartment,
where they couldn't be seen from the apartment's
only window. Rosie was to wait half an hour, then call
the cops and tell them she was being held hostage by
her son. After that, all Rosie had to do was stall, stall,

stall; all Cappy had to do was let himself be heard in the background every so often.

And when push came to shove, Simon assured them, they wouldn't have to put themselves in danger—he wouldn't think of allowing any harm to come to either of them. Let the cops in, explain how Simon had threatened to kill them if they didn't help him get away, then go treat yourselves to a fancy dinner someplace with the money Simon had so generously left behind, and never mind the senior/twilight discounts.

Before leaving, he'd traded clothes with Cappy and kissed his mother good-bye. The wrinkled cheek was surprisingly soft against his lips; the eyes were filled with tears. She cried easily, this old woman—but had she cried when she spent the blood money Grandfather Childs had given her to abandon her children? And did she cry when she spread her legs for that old man on the Murphy bed? Did she cry for her children then?

Of course not—so why should I cry for her? thought Simon as he closed the door behind him. Then he'd made a big stomping show of starting down the stairway, before doubling back quietly to ring the bell of the apartment next door.

"Who's there?" A shaky, phlegmy old voice. Perfect for his purposes: if the occupant was as feeble as she sounded, there would be no need to strong-arm her, as he'd originally planned. He might not even need to improvise a delayed-action fuse to trigger the explosion.

"Gas company, ma'am," Simon had called. "I'm afraid there may be a problem with your line."

* * *

Twenty minutes later he was on his way. He might even have passed the Bu-car containing Special Agents LaFeo and Kingmore, traveling in the opposite direction. He heard the explosion an hour later, from a phone booth near Deep Water, New Jersey, just east of the Delaware Memorial Bridge spanning the Delaware River.

"Hello, Mrs. Schantz? This is Joe from the gas company. Your readings are all clear now—as they say in the Navy, the smoking lamp is lit. . . . Yes, ma'am, I know the smell is strong—that's the anti-inflammatory I told you we were going to be pumping in. . . . I quite understand—I'm a pack-a-day man myself. What I want you to do, though, while I'm holding, I want you to flick that Bic for me, walk around the apartment, see if the flame wavers. . . . No, you can keep the Bic with our compliments. . . . Yes, ma'am, I'll wait."

While he waited, Simon held the phone at arm's length to avoid the percussion tinnitus syndrome shortly to be experienced by the hostage negotiator for the Atlantic City Police Department, currently holding the line for Rosie Delamour next door—unlike her, he knew what was coming.

And though he'd told himself he wasn't going to cry, afterward there were tears in his eyes as he replaced the receiver and walked slowly back to the Harley. He was an orphan now, he'd suddenly realized—a motherless, fatherless, sisterless child.

7

Dorie and Pender hit the hay early. It didn't take Pender long to drop off—within twenty minutes he was bleating and blatting like a Sun Ra solo scored by John Cage.

No such luck for Dorie, not with her first airplane ride looming at seven-fifty in the A.M. It was funny, she mused, how she'd never really thought of herself as an aviophobe. Probably because flying was so easy to avoid. But fear of flying was one of those sneaky phobias. It's not really a problem for me, you say: I don't like to travel anyway. And you never think about what came first, the fear of the chicken or the fear of the egg.

Plenty of time to think about all that now, however. And the longer she lay there listening to Pender snore, the more unfair it seemed. Wasn't this whole thing his idea in the first place? So how come he gets to sleep like an adenoidal baby while I lie here gnawing on my liver? She scooted over toward the warm center of the bed until she felt his hip warm and solid against hers.

"Hey, Pen? Pen, you awake?"

"Apparently."

"Tell me about your house."

"Hill. Woods. Canal. Bedrooms, lots of bedrooms. Pen sleep now."

"I wouldn't count on it. How come you have so many bedrooms if you live alone?"

Pender bowed to the inevitable. "Tinsman. The

lockkeeper. He used to add another bedroom onto the end of the house every time his wife had another kid. She had seven." A portentous pause—this was one of Pender's set pieces. "Only six bedrooms were added on." And another pause.

"How come?" Dorie rolled onto her side and pillowed both hands under her cheek the way she used to when she was a little girl—her daddy had been an excellent storyteller.

"The way the rangers tell it—every year they have a special Halloween program down at Great Falls: rangers in period costumes tell all the ghost stories and murder stories from the history of the canal, and they always end with Tinsman's Lock. The way they tell it, the last kid wasn't Tinsman's. His wife had been having an affair with a redheaded mule driver from Rock Creek. They say the lockkeeper cut her throat, then drowned the seventh baby in the canal. Some people claim to have seen her ghost wandering up and down the banks in a bloodstained nightgown, searching for her redheaded baby."

"Great, a ghost story," said Dorie with a mock shudder that turned real at the end, as mock shudders often do. "Remember one thing, buster: *I* don't sleep, *you* don't sleep."

Pender reached across his body with his good arm, and patted her shoulder. "You don't have a thing to worry about. They say she only walks on Halloween night."

"Pender."

"What?"

"Halloween is this coming Sunday."

"Is it really?" Wide-eyed and innocent; butter

wouldn't melt . . . , as his sister Ida would have said.

"Yeah—and you know what's amazing? For the first time since I can remember, I don't care—it doesn't matter."

"I remember you telling me Halloweens were always tough on you."

"And Sunday ones were the worst. 'Cause if it fell on a Sunday, that'd be three days I'd have to hide out in my house with the curtains drawn. Couldn't go shopping on Friday, because the store clerks might be in costumes with masks, on Saturday night people in masks might be coming and going from parties, and then of course the trick-or-treaters on Sunday."

"No trick-or-treaters out where I live."

"But don't you see, it doesn't matter anymore? I'd almost like to give it a try."

"Ask and you shall receive. Pool, the Liaison Support secretary, she and her roommate always do Halloween up real big, costume party, haunted house and all. If you want me to take you, I have a standing invitation."

"I'll have to get back to you on that," said Dorie. She suspected it was an idea that was going to seem less and less attractive, the closer to Sunday they got.

8

It was close to two in the morning when Linda let herself into the house. She hung her coat on a peg in the vestibule; as she limped past the answering machine in the living room, she saw the message light blinking, and stopped to check it out.

Mr. Pender, this is Judge Heinz. I hope you've received my letter by now. There are a few matters we need to go over. Please give me a call at your convenience.

He'd left a number. The machine was on a small table near the vestibule, along with the wire basket full of mail Linda had been saving for Pender. She found a letter from Noble J. Heinz, Attorney at Law, LaFarge, Wisconsin, jotted the telephone number on the back of the envelope, and left it on the top of the pile. Pender was due back late tomorrow afternoon—Linda had no intention of getting out of bed until then.

Or answering any Bu-calls. She retrieved her cell from the pocket of her coat and called her own office to leave a message for Pool, to the effect that she would not be coming into work tomorrow, and that if there were any calls from media or brass or especially OPR, could Pool possibly, please, stall them, hold them off, tell them she was dead, anything—Linda would call her on Monday to explain. And, oh yeah, thanks for the invite, but she'd have to pass on Halloween, because she was going to bed now and intended to stay there, not just through Halloween, but probably through Thanksgiving as well.

And exhausted as she was, it was only the knowledge that she really could sleep in as long as she wanted tomorrow that gave Linda the incentive to prepare for bed, instead of just throwing herself across the bedcovers and collapsing in the rancid clothes she'd been wearing for over eighteen hours.

Linda undressed in the bathroom, while seated on the toilet, pulling her slacks down over her shoes and tossing her dirty clothes into the mildewy rattan hamper. Then she washed up a little, brushed her teeth, and crossed the hall to her bedroom wearing only her shoes and braces, and leaning even more heavily than usual on her cane. Tomorrow, she reminded herself, she'd have to start wearing a bathrobe for the trip across the hall. Tonight, though, she was too tired even to pull on a nightie—she untied her shoes, slipped them off along with the braces, crawled under the covers naked, closed her eyes, and was asleep within minutes.

A dream. It had to be a dream. Simon Childs standing over the bed, holding a revolver in one hand, hiding the other hand behind his back. But not the Childs from the elevator video, with the self-assured manner and the easy slouch, nor the groomed and handsome Childs of the DMV photo, looking better with his silver hair and dapper 'stash than anybody has a right to on their driver's license.

No, this was a ragged, haggard caricature of Childs—no hair, no mustache, wearing an unzipped black leather bomber jacket over a hideous sport shirt of mustard yellow and dung brown.

"Where's your boyfriend, Skairdykat?"

Still clinging to the hope that it was only a dream, Linda tried to open her eyes. They were already open. She closed them instead, heard the springs creak and felt the mattress shift. When she opened her eyes again, he was sitting on the edge of the bed, grinning like the happiest madman in the asylum.

"I asked you where your boyfriend was. If you don't answer me, you'll have to answer to my friend here."

Slowly he drew his hand from behind his back. Linda was not surprised to see that he was grasping a snake by the neck. This was *her* dream: what else would he have had in his hand? She tried to draw back, but with his weight atop the covers, she found herself pinned beneath them. Not very dreamlike, she thought, trying to wriggle free—not very dreamlike at all.

"You're dead," she told him. "They found your body."

"Keep telling yourself that," he replied, slipping the revolver into the waistband of his high-water slacks. "It'll make the game more fun. But until we get started, you can avoid a good deal of unnecessary suffering by simply telling me where your boyfriend is, and when he's expected back."

Unnecessary suffering. Dream or no dream, Linda didn't like the sound of that; dream or no dream, she decided to play along. "I don't have a boyfriend, but if you mean Agent Pender, he's on vacation—I haven't heard from him in nearly a week."

"My misunderstanding. And when is Agent Pender

expected home?" There was nothing in Simon's voice to suggest sarcasm—or that he had tugged the covers down to Linda's waist.

"I don't know."

"I find that hard to believe." He looked up from her naked torso, searched her eyes.

Linda held his gaze. Though those were not a pair of eyes you wanted to be looking into while you were trying to hold on to your sanity, neither were the snake's—she could see its tongue flickering in and out at the edge of her peripheral vision.

He brushed his fingers across her stomach. "I'm still finding that hard to believe."

"Listen," she said, angered by the intimacy of the touch, "if I *were* expecting him momentarily, do you think I'd tell you?"

The hand began traveling up, past her chest; his long fingers gripped her chin and turned her head toward the snake. "Eventually," he said.

9

Simon triumphant! But even he was a little surprised by the ease with which all the pieces were falling into place. He shouldn't have been, he told himself: the great ones always make it look easy. Naturally the cops had bought the charred-corpse scenario. The key was suggestion, the planting of an assumption that became a fulfilled expectation. He didn't have to convince them that the body was his—they'd convinced themselves.

Nor did Simon deny there was an element of luck in all this. He was lucky the Harley had been available—it would have been a lot harder to hide the Lexus in the woods. He was lucky, too, that Skairdykat had failed to lock the front door behind her—but luck favors patience as well as preparation. Arriving before she did, having the patience to wait, to watch the empty house, instead of just breaking in, meant there were no signs of forced entry that might have alarmed her into locking up—or not entering in the first place.

As for the game itself, Simon had never doubted his abilities. *Unnecessary suffering . . . eventually:* more suggestion, gentle guidance. Simon's theory, Simon's genius: fear comes from within. You can't drive it in like a railroad spike; you have to plant it like a seed and nurture it until it blossoms.

True fear, however, is a bloom that demands time, patience, attention, and concentration, none of which Simon could provide until he knew when and how Pender was expected to return. And yet the traditional mainstay of the torturer—the infliction of pain, either gross or subtle—was not available to him. Not only was pain itself anodyne to fear, but the fear of pain was a mere avoidance reflex, like a worm shrinking from a hot needle, and as such, relatively uninteresting to Simon.

Still, he reasoned (and despite his having logged only a few hours of sleep since Ogallala, thanks to the crosstops he found his mind was as sharp as it had been all night), if the man wasn't home at two in the morning, he probably wasn't coming home. Even if he did, Simon would hear the car coming down the long drive, and still have the element of surprise on his side.

More likely, though, he'd have all night to play with Skairdykat. So he let her slip on a bathrobe—naked, she looked like a concentration camp victim; Simon much preferred Dorie's type—and helped her into the living room, where he laid a crackling fire with last winter's dry logs. Once again, it was all so easy: no need to tie her up; she wasn't going anywhere without her cane and braces. He didn't even have to gag her: this time of night there wasn't a living soul within a mile of Tinsman's Lock.

"Kind of chilly tonight," he said, sitting down next to her with the canvas travel bag on his lap, and the snake in the bag. "Does it ever snow around here?"

"I don't know. I just moved here, myself."

"I know—Gloria told me. By the way, do you know how she died?"

By the way? By the fucking way? Linda ignored the question, stared into the fire. How sane and casual he sounded when she wasn't looking at him.

"When I ask a question, I expect you to answer it. Remember what I said about unnecessary suffering?"

"Oh, that's a crock. You want me to be afraid of what you *might* do, so you don't actually have to *do* anything."

Simon was impressed. He was also beginning to suspect he was in for a tussle. She would fight him every step of the way, this FBI agent. He didn't mind—it was his game, and they had all night. "I'll tell you anyway. She was in the bath. We'd been together all night—just like you and I are going to be. *Hot* bath. No suds. The—"

"Yes!" Linda hadn't meant to shout.

"Yes, what?"

"Yes, I know how she died. Coral snake, neurotoxin, respiratory failure. So you can save *yourself* the trouble."

"But it sounds so clinical, the way you put it. It wasn't clinical at all. For one thing, the coral didn't *want* to bite her—I had to hold it up against her neck, press it right up tight against her jugular, then let its tail droop into the hot water. They have short fangs, the corals—they have to—"

"Shut up. Just shut the fuck up."

He boxed her ear. It was a trick he'd learned from Grandfather Childs. Very painful—even prizefighters hate to get whacked on the ear. One way or another, it seemed, the old man was always with him. "To be continued," he said. "Where's the kitchen?"

Linda felt as if she'd won a small battle—at least he'd dropped the pretense of civility when he slapped her. She resisted the temptation to provoke him further, though. She let him help her into the kitchen, kept her mouth shut while he made coffee.

Then he poured them each a cup, sat down across from her at the kitchen table, and it began again. Linda did her best to tune him out, but you can't close your ears like you can your eyes; you can look away, but you can't listen away. So she heard most of it, the worst of it, as Childs recounted in meticulous detail how Gloria had died.

And he was right; it wasn't clinical at all. He made

Gloria's death throes come alive; he acted out the pain, and how she'd gradually gone numb, how her eyelids had drooped, how a look of surprise had passed over those half-hidden eyes at the end, when she tried to draw a breath and her lungs would not respond.

A lousy way to die, thought Linda. But she could have guessed all that, extrapolated it from the condition of the corpse and the fax from Poison Control, if she'd wanted to. So all Childs had really accomplished, she realized, was to take the incentive out of the surrender-and-get-it-over-with option for her. Which left the fight-to-the-last-breath option. Physically, she told herself, she was no match for him—physically, she was no match for the Pillsbury Doughboy—but maybe she had a shot at outwitting him.

As in any fight, it was always a good idea to get your adversary distracted. "So how'd it go in Atlantic City? How's your mom?"

"A drunken hooer—a dead drunken hooer. How's yours?"

Touchy, touchy—that told her she was on the right track. "Did you mean to kill her, or was it an accident?"

Simon almost answered, then caught himself. Wrong game. "That's neither here nor there—I still haven't finished telling you about Gloria."

"You got to where Gloria's dead. That's pretty fucking finished. What'd you do, kill her twice?" When you were trying to convince somebody you were tough—when you were trying to convince yourself, for that matter—it helped to be an Italian from the Bronx. Swearing helped, too.

"Watch your language."

"Fuck you."

Simon was momentarily at a loss. He couldn't let her attitude stand, but if he let things get heated, he might find himself playing the game with a bloodied corpse; not much satisfaction there. "In case you've forgotten, Skairdykat, I do have the power of life and death over you."

"Big hairy deal. Every *strunz'* with a loaded gun has the power of life and death."

In a contest like this, Linda was beginning to realize, it also helped to have a fatal disease. She watched the steam curl lazily from her coffee, then took a tiny sip—still a little too hot to drink, but not bad for the Safeway house blend. Linda was starting to appreciate little things—that was also supposed to be one of the pluses of having a fatal disease. Yeah, right. Then it occurred to her: in the last hour or so, the odds of her dying from MS had dropped considerably.

"You're really asking for it," said Childs. "You understand that, don't you?"

Linda decided there might be a way to steer the conversation to her advantage. "Mr. Childs, I want to live. But sometimes it just isn't in the cards. You of all people ought to know that—you don't have much longer to live than I do. Oh—but I forgot. You're rich. You're mentally ill, at least by most people's standards, and you're rich. They don't execute sick, rich people in this country. If you give yourself up—if you let me handle your surrender—you'll be living the high life in some country club asylum, like that du Pont guy who killed that wrestler, long after this damn MS sends me to my grave."

"Excellent point," said Childs. "How's your coffee?"

The pleasant tone should have alerted Linda; instead she thought for a moment she had succeeded in getting him to consider another option. "Very good. I was just waiting for it to cool down."

He picked up her mug, dashed the contents in her face. "There," he said. "That'll cool it down a little quicker."

As if to show his contempt, Simon left Linda alone in the kitchen while he returned to the living room to fetch the travel bag. Unfortunately, he hadn't allowed her to put on her braces or bring her cane into the kitchen with her. Her face still stinging from the hot coffee, Linda was inching her chair backward toward the counter, bound for the knife drawer, when Simon returned. Without breaking stride or even glancing at Linda, he grabbed the top rung of her chair and dragged it back to the table; it might as well not have been occupied.

"I think it's time." He dropped the travel bag into Linda's lap. "Do you think it's time?"

"You're gonna do what you're gonna do."

"Well, yes. But you mustn't give up hope."

"Why not?" It might have been an attempt at irony—then again, it might not. Childs seemed to take it seriously enough.

"Because it will spoil the game," he said.

No surprises here, Linda reminded herself, as Simon slipped on the heavy leather gauntlet and reached into the travel bag. He frightens them, he custom fits their deaths—we knew all that. She braced herself, and if it's possible to shout at yourself in your interior monologue, she shouted.

Okay, asshole, I'll play your fucking game. Lord knows, I can't die any younger. Come on, whip it out, let's see what you got. Fuck, is that all? Not a very big one, is it? Kind of skinny, too. Black nose, black head, pretty bands, red-yellow-black-yellow-red-yellow-black down to the black tail. Yeah, that's right, a little closer, bring it a little closer. I love this, I want a better look. I love this snake I love this fucking snake. Forked tongue, flickering out. That's how they smell, it's just smelling me. Smelling the coffee. Wake up and smell the coffee. Good snake pretty snake I love it observe observe observe the red and black bands are wider than the yellow ones the red bands have little black flecks the pupils are round not slits like I thought yeah sure bring it right up to my fucking eye I love it I—

When she made her move, Linda went, not for the snake, and not for Childs, though she wanted to rip his face off, but for the glove. She reached around the snake, grabbed the gauntlet at the wrist with both hands while simultaneously throwing herself backward, and held on to the rough leather for dear life as her chair tipped over; she hit the floor still throttling the empty glove at arm's length.

Okay, I played your fucking game, thought Linda, as the snake slithered rapidly but gracefully through the kitchen door, with Childs in clumsy pursuit. *Now, where's my lovely parting gifts?*

One advantage to having been raised in his grandfather's house—Simon had learned to handle disappointment. Or at least to disguise it. It didn't matter

whether your birthday presents consisted of a savings
bond and an itchy sweater, or if your dinner was liver
and onions with brussels sprouts, you'd better not let
an expression other than stupefied gratitude cross
your mug or Grandfather would have your hide.
(None of this applied to Missy, of course—Missy
always got away with murder.)

So as he made his way back to the kitchen, Simon
reassured himself that he'd gotten his money's
worth out of the coral with Gloria. And as for that
pitiful creature crawling across the kitchen floor,
dragging her legs behind her? Useless—that was a
good word for her. Blame it on the disease—knowing that she was dying anyway rendered her unfit for
the game.

But there was always Pender's game. Pender would
make it all worthwhile, thought Simon, striding
across the room and dragging Linda back from the
counter—she was trying to pull herself up, probably
hoping to climb through the tiny window over the
sink. She turned, raked at his face with blunt and bitten nails. He caught her wrists, bent her arms back,
leveraged her down to her knees.

"Do you know what I'm going to do to you?" he
asked, kneeling in front of her, looking into her eyes.
He saw white-hot anger, but not a blessèd trace of fear.

"No, and I don't give a rat's ass," she said. She'd
have spat in his face, but she didn't want to give him
the satisfaction of watching her trying to work up
some saliva.

"I'm going to let you live," he said quietly. "I'm
going to make you watch while I blind your friend

Pender—slowly, one eye at a time—and then I'm going to let you both live."

"We'll dance on your grave," Linda snarled back. "If I have to lead him there and he has to hold me up, we'll dance on your fucking grave."

10

Darkness. Smell of dank cement, old brick and old timbers, damp cardboard and laundry soap, and the faintest whiff of decay from the far corners, the unexplored reaches of the cellar where generations of rodent corpses had long since crumbled to dust.

Linda was lying on her side with her hands behind her back and her wrists tied to her ankles with a length of clothesline; Childs had gagged her with the belt of her flannel bathrobe. She could hear a television overhead, somewhere off to her right. Sounded like Childs was listening to CNN.

Linda held her breath, straining to make out the words. Media coverage, she knew, was a two-edged sword for law enforcement in these situations— every piece of information broadcast to warn the public would likewise inform the fugitive. So if the arson investigators had figured out that the body in 5-B wasn't Childs, he would learn it along with everybody else. Then she could expect footsteps descending the basement steps, a bright light piercing the darkness, the resounding boom of a Colt .45 in an enclosed space.

On the other hand, if they still hadn't discovered that Childs was alive, there wasn't much hope of anybody calling to check on *her.* So either way, Linda told herself, she was screwed. And unless she could think of something between now and tomorrow afternoon, so was Pender.

After the big story—double murder in Georgetown, six dead in Atlantic City, including the fugitive serial killer—the sports came on. Something about the Redskins. In this day and age, how could you call a sports team the Redskins? It was not only demeaning, thought Simon indignantly, it was inaccurate. Native Americans were no more red than Gloria was yellow. She was ivory, that's what she was. Beautiful antique ivory.

Thinking about Gloria, Simon felt a stab of regret. Not over killing her, but over losing her. Naked, terrified, pliant, in the bed or in the bath, she'd been *his,* completely and entirely *his*—a relationship like that, you just naturally miss it when it's over.

Simon switched off the bedroom TV, lay back on Pender's bed. Underneath the gloss of the dexedrine he was dull and exhausted—he hadn't slept since Wednesday morning—but whether exhaustion would be soporific enough for someone with a snootful of crosstops and a history of sleep disorders was highly questionable.

On the other hand, he didn't want to knock himself out with one of his few remaining Halwanes. It seemed unlikely that in the space of three hours the cops would not only figure out he was still alive, but trace him here as well—but if they did come, he didn't want to be taken while he slept. Not without a fight—and not alive, either.

But he did have one of Zap's Ecstasy capsules left. He swallowed it dry, and while waiting for it to take effect he kept the blind rat away by thinking about the upcoming game. Pender's game. Searching the house earlier, after stowing Skairdykat in the cellar, Simon had learned that the information he'd failed to extract from her had been right in front of his nose the whole time, or at least the whole time they were in the kitchen. A note, stuck to the refrigerator with a magnet shaped like a banana: *P: United 970, dep SFO 7:50a, Thu, 10/28—arr Dul, 4:07 p.*

Four-oh-seven. Simon went over it in his head again. Dulles wasn't that far over the Virginia border. If the flight was on time, if Pender didn't check his baggage and the traffic wasn't horrendous, then the earliest he'd be arriving would be five; five-thirty or six more likely. Still daylight. Simon would wait inside—the vestibule would screen him from Pender.

But if for some unforeseen reason Pender decided to go around, to enter the house via the back porch, there was no cover in the living room—Simon would have to hide in that first bedroom and wait for him there. Either way, the Colt would be cocked and ready. If Pender ignored the order to freeze, Simon would kneecap him; if he obeyed it, Simon would secure him—the man was a cop: there had to be a pair of cuffs around here someplace—and the game would begin.

The only other question was whether to bring

Skairdykat upstairs or Pender down to the cellar. Simon decided to play that by ear. Or by eye, he thought with a chuckle. Then we'll see who dances on whose grave.

11

The natural habitat of the eastern coral snake is varied, from scrublands to woodlands to swamp verges, but the species is rarely found north of the thirty-fifth parallel: they don't much care for cold. And this particular individual had been born and raised under the lights of the reptilarium: he or she had no yearning for the wide open spaces, not when there was food under the house.

The coral had never hunted before, but neither had it ever been hungry before. (The instinct was programmed, anyway—nature's plan for reptiles didn't involve Mommy or Daddy Snake spending a lot of quality time with the young'uns, teaching them how to fend.) The mice under Pender's house were well fed (everything in Pender's house but the ficus in the living room was well fed) and had never been hunted by anything as fast and deadly as a coral snake before. *Mus musculus* v. *Micrurus fulvius fulvius* wasn't much of a contest.

Afterward, another programmed instinct kicked in, a thermal tropism: find warmth. The warmest place in the cold cellar was on the floor between the furnace and the water heater, but no sooner had the coral settled down than the thermostat on the furnace kicked in with a full-throated, percussive roar even a deaf snake could feel.

Once again, nurture affected nature's plan. The coral had been raised, and more important, fed, by humans; it had no fear of them—quite the opposite. And the next warmest place in the cold cellar was across the room, next to the human. For all the snake knew, there might even be more food by the human, after the mouse had been digested. And perhaps there was also a conditioned reflex at work: this human smelled like coffee; coffee was the first thing the coral smelled every morning when the humans arrived to turn on the warm lights, and feed it, and clean its cage.

Or maybe it was just lonely. If snakes even *get* lonely—they are among the most difficult of creatures to anthropomorphize. It *was* true, though, that this one had never lived alone—never even been alone until the scarlet king had made good its escape. And even if the coral didn't *crave* a companion, it certainly wasn't averse to one that smelled like coffee and pumped out heat at a steady 98.6 degrees Fahrenheit.

Humans are not without instincts of their own. The coral didn't make any noise, it didn't give off any warmth, and it wasn't actually touching her skin, only her wool bathrobe, but Linda sensed its presence. She wanted to crawl away, but it had taken her too long to achieve her current position, lying on her side, her knees drawn up in front of her as far as the rope permitted, with a jagged-edged chunk of brick behind her, wedged into place between the wall and her bound wrists.

But humans, as opposed to snakes, can talk themselves into going against their instincts. Linda told herself it was nothing—*nothing!*—and went back to sawing at the rope. It was hard work, with barely perceptible progress—she could saw for only a minute or so at a time, then had to rest her arms and shoulders for an equal period of time.

During one of these rest periods the *nothing!* squirmed more tightly against her, until it was an undeniable *something*. If Linda hadn't just had an up-close-and-personal encounter with the coral, it would have taken her much longer to identify just what that something was, pressing against her so quietly and insistently. Instead, a concrete visual image came to her sight-starved mind almost immediately. The black snout, the flickering tongue, the round pupils, the muscular writhing beneath the shiny tricolored bands. She moaned into her fuzzy flannel gag—but only once, and softly, before her sense of humor, or at least irony, came into play. What's next? she asked herself. What's fucking next, the thuggees of Kali?

Linda had drawn back in spite of herself. The rope tautened against the brick; the coral wriggled closer. To her surprise, Linda found its presence at least tolerable.

She *had* been afraid of snakes her whole life, she really had—Gloria had been with her the day their anthro class came all the way up to the Bronx Zoo primarily to see the primates (the *other* primates, their instructor had emphasized), when Linda had passed out at the door of the reptile house—but she was afraid of them no longer. Must have worked through it when Childs was thrusting the coral into her face. She'd read about that happening, on phobia.com.

Flooding, they called it: the most extreme and successful form of counterphobic programming. And of course some good old-fashioned information hadn't hurt: Childs said it hadn't wanted to bite Gloria; and it certainly hadn't bitten *her* even when she yanked it violently from Childs's grasp.

But even if she wasn't in any real danger from this serpent, Linda reminded herself, there was still the other snake, the human one, pacing the floor directly overhead. Quickly she went back to work. Freeing her hands might not help—she was still weaponless—but it sure wouldn't hurt.

Then it struck her—she wasn't weaponless. Or rather, she wouldn't be, if only she could get her hands free before Childs returned for her, or before the coral slithered away, whichever came first.

12

Simon hadn't thought about Halloween since he'd bought the masks for his game with Dorie a week and a half ago. But unable to sleep, and with the blind rat closing in on him, he wandered into the living room, poked up the fire, and channel-surfed the larger TV there until he found a pre-Halloween-weekend-horror-thon on one of the Turner channels. *Cat People,* with Simone Simon—"She was marked with the curse of those who slink and court and kill by night!"—was just ending and *Curse of the Cat People,* the quasi-sequel, was about to come on. A real stinker, as Simon remembered it from the Horror Club days. No curse, no cat people—it hadn't even scared Nervous Nellie.

The film proved to be a lot more enjoyable on Ecstasy, but not good enough to stay awake through. Eventually exhaustion and serotonin trumped the crosstops: Simon fell asleep in the Barcalounger. Not surprisingly, Nelson featured prominently in his dream. They were kids again—or kids still, however it works in dreams. They were bicycling through Tilden Park, as they often had. Nelson skidded to a stop, pointed to something in the bushes by the side of the trail. It was a body. A man's body, nude, facedown. Nelson ran away, leaving Simon alone with the body. Simon wanted to run away, too, but he knew some-how that Grandfather Childs was waiting at the head of the trail—he'd get a beating if he went running out like that scaredy-cat Nelson. He rolled the body over, brushed the mud, the damp leaves and clinging leaf mold, from the face.

"Who's that?" Grandfather Childs had somehow materialized, and was standing over him.

"It's Nelson, sir," said Simon. "That's what he looks like now." Simon had also turned into his pre-sent, grown-up, self, and the body was now in the tub of the master bathroom of 2500.

"Did you kill him?"

"Sort of. Sir." An adult now, Simon was no longer cowed by the old man—he just wanted to show him how he could do everything by the book.

"Sort me no *sort of*s, boy. You either did or you did not."

"Indirectly, sir. *I* glued him to the bathtub, but he turned on the water by himself."

"Going to bury him in the basement with the others?"

"You know about the others?"

"Of course I know about the others. Don't be stupid. And, boy?"

"Yes, sir?"

"While you're at it, dig yourself a hole this time."

"I'll see you in *H E* double *L* first," said Simon.

"Yes," said the old man in the dream. "Most likely you will."

In the basement, Linda was sure he'd left the horror movies on to torment her. The screams, the spooky organ music—it had to have been deliberate.

But it was also pointless. What kind of wusses does he take us for? she asked the coral, rhetorically. By now, she was as glad for its companionship as it seemed to be for hers, and as she went back to sawing at the rope binding her wrists, she would have been willing to stake her life—she was, in fact, staking her life—that at this point in their relationship, the coral was no more likely to bite her than she was to bite it.

By morning, however, that would all change.

XII

Tinsman's Lock

1

A cold snap had swept in overnight; when the breeze came up just before dawn, Simon could hear the brittle autumn leaves whispering to each other. A hundred, a thousand, ten thousand tiny conversations, all on the same subject: frost coming, death, a great falling.

Until then, enjoy the show, thought Simon, standing on the back porch with a blanket drawn over his bare shoulders. And what a show it was: the sun rising behind him; the dew sparkling on the brightly colored leaves and the grass, and turning even the cobwebs into strings of diamonds; the sunlight glinting off the still, dark green water of the canal; the dawn mist rising.

But on his way back into the house, Simon was startled from his reverie by the sight of a reflection in the glass door: tottering toward him, clutching a blanket around its shoulders like a refugee, was an unshaven, haggard scarecrow with eyes like two pee-

holes in the snow. He winked at it; Grandfather
Childs winked back. Shaken, Simon reached for the
door handle; so did Grandfather Childs.

The last strands of the rope parted around dawn.
There were no windows in the cellar, no visible cracks
in the plank flooring overhead, but enough light had
seeped in from somewhere for Linda to be able to
make out the outline of the coral. Thank you, God,
she whispered: of all the factors beyond Linda's control over the course of the long night—the cold, the
thirst, the pain, basically everything except the fear
and the endless sawing—the one she'd spent the most
time talking to God about was the coral. Please, God,
let it be there when I'm ready.

And it was, coiled loosely and still sound asleep, to
all appearances. Maybe it's hibernating, she told herself hopefully, as she drew her right arm from behind
her back, slowly, so as not to alert the snake, and in
stages, because that's the only way her stiff, sore
shoulder would move. Maybe it's hibernating and it
will just lie there all day.

Yeah, right. Hope springs eternal. For your fucking
throat. Frankly, Linda wasn't sure whether the feat she
had in mind could be accomplished even by a strong,
healthy individual, but she was relatively certain that
her chance of grasping the coral behind the head and
hanging on to it until Childs returned was better than
the chance that it would remain where it was.

As she waited for feeling and mobility to return to
her right hand and arm—the fingertips of the left
were an uncomfortable combination of numb and
pins-and-needles—Linda thought about all the ways

this could go bad on her. She'd seen how fast the
coral could move; she knew she'd only get the one
shot at it. If she missed, it would certainly escape; if
she grasped it incorrectly, it might turn on her. She
thought of Gloria. Unimaginable, to die that way, in
pain, alone, gasping for air.

And even if she grasped it correctly, how long
would she be able to hold on? If it were angry, if it
thrashed in her grip? If she fell asleep, if her attention
wavered for a—

No! She caught herself. This is where you came in,
Abrootz. You can go around on that merry-go-round
until Childs comes for you, or you can grab the bull
by the, I mean the snake first catch the snake then
worry about holding on to it but what if oh fuck just
do it you sound like a Nike ad just do it oh fuck oh
fuck oh—

2

One thing about insomnia: it made getting up at four-
thirty in the morning seem like the lesser of two evils.

Despite her threat, Dorie had let Pender sleep. She
also let him drive—all she had to do was shift the
lever into "R," then into "D" once they were out of the
driveway, and it was beddy-bye in the backseat for
Dorie; he wouldn't need her again until they turned
the car in at the airport.

Pender didn't miss the conversation. Instead of

turning on the radio, Pender went over the Childs case in his mind as he drove. Still unaware of the events of the previous evening, he was trying to put himself in Childs's place. Where does he go when he leaves Concord? A man with his money, wouldn't Childs have bought himself a hideaway somewhere? Possibly in another country. Mexico was closest, of course. Canada, however, was more reluctant to extradite prisoners who faced the death penalty.

Then there was Costa Rica, favored by your wealthier fugitives; Brazil—or do we have an extradition treaty with them now? Damn, I used to know that.

So never mind where he's going to go, concentrate on how he's going to get there. One thing for sure— almost for sure—he didn't drive that Volvo over either border. The airports and bus stations were already covered—how about on foot? Or . . .

He worked on the possibilities for most of the drive to the airport, and all he came up with after nearly two hours were a few long shots. Find out if Childs had paid any property taxes to foreign countries. See if he'd ever taken Missy out of this country—he might have a phony passport for himself, but would he have gotten one for her?

Once they'd dropped the car off, Pender turned his attention to Dorie. He understood enough about phobias by now to know that it was not flying per se that she feared, but the fear of flying. She was less afraid of a crash than she was that she'd lose control, have a panic attack, maybe pass out. So he didn't bother reassuring her about the safety of air travel or reciting the statistics that said you were more likely to die in your car within ten miles of home than in an airplane accident.

Instead, as they took their seats on the shuttle van at the Enterprise lot, he leaned as close to her as the brim of his Panama would allow and whispered into her ear that if she wanted to have a panic attack, that would be fine with him. And if she wanted to pass out, that would also be fine with him: he'd stay close enough at all times to catch her before she hit the ground and broke her nose again, then sling her over his shoulder and carry her onto the plane one-handed, flashing his badge as necessary. Which of his zero remaining good hands he would use to flash the badge, he didn't say.

He did tell her what wouldn't be fine with him, though, as the van pulled up in front of the United section of the SFO terminal. Quitting wouldn't be fine, giving in and giving up wouldn't be fine. So she didn't have to waste her psychic energy wondering whether to turn back, as that was no longer an option.

And no, the Pender treatment was not exactly in line with current psychiatric thinking. Desensitization was the modern style. First you talk it through; then you visualize; then you simulate; then one week you drive by the airport—but no closer—and the next week you walk through the terminal; and so on, until lo and behold, one year and Lord knows how many thousands of dollars in therapist fees later, maybe you'd be ready to fly.

But who was Pender to challenge the best minds of the psychiatric profession? Where did he get his degree? Why, at the University of Dorie, he would answer. He might not know dick about desensitization therapy, but he knew people, and he knew Dorie. She didn't need coddling, she needed flooding, a dare, a challenge. Something to arouse that lion heart.

At seven in the morning, the lines at the counter were still short. They checked their baggage through— Dorie's painting gear was in a footlocker and her clothes in a full-size suitcase that was never intended as a carry-on—and headed for the gate, with a detour to the same bar Pender and Sid had stopped at six days earlier. A Jim Beam on the rocks for Pender, a screwdriver for Dorie, on the theory that liquor was cheaper and quicker than Xanax, and didn't give you the shits or diminish your orgasm.

Not that they were planning to join the Mile High Club—even if Dorie had been willing, there was no way to cram two people their size into an airplane lavatory.

The worst part, for Dorie, was sitting in the boarding lounge waiting for the flight to be called. It wasn't Pender who got her through it, though—instead, it was a little boy, maybe four years old, wearing a devilish red-and-black Darth Maul mask, probably part of his costume for Halloween, and playing peekaboo over, under, and around the rows of molded plastic chairs.

The first time the devil's face popped up, it gave her a start, no denying that. But a start was all it gave her— she yelped and clutched her hand to her chest, then laughed weakly, same as most adults would have.

As for the tot, it was probably the first time he'd actually managed to scare somebody; he circled around the row and came around again, and again, and again, and each time Dorie laughed a little harder, not at the boy, but at the absurdity of it all.

"You sure you don't want me to tin the little bastard?" asked Pender as the kid came around for the fourth time.

"Are you kidding?" she replied. "The little bastard is a messenger from God."

"From God, eh? And what's the message?"

"The message is, Dorie Bell, you've wasted two-thirds of your life being afraid of being afraid. Why not unpucker, and enjoy the ride?"

"Now, *there's* an advertising slogan for you," said Pender. "United Airlines: Unpucker and Enjoy the Ride!"

3

A hot shower, a shave (but not the scalp: Simon had decided to let the stubble sprout, lest Grandfather Childs be tempted to make another unscheduled appearance), a good breakfast, a handful of crosstops, and a stout joint, and Simon was himself again. He'd been through some rough moments, what with the death of his mother and all, and for a while there he might have been closer to the precipice than he cared to think about, but that was all behind him. This morning's grandfather sighting was only a flashback, he told himself. Too many drugs lately—or at least too many of the wrong drugs in the wrong combinations. From now on he'd be sticking to crosstops and weed, the former for energy and clarity of purpose, the latter for imagination and creativity—all of which would be required for the game.

As would handcuffs and either a scalpel or a narrow-bladed knife—at any rate, something with a pointed, thrusting edge, as nasty-looking as it was sharp, to go along with the box cutter he'd picked up at Conroy Circle. As he searched the house, it occurred to Simon that if he wanted to hear Pender pleading for Skairdykat and Skairdykat pleading for Pender, then he'd have to leave both their mouths free. Which meant at least part of the game had to take place in the cellar, where, if pleading turned to screaming, the screams would be less likely to be heard down by the canal. Later in the afternoon, he decided, he would bring one of the kitchen chairs down to the cellar—for now, he would continue to search for the handcuffs, and further refine his game plan.

Pain had been no stranger to Linda Abruzzi in recent months, but she'd never known agony like this. Catch the snake first, worry about holding on to it later, was easier said than done.

Linda's sense of the passage of time was necessarily vague. It felt as if she'd been lying on her side at the foot of the stairs, holding the coral at arm's length and listening to Childs's footsteps overhead for days now (whenever it sounded as if he was approaching the kitchen, she would replace her gag and hide both the coral and the parted rope behind her back), but the dim cellar light told her it was still Thursday afternoon.

The living room television came on. From Linda's current location, she couldn't make out the program.

Sounded as if it might be *Rosie* or *Oprah* or *Sally Jesse Raphael*—at any rate, it was a female voice with an excitable audience, and the footsteps had stopped for a while.

No rest for Linda, though. And as if the pain, the thirst, and the hunger weren't bad enough, she had to fight the cramps that for the last few hours had been hopscotching unpredictably up and down her arm—now the thumb, now the shoulder, now the wrist, now the elbow. If she could have changed hands, she would have, but she couldn't trust the benumbed fingers of the left one anymore.

More insidious than the pain and cramping was the almost hallucinatory exhaustion. She'd been awake since yesterday morning. And unlike her pain, she knew, the exhaustion could well prove fatal. The coral was no longer thrashing, but neither had it gone back to sleep. Instead it was waiting, biding its time. And every so often, it tried her—a powerful, quicksilver-smooth shifting of the bands of muscle beneath the scales; she would tighten her grip and it would relax again. Waiting. Biding.

Just a little bit longer, she promised it in her mind. And when it's all over, I'll let you go. You can live here under the house forever and I'll bring you all the fat mice you can eat, and a hamster every Christmas.

The television fell silent; the footsteps began again. By the time Childs actually opened the cellar door and started down the steps, Linda had been visualizing the scenario for so long that it was almost as if it had already happened. He trots down the steps, she plays possum, he bends over her, she thrusts the coral at his eye, his neck, his—

The footsteps came halfway down the stairs, then receded; the cellar door closed again. The disappointment was crushing. Linda hadn't been willing to admit to herself how whipped she really was until she thought her ordeal was nearly over; now she didn't know how much longer she'd be able to hang on.

Oh, you scumbag, she called after him in her mind—get back here, you shitsucking scum—

The coral, perhaps sensing a moment of inattention, gathered itself and lunged for freedom. Linda's grip tightened reflexively, but she had it around the midsection now instead of behind the head; as she brought her left hand over to grab it higher, she felt a sensation like two needles sinking into the back of her left wrist.

4

It must have been quite a sight. The middle-aged couple, huge man with a Panama hat and a broken arm, big woman with a long brown braid and a broken nose, all but skipping down the ramp into the terminal.

"We did it!" Dorie exulted, still flushed with the glory of having licked her last phobia.

"You did it," said Pender. He was happy for her, of course, and not unmindful of his contribution, but mostly he was just glad to be out of goddamn coach. One first-class flight with Sid had been enough to spoil him forever.

Normally, Sid would have been waiting at the curb in front of the baggage claim. There are friends, and then there are friends who pick you up at the airport—Sid was the latter to Pender, and vice versa. Pender hadn't asked him this time, though—he wasn't sure Sid was still talking to him, after the stunt he'd pulled at SFO last Friday. So after they picked up Dorie's baggage, the suitcase and footlocker—and mirabile dictu, both arrived safely, sliding down the designated carousel in the designated airport—Pender hailed a cab.

The ride from Virginia to Maryland was Dorie's first experience with honest-to-God autumn foliage. Pender got a kick out of watching her—the expression on her face was MasterCard-ad priceless: not so much that of a kid in a candy shop as a teenage boy in a whorehouse.

Pender turned tour guide for the last leg of the drive, pointing out Civil War sites, detailing the history of the C&O. At the bottom of Tinsman's Lock Road, a canopy of yellow-leaved box elders shut out the sky. Dorie had never seen light like that before—where she came from, bowered light was always green.

Pender pointed out his driveway, warned the cabbie about the ruts. They jounced the last few hundred yards. Then, as the driver carried the luggage to the front doorstep, Dorie told Pender she wanted to see the canal while it was still daylight.

"Follow that path around the side of the house," Pender told her, "and keep going downhill until you see a woman in a bloodstained nightgown looking for a redheaded baby. I'll catch up as soon as I pay the man."

* * *

Phasmophobia—fear of ghosts. Despite her protestations last night, Dorie didn't have it, had never had it—after all, who ever heard of a ghost wearing a mask?

The path was steep and narrow; it wound down through a dense wood, then opened out suddenly on a scene Dorie longed to paint with all her heart, and doubted she could ever capture. Pender had been right—she would need to add a few new oils to her palette to get it all: the formal strips of color in the foreground, emerald green lawn, malachite green water, reddish brown canal wall built of rough-hewn, fitted sandstone blocks; the particulate air, the long black shadows, the horizontal light streaming in from dead ahead, but cut into dazzling vertical columns by the single row of flaming trees towering behind the towpath running along the raised berm of the far bank.

Impossible, though, to capture all that in a plein air, then paint in any of the detail—the footbridge, the miniature waterfall tumbling down the flume, the split-rail wooden fences, never mind the joggers and dog walkers on the towpath—before the light faded entirely.

Still, wouldn't it be something to try! If the weather held, she could set up her easel in the same spot a few days in a row, paint in one section at a—

"Well? Did I lie?" Pender caught up with Dorie as she mentally began cutting the scene into horizontal sections—the landscape defined its own verticality.

"It's beautiful, Pen. I can't wait to paint it. Or try, anyway. Where's the nearest art supply store?"

"We'll have to consult the yellow pages on that, scout," said Pender as they started back up the path to the house. "The last time I bought any art supplies, they came in a Crayola box with a built-in sharpener."

"I loved that built-in sharpener," said Dorie.

"Me too."

When they reached the house, Pender nodded toward the porch. "Let's go in that way—I want you to see the panorama."

"Technically, a panorama is an unbroken view or a series of pictures representing a continuous scene," Dorie explained as she trudged up the steps after him.

Pender stopped on the landing and turned back to her as if he had something important to say. Actually, he was just winded from the climb. "Did anybody ever tell you you were extremely argumentative?"

"Yes. I always took it as a compliment."

The view from the porch was spectacular, Dorie had to admit. It occurred to her, as Pender unlocked the sliding glass door, that she could paint from up here in the morning, then go down to the canal in the afternoon. It's a tough job, but somebody has to do it, she thought, following Pender into the house. God, I love my work.

5

Simon was ready. He'd been ready for hours, fussing around the house, watching TV, smoking a joint out on the porch, refining the game. At the last minute, he changed his mind about taking a chair down to the cellar beforehand. He was halfway down the stairs with it when it dawned on him that if Pender did enter the house through the porch door, he was as likely to head for the kitchen as the bedroom—best to leave everything as is.

Simon did an about-face on the steps. He was still in the kitchen when he heard a car coming down the drive. He raced into the living room, peeked out through the drawn blinds, saw the cab pulling up behind the Geo. He saw Pender climb out—nice hat, duude; wha' happen, somebody break your arm? Then he saw a second figure climbing out.

Simon's heart dropped—please let it be a cab-share—and when he recognized Dorie Bell, his jaw dropped as well. Last time he'd seen her, she was naked in the galvanized tub in the basement of 2500 and he was holding her head underwater. He knew she hadn't drowned, but as the only participant ever to have survived the fear game, she had somehow slipped into another dimension of Simon's consciousness, neither dead nor living; he wasn't quite as surprised to see her as he would have been to see, say, Wayne Summers—but it was a near thing.

As the cabdriver dropped the suitcase by the front door and went back for the footlocker, Simon raced into

Pender's bedroom, thinking furiously. Dorie's presence wasn't necessarily a bad thing. Snatch her first, put a gun to her head, he'd have himself a bargaining chip. Think Edward G. Robinson: Freeze, G-man, or I blow her brains out. Hero cop like Pender, he'll freeze all right. He'll do anything I tell him to do—she's his sweetie pie now. Some hero: he saves 'em and screws 'em.

And as he closed the bedroom door behind him, breathing hard, as engaged and excited as a soldier going into combat, Simon realized that having a second shot at Dorie was the only thing that could possibly have improved what was already promising to be the ultimate fear game. Not just a triple-header, but a chance to erase his only loss. Because when he was finished with Dorie (and this time he would insist on having a piece of what Pender had been enjoying, if it took him all night to get it in), the final score in the fear game would be *Childs: 27, World: Zip*—and that was without counting Zap, any of the old folks, any of the cops, or what's-his-name, Gloria's husband, the Chinese guy in the red bikini underwear.

Linda spat out her gag. Somehow she'd held on to the coral; she had it behind the neck again with her good right hand. She told herself not to panic—it hadn't gotten her that badly. Small mouth, short fangs, Reilly had said—they have to chew their way in. And hadn't Reilly also said the venom was only borderline lethal and that there was always a delayed reaction. Or had he said *often* rather than *always?* Or only *sometimes?* And how delayed—how much time did she have?

Related question: what was going on upstairs? Linda could hear Childs running from the kitchen to the living room, then into the bedroom wing. Was Pender home? She hadn't heard his footsteps yet—and she would have, heavy as he was. Which meant it might be too late to save herself, but she could still save him.

How? Concentrate—never mind the pain. Use it to focus. You wait until you hear a door, a heavy tread. Then you scream, *"Pender, watch out! Pender, Childs is here!"* If you can hear him upstairs, he can hear you downstairs.

But what if Childs already has a gun on Pender? Then all you've done is blow your only advantage—surprise.

No, you have another advantage: he's already told you he plans to blind Pender while you watch. So you know you have time; he's not going to shoot Pender as soon as he comes in. You also know he has to come back down to the cellar eventually. Wouldn't it be smarter to—

But by then the burning sensation had begun traveling up Linda's arm: when it reached her elbow, she understood that waiting for Childs to come to her was no longer a viable strategy.

6

As Pender crossed the living room, heading for the vestibule—the bags were still out on the front doorstep—he saw the basket of mail on the table beside the answering machine. The letter on top caught his eye. Noble J. Heinz—Ida's lawyer. The Judge, everybody in La Farge called him. An imposing, wintry man with arctic blue eyes and a mane of snowy hair. Always wore Clarence Darrow galluses and navy serge suits as dark as blue can be, and still be blue. But why would the Judge be writing him? He decided the baggage could wait.

"Where's the bathroom?"

Pender glanced up from opening the envelope. It was good to see Dorie standing in his living room. She was looking mighty fine, too. Her cheeks were rosy from the nippy air, the discoloration around her eyes had faded to a faint yellowish green, and the blue eyes themselves were as bright as if she were high. Maybe she was, thought Pender—maybe landscapes were her drug of choice. "First door on the right or third door on the left."

Inside Judge Heinz's envelope was a second envelope, with Pender's name written in Ida's Palmer Method handwriting. He opened it with a sharp pang of dread and unfolded a sheet of her familiar lavender stationery, so thin it was almost transparent.

May 29, 1997

Dear Eddie,

If you're reading this, that means I'm gone.

I've arranged to have some things sent on to you. The family papers and photo albums, Mom's jewelry, a few knickknacks from the Cortland house, et cetera.

Everything else has been left to the Down Syndrome Foundation. Judge Heinz is handling the estate, which he says is an attorney's dream. Most of my assets, including the title to the house, have already been transferred into a trust for the DSF, so Uncle Sam is going to reap precious little out of the transaction, which warms the cockles.

Cleland's is handling the auction, and Seland's Funeral Home will haul my carcass up to the crematorium in La Crosse. They have strict instructions not to bring anything back. No tarted-up corpse in an overpriced casket for me, no cremains in an overpriced urn. Ashes are ashes and dust is dust, and it is ghoulish superstition to treat them as if they were anything else.

As for a funeral or memorial service, you know how I feel about that sort of thing. I didn't bury Walt, I didn't bury Stanley, and I won't have you burying me. If you want to, you can raise a glass in my memory, but don't go off on a bender on my account.

I guess that's about it, except to tell you that I love you dearly, as did Walt and Stanley, and that no big sister was ever prouder of her little brother than I am of you.

Your Loving Sister,
Ida

Pender was still trying to digest all that—in fact, he was still trying to digest the first sentence—when Dorie appeared in the doorway leading to the bedroom wing. "Pen?"

He looked up. The high color of a moment ago was gone, leached from her face. "Dorie, what—"

As Dorie shuffled reluctantly into the room, chin in the air, hands in the air, Pender saw first a pistol barrel against the back of her neck, then a hand yanking her tightly by the roots of her braid, then a bald Simon Childs behind her, turning her, angling her body toward Pender, to keep it between Pender and himself.

"You move, she dies," said Childs.

Everybody dies, thought Pender, letting Ida's letter slip from his fingers; the flimsy lavender sheet fluttered slowly to the floor.

Twelve steep wooden steps, each with a lip that overhung the step below. Wall and railing on the left, ascending; sheer drop to the cellar floor on the right. Holding the thrashing coral aloft in her right hand, Linda grabbed the railing with her damaged left hand and hauled herself to a standing position. The pain shooting up her arm was . . . excellent. First rate.

By raising her left knee, she managed to lift her floppy left foot high enough to clear the first tread. When the sole was planted firmly on the bottommost step she leaned forward, put her weight on it, and by straightening the left leg she managed to drag the trailing right foot up to the step, though not without banging her toes on the overhanging lip.

One down, eleven to go.

Simon was feeling pretty good about himself. Large and in charge. This was going to be the best game ever, he told himself. Early as it was, he was already feeling connected with Pender—merely by looking at him, Simon could tell he'd just learned about his sister's death.

He knew better than to take the credit for it right away, however. Simon didn't want to drive the hulking Pender into a rage—not until he had him secured, anyway. But first he needed to take care of the superfluous Miss Bell. Having her around was making him too self-conscious—it was like having a ghost at your elbow.

No good—it was no good, trying to climb the stairs standing. Linda's left hand had lost most of its gripping strength, her fingers were too numb to feel the rail, and the pain traveling up her left arm made her pay dearly when she tried to raise the arm above her shoulder. Every time her hand slipped from the rail, she flailed the other hand to keep her balance, further inflaming the already infuriated coral.

She dropped to her knees on the third stair; three down, nine to go.

Childs marched the two of them back into the bedroom where he'd first surprised Dorie, ordered her onto the bed with her hands on either side of the centermost vertical rail of the brass headboard, then ordered Pender to cuff her wrists behind it.

Yes, thought Pender, trying to hide his eagerness. Perfect. His last girlfriend had been a DEA agent, somewhat unstable, like most DEA, and a hellcat in the sack. She liked to play mild bondage games, with herself as dominatrix—that's what the cuffs were doing under the bed in the first place. Pender didn't mind—at least that way she did all the work—but he didn't trust her as far as he could throw her. Which was why he had stashed a spare key under the mattress, at the head of the bed, where he could reach it even while cuffed to the headboard.

But how to let Dorie know, with Childs standing over them? Pender leaned across her body, fumbling one-handed with the cuffs. "Under the mattress," he whispered. Probably not loud enough, but Childs was leaning closer; Pender could smell his own aftershave on the man. Sensing his chance, he whirled around, trying to club Childs with the elbow of his cast.

Childs jumped back; the blow missed. Dorie saw the barrel of the Colt come crashing down across the back of Pender's neck. Pender's hat went flying; he fell limply across her, knocking the wind out of her. With his weight across her chest, she couldn't draw a breath. She started seeing stars; the white hat was a pinwheel, rolling on its brim across the floor. Then, as her consciousness began slipping away to a pinpoint of light, the crushing weight came off her; she sucked in a great gulping breath.

Pender lay on the floor, unmoving; Simon was stretched out across Dorie, clicking the handcuffs into place behind the rail. She tried to knee him. He avoided her easily, then knelt painfully across her thighs while he gagged her with one of Pender's garish neckties.

This is the last time I'll ever see him, thought Dorie, as Simon dragged Pender out of the bedroom by the ankles. By *him,* she meant Pender—she was pretty sure she'd be seeing Simon again.

To keep from toppling backward as she knee-walked up the stairs, Linda had to lean forward, bending at the waist (she hadn't forgotten her old friend

Lhermitte and his lightning bolt), and leaning awkwardly on her left elbow to keep from falling onto her face.

By the sixth step—*fuck this excellent pain, fuck this excellent, first-rate pain,* was her mantra—her knees were killing her, and both insteps were bruised from banging against the overhanging tread, but she could hear Childs and Pender talking in the kitchen. At least when she reached the top, it would be over, she told herself: she wouldn't have to drag her sorry ass the rest of the way across the house.

Eight down, four to go.

7

A sense of rising, of swimming upward through blackness, shedding dreams as he rose to the surface. The swimmer, the dreamer—he had no sense of himself *as* himself yet—heard a voice, echoic and distorted. For a moment he was a boy again, playing a joke on his mother, holding his breath at the bottom of Little York Lake to frighten her.

With the memory came identity; when Pender knew who he was, the rest came flooding back. It was the second time in four months he had been separated from his senses. Back in July, a blow to the head had launched him on one of those so-called near-death experiences, white light, tunnel, a visit from his dad in dress blues—the whole nine yards. This time, there'd been only chaos, and his dreams were not so much dreams as swirling fragments.

Pender opened his eyes, found himself lying in a contorted position on his side on the kitchen floor, with his left arm drawn painfully behind his back and cuffed at the wrist to his right ankle. Looking up sideways, he saw Childs sitting on a straight-backed kitchen chair.

"Sorry about your sister," Childs said in a conversational tone.

Pender assumed he'd read the letter; he mirrored Childs's tone—stay calm, keep the hostage-taker calm. "She had a good life."

"I didn't mean I was sorry she was dead—I meant I was sorry I had to kill her."

"No shit? Did you off Judge Crater and the Ramsey girl, too?"

"No—neither of them had killed my sister."

"I didn't kill your sister. The doctor said she died of a congenital heart condition."

"Congenital—that means she had it for forty-nine years. Why is it, do you think, that her heart gave out while she was struggling with you?"

"Struggling? She was trying to save me from getting my brains bashed out by you."

Simon let it pass—he wasn't here to argue. "Almost biblical, don't you think? The retribution, I mean— my killing your sister in return for your killing mine. I have to tell you, though, I didn't really want to kill Ida, fitting as it might have been. I thought she was a very nice lady, right up until the moment I broke that blue capsule into her hot toddy. If it's any consolation to you—it was to me—she was dead by the time she hit the floor. As I say, I didn't want to do it—but I couldn't take a chance on her telling you about our conversation. Would you like to hear about our conversation, Eddie? Or should I call you Pen, like that hooer waiting for me in the bedroom?"

Pender wanted to kill Childs of course—he wanted to kill him as badly as he'd ever wanted anything in his life. Instead, he reminded himself that the most important thing he could do at the moment was to work the problem.

And the problem—how to get loose, at least long enough to dial 911 on the phone in his pants pocket—was in the present. If Childs had killed Ida, that was in the past—nothing he could do would bring her back. And Childs's threat about Dorie belonged to the future, and was of no account. When your enemy threatens you, he's either lying, which means he's scared, or he's stating his intentions, which gives you more data to work with. The more data, the more better. "Call me anything you want. And, yes, I'd like to hear about your conversation."

Childs leaned back, laced his arms behind his head, and crossed his legs casually at the ankle—not an easy thing to do in a straight-backed chair. "It was very illuminating. For some reason, Ida was under the assumption that my name was Bellcock."

The name hit Pender like a slap. Ida had been a tough old bird—she wouldn't have told Childs squat, no matter how much he'd threatened or cajoled or even tortured her. But Pender himself had given her permission to talk to Bellcock—maybe Childs wasn't bullshitting about killing her after all.

"She told me all about Stanley, and Dr. Walt—this is Dr. Walt's gun I'm holding now," Childs continued. "She also told me all about what a naughty boy her little brother Eddie was. How he threw a firecracker down the chimney and nearly blinded himself. How he never got over it. How as a boy, he wouldn't let himself be blindfolded for a game of pin the tail on the donkey. And even at Stanley's birthday party, grown man, big-shot G-man, he wouldn't even play bust the piñata."

You wanted data, you got it, thought Pender, as Childs began removing an assortment of implements from the drawer next to him, and showing each one to Pender with a stage magician's flourish before setting it down carefully on the table—folding Buck knife, which he ostentatiously unfolded, apple corer, box cutter.

More data, Pender told himself. Keep working the problem. So Childs knows. About your fear. So what? Pain, darkness, death—one way or another it was going to be pain, darkness, death. Nothing else has changed. The phone is still in your pocket. Six inches away—might as well be six feet.

But there was still the possibility that Dorie had heard him and found the handcuff key under the mattress. If she'd already freed herself and called 911 or gone for help, all Pender had to do was hang on awhile longer. Just hang on. And stall like a mo-fo. A fearless mo-fo from the Eff Bee Fucking Eye. And keep on collecting data: "What have you done with Abruzzi?"

Skairdykat! Thanks for reminding me, thought Simon, as he tested the point of the Buck knife on his thumb—he'd been so caught up in the moment, so dialed in to Pender, that he'd almost forgotten Skairdykat. He'd also almost forgotten that the game, the doubleheader, would have to take place in the cellar, where no one would hear them scream—no one except Dorie, that is. "Nothing, yet. Would you like to see her?"

"Yes—yes, I would."

"She's in the cellar—all you have to do is hump your way across the floor and down the stairs. I'll hold the door for you."

Dorie had rattled the headboard until her wrists were sore. Leave it to Pender, she thought. The house looks like it's going to fall down any minute, but the bedstead couldn't be sturdier. She kept picturing Childs coming through the door, covered in Pender's blood, and throwing himself on top of her. Horrible as the image was, she knew that would be her best—and last—chance to kill him before he killed her.

But this time, Dorie promised herself—and Pender, and all the others—if she did through some miracle survive this second attack, there would never be a third. She'd kill him first, with her bare hands if necessary.

And as she waited on the bed to kill or be killed, with absolutely no idea that the key to her survival was only inches away, under the mattress beneath her head, Dorie found herself thinking back to the first time she had met Simon Childs. It was at the convention, in the welcoming suite of the Olde Chicago. The name tags had been specially prepared: a blank space for your name on the first line, the printed words *A Person With* on the second, and on the bottom line you were supposed to print the name of your phobia, using the *-ia* suffix, not the *-ic*. Like the name PWSPD, this was all in line with current thinking: a phobia was something you had, not something you were.

And although romance was the last thing Dorie'd had in mind when she got up the courage to leave the central coast for the first time in three years, the moment she saw the tall, handsome, silver-haired man standing behind the registration table, she was prepared to revise her expectations.

Simon Childs
a person with
Katapontismophobia

read his name tag.

"That's a new one on me," said Dorie.

"Fear of drowning," he explained. "The verb *katapontidzo* means 'to hurl into the sea.' The noun *katapontidzes* means 'pirate,' but I guess there were more people who were afraid of drowning than of pirates."

"I *like* pirates," Dorie declared.

"Aargh," said the handsome Mr. Childs, squinching up one eye. It was the worst Long John Silver impression Dorie had ever seen, but hilarious in context—she'd laughed so hard her boobs bounced. And it turned out, when he saw her name tag, that Simon was the first person she'd ever met, not excluding her current therapist, who knew what prosoponophobia meant without having to be told. She thought she might have found a lover; she *knew* she'd found a friend.

Honey, you sure can pick 'em, Dorie told herself; a moment later a shot rang out, and the screaming began.

Eleven down, one to go. Linda heard Childs tell Pender he'd hold the door. She was still on her knees—no time to stand up, even if she'd had the strength; as it was, she barely had time to hide the coral behind her back before the door opened.

Childs looked down at her in surprise; behind him, through his legs, she could see Pender on his side on the kitchen floor. "Well, would you look at that, Eddie Pen," said Childs. "Would you look what gnawed itself loose?" He raised one foot as if to shove her back down the stairs.

Linda flinched but remained upright. She would take the leg if necessary, but she wanted the face, or at least the neck.

"And what's that behind your back, Skairdykat? Biiiig scairdykat knife? It's not a gun—I know, I searched the cellar." He knelt, extended a hand; the gun was in his other hand, out of reach. "C'mon, fork it over."

Closer, thought Linda, as the coral thrashed frantically behind her back; the face—I want the face.

"C'mon, Skairdykat, give it to Simon before he has to take it away from you and stick it where the sun don't—"

Close enough.

8

One thing all criminal defense attorneys (along with a majority of cops and the few prosecuting attorneys who are willing to admit it) will tell you is that the only thing most eyewitnesses are good for is impressing juries. The truth is usually quicker than the eye, and the assumption is quicker than either, even for a trained observer like Pender.

He didn't know, for instance, that Linda was on her knees—he'd seen her through Childs's legs from the torso up and assumed she was standing on a lower step. He saw Childs kneel, heard him taunting her, heard the word *knife,* and assumed that's what she had for a weapon. He saw Linda lunge, heard the gun go off, saw her topple forward, and assumed she'd been shot. When Childs rocked backward and the Colt went flying, Pender continued to assume that Abruzzi had somehow slashed him, and it wasn't until Childs, still on his knees, turned blindly toward Pender, that Pender began to understand what had happened.

Or perhaps *understand* is too strong a word. A gun, a knife, a billy, even a sharp screwdriver—those were items commensurate with understanding. But a man on his knees, clawing with both hands at a thrashing snake dangling from his left eye? You don't understand something like that; you just accept it.

Or reject it—doesn't matter. What matters is Dr. Walt's Army Colt under the table, less than six feet away. Pender braced his left leg—his only free limb—against the cabinet and shoved off, bellowing to Dorie, over Simon's shrieking, that the handcuff key was under the mattress, as he began hump-crawling his way across the splintery plank floor of the kitchen.

The shot, the womanish shrieking—Dorie assumed the worst. The next few seconds were as bad as any she'd experienced in the last week—and that was saying something. When she heard Pender shouting that the key was under the head of the mattress, it was like whiplash, emotional whiplash. She recovered quickly, tried to puzzle it out. Easier to say that the key was under the mattress than to reach it, if you were lying on your back with your arms cuffed through the headboard.

Guess what, though: it's possible. You have to scooch way up, and contort yourself as far onto your side as you can, and pronate both wrists no matter how tight the cuffs are, and slide your fingers under the mattress, which is pressed tight against the box spring by your weight, so you have to scooch even farther to the side, which puts more strain on your wrists—but it can be done. If the key is less than a finger's length from the edge, you can find it, you can slide it out. And then if you crane your head at an angle that would break an owl's neck, so you can see what you're doing, and get the key inserted in the keyhole without dropping it—whatever you do, don't drop it—and turn the key, you'll hear the sweetest sound you've ever heard.

Click.

* * *

Dorie followed the sound of the bellowing and shrieking into the kitchen, quickly knelt behind Pender, unlocked his cuffs. As Pender scrambled to his feet, he saw Childs rising to his knees, moaning, one hand still clapped to his eye, blood leaking out between the fingers; his other hand was flailing the air as if he were blind. Pender punted him in the ribs to knock him over, then kicked him in the head a few times, until he lay still. Subduing the suspect, it was called.

As Pender cuffed Childs, Dorie knelt by the woman lying across the cellar doorway. "Are you all right?"

"I'm bit."

"You're hit?" Dorie had heard a shot, not a snake.

"Bit. Coral snake got me," said Linda. "It got Childs worse, though," she added—there was a world of triumph in those five words.

Pender was already on the line with the 911 operator. "What kind of snake, did you say?"

"Eastern coral." Linda raised her head wearily. "Tell 'em Animal Control had the antivenin at Conroy Circle."

"Eastern coral, antivenin, Conroy Circle—got it," said Pender, who had no idea what she was talking about.

Dorie hauled Linda—she assumed it was Linda Abruzzi—the rest of the way up the steps into the kitchen. The woman looked like hell—her thin face was dark and puffy and both eyelids were drooping. Dorie glanced over at Childs, who hadn't moved since Pender had "subdued" him. "Is he dead?" she asked Pender when he got off the phone.

"Not yet."

"Is he *going* to die?"

"I don't know." Pender sat down on the floor next to Linda, helped her turn over onto her back, and cradled her head on his lap. "I guess you're our resident snake wrangler," he told Linda, not so much for information as to give her something to do with her mind, to help keep her present and awake. He didn't know much about snake bites, but he knew you didn't want the victim slipping away. "What do you think?"

Although it was getting hard to concentrate on anything besides the pain, and drawing her next breath, Linda tried to piece together what little data she had. The coral had bitten Gloria, and she was dead. Linda herself had been bitten before Childs, and she was still alive. It had only nipped her on the back of her wrist, though—Childs got it in the eye. And he had to have received twice as much venom— the enraged coral had gone for him with a vengeance and hung on for dear life, or rather, grim death. But he also weighed nearly as much as Linda and Gloria combined. And there was that delayed reaction Reilly had mentioned.

"If we're both alive . . . when the antivenin . . . gets here," she told Dorie between gasps, "I think we'll both make it."

"That's all I wanted to know," said Dorie, turning toward the revolver she'd seen under the table when she entered the kitchen. But it was no longer there— it was on the floor beside Pender. "Could I see the gun for a second?" she asked.

* * *

Pender had probably done Simon a favor, knocking him out like that. Not only had he released Simon from his agony for a few minutes, but while Simon was unconscious his respiration and heart rate had slowed appreciably, thereby retarding the progress of the neurotoxin through his bloodstream.

Alive . . . antivenin . . . make it, somebody said. Woman's voice. He wasn't sure where he was or what had happened, but somehow, through the fog and the pain, he understood they were talking about him. He pictured a nurse in a crisp white uniform. See, you're going to make it, he told himself, slipping back into the darkness to get away from the pain. There's nothing to be afraid of, after all.

Dorie was on her feet, standing over Pender, reaching her hand out for the Colt.

"I think it would be better if I held on to it for a while," he told her. They both understood what she was asking; they also knew what his answer had been.

"Suit yourself," she said, picking up the Buck knife from the table.

"What are you planning to do with that?"

"Cut his throat," said Dorie, matter-of-factly.

"Don't do it," Pender said. "Please."

"Why not?"

"You know why not."

"No, I don't," said Dorie, looking down at the knife in her hand. She was almost certain she could have shot Simon—though she had never fired anything but a twenty-two in her life, and then only at a paper target—but she was far from sure she'd have the nerve to kill him with this. "Why don't you tell me?"

"Because . . . I don't know, because it's wrong." Pender was surprised to find himself fumbling for words. "Because it brings us down to his level."

Dorie cocked her head, listening not to Pender, but to the faint sound of a siren in the distance. It was now or never; she knelt beside Simon, her back turned to Pender. Simon's face was dark. One eye was a bloody mess, the strangely naked eyelid of the other was at half-mast, but fluttering as if he were struggling to open it.

"Get back," called Pender, easing himself out from under Linda, edging away so as not to deafen her if he had to fire. "Get away."

Dorie tilted Simon's head up, held the point of the blade against his throat. "You'll have to shoot me first," she said, without turning around.

As if in answer, the gun barked twice. The body jumped; the sound of the shots reverberated around the kitchen. Dorie still hadn't moved. Slowly she pulled the knife back—it was still unbloodied; now she'd never know whether she could have done it— and saw a dark, viscous liquid oozing from two holes in the side of Simon's mustard yellow and dung brown sport shirt, just below the heaving rib cage. As she watched, the heaving slowed, then stopped; so did the trickle of blood and bile and enteric fluid. She turned to Pender, her ears still ringing.

"We have about two minutes to get our stories straight," he said, as the sound of the sirens grew louder. "Linda, honey, you still with us?"

She raised her head weakly. "You guys work it out."

"Hang on," Pender told her. "The ambulance is almost here."

Hang on? thought Linda, closing her eyes and letting her head fall back to the hard plank floor. I've been hanging on for twelve fucking hours—when do I get to let go?

Epilogue
October 31, 1999

The cold, clear weather held for three more days. Dorie finished *Sunset: Tinsman's Lock* as the sun dropped behind the raised berm of the canal while Pender, bundled in blankets and medicating his bruised cervical vertebrae with Jim Beam and Vicodin, dozed beside her on a folding lawn chaise. The last touch was a solitary figure on the towpath—just a vertical dab of black against the horizon, with the thinnest penumbra of violet her finest brush could manage, to give it that magical twilight shimmer.

Neither of them felt much like going to Pool's Halloween party that evening. Like soldiers after a battle, they found they preferred each other's company, partly because they could talk about what they'd been through with someone who'd been there and would understand, and partly because they didn't have to. (For the same reason, Pender had put off his meeting with the real Arthur Bellcock for at least another week.) In the end the decision was made by default, one of those, "I'll go if you want to go; well, *I'll* go if *you* want to go" deals.

Pool's roommate met them at the front door of the frame house near Annandale. Slender, late forties, clinging black dress, waist-length gray polyester wig. Pender introduced her as Bunny.

She corrected him. "Tonight it's Morticia. I'm glad you came, Ed. I've never seen her so down. I've tried everything—maybe you can talk to her."

"Where is she?"

"In the bedroom." Bunny turned to Dorie, who was wearing the same outfit she'd worn the night she and Pender had met, and gave her the once-over. "Hag or drag?"

"Beg pardon?"

"Costume. There's a gorgeous décolleté witch outfit we could stuff those into, or I could loan you a tuxedo like Julie Andrews wore in *Victor/Victoria.*"

"Tuxedo," said Dorie.

"Spoilsport," said Pender.

Pender rapped on the bedroom door.

"Go away."

"It's Ed Pender."

The door opened. The woman who ran the FBI was costumed as Gomez Addams, to Bunny's Morticia. Tuxedo with absurdly wide lapels, dark hair slicked down and parted in the middle, pencil mustache, penciled in.

Pender gave her a hug. He'd always thought of Pool as an iron woman and was surprised how light and fragile she felt in his arms. "She was the first one, Ed."

"The first one?" They disengaged, sat on the edge of the bed together.

"The first one I ever lost."

Pender thought back, realized she was right. It was in 1979 that he had joined Steve McDougal in Washington to help set up the Liaison Support Unit. Pool arrived a year later, and no, the LSU had never lost an agent in the line of duty. "Do you want to hear about it?"

"I read the file. I meant to tell you, I was so sorry to hear about your sister."

"Thanks," said Pender. "Finding out about it the way I did, somehow it's still not real to me. I mean, part of me knows Ida's dead, but part of me still feels like I could pick up the phone and call her."

"I kind of feel like that about Abruzzi—as if when I open her office door tomorrow, she's going to be there behind the desk as usual, grinning up at me from behind a stack of autopsy reports. She never complained, Ed—sometimes she was so tired I had to help her up from her chair, but she never let up and she never complained."

"She saved our lives," said Pender simply. "Mine and Dorie's."

"I know." Pool brightened a little. "Hey, guess what's in the works? Hall of Honor. She's going in as a Service Martyr."

"No shit!" Pender was impressed. The Hall of Honor was for special agents killed in the line of duty; the Service Martyr plaque was reserved for those who died as a direct result of adversarial action. As of three days ago there'd been only thirty-three Service Martyrs in the entire history of the Bureau; now there were thirty-four. "There's not gonna be any problem about her not being an SA?"

"There'd better not be. She told me once that the day she got to write *Special Agent* in front of her name was the proudest day in her life. So that's what it's going to say under her picture in the Hall: 'Special Agent Linda Abruzzi.' And her parents are getting a Memorial Star, and that's going to read 'In Memory of Special Agent Linda Abruzzi.' And if either of those things doesn't happen," Pool continued, with the air of one who knows where the bodies are buried and has snapshots of the funeral to prove it, "then the divorce rate in the highest echelons of the Bureau is going to spike like you wouldn't believe."

"I'll bet." There used to be a saying among LSU agents: If you can't get God on your side, get Pool.

"Speaking of the highest echelons, I have it on good authority that the OPR is going along with your story about how Childs pulled a knife on Miss Bell, and you had to shoot him to save her."

"What do you mean, going along with my story?"

"I mean, *I* don't buy it. In your statement, you said you sent her over to check on Childs—if Childs had been in any condition to pull a knife, you never would have let her anywhere near him. Not that I care—I only wish you'd shot him lower and slower."

Pender leaned forward confidentially. "This doesn't leave the room, but the truth is, if I hadn't shot him when I did, Dorie would have used that knife to cut his throat."

"The more I learn about that woman, the better I like her," said Pool.

Talking to Pender must have helped—Pool decided to attend her own party. They found Dorie downstairs, giving out trick-or-treat bags to the vampires, ghosts, and Power Rangers as they emerged from the haunted house in the basement. She had changed her mind about the tux and was wearing a witch costume cut so low and sexy it would have convinced Billy Graham to convert to Wicca.

"Oh, Pen," she cried, from under her conical hat. "Aren't they cute?"

"They sure are," said Pender, waggling his eyebrows.

"The kids, you lech—I mean the kids. Especially the little girls, the ballerinas and the fairy princesses—my God, I just want to eat 'em up."

"This is all new to you, isn't it?" asked Pool.

"It's my first Halloween since—I guess since I was three."

"No problem with the masks?"

"There *was* one kid. It was a boy, he must have been fourteen or fifteen. He was wearing—I don't even know what to call it—a ghoul or a zombie mask or something like that. It had these gaping wounds, and there was this fake eyeball hanging by a string from this gory eye socket. He had his little sister with him—I could tell by his body language he wasn't real thrilled about it. I didn't see him coming—I just turned around and there he was. I jumped about a mile—almost peed my panties—and when I finally came down, I said, 'Jeez, you scared me.' And he brings his face right up next to mine, and you know what he says? He says, 'It's Halloween, lady—that's the general idea.' "

Pender laughed, raised his glass. "To Halloween," he said. "To ghosties and ghoulies and long-legged beasties, and things that go bump in the night."

"That's not how it goes," said Dorie. "First of all, it's not *to,* it's *from.* Second of all, you left out the most important line:

From ghosties and ghoulies and long-leggety beasties
And things that go bump in the night,
Good Lord, deliver us!

"Amen," said Pool.
"I'll drink to that," said Pender.

Don't miss Jonathan Nasaw's
spine-chilling thriller

The Girls he Adored,

also featuring FBI Agent E. L. Pender.

1

"I'll save you some time," said the prisoner, shuffling into the interview room in his orange jumpsuit, fettered and manacled, wrists cuffed to a padlocked belt around his waist, and a scowling sheriff's deputy at his elbow. "I'm oriented times three, my thought processes are clear, and my mood and affect are appropriate to my circumstances."

"I see you're familiar with the drill." The psychiatrist, a slender blond woman in her early forties, looked up from behind a metal desk bare except for a Dictaphone, a notepad, and a manila folder. "Have a seat."

"Any chance of getting these things off?" The prisoner rattled his fetters dramatically. Slight, an inch or so below medium height, he appeared to be in his late twenties.

The psychiatrist glanced up at the deputy, who shook his head. "Not if you want me to leave you alone with him."

"I do, for now," said the psychiatrist. "He may need a hand free later for some of the standardized tests."

"I'll have to be here for that. Just pick up the phone when you're ready." A black telephone was mounted on the wall behind the psychiatrist. Beside it was an inconspicuous alarm button; an identical button was concealed on the psychiatrist's side of the desk. "And you, siddown."

The prisoner shrugged and lowered himself into the unpadded wooden chair, tugging with manacled hands at the crotch of his jumpsuit, as if it had ridden up on him. His heart-shaped face was just this side of pretty, with long-lashed eyes and lips like a Botticelli angel. He seemed to be bothered by a lock of nut brown hair that had fallen boyishly across his forehead and over one eye, so as the guard left the room, the psychiatrist reached across the desk and brushed it back for him with her fingers.

"Thank you," said the prisoner, looking up at her through lowered eyelids. The glitter of mischievous, self-satisfied amusement had faded from his gold-flecked brown eyes—but only for a moment. "I appreciate the gesture. Are you a defense whore or a prosecution whore?"

"Neither." The psychiatrist ignored the insult. Testing behavior, she told herself. He was trying to control their interaction by provoking an aggressive response.

"Come on, which is it? Either my lawyer hired you to say I'm insane, or the DA hired you to say I'm not. Or were you appointed by the court to see if I'm fit to stand trial? If so, let me assure you that I am perfectly capable of understanding the charges against me and assisting in my own defense. Those are the criteria, are they not?"

"More or less."

"You still haven't answered my question. I'll rephrase it if you'd like. Have you been hired by the defense, the prosecution, or the court?"

"Would it make a difference in how you respond to my questions?"

The prisoner's demeanor changed dramatically. He lowered his shoulders, arched his neck, cocked his head to the side, and formed his next words carefully, almost primly, at the front of his mouth, speaking with just a trace of a lisp. *"Would it make a dif-fer-ence in how you respond to my questy-ons?"*

It was a remarkably effective imitation of her own bearing and manner of speaking, the psychiatrist realized. He had her nailed, right down to the hint of sibilence that was, after years of speech therapy, all that remained of a once ferocious, sputtering, Daffy Duck of a speech impediment. But the parody was more affectionate than cruel, as if he'd known and liked her for years.

"Of course it would," he went on in his own voice. "Don't be disingenuous."

"I suppose you're right." The psychiatrist sat back in her chair, trying to maintain a professional demeanor despite the hot blush blooming in her cheeks. "That was an excellent imitation, by the way."

"Thank you!" Jail garb, fetters, and circumstances notwithstanding, the prisoner's grin lit up the bare room. "Want to see my Jack Nicholson?"

"Perhaps some other time," she replied, sounding to her annoyance every bit as prim as his imitation of her. She caught herself touching the top few buttons of her beige blouse with fluttering fingertips, like a schoolgirl who'd noticed her date glancing surreptitiously at her chest. "We have quite a bit of work ahead of us today."

"Oh! Well then, by all means, let's get on with it." The prisoner flapped his manacled wrists, as if he were shooing pigeons away; his chains rattled musically.

"Thank *you*." She leaned forward and pressed the power button on the voice-activated Dictaphone. "I'm Dr. Cogan, by the way."

The psychiatrist had been hoping he would respond in kind—thus far the prisoner had refused to give his name to the authorities. But all she got from him was a cheerful "Pleased to meetcha," and a cavalier, if truncated, wave of his cuffed right hand.

She tried again, more directly. "And your name is . . . ?"

"Call me Max."

"I notice you haven't quite answered my question."

"I notice you haven't *quite* answered mine. Who hired you?"

She'd been hoping he'd let it drop; now she had to answer, or risk losing his cooperation. "The court, indirectly: I was hired by a firm that contracts its services to the county."

He nodded, as if she'd confirmed something he already knew. She waited a moment, then prompted him. "And your name?"

"Like I said, call me Max." He looked up. Really, that's the best I can do, said his embarrassed grin; I win, said his eyes.

The psychiatrist moved on. "Nice to meet you,

Max. As you're probably aware, we have some standard tests we need to get through—"

"MMPI, Rorschach, thematic apperception, maybe a sentence completion if you're really trying to pad your hours—"

"—but first let's just chat for a few minutes."

"By chat, if you mean conduct a clinical interview, beginning with a question to be asked in an open-ended manner and designed to elicit the patient's own perception of the problem"—he had to stop for a breath—"or difficulty that has led him or her to seek treatment, let me save you some time: My diagnosis is dissociative amnesia, possibly a dissociative fugue state."

Then you're not really oriented times three, are you? thought Dr. Cogan, breaking off eye contact to look through the manila folder. "I'm curious, Max. You seem to be quite familiar with psychiatric terms and procedures. Might you have worked in the mental health field?"

"Might have." Then, thoughtfully: "Of course, I also might have been a patient in a locked facility. I mean, considering the circumstances under which I was found."

"That sounds like a good place to start. Tell me about the circumstances under which you were found."

"Well, Dr. Cogan, it's like this." The prisoner leaned forward in his chair. His breathing had grown shallower, and the glitter in his eyes was darker and more pronounced. The psychiatrist had the impression that for the first time since he'd entered the room, his interest was fully engaged. "The first thing I remember is finding myself sitting in a car next to the body of a young woman who had recently been dis-emboweled."

Disemboweled. It struck Irene Cogan as odd how one simple word could be so much more evocative than a three-page coroner's report describing in clinical detail "a semicircular ventral incision beginning one and a half centimeters above the right iliac crest, extending downward to three centimeters above the pubic symphysis, then describing an upward arc to the top of the left iliac crest, with resulting extrusion of both large and small bowel. . . ."

She looked up from the manila folder. The prisoner was waiting for her next question with an eager grin, his gold-flecked eyes shining, looking for all the world like a man enjoying a terrific first date. Momentarily jarred out of her professional detachment, Dr. Cogan switched onto automatic pilot, lobbing one of the interviewee's last words back at him in lieu of a real question. "Recently? How recently?"

The prisoner shrugged easily—or as easily as the fetters would allow. "I dunno, thirty, forty seconds. She was still sitting up."

2

The bureau liked its agents to be young and fit, to wear conservative suits, and to carry regulation weapons in over-the-kidney holsters. At fifty-five, Special Agent E. L. Pender was two years from mandatory retirement, overweight and out of shape, and beneath a plaid sport coat his boss had once described as being loud enough to spook a blind horse, he carried a SIG Sauer P226 9mm semiautomatic in a soft calfskin shoulder holster.

"Enjoy your stay in San Jose, Agent Pender," said the young flight attendant, giving him the obligatory doorway send-off. What with all the forms that had to be filled out in order to carry a weapon on a commercial flight, it was impossible for an armed FBI agent to travel incognito these days. "Thank you for flying United."

"Thank *you*, dear." Pender tipped his trademark hat, a narrow-brimmed green-and-black houndstooth check with a tiny feather stuck into the band. Beneath it, he was bald as a melon. "You know, the time was when I'd have asked a pretty gal such as yourself for her phone number."

"I'll bet." The stewardess smiled politely.

"Would I have gotten it?"

The smile never wavered. "My parents didn't let me date much when I was seven, Agent Pender."

Pender's luck wasn't much better at the rent-a-car counter. The clerk knew nothing about the midsize sedan that was to have been reserved for him, so he was forced to squeeze his six-four, two-hundred-and-fifty-pound frame behind the wheel of a Toyota Corolla.

At least the car had AC and a respectable sound system. Pender set the temperature control to blue and the volume control to high, found an oldies station on the FM band, and sang along in a sweet, surprisingly soulful tenor as he drove. A full hour passed before they played a song to which he didn't know all the words.

Strictly speaking, from the standpoint of professional courtesy, Pender should have notified the local FBI resident agency before showing up in Salinas to interview a murder suspect currently being held in the county jail. But according to the grapevine, the RA's collective nose was still out of joint from the previous summer, when the bureau had brought down agents from the San Francisco field office to take over a high-profile kidnapping investigation—they wouldn't be likely to welcome an interloper like Pender with open arms.

Also strictly speaking, Pender should have checked in immediately with the Monterey County Sheriff's Department. But before he requested an interview with the prisoner, he first wanted to speak to the arresting officer, and local cops tended to be overly protective of their own.

According to Pender's information, obtained for him by one of Liaison Support's overworked clerks, Deputy Terry Jervis lived in a town called Prunedale. They'd had a few chuckles over that back in Washington. "Prunedale, home of regular folks," and so on.

He found the place without any difficulty—one thing about working for the government, you could always get hold of a decent map. The house was a small, well-tended ranch with sprayed-stucco walls and a few rounded arches thrown in so they could call it mission style, perched on a hillside in the sort of semirural neighborhood where half the houses were trailers, and half the trailers were probably meth labs.

A spindly lemon tree was tied to a stake in the middle of a rocky but carefully trimmed front lawn; tidy flower beds lined the short walk from the driveway to the front door.

Pender rang the bell, then backed down from the low doorstep so his height wouldn't be intimidating. The woman who opened the door as far as the chain permitted was black, solid, broad in the beam, and low to the ground. It occurred to Pender that this might be Jervis—she had a cop's wide ass, and the arrest report hadn't been gender-specific.

"Yes?"

"Special Agent Pender, FBI. I'm here to see Deputy Jervis."

"Terry's resting. Could I see your shield, please?"

If not the cop, then the cop's wife—only a cop's wife would say "shield" instead of "badge." Pender tinned her, flipping his wallet open to show her his old Department of Justice badge with the eagle on the top and the blindfolded figure in the pageboy haircut holding the scales of justice in one hand and a sword in the other.

"You have a photo ID?"

"Here you go."

She glanced from the picture on the laminated card to his face and back again, then closed the door. The chain rattled; the door opened wider. "Come on in."

Pender took off his hat as he stepped through the doorway. "Thank you, Mrs. Jervis."

The woman frowned. "I'm Aletha Winkle."

Pender winced exaggeratedly. "Sorry. That's my job—stumbling to conclusions."

She ignored the apology. "Hey, Terry," she called over her shoulder. "There's an FBI man here to see you."

The response was a muffled "Okay." Pender followed Winkle down a short hallway, past a small living room furnished largely in wicker, and into a white-and-pink bedroom—everything from the bed-clothes to the bureau, the rug to the ceiling fixture, was either white or pink.

Pender froze in the doorway—the pale woman sitting up in bed was pointing a semiautomatic pistol at his midsection. He threw up his hands. "FBI—take it easy there, Deputy."

"Sorry," Terry Jervis hissed through clenched teeth, lowering the gun. "They tell me the guy was making threats—we were worried he might send somebody to carry them out."

Deputy Jervis had spiked blond hair and washed-out blue eyes. The lower half of her face was heavily bandaged, and her jaw was wired shut. Her pajamas were pin-striped, black on pink.

"I understand." Pender lowered his hands. "Does it hurt to talk?"

"Some."

"I apologize in advance—I wouldn't be here if it weren't important. I'd be grateful for anything you can tell me."

"This is where I get off," said Aletha Winkle. "Call me if you need me, honey." She stooped, plumped the smaller woman's pillows, kissed her high on the fore-head. On her way out of the room she waggled her forefinger in Pender's direction. "Don't you tire her out, now!"

"Scout's honor," replied Pender.

Jervis smiled weakly. "Aletha's a little overprotective."

"I noticed—and God bless her for it." In Pender's experience, some lesbians, like most minorities, tended to regard even a pleasantly neutral tone as barely disguised disapproval. But Pender was a proponent of what was known as the affective interview, so he made sure to add an extra dollop of warmth to his voice as he returned the grin.

"Take a load off." Deputy Jervis pointed to the small, pink-cushioned chair in front of the pink-and-white mirrored vanity, then set the pistol down carefully on the bedside table, next to a framed photo of herself and Winkle, posed in front of the house with their arms around each other's waists. It had probably been taken on the day they moved in—a yellow Drive-Yr-Self moving van was parked next to a green Volvo station wagon in the driveway.

"You really need that?" asked Pender, nodding toward the gun. He knew the model well—Glock .40s were now standard issue for recruits at the FBI Academy.

Jervis nodded sheepishly. "I know it's dumb, I know he's behind bars, but he's still got me spooked. If you never saw the fucker, then you can't imagine how fast the fucker can move."

"Probably not." Pender picked up the delicate-looking chair, positioned it a few feet from the side of the bed at a forty-five-degree angle—the recommended interviewing position—and sat down carefully with his hat in his lap.

"Have your people found out anything more about the son of a bitch?"

Pender shook his head. "Dead end. He wasn't carrying any ID—no wallet, just a roll of cash—and it was the victim's car. His prints are a mess, old grafts on the interior surfaces of both hands. No matches so far—the lab's working on a reconstruction." Pender scraped his chair a little closer to the bed—a signal to the interviewee that it was time to get down to business. "Tell me about the bust—how'd you take him down?"

"Routine traffic stop. Eastbound maroon Chevy Celebrity with California plates rolls through a red on Highway Sixty-eight, near Laguna Seca. Male driver, female passenger. I hit the lights, he hits the gas. I call in the pursuit; he pulls over a few seconds later. As I'm approaching the vehicle, I see the driver leaning over toward the female passenger—I figure he's fastening her seat belt for her. Then he turns toward me, big smile, what's the problem officer? At this point I haven't even unsnapped my holster. Routine traffic violation, maybe a warning on the seat belt.

"But when I look in, I see this blond girl, couldn't have been more than eighteen, she's sitting straight up holding her stomach with both hands. She's wearing a white sweater that looks like it's dyed in overlapping bands of red at the bottom, and she has the strangest expression on her face. Just, you know, *puzzled*—I'll never forget that expression. I ask her if she's okay, she lifts up her sweater with both hands, and her guts spill out onto her lap."

Jervis closed her eyes, as if to shut out the memory. Pender wouldn't let her. "What happened next?"

"He has the knife in his left hand—before I can react he brings it up so fast and hits me so hard I thought he shot me at first. It was like my mouth exploded—I'm falling backward, spitting out blood and teeth, trying to draw my weapon. He's on top of me before I hit the ground. I can't get my weapon out, but I'm hanging onto the holster for dear life."

Jervis winced again; her hand went to her jaw. "That's all I remember—they tell me he was trying to yank my belt off when the backup unit pulled up, and I was holding onto the holster so hard they had to pry my hands away."

"But you're down as the arresting officer."

A rueful chuckle. "Charity collar. It was a twelve-inch bowie knife—a souvenir from the Alamo, I heard. Busted out all the lower molars on the right side, all the uppers on the left. He just barely missed my tongue or I wouldn't be talking to you now."

Her pale complexion was turning chalky; her glance strayed toward the bottle of Vicodin on the white wicker bedside table.

"And here I promised Miss Winkle I wouldn't wear you out," said Pender. He knew he didn't have much longer; he cut to the question he most needed to ask the only person who'd seen the victim alive. "One more thing, then I'll leave you in peace. It's about the girl. You say she was blond?"

"Yes, sir."

"Could you be a little more specific—was it platinum blond, ash blond, something like that?" Careful not to lead her where he hoped she'd take him.

And she did: "No, sir, it was more of a reddish blond."

"Would that be the color people sometimes refer to as strawberry blond?"

"Yes, sir, that's it exactly." It was obvious that every word was causing her pain.

Pender patted her pale freckled hand as it lay on the pink comforter. "That's okay. That's okay, dear. You've been a great help—you don't have to say another word."

Aletha Winkle gave Pender a dark look as she bustled into the room.

"I'll let myself out," Pender said.

"And next time call first."

"Yes, ma'am, I'll be sure to do that," replied Pender meekly.

Pender's chagrin didn't last long. In fact, as he strode down the flower-lined front walk, he was tum-te-tumming "And the Band Played On," a tune written by Charles B. Ward and John F. Palmer in 1899, but still familiar enough nearly a century later that at the 1997 inaugural meeting of the team charged with investigating the disappearances of nine females from nine widely separated locales over the past nine years, Steven P. McDougal, chief of the FBI's Liaison Support Unit, was able to recite the first few lines of the chorus by heart, confident that it would be recognized by every agent in the room:

Casey would waltz with a strawberry blond
And the band played on.
He'd glide 'cross the floor with the girl he adored
And the band played on.

Thus McDougal dubbed the phantom kidnapper Casey, after the only characteristic the missing females had in common: the color of their hair. But it was Ed Pender who sang the next two lines of the song in his sweet tenor:

His brain was so loaded it nearly exploded
The poor girl would shake with alarm.

The room went dead quiet; McDougal broke the silence.

"Ed has a bad feeling about this one, boys and girls," he announced, leaning back in the leather chair at the head of the conference table, peering professorially over his half glasses. "Let's help him make it go away."

Since that initial meeting, two more strawberry blonds had been reported missing under suspicious circumstances, but the FBI still hadn't gone public with the investigation, largely because not a single body had come to light. Then in June 1999, Monterey County sheriff's deputy Terry Jervis made what she thought would be a routine traffic stop, and everything changed.

Casey, you son of a bitch, thought Pender as he squeezed himself back into the blue Corolla. You son of a bitch, we've got you now.

**POCKET
BOOKS**

The Girls He Adored
Jonathan Nasaw

The man in the prison cells calls himself Max. He
admits to killing the cop who found him sitting in a
car beside the still-warm body of a disembowelled
young woman, but he claims to be suffering from
DID, the multiple-personality disorder that is a
common alibi for the worst criminals. Assigned to
assess the truth of Max's defence is strawberry
blonde psychiatrist Irene Cogan. When Max
masterminds his bloody escape from prison and
kidnaps Irene, he agrees to undergo a course of
therapy, during which Irene is introduced to a
succession of his alters – his alternative
personalities. To her alarm, it seems that one of
them has a distinctly unhealthy penchant for
strawberry blondes.

And it looks like it will be up to FBI Special Agent
E.L. Pender, who has been on Max's trail for over a
decade, to find them before Irene discovers exactly
what that penchant entails . . .

ISBN: 0 7434 1507 8

PRICE £5.99

POCKET
BOOKS

Puppets
Daniel Hecht

The New Jersey State Police had started calling him
Howdy Doody, after the famous TV puppet of the
1950s. Three people killed in northern New Jersey,
then three in Manhattan and another in the Bronx.
All of them hung up with strings attached to their
limbs like puppets, and objects arranged in
geometric patterns throughout the murder scene.
The murderer had been caught in New York city
several months previously.

Then State Police detective Mo Ford found another
victim, killed and arranged in exactly the same
way . . .

'A fast, effortless, intriguing story, bolstered
by real substance' *Daily Mirror*

ISBN: 0 7434 2896 X

PRICE £6.99

POCKET BOOKS

This book and other **Pocket** titles are available from your bookshop or can be ordered direct from the publisher.

0 7434 1507 8	**The Girls He Adored**	**Jonathan Nasaw**	£5.99
0 7434 2896 X	**Puppets**	**Daniel Hecht**	£6.99

Please send cheque or postal order for the value of the book, free postage and packing within the UK; OVERSEAS including Repubilc of Ireland £2 per book.

OR: Please debit this amount from my:

VISA/ACCESS/MASTERCARD ....

CARD NO..

EXPIRY DATE...

AMOUNT £...

NAME...

ADDRESS..

....

SIGNATURE..

Send orders to SIMON & SCHUSTER CASH SALES
PO Box 29, Douglas, Isle of Man, IM99 1BQ
Tel: 01624 677237, Fax 01624 670923
e-mail: bookshop@enterprise.net

Please allow 14 days for delivery.
Prices and availability subject to change without notice.